ALIVE IN SHAPE AND COLOR

Office Girls by Raphael Soyer

ALIVE IN SHAPE AND COLOR

17 PAINTINGS BY GREAT ARTISTS AND THE STORIES THEY INSPIRED

EDITED BY
LAWRENCE BLOCK

PEGASUS BOOKS

NEW YORK LONDON

ALIVE IN SHAPE AND COLOR

Pegasus Books Ltd.
148 W 37th Street, 13th Floor
New York, NY 10018

First Pegasus Books cloth edition December 2017

Interior design by Maria Fernandez

Frontispiece: Raphael Soyer (1899–1987). *Office Girls,* 1936.
Oil on canvas, 26 ⅛ × 24 ⅛ in. (66.4 x 61.3 cm).
Whitney Museum of American Art, New York; purchase 36.149
Digital Image © Whitney Museum, N.Y.

Library of Congress Cataloging-in-Publication Data is available.

ISBN: 978-1-68177-561-6

10 9 8 7 6 5 4 3 2 1

Printed in the United States of America
Distributed by W. W. Norton & Company

CONTENTS

FOREWORD
BEFORE WE BEGIN . . .

Here, Gentle Reader, is the foreword as I initially wrote it:

Months before the December publication of *In Sunlight or in Shadow: Stories Inspired by the Paintings of Edward Hopper*, it had already become clear that the book was destined for success. The pantheon of contributors had turned in a stunning array of stories, and the huge in-house enthusiasm at Pegasus Books guaranteed the book would be well published.

So what would I do for an encore?

I considered—and quickly ruled out—putting together the mixture as before, another anthology of Hopper-inspired stories. The man left us a large body of work, and one could point to any number of paintings as likely to evoke stories as the ones already chosen, but it was clear to me that one trip to that well was enough.

So what other artist might stand in for Edward Hopper in a second volume?

No end of names came up, and not one of them struck me as promising. In each instance, one could imagine a story flowing out of a painting by the proposed artist. Andrew Wyeth, Piet Mondrian, Thomas Hart Benton, Jackson Pollock, Mark Rothko—any of these masters, figurative or abstract, might inspire a single intriguing story. But a whole book's worth?

I couldn't see it.

And then the penny dropped. Perhaps a whole roomful of artists could do what a single artist could not.

Seventeen writers producing seventeen stories based on seventeen paintings—each by a different artist.

Alive in Shape and Color.

I didn't like the title quite as much as *In Sunlight or in Shadow*—and still don't, I have to admit. But it would do to get us started.

I took a deep breath, poured myself a cup of coffee, and began drafting an email to potential contributors.

An invitation to contribute to an anthology is an honor, right?

Well, of course it is. And yet I find myself thinking of the visitor who somehow aroused the ire of the local citizenry, some of whom had expressed their displeasure by tarring and feathering the fellow and riding him out of town on a rail.

"But for the honor of the occasion," he reported, "I'd have preferred leaving town in a more conventional fashion."

The honor of an anthology invitation brings its own tar and feathers. One has to write something, and the cash return for one's time and effort is essentially token payment. It's always been clear to me that to ask someone for a story is to ask that person for a favor.

Sometimes, of course, it all redounds to the writer's benefit. When I look back at the stories I've written for other people's anthologies, I have much to be grateful for. A couple of stories about a cheerfully homicidal young woman, all written almost grudgingly for friends of mine compiling anthologies, led to a novel, *Getting Off*. A short story I'd long ago promised for a collection of private eye stories revived Matthew Scudder when I'd assumed I was done writing about him. (The story, "By the Dawn's Early Light," was my first sale to *Playboy*, won me my first Edgar Award, grew into *When the Sacred Ginmill Closes*, and led over the years to a eight more short stories and a dozen more novels about Mr. Scudder.)

So I can't say I regret those anthology invitations I've received. Still, I issue them diffidently, knowing that they're always, to some extent, an imposition.

In this instance, I knew where to start. I invited all sixteen *ISOIS* contributors. They'd been a pleasure to work with, and their stories were superb—and I could only hope that at least a few of them would re-up for another tour of duty.

Megan Abbott had to pass, explaining she had way too much work on her plate. Stephen King, who'd surprised me by letting his love for Hopper lure him into *ISOIS*—and whose story won him an Edgar nomination—was able to resist this time around. Robert Olen Butler liked the idea of *Alive in Shape and Color* (which I think I'll call *AISAC* for the rest of this introduction); he chose an artist and a painting, then had to bow out when he learned his publisher had committed him to a lengthy book tour that ate up all his time.

But everybody else accepted.

Now I have to tell you that this flat-out astonished me. I sent out a few more invitations, to David Morrell, Thomas Pluck, S. J. Rozan, and Sarah Weinman. And they accepted, too.

All the stories for *ISOIS* were new, specifically written for the book, and *AISAC* was similarly conceived. But David Morrell responded to my invitation by stating that he not only liked the premise but that he'd written the story thirty years ago. He sent along "Orange Is for Anguish, Blue for Insanity," and it wasn't hard to see what he meant. (It was just as easy to see why it had won a Bram Stoker Award when it was published.)

So the possibility exists that a few of you may have read David's story before. I don't think you'll mind reading it again.

And you could think of it as a bonus, because we'd have eighteen stories this time around, one more than *ISOIS*. I didn't see that as a problem, and neither did the good folks at Pegasus.

Eighteen stories? Um, better make that sixteen.

One thing to know about writing is that it doesn't always work out the way you'd hoped. It's a rare anthology to which a writer doesn't fail to deliver a promised story.

This happened with *ISOIS*. One writer picked a painting and agreed to write a story, and an onslaught of personal problems made work of any sort out of the question. By the time he let us know his story was just not going to happen, we'd already acquired reproduction rights to his chosen painting, *Cape Cod Morning*. If we couldn't have the story, at least we could have the painting—and used it as a bonus frontispiece for the book.

This time around, Craig Ferguson found himself unable to deliver. He'd picked a Picasso painting, but the story never came, and his own schedule grew impossibly demanding, with the added time commitment of a new show on SiriusXM radio. He apologized profusely and said he hoped I could understand.

I understood all too well.

Because I too found myself unable to deliver a story.

I'd picked a painting very early on, around the time I was readying my letters of invitation. My wife and I were at a portrait show at the Whitney in New York City, and an oil by Raphael Soyer stopped me in my tracks. I'd never seen it before, knew next to nothing about the artist, and figured it was as perfect a source of fictional inspiration as anything of Hopper's.

Eventually I got around a thousand words written. But I didn't like what I'd done, nor did I see where to go with it.

Now, I sold my first story in 1957, so I've been doing this for sixty years. And I've been getting the message lately that it may be something I can't do anymore. A few years ago it seemed to me that I might be ready to stop writing novels, and while I've turned out a book or two since then, I don't expect to do another. There have been a few short stories and novellas in recent years, and there may be more in what time I have left—but there may be not.

And that's okay.

If I'd promised the Soyer-inspired story for someone else's anthology, I'd have long since sent regrets and apologies. But it seemed unpardonable for me to bow out of my own book, and so I banged my head against that particular wall longer than I needed to. Eventually it dawned on me that a book with such fine stories by so distinguished a list of contributors could make its way in the world without a story of mine.

And just because I'd failed to deliver the story didn't mean you'd have to make do without the painting. Even as *Cape Cod Morning* functioned admirably as the frontispiece illustration for *In Sunlight or in Shadow*, so does *The Office Girls* serve beautifully in that capacity in *Alive in Shape and Color*. And, as before, I'll extend an invitation to y'all. Feel free to come up with a story of your own based on Raphael Soyer's evocative painting. Dream it up—and, if you're so inclined, write it down.

But don't send it to me. I'm done here.

And that would have been that, but for an email from Warren Moore, whose Salvador Dali–inspired story is one of the special treats awaiting you. He reminded me that I had in fact published a story twenty years ago that fit AISAC's *requirements quite comfortably. "Looking for David" grew out of my own teenage exposure to a copy of Michelangelo's statue in Buffalo's Delaware Park, the recollection triggered by the sight of the original on a 1995 visit to Florence. Matthew Scudder's in Florence with his wife, Elaine, when a chance encounter with the principal in an old case fills him in on what Paul Harvey used to call "the end of the story"—a story that begins in Buffalo, plays out in New York, and winds up on the banks of the Arno.*

A perfect fit for the book, but could AISAC *include a second previously published story? I could argue the case either way, so I handed off the decision to Claiborne Hancock at Pegasus, who didn't hesitate to vote aye. And so* AISAC *has seventeen stories after all, with Michelangelo's* David *joining Rodin's* The Thinker *in the sculpture gallery.*

But we've kept Raphael Soyer's The Office Girls *as a frontispiece, a bonus painting that may inspire you as it didn't quite manage to inspire me.*

—Lawrence Block

JILL D. BLOCK *lives in New York City, where she is a writer and an attorney, but not always in that order. Her writing is inspired by the world around her—including, in this case, Art Frahm's* Remember All the Safety Rules, *which hangs in her apartment. Her legal work, on the other hand, is inspired by a fear of being fired.*

She has had short stories published in Ellery Queen's Mystery Magazine, *and in the anthologies* Dark City Lights *and* In Sunlight or in Shadow. *She is coming perilously close to finishing her first novel (which, she acknowledges, will be her only novel unless she writes a second).*

Remember All the Safety Rules by Art Frahm

SAFETY RULES

BY JILL D. BLOCK

DAY ONE

This was my third time, and I knew exactly what to expect. I got downtown early, so I had time to stop at Starbucks when I got off the subway. I was upstairs, in the appointed room, at 8:55. I found a seat, took out my magazine, flipped past the fashion ads, and was already pretty well into Graydon Carter's piece on Trump by the time things got started. The lady told us to tear our cards along the perforated fold, and after she collected the bottom piece, she turned on the instructional video.

I wasn't at all surprised when a court officer came into the room, about thirty minutes after the video ended, to call for the first group. I knew the drill—twenty or twenty-five of us would be taken up to a courtroom where they'd be selecting a jury. Everyone else would stay here, and other groups would be called for throughout the day and maybe into tomorrow. Three days tops, and I'd have done my civic duty. I hoped that I would be called

3

in this first group—early in, early out. Maybe I'd even have time to look for boots before I headed back uptown.

I did that thing I do, keeping count as he called out names. He read loudly, with the bored authority of a man with a badge, from the stack of cards he was holding, struggling now and then with the pronunciation. I stopped counting when I got to eighty-five and he kept going. I looked around the room—six chairs per row on each side of the center aisle and what looked to be about twenty-five rows. Not every seat had been filled, but it was pretty close. So there were maybe 250 of us? 260? I was trying to do a rough count of how many people were still seated when I heard my name. I put my magazine in my bag, picked up my empty coffee cup, and stepped into the crowd that was making its way toward the door at the back of the room and out into the hallway. The clerk continued to call out names.

It's funny what happens when the rules change. I had walked in less than an hour earlier, feeling like I owned the place, knowing exactly where to go, what to do, what to expect. *Jury duty, yeah, yeah. Maybe I can find a place to get a manicure during the lunch break.* And then, there I was, just as lost as everyone else, awaiting instructions and following the crowd into the unknown.

"So that should be everyone." The clerk kept talking as he moved through the crowd. "If you didn't hear your name, check the postcard you received in the mail that told you to come here today. If your postcard says September 27, 2016, and room 311, you are in the right place, and you are coming with me. If your postcard says anything other than September 27, 2016, and room 311, you are in the wrong place. If you are in the wrong place, you need to go to the central clerk's office, room 355. Everyone else, we are going to the ninth floor, part forty-two. Please follow me."

It took more than forty-five minutes to get us all upstairs and into the court-room. We were like a class of unruly kindergarteners. We filled all the seats, and there were people standing along the sides and at the back of the room. The judge introduced himself, apologized for there not being enough seats, and thanked us for being there. He introduced the prosecuting attorneys, the defense attorneys, and the defendant, and explained that we were the group from which the attorneys would be selecting a jury of twelve. Why so many people? Well, he explained, the trial is expected to go for four months. Four days a week, ten to five, through January. A collective gasp was followed by a din of whispered conversations. He let us settle down, and then he talked a little bit about how the jury system works. He said that he recognized the sacrifice that each of us had made just by coming in today, not to mention what would be required of the jurors who were selected to serve on this case. Then he asked us to take a few minutes to think, to reflect, to determine, based solely on the schedule he had described, if we would not be able to serve on this jury. He was good. He made you feel like you owed him something, like you really needed to dig deep, to find a way to give of yourself in support of this very fundamental tenet of our legal system. Like if you said you couldn't do it, you would be letting him down. He said that if we thought we could do it, we were to take a questionnaire from the clerk, go out into the hall and fill it out, then give it back to the clerk when we were done and come back on Friday. If we thought we could not, we were to have a seat. He and the attorneys would meet privately with each of those who stayed, one at a time.

I took a seat.

I spent the rest of the day bored out of my head, with no electronics permitted in the courtroom. It was freezing in there. I kept myself busy watching how they lined people up, as if understanding the system would give me some control over it. They had five people get up at a time, going in order from where we were sitting on the benches. They would have the next five come up when there was one person left on line, waiting outside the closed door. I tried to keep track of how many people ended up taking a questionnaire after they came out from having their private conversation, and how many were given back their card, told to go back to the room we'd started in, presumably to be dismissed. There were seven people left ahead of me when they sent us to lunch and told us to be back at two fifteen. When I got back, I was behind someone who had apparently never been through a metal detector before ("What? I need to take off my belt?"), so I was one of the last people to get back into the courtroom. Instead of there being seven people ahead of me, I was now sitting in the back row, with only four people behind me. All afternoon, it was more of the same, more sitting, more waiting. And then, finally, it was my turn to go in. The judge introduced himself and the lawyers again, and I introduced myself. I explained to them that my job made this impossible for me. That my position at the bank requires redundancy, that there always needs

5

to be someone there who does what I do. They asked how many of us there are, who was covering for me that day, and what happens when one of us gets sick or goes on vacation. I wondered what I should have said instead, if they would have asked me for proof if I'd said I had life-saving surgery scheduled. The judge thanked me for my time and told me to fill out a questionnaire and be back on Friday.

DAY TWO

We'd been told to report to a bigger courtroom, but they were still a couple of seats short for everyone who came back on Friday. It turned out that my group from Tuesday was the second group—they'd done the same thing with another group two weeks before, and this was day two for everyone who had filled out a questionnaire. The judge began by telling us that we were the group from whom the attorneys would be selecting a jury for the 1978 kidnapping and murder of Milo Richter. I felt myself take a breath. Micheline! All of a sudden, it made perfect sense. I was there for a reason. The judge explained that familiarity with the case was not a reason anyone would be dismissed. He acknowledged that some of us might know quite a lot about it, and others of us might never have heard of it, but either way that alone didn't matter.

He explained how jury selection would work. They would call sixteen names at random, and those sixteen people would sit in the jury box, where the judge would ask them each a series of questions. The attorneys might decide, based on the answers to the judge's questions, that one or more of the sixteen were not right for this case, and they would be dismissed. More names would be called, and the judge would ask the new people the same questions. Once they had sixteen who made it past the judge's questions, the attorneys would address them as a group. All of this would happen in the courtroom. Each of us would be present. No phones, no computers. He started talking about the importance of an impartial jury, and I stopped listening.

Micheline. I hadn't thought of her in years, but I could picture her in my mind like I'd seen her yesterday. Those braids. At school, everyone called her Braidy. Braidy Grady. Because Micheline was too long, too hard to say, too foreign for our sleepy New Jersey town. But I only ever called her Micheline.

I'd practiced, alone in my room, learning to say it right, like she did, like her mother did.

Micheline and I were best friends. I'd chosen her, from a classroom full of first graders, the way you might choose the best-looking apple from a bushel at a farmstand. She was my first friend who was truly my own, whose mother wasn't already friends with mine, who hadn't been shoved toward me, told to go play, while the grown-ups talked. Of course I'd chosen her. From the first moment I looked at her, I couldn't look away. She was different, not like the rest of us. Not just her name, but her manners, her accent, her clothes. She was wearing Petit Bateau, and the rest of us were wearing Danskin outfits that our mothers brought home from JCPenney.

Everyone wanted to be her friend. Even Mrs. Turner, with her thick ankles and glasses hanging on a chain around her neck, was utterly enchanted by Micheline. What was so amazing to me, even then, at six years old, was that she chose me back. She was my best friend and I was hers, with an unquestioning certainty that I have never known since. About anything. We were Braidy and Nicki. Micheline and Veronica.

The judge sent us out into the hallway for a ten-minute break. He said that when we returned, they would assemble the first group of sixteen and we would get started, going all day, with a break for lunch from one to two fifteen. I picked up my bag, turned on my phone and joined the crowd exiting the courtroom. *Please pick me, please pick me, please pick me*, I said to myself. Waiting in line to use the ladies' room, I scrolled through the emails that had come in while my phone was turned off. *Please pick me, please pick me, please pick me*. I put my phone away, without having opened any of the emails. *Let me do this*, I thought. *Let me fix it. Let me do this for Micheline.*

It was twenty-five minutes by the time we were all back inside, seated and ready to go. The clerk began reading names from the cards he pulled from one of those metal barrels that you turn with a crank. *Please pick me, please pick me, please pick me*. He read a name, and then spelled it, first then last, I guessed to make sure the court reporter would get it right. I sat up straight in my seat and shifted a little to the left so that if he looked up, the clerk would have a clear view of me. He'd called ten names. Six to go. I closed my eyes and took a slow breath in. *Please pick me, please pick me, please pick me.*

He didn't pick me.

I was disappointed, but I knew that there would be other opportunities for my name to be called. I paid attention to what the judge was saying to the sixteen they'd chosen. He asked the same questions, in the same order, to each person, one by one. By the time he started asking the fourth person, I had the questions memorized. "Where in Manhattan do you live?" "Where are you from originally?" "How much school did you complete?" "Are you currently working?" "What type of work do you do?" "With whom do you share your home?" "Are your children school-aged?" This was going to be easy. I had lived on the Upper East Side for almost thirty years, since I moved there after grad school. I lived alone, didn't have kids, didn't work with kids. "Have you or a close friend or family member been the victim of a crime?" "Do you have any close friends or family in law enforcement?" "Do you know anyone who has been charged or convicted of a crime?" "What do you like to do in your spare time?" Most of the people answering the questions spoke so softly that I couldn't really hear what they were saying, even though the attorneys kept asking them to speak up. The people sitting in the front rows on the right side of the room, closest to the jury box, laughed at one lady's answer to the question about who she lived with. I looked over and saw that the judge was smiling, too. I wondered what she'd said.

When the guy in the Buffalo Bills shirt answered yes, that he or a close friend or family member had been the victim of a crime, the judge asked if he had described it in his questionnaire, and the guy said yes. Oh, shit. I remembered the question, but I had answered it without much thought. I was pretty sure I answered no. Or if I said yes, I had only been thinking about the time my wallet was stolen in Paris, so I probably just wrote something like "pickpocketed, 1984." I hadn't been lying. Not on purpose, anyway. I honestly didn't think of Micheline that way. We were eight years old.

The fact that I hadn't said anything about it in my questionnaire felt like another sign that I was supposed to be there. That I was there for a reason. Before knowing what this case was about, I totally could have answered that question "yes," and I could have written something about what happened, and I was pretty sure that would have been enough to get me sent home. Which, at the time, was what I wanted, right? So it wasn't like I didn't mention it on purpose. I *wanted* to get released. If I'd thought of it, I *would* have said yes.

After the judge finished asking his questions to the seventh person, we broke for lunch. I walked and walked, trying to decide what I should do. Should I tell them, or should I not? Of course I knew that I should. There was a reason they were asking the question. And we had sworn, or taken an oath or something, that we would tell the truth. But I also knew that if I told them it would prejudice them against me. They would assume I couldn't be impartial. That I couldn't distinguish between this case and what happened to Micheline.

After lunch, they picked up where they'd left off. The judge continued to ask the same questions, and the people in the jury box continued to answer them. I closed my eyes.

All of a sudden, I had this memory. It was vivid like a dream, but I was wide-awake, perfectly conscious of where I was, sitting in the courtroom, with the hum of questions and answers in the background. We were in second grade. I knew that because Ms. Jordan was there, and we had her for second grade. We loved her, because she was so young and pretty. Especially after Mrs. Turner the year before. A policeman came to our class that day, to talk to us about traffic safety. Stuff like looking both ways and only crossing at the corner. When the policeman finished and asked if anyone had any questions, two kids raised their hands, Timmy something, who moved away the summer after fifth grade, and Micheline. Timmy asked the policeman if he'd ever shot a gun. And then Micheline asked what were the safety rules for walking past a haunted house.

Everybody laughed, including the policeman and Miss Jordan. But I knew she didn't mean to be funny. Micheline and I walked to and from school together every day. It seemed impossible, thinking back, that our parents allowed it. We were six or seven years old. But it really was a different time. All the kids from school who lived out toward the lake walked in the same direction at the same time. Not quite together, but none of us really alone. Micheline and I lived the farthest out, so it was always just the two of us when we passed the Red House.

We had already come up with some safety rules of our own. We had to hold our breath while we were passing the house. We'd breathe in a big gulp of air at the mailbox, and we'd hold it until we got to the tree on the other side and touched it with our hand. We walked as fast as we could, but we couldn't

9

run. And we couldn't look at the house. We would look straight ahead, and we would try not to blink. I don't know why we didn't just cross the street.

After the judge finished questioning the last person, he talked to the attorneys for a few minutes. He asked the people in the jury box to wait around in the hall for a little bit in case the attorneys had any questions for them, and the rest of us were done for the day. We were told to be back on Monday at ten. It was nice out, and too late to go to the office, so I decided to walk home.

I hadn't really believed the Red House was haunted. I don't think I even knew what *haunted* meant. It was an old house, the paint faded and peeling, and no one lived there. The front lawn was overgrown, and the driveway didn't get shoveled when it snowed. One of the steps up to the front porch was broken. I remembered when I was home from college for a visit, and I saw that it had been torn down, that a new house had been built on the property. I couldn't believe it—the Red House was gone. I asked my mother what she knew about it, who had owned it and when they'd sold it. She said she didn't know what I was talking about. The old red house? That she'd driven by thousands of times? Maybe tens of thousands of times? The one Dad used to call a "goddamn eyesore"? Nope. She had no recollection.

I was careful to stay busy, not wanting to spend the weekend thinking about the case. The judge had told us that we were not to talk or read about it, and that we had to avoid any articles or news stories or conversations about it. He said it was okay for us to tell people which case it was that we were being considered for, but that was it. I decided not to. I didn't want to risk anyone saying something to me about it. Or about Micheline.

I never understood why, but Micheline's disappearance hadn't gotten the national attention that the Milo Richter case got just a few years later. It was, of course, a huge deal where we lived. I didn't really know how much I remembered, and how much I knew from having read or been told about it since. What I knew was that Helene had gone in to wake Micheline up for school, and her bed was empty. She was gone. Her father was out of town for work, so it had been just the two of them at home. Their back door wasn't locked. But lots of people used to leave their doors unlocked. Helene had been drinking. In the newspaper articles I read later, there was a lot of attention to the fact that there had been an empty wine bottle in the trash and a half-empty bottle on the counter. She'd fallen asleep on the couch. Whatever had happened in the house, she slept through it.

Helene wasn't like the other moms, and she didn't have many friends. She and Pete met when he was working in France. They'd moved from Paris when Pete got transferred to his company's New York office, the summer before Micheline and I started first grade. Helene wasn't one of the moms who came on class trips, or who volunteered in the school library or helped with the Halloween parade. My mom had been very critical of her. Probably all the moms were. I was sure it didn't help that I would come home from Micheline's with stories about how Helene said I could call her Maman, how she sprayed us with her perfume, or that she let us help her bake and how she'd laughed at the mess we made, that we'd gotten powdered sugar everywhere. At my house, Micheline called my mom Mrs. Ellis, and as a treat we were sometimes allowed to eat TV dinners on tray tables in the den. My mom had said it just didn't seem right that Helene had dressed so nicely for the funeral, that she'd put on lipstick and a scarf. I remembered my mom saying to my dad, "What kind of mother would even think to put on a scarf to go to her child's funeral?"

DAY THREE

Please pick me, please pick me, please pick me. The day started with the clerk choosing people to replace the two who had been let go based on the judge's questions. I tried to remember who had been sitting in the empty seats, what they'd said that got them sent home. The clerk turned the crank and pulled out a card identifying the new person for seat number three. *Please pick me, please pick me, please pick me.* Not me. Next name, for seat number nine. Not me. The judge asked his same questions of each of the new people. When he was done, he and the attorneys had a whispered conversation, I guessed to make sure the two new people were okay, and then said he was just about ready to give someone else a chance to talk. He explained a little about the voir dire process and told us in the audience that we should pay attention and think about how we would answer the questions being asked, and then he turned it over to the assistant district attorney.

I liked her at first. She seemed like she was going to be good. She spoke loudly and with authority, and seemed comfortable speaking to a group. She talked about the evidence that she and her team were going to present and what it was going to prove. She also talked about the evidence the defense attorneys were likely to present. When she started asking questions, you could see that she'd memorized the names of who was sitting in which chair. "Ms. Cantone, you will you be able to listen to the evidence and use your common sense to determine if it is reliable, right?" Ms. Cantone said yes. "And you, Mr. Wald. You too? Will you be able to apply your life experience and common sense to the evidence that is presented?" Mr. Wald said yes. "Everyone else? Is there anyone here who will not be able to use your common sense? Mr. Lometo? Am I saying that right?" I could see that poor Mr. Lometo didn't know which of her questions he was supposed to answer.

She explained that the prosecution's first witness would be Wendy Richter, Milo's mother, and she was likely to be very emotional during her testimony. "It has been thirty-eight years since Milo was kidnapped and murdered. Does anyone—?"

"Objection. Allegedly kidnapped and murdered."

The judge turned to the people in the jury box. "Unless it is proven that a kidnapping and murder took place, please keep in mind that it is only alleged to have occurred. Go ahead."

She began again, emphasizing the word *alleged* like she was indulging a petulant child, asking if anyone thought that it was time that Wendy Richter "just get over it already"? A collective no. When she asked if everyone could agree that real life isn't like an episode of *Law & Order*, I tuned her out.

For a long time I believed that what happened to Micheline was my fault. One day, when we were walking by the Red House on our way home from school, something made me look. I barely turned my head at all, moving my eyes way to the left so I could see. And then I stopped and turned. A man was sitting on the front steps, pulling at the splintered wood of the broken step. I grabbed Micheline's hand and pointed. "Look! A monster." We ran to my house as fast as we could. We didn't say anything about it to my mom. I was afraid that we'd get in trouble for having broken the Red House Rules. I wondered what would have happened if we'd told someone what we'd seen. If everything might have turned out differently.

We saw the Monster three more times after that. Twice, he was sitting in a dirty white car parked in front of the Red House, and once he was on the porch, standing by the front door, smoking a cigarette. He was a regular-looking guy, a grown-up but not old, with glasses, long hair, and baggy clothes. That last time we saw him, he smiled and waved to us. We were terrified.

The lawyer continued to ask these rhetorical questions, and the people in the jury box continued to give all the right answers. "As jurors, you will be required to follow the judge's instructions. Will you be able to do that? Yes? Ms. Chen? Mr. Frawley?" "Just because someone is uneducated, do you think it is possible for them to be truthful?" It was frustrating. Her questions were so dumb. How was this going to help her decide who should be on the jury? I took out my book and read until we broke for lunch.

The defense attorney was better. At least I could tell what he was trying to learn about the people he was questioning. He spent a lot of time talking before he started asking questions. He talked about the burden of proof and reasonable doubt and the presumption of innocence. He talked about the challenges in the prosecutor's case, that there were no eyewitnesses, no DNA, no video footage from security cameras. That Milo's body had never been found.

Micheline's body was found in the lake three days after she disappeared. She'd been strangled and was already dead when she was put in the water. I didn't know any of that at the time. It was years later before I was able to get my mom to really talk to me about it. What do you tell an eight-year-old whose best friend has been taken from her bed, while her mother slept, murdered and thrown in the lake?

I'd known right from the start that she was missing. That first morning, everyone was too freaked out to make up an age-appropriate story. After her body was found, my mom told me that Micheline was someplace so far away that she was not ever going to be able to come back. I only figured out that she was dead because some of the churchier kids at school said that she was in heaven. My mom must have heard or read somewhere that it was important to get me to talk about my feelings, so when she put me to bed that night, instead of telling me some sanitized version of the truth, she asked me to tell her what I thought had happened. I said it was the Monster. That the Monster from the Red House had gotten her. My mom said later that she'd figured that that was as good a story as anything she and my dad were going to come up with, so she gave me a hug and lay down with me until I fell asleep.

The lawyer asked a bunch of questions about IQ and psychological testing. Had anyone ever had their IQ tested? Were people familiar with the Myers-Briggs personality test? He didn't ask yes-or-no questions like the other one had. He asked different people, sort of jumping around, what their experience was, or if they had an opinion about something. He talked about mental illness, and asked people what kind of contact they'd had with mentally ill people. He said that there would be testimony about the defendant having used drugs for several years in the 1980s and '90s. He asked how knowing that about the defendant might affect what they thought about him, about his likelihood to commit other crimes. Same thing with domestic violence. There had been a couple of incidents of domestic violence between him and his ex-wife. I could see what he was doing. He was putting it all out there. Not pretending for a minute that this guy was an angel. But asking these questions to see who was going to be able to listen to all of this ugly stuff about him and not automatically assume he'd done this other thing.

The Monster was never caught. Or if he was, he was never connected with Micheline's case. Other than that one conversation with my mother, when I told her that I knew the Monster had taken her, no one ever spoke to me about it. There was no kind lady cop asking me to draw her a picture of the Monster, no spunky school psychiatrist committed to helping me find language that the adults would understand. It was 1971. Life went on.

Helene and Pete moved away pretty soon after Micheline disappeared. Eventually, my mom told me that she'd heard they split up, that Helene had gone back to France. I studied in Paris my junior year of college. I spent the whole time I was there hoping to find Helene, but not really looking for her, thinking that I'd run into her on the Metro or in a café, afraid of what would happen if I did. I wanted to see her so I could apologize, and so she could tell me that it wasn't my fault. I found her obituary on the internet a few years ago. It turned out she'd died in 1982, more than a year before I went to France.

The defense attorney spent the most time talking about confessions. There would be evidence, he said, that the defendant had confessed, to various people at various times. He asked why a person might confess to a crime he didn't commit. The defendant, who he said had an IQ of sixty-seven, and had been diagnosed with psychotic hallucinations, had confessed to the cops after seven hours of interrogation, most of which was not recorded. He'd been in prison for the last four years, awaiting trial.

The defense attorney said that there had been no witnesses to the alleged kidnapping, and he asked the jurors what they could imagine might have happened instead. What other explanation besides kidnapping could there be for Milo's disappearance? People answered that he could have run away, or maybe he got lost. Were they saying that Micheline might have run away? No way. She wouldn't have done that. Or that Helene had done something to hurt her? That was impossible.

The defense attorney finished a few minutes before five and we were told to be back at ten the next morning. It had been a grueling day, and all I'd done was watch and listen. I just wanted to go home and get in bed, to stop thinking, stop remembering.

DAY FOUR

The judge thanked us for our continued patience and explained that not getting chosen to serve on this jury did not mean anything other than that the attorneys did not happen to agree that you were right for this particular case. He told us what was going to happen next. The clerk was going to read the names of those people in the group of sixteen who would be members of the jury. "Please stand if the clerk calls your name. Everyone else, remain seated." I noticed that it was that same clerk from that first morning in the big room downstairs. Maybe he'd been there in the room with us all along. "Seat number three, Alicia Mason." She stood up. "Seat number fourteen, Roberto Diaz". He stood up. We waited for the clerk to call the next name. Silence.

It took a minute for us to realize that that was it. That after all that, they had chosen two people. This was going to take forever.

The judge told the fourteen people who were being let go what they needed to do, and then they swore in the two people who made it. After that, the two were told to go with the court officer to exchange contact information. The judge told them to plan to be back next Monday.

From where I was sitting, in the third row behind the defense table, I could see the back of the defendant's shaved head, the roll of fat at the base of his skull. He was eighteen years old when Milo disappeared, thirty-eight years ago. He worked at the deli where Milo was going to stop to buy a snack for his lunch. He had a history of drug use and domestic violence. He'd fucking confessed. It would be so easy to convict him. But what if he hadn't done it? They said he'd been interrogated for seven hours before he gave his confession. And it was apparently pretty clear that he was mentally ill. He had an IQ of sixty-seven. I didn't know what a normal IQ score might be, but sixty-seven didn't sound good. Did he have the intelligence of an eight-year-old? When I was eight, I told my mother that the Monster from the Red House had taken Micheline.

The clerk was turning the crank, picking sixteen new names from the barrel. Just like before, he would read the name, and then spell it, first then last. It had become background noise, easy to ignore. I looked over and saw that they'd already filled nine seats when I wasn't paying attention. I closed my eyes. This experience was going to be brutal for everyone involved. *Don't pick me, don't pick me, don't pick me.* I had thought in the beginning that this was going to be my opportunity to make things right for Micheline. But I could see that there would be no good outcome here. *Don't pick me, don't pick me, don't pick me.* The reality was that no one would ever know what had really happened. And maybe that was okay. How was knowing what happened going to help anyone? Maybe closure was overrated. Maybe that was the reason I was there, that was what I was meant to learn. I had heard enough. I didn't need to listen anymore. I reached down to get my book from my bag on the floor.

"For seat number eleven, Veronica Ellis. V-E-R-O-N-I-C-A E-L-L-I-S."

The judge's questions went a little bit faster. We knew by now what to expect. He finished with the lady next to me, Ms. Rosalia, at about ten to one, and the judge said we would break a little early for lunch, that we should be back at 2:15. I found an empty bench in the sun in the park next to the courthouse. I leaned back and closed my eyes.

Had I or a close friend or family member been the victim of a crime? I didn't know what the right answer was. I could say no. It was forty-five years ago. We were children. I didn't know what had happened. I wasn't a witness; I had never been questioned; I had no personal knowledge of the case or the investigation. It was ancient history. I hadn't even thought about it in years. Not until all of this.

This wasn't fair. It shouldn't have been up to me. It should be up to the attorneys to figure it out. They were the ones getting paid for this, not me. I decided then that it was out of my hands. I had sworn to tell the truth, so I would. Had I or a close friend or family member been the victim of a crime? I would say yes. When the judge asked me if I had described it on my questionnaire, I would say no. When the judge asked if I wanted to speak with them privately about it, I would say yes. I would tell them that I had known Micheline Grady. Maybe they would be familiar with the case, maybe not. Whatever questions they asked, I would answer. Let it be someone else's problem.

I sat on the bench until ten after two. I went inside, through the security line, and up to the courtroom. The court officer directed those of us who had been in the jury box to go back to our same seats. We waited for the people in the audience, the people not yet chosen or released, to get settled.

"Good afternoon. Ms. Ellis, right?"

"Yes."

"Where in Manhattan do you live?"

"On the Upper East Side."

"Where are you from originally?"

"New Jersey."

"How long have you been living on the Upper East Side?"

"About twenty-eight years."

"How much school did you complete?"

"I have a master's degree."

"In what field?"

"Finance. I have an MBA."

"And are you currently working?"

"I am."

"What type of work do you do?"

"I'm in banking. I work in the treasury department of a bank."

"We spoke about that. Required redundancy, right?"

"Yes. That was me."

"With whom do you share your home?"

"I live alone."

"Have you or a close friend or family member been the victim of a crime?"

My heart was pounding. I wondered if Ms. Rosalia could hear it from seat number ten.

"Yes."

"I'm sorry to hear that. Will it affect your ability to be impartial in this case?"

Wait, what? Go back. That wasn't what he was supposed to ask me.

"Umm, no. I don't think so. I mean, no. It won't."

He was supposed to ask if I had described it on my questionnaire. What am I—?

"Do you have any close friends or family in law enforcement?"

"No."

Wasn't someone going to say something? Was anyone even paying attention? I looked over at the attorneys sitting at their tables. Someone should say something.

"Do you know anyone who has been charged or convicted of a crime?"

"No."

"And what do you like to do in your spare time?"

"I, umm—I practice yoga. I like to read and watch TV. I do crossword puzzles."

"Very good. Thank you, Ms. Ellis. Next is Mr. Colon?"

Previously a television director, union organizer, theater technician, and law student, **LEE CHILD** *was fired and on the dole when he hatched a harebrained scheme to write a best-selling novel, thus saving his family from ruin.* Killing Floor *went on to win worldwide acclaim.* The Midnight Line, *the twenty-second Reacher novel, was published in November 2017.*

The hero of his series, Jack Reacher, besides being fictional, is a kindhearted soul who allows Lee lots of spare time for reading, listening to music, and watching Yankees and Aston Villa games.

Lee was born in England but now lives in New York City and leaves the island of Manhattan only when required to by forces beyond his control. Visit Lee online at www.LeeChild.com for more information about the novels, short stories, and the movies Jack Reacher *and* Jack Reacher: Never Go Back *starring Tom Cruise. Lee can also be found on Facebook.com/LeeChildOfficial, Twitter.com/LeeChildReacher and YouTube.com/LeeChildJackReacher.*

Bouquet of Chrysanthemums by Auguste Renoir

PIERRE, LUCIEN, AND ME

BY LEE CHILD

I survived my first heart attack. But as soon as I was well enough to sit up in bed, the doctor came back and told me I was sure to have a second. Only a matter of time, he said. The first episode had been indicative of a serious underlying weakness. Which it had just made worse. Could be days. Or weeks. Months at most. He said from now on I should consider myself an invalid.

I said, "This is 1928, for fuck's sake. They got people talking on the radio from far away. Don't you have a pill for it?"

No pill, he said. Nothing to be done. Maybe see a show. And maybe write some letters. He told me what people regretted most were the things they didn't say. Then he left. Then I left. Now I have been home four days. Doing nothing. Just waiting for the second episode. Days away, or weeks, or months. I have no way of knowing.

I haven't been to see a show. Not yet. I have to admit it's tempting. Sometimes I wonder if the doctor had more in mind than entertainment. I can

21

imagine choosing a brand-new musical, full of color and spectacle and riotous excitement, with a huge finale, whereupon all of us in the audience would jump to our feet for a standing ovation, and I would feel the clamp in my chest, and fall to the floor like an empty raincoat slipping off an upturned seat. I would die there while the oblivious crowd stamped and cheered all around me. My last hours would be full of singing and dancing. Not a bad way to go. But knowing my luck it would happen too soon. Some earlier stimulus would trigger it. Maybe coming up out of the subway. On the steep iron-bound stairs to the Forty-Second Street sidewalk. I would fall and slip back a yard, in the wet and the dirt and the grit, and people would look away and step around me, like I was a regular bum. Or I might make it to the theater, and die on the stairs to the balcony. I no longer have the money for an orchestra seat. Or I might make it to the gods, clinging to the stair rail, out of breath, my heart thumping, and then keel over while the band was still tuning up. The last thing I would hear would be the keening of violin strings all aiming for concert pitch. Not good. And it might spoil things for everyone else. The performance might be canceled.

So in words I have always used, but which are now increasingly meaningless, a show is something I might do later.

I haven't written any letters either. I know what the doctor was getting at. Maybe the last word you had with someone was a hard word. Maybe you never took the time to say, Hey, you're a real good friend, you know that? But I would plead innocent to those charges. I'm a straightforward guy. Usually I talk a lot. People know what I think. We all had good times together. I don't want to spoil them by sending out some kind of a morbid goodbye message.

So why would anyone write letters?

Maybe they feel guilty about something.

Which I don't. Mostly. Hardly at all. I would never claim a blameless life, but I played by the rules. The field was level. They were crooks too. So I never laid awake at night. Still don't. I have no big thing to put right. No small thing either. Nothing on my mind.

Except maybe, just possibly, if you pushed me really hard, I might say the Porterfield kid. He's on my mind a little bit. Even though it was purely business as usual. A fool and his money. Young Porterfield was plenty of one and had plenty of the other. He was the son of what the scandal sheets used to call a

Pittsburgh titan. The old guy turned his steel fortune into an even bigger oil fortune, and made all his children millionaires. They all built mansions up and down Fifth Avenue. They all wanted stuff on their walls. Dumb fucks, all of them. Except mine, who was a sweet dumb fuck.

I first met him nine years ago, late in 1919. Renoir had just died in France. It came over the telegraph. I was working at the Metropolitan Museum at the time, but only on the loading dock. Nothing glamorous, but I was hoping to work my way up. I knew some stuff, even back then. I was rooming with an Italian guy named Angelo, who wanted to be a nightclub performer. Meantime he was waiting tables at a chophouse near the stock exchange. One lunchtime a quartet of rich guys showed up. Fur collars, leather boots. Millions and millions of dollars, right there on the hoof. All young, like princes. Angelo overheard one of them say it was better to buy art while the artist was still alive, because the price would rise sharply when he was dead. It always did. Market forces. Supply and demand. Plus enhanced mystique and status. In response a second guy said in that case they'd all missed the boat on Renoir. The guy had seen the news ticker. But a third guy, who turned out to be Porterfield, said maybe there was still time. Maybe the market wouldn't react overnight. Maybe there would be a grace period, before prices went up.

Then for some dumb reason Angelo buttonholed Porterfield on his way out and said he roomed with a guy who worked for the Metropolitan Museum, and knew a lot about Renoir, and was an expert at finding paintings in unlikely places.

When Angelo told me that night I asked him, "Why the fuck did you say that?"

"Because we're friends," he said. "Because we're going places. You'd do the same for me. If you overheard a guy looking for a singer, you'd tell him about me, right? You help me, I help you. Up the ladder we go. Because of our talents. And luck. Like today. The rich man was talking about art, and you work at the Metropolitan Museum. Which part of that was not true?"

"I unload wagons," I said. "Crates are all I see."

"You're starting at the bottom. You're working your way up. Which ain't easy. We all know that. So you should skip the stairs and take the elevator whenever you can. The chance doesn't come often. This guy is the perfect mark."

"I'm not ready."

"You know about Renoir."

"Not enough."

"Yes enough," Angelo said. "You know the movement. You have a good eye."

Which was generous. But also slightly true, I supposed. I had seen reproductions in the newspaper. Mostly I liked older stuff, but I always tried to keep up. I could tell a Manet from a Monet.

Angelo said, "What's the worst fucking thing that could happen?"

And sure enough, the next morning a messenger from the museum's mail room came out into the cold to find me and give me a note. It was a nice-looking item, on heavy stock, in a thick envelope. It was from Porterfield. He was inviting me to come over at my earliest convenience, to discuss an important proposition.

His place was ten blocks south, on Fifth, accessed through bronze gates that probably came from some ancient palace in Florence, Italy. Shipped over in a big-bellied boat, maybe along with the right kind of workers. I was shown to a library. Porterfield came in five minutes later. He was twenty-two at the time, full of pep and energy, with a big dumb smile on his big pink face. He reminded me of a puppy my cousin once had. Big feet, slipping and sliding, always eager. We waited for a man to bring us coffee, and then Porterfield told me about his grace-period theory. He said he had always liked Renoir, and he wanted one. Or two, or three. It would mean a lot to him. He wanted me to go to France and see what I could find. His budget was generous. He would give me letters of introduction for the local banks. I would be his purchasing agent. He would send me second-class on the first steamship out. He would meet all my legitimate expenses. He talked and talked. I listened and listened. I figured he was about 80 percent the same as any other rich jerk in town, with too much bare wallpaper in his dining room. But I got the feeling some small part of him really liked Renoir. Maybe as more than an investment.

Eventually he stopped talking, and for some dumb reason I said, "Okay, I'll do it. I'll leave right away."

Six days later I was in Paris.

It was hopeless. I knew nothing and no one. I went to galleries like a regular customer, but Renoir prices were already sky-high. There was no grace period. The first guy in the chophouse had been right. Not Porterfield. But I felt duty bound, so I kept at it. I picked up gossip. Some dealers were worried Renoir's kids would flood the market with canvases found in his studio. Apparently they were stacked six deep against the walls. The studio was in a place called Cagnes-sur-Mer, which was in the hills behind Cannes, which was a small fishing port way in the south. On the Mediterranean Sea. A person could get to Cannes by train, and then probably a donkey cart could take him onward.

I went. Why not? The alternative was passage home, to a job I was sure was already gone. I was absent without leave. So I took the sleeper train, to a hot and tawny landscape. A pony and trap took me into the hills. Renoir's place was a pleasant spread. A bunch of manicured acres, and a low stone house. He had been successful for many years. No kind of a starving artist. Not anymore.

There was no one home, except a young man who said he was a good friend of Renoir's. He said his name was Lucien Mignon. He said he lived there. He said he was a fellow artist. He said Renoir's kids had been and gone, and Renoir's wife was in Nice, staying with a friend.

He spoke English, so I made sure he would pass on all kinds of sincere condolences to the appropriate parties. From Renoir's admirers in New York. Of which there were many. Who would all like to know, for reasons I made sound purely academic and even sentimental, exactly how many more paintings were left in the studio.

I figured Mignon would answer, being an artist, and therefore having a keen eye for a buck, but he didn't answer. Not directly. Instead, he told me about his own life. He was a painter, at first an admirer of Renoir, then a friend, then a constant companion. Like a younger brother. He had lived in the house for ten years. He felt despite the difference in their ages, he and Renoir had formed a very deep bond. A true connection.

It sounded weird to me. Like why people get sent to Bellevue. Then it got worse. He showed me his work. It was just like Renoir's. Almost exactly copied, in style and manner and subject. All of it was unsigned too, as if to preserve the illusion it might be the master's own product. It was a very odd and slavish homage.

The studio was a big, tall, square room. It was cool and light. Some of Renoir's work was hung on the wall, and some of Mignon's was hung beside it. It was hard to tell the difference. Below the pieces on display, there were indeed canvases stacked six deep against the walls. Mignon said Renoir's kids had set them aside. As their inheritance. They were not to be looked at and not to be touched. Because they were all very good.

He said it in a way that suggested somehow he had helped make them all very good.

I asked him if he knew of any other canvases as yet unspoken for. Anywhere in France. In answer he pointed across the room. Against another wall was a very small number of items the kids had rejected. Easy to see why. They were all sketches or experiments or otherwise unfinished. One was nothing more than a wavy green stripe running left to right across a bare canvas. Maybe a landscape, started and immediately abandoned. Mignon told me Renoir didn't really like working out of doors. He liked being inside, with his models. Pink and round. Village girls, mostly. Apparently one of them had become Mrs. Renoir.

One of the rejected canvases had the lower half of a landscape on it. A couple dozen green brushstrokes, nicely done, suggestive, but a little tentative and half-hearted. There was no sky. Another abandoned start. A canvas laid aside. But a canvas later grabbed up for another purpose. Where the sky should have been was a still life of pink flowers in a green glass vase. It was in the top left of the frame, painted sideways onto the unfinished landscape, not more than about eight inches by ten. The flowers were roses and anemones. The pink colors were Renoir's trademark. Mignon and I agreed no one did pink better than Renoir. The vase was a cheap thing, bought for a few sous at the market, or made at home by pouring six inches of boiling water into an empty wine bottle, and then tapping it with a hammer.

It was a beautiful little fragment. It looked done with joy. Mignon told me there was a nice story behind it. One summer day Mrs. Renoir had gone out in the garden to pick a bouquet. She had filled the vase with water from the pump, and arranged the stems artfully, and carried it into the house through the studio door, which was the easiest way. Her husband had seen it and was seized with desire to paint it. Literally seized, Mignon said. Such was the artistic temperament. Renoir had stopped what he was doing and grabbed the nearest available canvas, which happened to be the unfinished landscape, and he had stood it vertically on his easel and painted the flowers in the blank space where the sky should have been. He said he couldn't resist their wild disarray. His wife, who had spent more than ten minutes on the arrangement, smiled and said nothing.

Naturally I proposed a deal.

I said if I could take the tiny still life for myself, purely as a personal token and souvenir, then I would buy twenty of Mignon's works to sell in New York. I offered him a hundred thousand dollars of Porterfield's money.

Naturally Mignon said yes.

One more thing, I said. He had to help me cut the flowers out of the larger canvas and tack the fragment to stretchers of its own. Like a miniature original.

He said he would.

One more thing, I said. He had to paint Renoir's signature on it. Purely for my own satisfaction.

He hesitated.

I said he knew Renoir had painted it. He knew that for sure. He had watched it happen. So where was the deception?

He agreed fast enough to make me optimistic about my future.

We took the half-landscape, half-flowers canvas off its stretchers, and we cut the relevant eight-by-ten rectangle out of it, plus enough wraparound margin to fix it to a frame of its own, which Mignon assembled from wood and nails lying around. We put it all together, and then he squeezed a dot of paint from a tube—dark brown, not black—and he took a fine camel-hair brush and painted Renoir's name in the bottom right corner. Just *Renoir*, with a stylized first capital, and then flowing lowercase letters after it, very French, and very identical to the dozens of examples of the real thing I could see all around.

Then I chose twenty of his own canvases. Naturally I picked the most impressive and Renoir-like. I wrote him a check—*one hundred thousand and 00/100*—and we wrapped the twenty-one packages in paper, and we loaded them into the pony cart, which had waited for me, per my instructions and Porterfield's generous tip. I drove off with a wave.

I never saw Mignon again. But we stayed in business together, in a manner of speaking, for three more years.

I took a room in Cannes, in a fine seafront hotel. Bellboys brought up my packages. I went out and found an art store and bought a tube of dark brown oil and a fine camel-hair brush. I propped my little still life on the dresser and copied Renoir's signature, twenty separate times, in the bottom right corners of Mignon's work. Then I went down to the lobby and cabled Porterfield: *Bought three superb Renoirs for a hundred thousand. Returning directly.*

I was home seven days later. First stop was a framer's for my still life, which I then propped on my mantelpiece, and second stop was Porterfield's mansion on Fifth, with three of Mignon's finest.

Which was where the seed of guilt was planted. Porterfield was so fucking happy. So fucking delighted. He had his Renoirs. He beamed and smiled like a kid on Christmas morning. They were fabulous, he said. They were a steal. Thirty-three grand apiece. He even gave me a bonus.

I got over it pretty fast. I had to. I had seventeen more Renoirs to sell, which I did, leaking them out slowly over a three-year span, to preserve their value. I was like the dealers I had met in Paris. I didn't want a glut. With the money I got I moved uptown. I never lived with Angelo again. I met a guy who said RCA stock was the thing to buy, so I did, but I got taken for a ride. I lost most everything. Not that I could complain. The biter bit, and so on. Sauce for the fucking goose. My world shrunk down to a solitary life in the uncaring city, buoyed up by the glow of my roses and anemones above the fireplace. I imagined the same feeling inside Porterfield's place, like two pins in a map. Twin centers of happiness and delight. He with his Renoirs, and me with mine.

Then the heart attack, and the guilt. The sweet dumb fuck. The big smile on his face. I didn't write a letter. How could I explain? Instead, I took my Renoir off the wall, and wrapped it in paper, and walked it up Fifth, and through the bronze Italian gates, to the door. Porterfield wasn't home. Which was Okay. I gave the package to his flunky and said I wanted his boss to have it, because I knew he liked Renoir. Then I walked away, back to my place, where I continue to sit, just waiting for the second episode. My wall looks bare, but maybe better for it.

NICHOLAS CHRISTOPHER *is the author of six novels,* The Soloist, Veronica, A Trip to the Stars, Franklin Flyer, The Bestiary, *and* Tiger Rag; *nine books of poetry, most recently,* On Jupiter Place *and* Crossing the Equator: New and Selected Poems 1972–2004; *a nonfiction book,* Somewhere in the Night: Film Noir and the American City; *and* The True Adventures of Nicolò Zen, *a novel for children. His books have been widely translated and published abroad. He lives in New York City.*

Girl with a Fan by Paul Gauguin

GIRL WITH A FAN

BY NICHOLAS CHRISTOPHER

1

On the fifth of June, 1944, a young man stepped off the 9:13 train from Lyon, squinting into the morning light. Tall and slender, he had an asymmetrical face: the right eye higher than the left, the left cheek planed more sharply than the right. He was wearing a brown suit, black shirt, yellow tie, and brown fedora. His suit was rumpled, his boots scuffed. He was carrying a leather briefcase with a brass lock. His pants cuffs were faintly speckled with yellow paint.

He cast a long shadow as he walked down the platform. Halfway to the station, two men in leather coats came up from behind and gripped his arms. One of them pressed a pistol into his side, the other grabbed his briefcase. They veered away from the station, guiding him roughly down an alley to a waiting car. A man in dark glasses was behind the wheel. He was bald, with an eagle tattooed at the base of his skull.

After frisking the young man and taking his wallet, the two men pushed him into the rear seat, pressed between them. The driver glanced at him in the rearview mirror and said, "Hubert Ditmar, welcome to Arles."

The man on his right rifled his wallet. He removed eleven francs, a photograph of a blond woman in a red coat, and three calling cards:

LOUIS VINCENT

STOCKBROKER

CLERY & FENNIEL

15 RUE DE MARIBEL

BRUSSELS, BELGIUM 63 21T

Also a Belgian identity card in that name which listed his eyes as brown, hair black, height five ten, date of birth November 30, 1908, in Liège.

His actual date of birth was November 29, 1908, in Orléans, and his real name was neither Hubert Ditmar nor Louis Vincent.

2

Since beginning his assignment four months earlier, Hubert Ditmar had feared this day would come. He had planned to be in Arles until evening, returning to Lyon on the 6:10 express. He had made these day trips before—to Avignon, Rouen, Limoges, Perpignan—the shorter the stay, the better. His superiors praised him for his resourcefulness and grit, but he feared that he was overexposed, and that this trip, slated to be his last, might require him to summon a different kind of courage.

They drove past wide cornfields and meadows carpeted with lavender, through a beech forest, and then more cornfields. Hubert kept his eyes fixed on the road. The men ordered him to empty his pockets. Fountain pen, latch key, briefcase key, penknife, pipe, tobacco pouch, train ticket. They also took his topaz ring and his amber wristwatch, the back of which was engraved L.C.V.

The man on his right unlocked the briefcase and sifted through the contents. There was a blank sketch pad and a set of twelve colored pencils in a leather case. A railroad map of France. And two brown folders, one containing stock listings and market charts, the other two typewritten pages in a language the man had never seen before.

"What is this?"

"A financial report," Hubert said.

"The language."

"Catalan."

"A financial report without numbers?"

"The numbers are spelled out."

The man on Hubert's left threw an elbow into his side, expertly, so it knocked the wind out of him but didn't crack a rib.

The driver glanced back at the pages. "It's code," he said.

"Whatever it is, you will translate it for us," the man on the left said.

It wasn't a question.

"I don't know the language," Hubert said, bracing himself for another blow. It came from his right and this time cracked a rib.

And he screamed.

3

When they arrived at 2 Place Lamartine, a yellow two-story house, a green-and-yellow parrot flew off the roof into the forest. The guard at the entrance, an SS corporal, snapped to attention as the men stepped out of the car. Hubert was doubled over in pain. The men dragged him to the door. Hubert glanced up at a green patch of sky reflected in a window before losing consciousness.

He came to a half hour later when someone slapped him twice. He was seated, his hands and feet bound to a wooden chair. A ring of flood lamps were directed at him, beyond which he could see nothing. The room was dank, its low ceiling crisscrossed by pipes. A basement. His jacket and shoes were gone, his shirt torn open, and his tie was noosed around his neck.

A slow, smooth voice addressed him from the darkness.

"We won't waste time on the fact your name is not Louis Vincent."

"That is my name."

"And you traveled here from Lyon?"

"Yes."

"Before that?"

"Paris."

"We've already allowed you one lie. You don't get a second. Again: before Lyon?"

Hubert hesitated. "Geneva."

"You traveled across the Swiss border to Lyon in a hired car, correct?"

"Yes."

"What was your business in Geneva?"

"Banking. At the Credit Montray."

"That is another lie."

Before he could respond, Hubert heard a shuffle behind him, followed by someone pulling the tie tight around his throat. So tight he thought he would pass out again. Just as suddenly, he was released, gasping for air.

"In Switzerland you visited Signor Ugo Bartello, correct?"

Hubert nodded

"What is your business with him?"

"His investments."

"Stocks, bonds? Don't lie."

"No."

"What investments, then?"

Hubert caught a whiff of musk—the cologne the man who choked him was wearing.

"You'll tell us eventually. Spare yourself."

"Art," Hubert said.

"Bartello is a collector?"

"Yes."

"And why is he consulting you, a stockbroker?"

"Because I know art. I purchase for him."

"How do you know art?"

"I studied to paint."

"But you became a stockbroker."

"I was not good enough as a painter."

"You are good enough to forge."

"What?"

Again his tie was pulled tight. He felt the blood trapped, pounding, in his head. His lungs contracting. Ten, twenty seconds ticked by. He thought his heart would burst. He was released again. The cologne scent was stronger. The room was spinning.

"You're a forger. You copy the paintings Bartello steals from the Reich. Is that not true?"

Hubert couldn't catch his breath. "Yes."

"Bartello's thieves steal them and replace them with your forgeries. By decree, all the artwork in France is now property of the Reich. We've been storing it in warehouses before transporting it to Germany. By 1946 we will have secured every article the Reich Ministry has requested, including the paintings Bartello has stolen. He is an Allied pimp." He paused. "We know why you are in Arles, Monsieur Ditmar."

Hubert thought he was going to throw up. The restraints were cutting into his wrists and ankles. His cracked rib felt like a knife in his side.

"Most of the Van Goghs are already in Berlin," the voice continued. "But, just as Bartello broke into our warehouses, we penetrated his network of scouts and couriers, of whom you are one. We fed him the false information that certain lost paintings of Gauguin's were unearthed and awaiting shipment at the Marchand Gallery. There are no Gauguins, and the Marchand Gallery is closed. He sent you to study the paintings first-hand, correct?"

"Yes."

"As a forger and a thief, you will be hanged. Unless . . ."

Hubert waited.

"We don't care about you. It's Bartello we want. When the Italian government fell, he had enough connections to escape. Now we cannot touch him because he is in Switzerland with the paintings, whereabouts unknown. He keeps his thieves two steps removed from him. They don't even know who they're stealing for, only that he pays them plenty. He must pay you even more. You are one of the few who has gotten near him, personally. Who can give us his location. If you do—when you do—along with the names of your comrades and a list of the paintings you've forged, you will be imprisoned but not hung."

If Hubert could have smiled, he would have. "It's the list of paintings you really want," he said, against his better judgment. "You don't know which ones are forgeries."

"Of course we do," the voice said sharply. "We want your confirmation."

They don't know because I am a better painter than they expected, Hubert thought. But now he held his tongue.

"You will confirm the forgeries in your confession. When they are no longer required as evidence, they will be burned. Do you understand?"

He felt the tie tighten slightly around his throat.

"Yes."

The tie went slack and the cologne scent disappeared. A man walked toward him out of the lights. Hubert could not see the man's upper body, just his black pants and shoes and the hypodermic in his hand.

"This will help you tell the truth," the man said. A different voice. He pulled Hubert's shirt over his left shoulder and plunged the needle into his arm.

The first voice, in the darkness, said, "Do you know where you are, Monsieur Ditmar?"

"I am in Arles."

"Do you know what house this is?"

Hubert shook his head, blinking into the lights.

"You are in the Yellow House."

Though his face was frozen in pain, Hubert's expression betrayed his surprise.

"Of course you know what that means. This is where Van Gogh lived. Gauguin visited him for nine weeks in the fall of 1888. They painted upstairs. The house now has the honor of serving as district headquarters for the Gestapo. Think before you speak: the first thing you will tell us is Signor Bartello's address." The lamps dimmed, and a short, thin, bespectacled man wearing a black uniform and knee-high boots stepped out of the shadows. "This won't take long," he said, lighting a cigarette.

4

On the island of Hiva Oa, at the center of the Marquesas chain, a young woman was walking through a mountain forest on the first of May, 1902. It was close to sunset on a hot afternoon. On either side of the dirt path, emerald ferns fanned out brightly. Clusters of red and orange flowers rose up like flames. Bamboo stalks ticked in the breeze. In the higher mountains a light rain was falling.

The woman's name was Tohotaua. She had red hair—unusual for a Marquesan—and deep brown eyes. She walked lightly in her bare feet. Her white pareo was tied beneath her bare breasts and broke above her ankles. Eighteen years old, she was the wife of Haapuani, the sorcerer of Hiva Oa. Only twenty-five years old, Haapuani was much feared by the islanders for his magic and his daring feats. It was said he could levitate, turn stones to water, and revive a fallen bird. When there was a new or full moon, he drank a powerful tea brewed from durian seeds and danced all night on the rocky cliffs that rose high above the sea. He wore a scarlet cape with a yellow sash and carried an ironwood scepter on which he had carved animals' faces. His black hair fell below his shoulders, adorned with a spray of frangipani flowers by his left ear. Tohotaua had married him on her fourteenth birthday. Her father, chieftan of the neighboring island of Motane, conducted the ceremony in the Yellow Forest at the northern tip of Hiva Oa, where all the flowers were yellow and the palm fronds gold.

The path she was on led to a wide valley, beyond which was a smaller clearing with a cluster of teak houses. The largest of these had a kitchen and bedroom on the ground floor and a studio up a dozen outdoor steps. The studio was adorned with greenstone tiki and wooden sculptures. Sketches and paintings in various states of composition were tacked to the walls. There was an easel at the center of the room that faced an ornately carved chair.

Tohotaua climbed the steps, lifting the hem of her skirt, and peered into the studio. She had arrived early, and the painter was not there. She walked around the room, examining the paintings and artifacts and pausing by the chair. The smell of oil paints and incense was strong. She went downstairs and found his cook, Vaeoho, preparing a pungent yam soup. She told Tohotaua that the painter had gone to the stream to bathe.

Tohotaua returned to the front of the house and was startled to find her husband at the foot of the steps. She didn't know how he could have gotten there so fast without her seeing him.

"Did you follow me?"

"I came from the other direction," he said, pointing to a steep hill a few hundred yards behind the house. She knew there was no path there and that it was nearly impassable because the ground was so rough and the bamboo and vines so densely packed. But she had learned to expect such things of her husband, and she knew that he never lied.

"I want to watch him paint you."

"Have you spoken to him?"

"I don't have to speak to him. You are my wife." Sometimes, when the light was failing, his eyes seemed to be the same color as his cape. He smiled and his voice softened. "But, yes, I did speak to him this morning."

There was a stone bench at the other end of the clearing from which the sea was visible, a thick blue line above the treetops. She took his hand and led him to it. "We can wait here," she said, and they sat side by side as the sun arced down through the mist and set fire to the water.

5

The Widow Venicasse was Van Gogh's landlady in 1888. She also owned the restaurant in the pink building next door. Van Gogh and Gauguin often ate supper there, sitting silently, their shirts and jackets smeared with paint. They invariably ordered the beef stew or roast chicken and a carafe of cask wine. After living in the Yellow House for several weeks, Gauguin told the widow that having the restaurant next door was a blessing. "Vincent likes to cook soup," he said, "but he mixes his ingredients according to color, not taste." She would regale her customers with this anecdote long after the two artists were dead and celebrated.

Marie Venicasse, the daughter of a provincial doctor, married a hotel keeper in Arles. Widowed at forty, she lost their twelve-room hotel near the public gardens to creditors, rented out their former home, the Yellow House, and bought the restaurant, where she lived in a small second-floor apartment. She had one daughter, Vanessa, born in 1877, a pretty girl who resembled her mother when she was young—petite, with brown eyes, delicate features, and flaming red hair. Vanessa married a glazier, Michel Lavoir, and lived happily with him on the other side of the city until he was conscripted and killed at the Battle of Passchendaele in 1917. They had a son who died of cholera a year later. When her mother died in 1919, Vanessa had lost her entire family in just three years. It broke her. She fell ill and nearly died herself. She had inherited the Yellow House and the restaurant, and finding it too painful to remain in the cottage she had shared with her husband and son, she moved to her mother's old apartment and made her living running the restaurant and renting out rooms in the Yellow House. She had never expected to become the second Widow Venicasse and did not permit anyone to address her as such. Nevertheless, like her mother, she spent her days overseeing a cook, waitress, dishwasher, and handyman. Ten years later, when the country was plunged into depression, and another war was brewing, she considered herself fortunate to have a reliable income. By then she was fifty-three, still spry, but feeling much older inside.

Before all of that, in the fall of 1888, when she was eleven, her mother frequently sent her to the Yellow House with a box lunch for the two painters. It was usually ordered by Gauguin when Van Gogh had the urge to make soup. While Van Gogh often painted in the countryside, and preferred to be alone when he worked in his studio, Gauguin was glad to have Vanessa sit in the corner and chat with him while he painted. He made up fantastical stories that held her rapt. About birds in Martinique that change color according to the season, and a Siamese man who crossed the bottom of the Rhone in stone slippers, breathing air from goatskins. Vanessa in turn told him a story about her father when he was a young sailor on a tropical island.

"He found a magical red conch shell through which he was able to sing to me at night. His voice carried over two oceans. I would lie in bed and listen, and in the background I could hear waves breaking." She shrugged. "Do you think I really heard him?"

"Of course you did. One day I will live in such a place, and when I do I will look for a red conch shell."

"And sing?"

"Yes, to you and to my children."

"Thank you." She hesitated. "My mother said you don't see them so much."

"No, not so much. I need to paint, always in new places."

"Not at home."

"My home is where I go with my paints."

Vanessa thought about this, and felt sorry for his children but happy that he was with her and that, for now, he had made the Yellow House his home.

Six years earlier, he had quit his job as a stockbroker and left his Danish wife and their five children in Copenhagen. He sent money home, but he himself rarely returned. Martinique, Brittany, and Arles were his first stops on the way back to Martinique, and after that Tahiti and the Marquesas.

One cold afternoon in late December, Vanessa brought Gauguin a pot of tea. He was working on a painting of Van Gogh painting sunflowers. Vanessa told him she was looking forward to Christmas. The previous year her mother had knitted her a bright yellow scarf with orange trim. Gauguin turned around and told her that, as a Christmas present, he would paint her portrait as soon as he completed the sunflower canvas. Excited by his promise, Vanessa rushed home and told her mother.

But Gauguin's stay in Arles ended abruptly when Van Gogh had an accident and was rushed to the hospital by the police. Vanessa did not learn the circumstances of that accident for some time, but when she next saw Van Gogh, on Christmas Eve, his head was bandaged and he was being tended by his brother, Theo, who had taken the train from Paris. Theo and Gauguin left for Paris together several days later.

Before walking to the train station, Gauguin went by the restaurant for an omelette and coffee. The Widow Venicasse came out to say goodbye, and Vanessa trailed her with a large envelope that she handed to Gauguin.

"I'm sorry you have to leave," Vanessa said. "This is your Christmas present."

Inside the envelope was a white feather fan with a red dot above the handle. Gauguin took the fan from Vanessa and looked up at her mother.

She nodded her assent. "It is hers to give. Her most prized possession."

"I cannot take it," he said.

"I want you to have it," Vanessa said.

"As a young man, my husband was in the navy," the widow said. "He brought it back from Java."

"It's very beautiful," he said. "You're sure you want to give it away, Vanessa?"

"I'm sure."

"Thank you. I will carry it with me for luck. And I will return here one day and paint your portrait."

6

Hubert Ditmar woke to pealing bells. It was morning. He was no longer in the basement of the Yellow House but in a second-floor room with a single window and blackout drapes. A gap in the drapes revealed steel bars, recently installed. The room was a cell. He was lying on a cot, stripped to his underwear, under a thin blanket. There was a small table and a chair on which his clothes had been piled. Looking around, he realized his field of vision was cut in half because his left eye was swollen shut.

They had beaten him more than they needed to, even after he signed his confession. The short officer struck him so hard that blood shot out of his nose. He hit him again and again. His cheeks were gashed, his lips caked with blood, and he was deaf in his left ear.

Hubert had lied to them about everything, exactly as he was trained to do under such circumstances. He told them the two pages of Catalan were indeed code, and that Bartello kept all the paintings in a vault in Bern. He gave them a list of the forgeries he claimed to have painted, most of which were the originals that he had never laid eyes on. In fact, the paintings stolen back from the Germans had been transported along a tortuous route by a chain of brave men and women in trucks, automobiles, and mule carts, and then on horseback over the Pyrenees and across obscure mountain roads in Spain, to neutral Portugal. The paintings were warehoused in Porto, at the mouth of the Douro River, and guarded by Free French agents from London.

The door to Hubert's cell was unlocked by a uniformed guard who ushered in a woman with graying red hair who carried a tray. "Give it to him," the guard said, "and don't speak."

She approached Hubert slowly, staring at his face, trying not to betray her horror. He turned his one eye toward her, but his expression remained blank. His was one of the worst beatings she had seen since the Germans commandeered the Yellow House. What could he have done? She knew the Germans allowed her to see their prisoners up close in order to keep her frightened. To make her see what would happen to her if she crossed them.

She had brought Hubert a bowl of soup and a scrap of stale bread. The Germans always watered down the soup and removed the meat. They told her that criminals, enemies of the Reich, were lucky to be getting food at all. Sometimes, if she was sure they weren't watching, she would add a couple of spoonfuls of real soup to the bowl. Today she hadn't had the opportunity.

She set the tray down and tried to force a smile for Hubert. But he didn't notice.

"Get out," the guard said.

7

On the night of June sixth, word reached Arles that the Allies had landed in Normandy. American paratroopers were dropping from the sky. Warships were bombarding the coastline. The Resistance had waited a long time for this day. In the south, their brigades were mobilizing around the main cities. Forty-nine commandos, led by Captain Alain Deschalles, a pharmacist before the war, entered Arles on the morning of the seventh. Some penetrated deep into the city and took refuge in safe houses. Deschalles's ferocity in combat and his defiance—wearing a red jacket, making himself a target, to taunt the Germans—had put him at the top of their most-wanted list. They had murdered his wife and son and burned down his pharmacy in Avignon. Some of his men felt he was on a suicide mission. They were amazed that a man who made his living mixing potions and measuring out pills had become so adept with a machine gun and a hunting knife. But however reckless he was with his own life, he tried to minimize the danger to them.

Deschalles's orders were to execute simultaneous strikes on the German military command center on the Rue Vertier and the Gestapo's headquarters at 2 Place Lamartine, killing as many Germans as possible and destroying their communications equipment. There was also a high-priority prisoner at Gestapo headquarters who was to be extracted if he was still alive. Deschalles was given the man's name and description and told that his arrest would have set in motion a long-standing protocol: to provide the Germans with as much disinformation as possible. Deschalles knew that, however carefully crafted, lies offered up during interrogation had a brief shelf life. He had to move swiftly, and he planned to lead the Gestapo raid himself.

Vanessa Venicasse was shredding cabbage in the restaurant kitchen when she learned of the Allied invasion. She couldn't quite believe it. She had feared that this war would drag on for many years. The capitulation of the Vichy regime had been so rapid, and its collaboration so complete, that she had begun to lose hope for France. Maybe the Allies wouldn't want to shed blood for a puppet nation.

She knew that the Gestapo's reaction to this news would be to lash out even more viciously—if that was possible. She advised her staff to keep their heads down and say nothing. When only five Germans from the Yellow House sat down for lunch, she thought it must be that the rest had lost their appetites. Then she learned that there had been a police action to which most of the Gestapo agents were summoned. She wondered if it was an open rebellion inspired by the invasion. In fact, it was an ambush, engineered by Deschalles, in order to draw as many Germans as possible away from their respective headquarters. He had three snipers take positions on rooftops in the city center, and at eleven o'clock sharp, begin shooting every German soldier they spotted on the streets. Between them, the snipers killed nine Germans, setting off an all-out manhunt. One sniper was killed trying to flee, but the other two escaped and at noon joined Deschalles and seventeen of their comrades as they stormed the Yellow House.

The Gestapo agents and SS soldiers were caught off guard. Ten were killed and four soldiers taken prisoner, while Deschalles lost only two men. As soon as the way was clear, he crept up the stairs with one of his lieutenants and rushed the guard outside Hubert's cell, knocking him to the floor. Deschalles slit his throat and kicked down the door.

Hubert was battered and bloody. He had bruises on his chest and arms. With difficulty, Deschalles and his lieutenant put on Hubert's clothes, moving him as gently as they could. Deschalles figured he had ten minutes to get his men and Hubert out of the Yellow House. He didn't know if any of the Germans had managed to call for help before their radio transmitters were smashed, but it seemed likely.

He guided Hubert downstairs. Madame Venicasse was just outside the door with her staff. Despite the mayhem, she was calm.

"Thank god he's still alive," she said.

"I need to get him out of here, madame. He needs a doctor."

They followed Deschalles into the courtyard between the Yellow House and the restaurant. Two of Deschalles's men had lined up the four captured soldiers against a wall. Hands on heads, three of the soldiers kept their eyes fixed straight ahead. The fourth, the youngest, had wet his pants and was weeping.

Deschalles turned to Hubert. "Is the pig who beat you here?"

Hubert squinted at the soldiers. It took a few seconds for him to focus. He nodded toward the short captain at the end of the line.

Deschalles approached him. "You beat him, little man?"

The captain glared at him.

Deschalles whipped his revolver up from his hip into the captain's cheek, crunching the bone, shattering his spectacles. And then across the other cheek. And then his mouth.

The captain doubled over and spat out some teeth, and Deschalles turned to Madame Venicasse. "Please go into the restaurant," he said. "We'll join you in a moment."

Deschalles shoved the captain back against the wall and stuck the gun barrel under his chin.

Inside the restaurant, Madame Venicasse braced herself for the gunshots that reverberated in the courtyard. One shot followed by three others and then four more as Deschalles and his men fired into the soldiers' chests.

They seated Hubert. A few tables away, the Germans who had come for lunch were sprawled on the floor in their own blood. The food from their upended tables was scattered around them. Hubert sipped water and swallowed a piece of cheese.

Deschalles kneeled beside his chair. "You're safe now. We're going to get you out of here. The Allies invaded at Normandy. Everything has changed."

Hubert stared at him, dazed.

"What were you doing here?" Deschalles said.

"Paintings," Hubert said haltingly. "Stealing them back from the Germans. Renoir, Monet, Rousseau—our treasures."

Madame Venicasse brought over a wet cloth and bandages and poured a shot of brandy into Hubert's glass.

Deschalles stood up. "Gather the others," he shouted to one of his men.

The two delivery vans they had arrived in were parked around the corner, drivers at the ready, engines idling.

"Madame," Deschalles said, "you must come with us."

"I am not leaving my home."

"The Germans will kill you. You have no choice."

"I'm grateful to you, but I do have a choice. Tie me up, gag me, and lock me in the storeroom. I will say you overpowered me."

Deschalles shook his head, but didn't pursue it further. He was running out of time.

"It's complicated," Hubert stammered, trying to finish his explanation. "Primary mission was Lyon . . . paintings of Gauguin's from the Marquesas."

Deschalles, intent on gathering his men, was only half listening. But Madame Venicasse heard every word and grew animated.

"Where he died," she said.

Hubert nodded.

"I knew him," she said. "When I was a girl. I watched him paint."

Three weeks later, still recuperating in a safe house in Nantes, Hubert heard that the RAF had bombed Arles, pinpointing targets: the German garrison, their trains and armored vehicles, and the Yellow House, which was still Gestapo headquarters. He wondered if Madame Venicasse had survived. He made inquiries, but no one seemed to know.

8

Tohotaua watched the cook, Vaeoho, climb the stairs to the studio and reemerge ten minutes later. A green-and-yellow parrot flew out of the forest and perched on the roof just as the painter appeared, returning from the stream. He was wearing a straw hat, white jacket, and baggy green pants. He carried a cane and walked slowly, with a limp. He was pale, his hands blotched with liver spots, his feet bloated inside straw sandals. His health, shaky when he arrived on the island three years before, was far worse now. He wore spectacles all the time, and a jacket or raincoat even in the heat of day.

He waved to Tohotaua and Haapuani on the bench and hobbled straight to the house and up to his studio. When they joined him, he had his back to them. He was mixing paints and spreading them on his palette. The room was bright with candles and lanterns that the cook had lighted. A smoky amber light suffused the air. On a table beside the easel there were tubes of paint, two tins filled with brushes, and a red conch shell. The painter turned and bowed to them. Haapuani sat on a stool in the corner, and Tohotaua walked over to the ornate chair, where she found a white fan. She sat down and examined it. The pure white feathers did not belong to any bird she had ever seen in the islands. She ran her finger around the red dot inside a white circle, inside a larger black circle, on the handle.

When the painter finished mixing his paints and turned to her, she held the fan as she imagined he wanted her to: in her right hand, the handle propped vertically on her left thigh, the feathers covering her right breast. That felt natural. He nodded his approval and motioned her to lean more to the left, pressing her palm into the seat of the chair and raising her left shoulder as her weight shifted. She settled herself and gazed, not at the painter or her husband, but through the open doorway, across the clearing, to the darkness flooding the forest.

9

In a black coat and yellow scarf, Madame Venicasse climbed the steps of the Musée des Artes in Montpellier. She had taken the bus from Arles, where she lived in an apartment on the Rue du Bac, overlooking the Rhone. Her two calico cats liked to sit on the balcony among her sunflowers. Her property was destroyed in an air raid shortly after the Allied invasion. All that survived, uncovered in the rubble, was a small strongbox that had been concealed under a floorboard. It contained a gift from Vincent van Gogh to her mother: two signed sketches he did in anticipation of painting their house in oil. Madame Venicasse sold the sketches to a dealer in Marseilles, and for the rest of her life lived comfortably off the proceeds.

Badly damaged in the war, the museum had recently reopened after three years of repairs. Madame Venicasse's shoes clicked on the marble steps. She paid two francs at the reception desk, and after consulting the clerk, walked down a corridor, turned right, then left, through galleries of paintings by Cezanne and Matisse, Picasso and Braque, into a gallery devoted to the works of Van Gogh and Gauguin.

The painting she had come to see occupied a prominent position on the far wall. She sat down on the bench before it and met the gaze of the girl in the white dress, who had brown eyes and red hair like her own. In her hand was the white fan Madame Venicasse had given the painter sixty years before. He never returned to Arles to paint her portrait. Never sang to her from his island through a conch shell. But in the last year of his life, she thought, wiping away a tear, he had painted this girl on the other side of the world holding her fan and had preserved a precious vestige of the Yellow House, of her childhood, somehow knowing that she would see it one day.

Many of **MICHAEL CONNELLY**'s *novels concern Detective Harry Bosch of the Los Angeles Police Department. Harry's given name is Hieronymus, and even as he has had a longstanding relationship with Edward Hopper's* Nighthawks, *so does his namesake's* The Garden of Earthly Delights *particularly resonate with him; its third panel inspired this story.*

The Garden of Earthly Delights (third panel) by Hieronymus Bosch

THE THIRD PANEL

BY MICHAEL CONNELLY

etective Nicholas Zelinsky was with the first body when the captain called for him to come outside the house. He stepped out and pulled the breathing mask down under his chin. Captain Dale Henry was under the canopy tent, trying to protect himself from the desert sun. He gestured toward the horizon, and Zelinsky saw the black helicopter coming in low under the sun and over the open scrubland. It banked and he could see FBI in white letters on the side door. The craft circled the house as if looking for a place to land in tight circumstances. But the house stood alone in a grid-work of dirt streets where the planned housing development was never built after the big bust a decade earlier. They were in the middle of nowhere seven miles out of Lancaster, which in turn was seventy miles out of LA.

"I thought you said they were driving out," Zelinsky called above the sound of the chopper.

"The guy I talked to—Dixon—said they were," Henry called back. "Probably realized that would take them half the day driving up here and back."

The helicopter finally picked a landing spot and came down, kicking up a dust cloud with its rotor wash.

"Dumb shit," Henry said. "He lands upwind from us."

One man got out of the chopper as the pilot killed the turbine and the rotor started free spinning. The man wore a suit and dark aviator glasses. With one hand he held a white handkerchief over his mouth and nose to filter the dust. With the other he carried a tube used to carry blueprints or artwork. He trotted toward the canopy.

"Typical Fed," Henry said. "Wears a suit to a multiple-murder scene."

The man in the suit made it to the canopy. He put the tube under one arm so he could shake hands and still keep his handkerchief over his mouth and nose.

"Agent Dixon?" Henry asked.

"Yes, sir," Dixon said. "Sorry about the dust."

They shook hands.

"That's what happens when you land upwind from a crime scene," Henry said. "I'm Captain Henry, LA County Sheriff's Department. We spoke on the phone. And this is our lead detective on the case, Nick Zelinsky."

Dixon shook Zelinsky's hand.

"Do you mind?" Dixon said.

He pointed to a cardboard dispenser on one of the equipment tables containing breathing masks.

"Be our guest," Henry said. "You might want to put on the booties and a spacesuit along with the mask. A lot of chemicals floating around in the house."

"Thank you," Dixon replied.

He went to the table and put the tube down as he swapped his handkerchief for a breathing mask. He then took off his jacket and pulled on one of the white plastic protection suits followed by the paper booties and latex gloves. He pulled the suit's hood up over his head as well.

"I thought you were driving out," Henry said.

"We were, but then I got a window on the chopper," Dixon said. "But it's a short window. They need it this afternoon for a dignitary surveillance. So should we go in, see what you've got?"

Henry gestured toward the open door of the house.

"Nick, give him the grand tour," he said. "I'll be out here."

Dixon stepped through the threshold into a small entranceway that had been remodeled as a mantrap with fortified doors on either end. It was typical of most drug houses. Zelinsky stepped in behind him.

"I assume the captain filled you in on the basics when you talked," Zelinsky said.

"Let's not assume anything, Detective," Dixon said. "I'd rather get the rundown from the case lead than the captain."

"Okay then. This place was a sample house built before the crash in oh-eight. Nothing else was ever built out here. Made it perfect for cooking meth."

"Got it."

"Inside we have four victims—all in different parts of the house. Three cooks and a guy you would call the house security man. There are several weapons in the house, but it looks like nobody got off a defensive shot. It looks like they were taken out by fucking ninjas, to tell you the truth. All four are heart shot with arrows. Short arrows."

"Crossbow?"

"Most likely."

"Motive?"

"It doesn't appear to be robbery because there are bags and full pans of product in all the rooms and all of it readily visible for the taking. It just looks like a hit-and-run. And there is something else we didn't put out on the bulletin that I think you'll want to see."

"On the phone I think the captain mentioned this is a Saints and Sinners operation."

"That's right. Lancaster and Palmdale is their territory and this is their place, so it's not looking like a turf thing either."

"Okay, let's see the rest."

"First, your turn. What made the FBI jump on the bulletin we sent out?"

"The arrows. The crossbow. If it connects to something else we have working, I will tell you once I confirm it."

Dixon stepped through the second door and paused to look at the front room of the house. It was furnished like a normal living room, with two leather couches, two other stuffed chairs, a coffee table, and large flat-screen television on the wall. There was another smaller screen on the coffee table, and it was quadded into four camera views of the scrubland and desert surrounding the house.

There was a dead man sitting on the couch in front of the security screen, his body turned to the left, his right arm reaching across his body toward a side table where a sawed-off shotgun waited. He never got to it. A black graphite arrow had pierced his torso, back to front, a heart shot, as Zelinsky had said, penetrating the leather vest he wore with the Saints & Sinners motorcycle club logo—the grinning skull with devil horns and angel halo tilted at a rakish angle. There was very little blood because the arrow had struck with such high velocity that the entrance and exit wounds sealed around its shaft.

"We have this guy as victim number one," Zelinsky said. "Name is Aiden Vance, multiple arrests for drugs and acts of violence—ADWs and attempted murders. Did a nickel up in Corcoran. Your basic motorcycle gang enforcer. But it looks like they got the drop on him here. He apparently didn't see them coming on the monitors, didn't hear them pick the lock or come through the mantrap. Until it was too late."

"Neat trick," Dixon said.

"Like I said, ninjas."

"Ninjas? More than one?"

"Doesn't feel like a one-man op, you ask me."

"The cameras—are there digitized recordings?"

"No such luck. Purely for live monitoring. I guess they didn't want digital evidence of their own goings and comings here. It could have put them away."

"Right."

They proceeded farther into the house. There were several evidence technicians, photographers, and detectives working throughout. Yellow evidence markers were placed on the floor, on furniture, and on walls everywhere Dixon looked. The place had been used as a cookhouse for crystal meth, which was the main income stream for the Saints & Sinners. Zelinsky explained that this was only one of several such houses operated by the group and scattered through the desert northeast of Los Angeles, where the finished product was shipped to and distributed to dealers and then to the hapless victims of the devastatingly addictive drug.

"The starting point," Dixon said.

"Starting point of what?" Zelinsky asked.

"The trail of human misery. What was cooked in this house destroyed lives."

"Yeah, you could say that. A place like this—it was probably producing seventy, eighty pounds a week."

"Makes it hard to feel sorry for these people."

It was a three-bedroom house and each bedroom was a separate cookroom that was probably in operation twenty-four hours a day with two or three shifts of cooks and security men. In each cookroom there was another body pierced by an arrow and sprawled on the floor. Each one a man in a protection suit and wearing a breathing mask. No blood, just a clean heart shot each time. Zelinsky gave Dixon their names and criminal pedigrees as part of the tour.

Dixon didn't seem to care who they were, just how they died. He squatted down and studied the arrows protruding from each of the bodies, seemingly attempting to find some clue or confirm something from the markings on each shaft.

Zelinsky took Dixon into the master bedroom last because there was the only anomaly and the only visible blood. The victim there was on the floor on his left side. The sleeve of his protection suit had been pulled back, and the right hand was cleanly severed at the wrist.

"Guys," Zelinsky said. "Give us some space."

Two forensic technicians stepped back from the wall where they had been working. There above a meth drying pan on a folding table was the victim's severed hand, pinned to the wall by the long-bladed knife most likely used to hack it off the body. The fingers had been manipulated. The thumb and first two fingers were up and tightly together, the second two were folded down over the palm. On the wall surrounding the hand was a circle drawn in the victim's blood.

"Seen anything like that before, Agent Dixon?" Zelinsky asked.

Dixon didn't answer. He leaned down and in close to the wall and studied the hand. Blood had dripped down the wall, into the drying pan below.

"Kind of like the Cub Scouts salute, if you ask me," Zelinsky added. "You know, two fingers up?"

"No," Dixon said. "It's not that."

Zelinsky was silent. He waited. Dixon straightened up and turned to him. He held his hand up, making the same gesture as the hand pinned to the wall.

"It's the gesture of divinity often seen in the paintings and sculptures of the Renaissance period," Dixon said.

"Really?" Zelinsky said.

"Have you ever heard of Hieronymus Bosch, Detective Zelinsky?"

"Uh, no. What or who is that?"

"I've seen enough here. Let's go outside and talk."

Under the canopy they cleared space on a table and Dixon took the end cap off the cardboard tube. He slipped out a rolled print of a painting and stretched it out on the table, using the boxes of latex gloves and paper booties to weight the ends.

"This is a to-scale print of the third panel of a painting that hangs in the Prado in Madrid, Spain," Dixon said. "The original is five centuries old, and the artist who painted it was named Hieronymus Bosch."

"Okay," Zelinsky said, his tone betraying in the one word that he knew that an already weird case was about to go weirder.

"It's part of a triptych—three panels—considered to be Bosch's masterwork. *The Garden of Earthly Delights.* You may never have heard of this guy, but he was sort of the dark genius of the Renaissance. While Michelangelo and Leonardo da Vinci were painting angels and cherubs down in Italy, Bosch was up in northern Europe creating this nightmare vision."

Dixon gestured to the print. It was a tableaux of vicious creatures torturing and maiming humans in all kinds of religious and sexually suggestive ways. Sharp-toothed animals moved naked men and women through a dark labyrinth leading toward the fires of hell.

"Have you seen this before?" Dixon asked.

"Fuck no," Zelinsky said.

"Fuck no," added Captain Henry, who had stepped over to the table.

"The first two panels, which I don't have here, are bright and blue because they are about earthly matters. The first is a depiction of Adam and Eve and the garden and the apple and so forth, the creation story from the Bible. The second—the centerpiece—is about what came after. The debauchery and life without moral responsibility and respect for the word of God. This, the third panel, is about Judgment Day and where the wages of sin lead to."

"All I can say is this guy had one hell of a warped mind," Henry said.

Dixon nodded and pointed to a face at the center point of the panel.

"That's supposedly the artist there," he said.

"Pious son of a bitch," Henry said.

"Okay," Zelinsky said. "So he was a dark fucking guy and all of that, but he's been dead five hundred years and is not our suspect. What are you telling us? What do we have here?"

"You have the third panel uprising," Dixon said.

"What the fuck is that?" Henry asked.

Dixon tapped his finger on several images on the print.

"Let's start with the arrows," he said. "As you can see, the weapon of choice here is the arrow. Supposedly, the arrow in Bosch's work symbolized a message. This is what the scholars tell us. The arrow shooting from one individual to another meant the sending of a message. So there is that, and there is this."

Now Dixon tapped heavily on a specific point on the print. Both Zelinsky and Henry leaned down over the table to see the tiny detail. Depicted in the lower left quadrant of the panel was a man being pressed against what looked like the slab of a tomb by a demon animal with a round blue shield on its back. A knife piercing a severed hand was stabbed into the shield. The fingers of the hand were configured like those of the hand attached to the wall inside the cookhouse behind them.

"So what are we talking about?" Zelinsky asked. "Religious zealots, end-of-the-world nutjobs, what? Who exactly are we looking for?"

"We don't know," Dixon said after a pause. "This is our third scene like this in fifteen months. The commonality is the targets are purveyors of human misery."

He gestured toward the house.

"They make meth here," he said. "This starts the trail to addiction and human misery. In March we found a similar scene in a warehouse in Orange County used by human traffickers. Three dead there. Graphite arrows. Purveyors of human misery."

"Sending a message," Zelinsky said.

Dixon nodded.

"Four months before Orange County we were in San Bernadino, where four members of a Chinese triad were slaughtered in the kitchen of a noodle restaurant. They were involved in extortion and smuggling in workers from mainland China to work in kitchens as slave labor while the triad held family members hostage back home. Three scenes, eleven dead, all of it tied together by this painting and this panel specifically. A piece of it re-created at all three scenes."

"By who?" Zelinsky asked. "You have any suspects?"

"No identified suspects," Dixon said. "But it's a group that calls itself T3P. Short for The Third Panel. Within a day, maybe two, they will reach out to you in some way to take responsibility for this and to vow to continue the work they believe law enforcement is failing to do."

"Jesus Christ," Henry said.

"We believe they are an offshoot of something that started in Europe two years ago. It was the five hundredth anniversary of Bosch's death and his work was displayed in a Holland exhibition that drew tens of thousands and probably sparked the uprising. Since then, there have been similar multi-death attacks in France, Belgium, and the UK—all of them targeting the purveyors of human misery."

"It's sort of like they're terrorists against the bad guys," Henry said.

Dixon nodded.

"An international meeting with Interpol and Scotland Yard is scheduled for early next month," Dixon said. "I'll make sure you get the details."

"What I don't understand is why you haven't gone public with this," Henry said. "There's gotta be people out there who have to know who these people are."

"We most likely will after the international meeting," Dixon said. "We'll be forced to. But up until now we hoped the two cases were it and we'd have the chance to quietly identify and move in on them."

"Well, this one is going to go public," Henry vowed. "We are not going to wait around for fucking Interpol."

"That's a decision above my pay grade," Dixon said. "Right now I just came out to confirm the connection and I need to get the helicopter back. The special agent in charge of the Los Angeles Field Office will be reaching out to the sheriff's department to discuss task force operations locally."

Dixon turned toward the helicopter. The reflection off the cockpit windows made it impossible to see the pilot. Dixon raised his arm and twirled a finger in the air. Almost immediately the turbine engine turned over and the rotor blade began to slowly turn. Dixon started peeling off the protection suit.

"Do you want to keep the print?" he asked. "We have others."

"I would, yes," Zelinsky said. "I want to study the fucking thing."

"Then it's yours," Dixon said. "I just need the tube—my last one."

The helicopter blade started kicking dust up again. Zelinsky reached up and grabbed one of the canopy's cross struts when the tent threatened to go airborne. Dixon put his suit jacket back on but kept the mask on to guard against breathing the dust. He picked up the empty tube and re-capped it, then tucked it under his arm.

"If you need anything else you know where to reach me," he said. "We'll talk soon, gentlemen."

Dixon shook their hands, then trotted back toward the helicopter as the turbine began to obliterate all other sound. Soon he was inside the cockpit and the chopper lifted off. As it rose Zelinsky saw that the *F* in the FBI decal was starting to peel off in the down draft from the rotor.

The craft banked left and headed south, back toward LA.

Zelinsky and Henry watched it go, keeping a steady altitude of no more that two hundred feet above the hardscape. As it headed toward the horizon the sheriff's men then noticed the kick up of dust from an approaching vehicle. It had lights in its grill that were flashing and it was moving fast.

"Now who the hell is this?" Henry asked.

"They're in a hurry, that's for sure," Zelinsky added.

The vehicle took another minute to get to them and when it arrived it was clear it was a government vehicle. It pulled to a halt behind the other vehicles scattered on the road in front of the cookhouse. Two men in suits and sunglasses got out and made their way to the canopy tent.

They pulled badges as they approached, and Zelinsky recognized the FBI insignia.

"Captain Henry?" one of them said. "Special Agent Ross Dixon with the bureau. I believe we spoke earlier? This is my partner, Agent Cosgrove."

"You're Dixon?" Henry said.

"That's right," Dixon said.

"Then who the hell was that?" Henry said.

He pointed toward the horizon where the black helicopter was now about the size of a fly and still getting smaller.

"What are you talking about, Captain Henry?" Cosgrove asked.

Henry kept his arm up and pointing at the horizon as he began to explain about the helicopter and the man who had gotten off it.

Zelinsky turned to the equipment table and looked at the print of the third panel. He realized that the only thing the man from the helicopter had touched before gloving up was the cardboard tube, and he had taken it with him. He moved the boxes that weighted the print and flipped it over. On the back there was a printed message.

$$T_3P$$

WE SHALL NOT STOP

PURVEYORS OF MISERY

BE WARNED

$$T_3P$$

Zelinsky stepped out from the cover of the canopy and looked off toward the horizon. He scanned and then sighted the black helicopter. It was flying too low to be picked up on FAA radar. It was no more than a distant black dot against the gray desert sky.

In another moment it was gone.

A former journalist, folksinger, and attorney, **JEFFERY DEAVER** *is an interna-tional number one bestselling author. His novels have appeared on bestseller lists around the world; they're sold in 150 countries and translated into twenty-five languages.*

The author of thirty-seven novels, three collections of short stories, and a nonfiction law book, and a lyricist of a country-western album, he's received or been shortlisted for dozens of awards. His The Bodies Left Behind *was named Novel of the Year by the International Thriller Writers association, and his Lincoln Rhyme thriller* The Broken Window *and a stand-alone,* Edge, *were also nominated for that prize. He's a seven-time Edgar nominee.*

Deaver has been honored with the Lifetime Achievement Award by the Bouchercon World Mystery Convention and the Raymond Chandler Lifetime Achievement Award in Italy.

His book A Maiden's Grave *was made into an HBO movie starring James Garner and Marlee Matlin, and his novel* The Bone Collector *was a feature release from Universal Pictures, starring Denzel Washington and Angelina Jolie. Lifetime aired an adaptation of his book* The Devil's Teardrop.

While his father was an accomplished painter and his sister is a talented artist, Deaver's last foray into art involved fingerpainting; sadly, his opus no longer exists, as his mother insisted that it be scrubbed off his bedroom wall.

The Cave Paintings of Lascaux

A SIGNIFICANT FIND

BY JEFFERY DEAVER

A crisis of conscience. Pure and simple. What are we going to do?" He poured red wine into her glass. Both sipped.

They were sitting in mismatched armchairs, before an ancient fireplace of stacked stone in the deserted lounge. The inn, probably two hundred years old, was clearly not a tourist destination, at least not in this season, a chilly spring.

He tasted the wine again and turned his gaze from the label of the bottle to the woman's intense blue eyes, which were cast down at the wormwood floor. Her face was as beautiful as when they'd met, though a bit more worn, as ten years had passed, many of which had been spent outside under less-than-kind conditions; hats and SPF 30 could only give you so much protection.

"I'm not sure. I'm really at a loss," Della Fanning said in answer to her husband's question. She brushed her dark blond hair from her eyes.

Roger, fifteen years older, was considerably more weathered than she, though, he believed (on a good day), the toll from the out-of-doors gave him character, bestowing a ruggedness on his face. His thick hair, cut short, was largely the brown of his youth, dotted with strands lightened blond by the sun and gray from his age.

He stretched and felt a bone pop. It had been a busy, exhausting day. "There are two sides to it. You know, one says do the right thing. But it's not as easy as that."

She offered, "And sometimes you have to choose what looks like the wrong thing, if it's for the greater good."

He asked, "Do you think that's what we should do?"

They were interrupted by the innkeeper, who stuck his head in the door and, smiling, asked in French if they wanted anything else. Roger glanced at the clock. 11:00 P.M.

He and Della were fluent and he answered, no, but thanks. Della added, "*Bonne nuit.*"

Roger waited until the man was gone and then mused, "Doing the right thing." He shook his head and sipped more of the mild wine, *un vin du Provence*.

Yes, this was a complicated dilemma. It had occupied his thoughts, and, he was sure, Della's as well, for the better part of the past day.

Though the genesis of the conflict was far older: seventeen thousand years, give or take.

—•—

Last week the couple had flown to Paris and taken the train to this region of France to attend a conference on the cave paintings of Lascaux.

These were one of the greatest archaeological finds in history: Nine hundred colorful paintings, primarily animals, outlines of hands and symbols, created by tribes during the Upper Paleolithic era—the late Stone Age. The caverns were located near Montignac, in the Dordogne region of southwestern France.

The conference was one of several over the past few years attended by archaeologists like Roger and Della Fanning, as well as anthropologists and environmental scientists and French Interior Ministry officials, who were troubled by the accelerating degradation of the caves, which were presently closed—to all but a few researchers. Humidity, mold, and bacteria were taking their toll, in some cases so severely that the paintings had all but disappeared. This gathering was meant to try to find solutions to the ecological problems plaguing the caves, as well as to offer recent insights from the scholarly analysis of the artwork and to give attendees the chance to present papers on recent developments in the exploration of "decorated caves," as they were called, in this region and elsewhere.

Yesterday, Sunday, had been the last day of the conference. In the afternoon Della attended one session—recent attempts to attack a new strain of mold threatening portions of the caves—and Roger another, a presentation of a paper on the possible meaning of the abstract symbols on the walls.

During a break Roger found himself sipping coffee beside a man who fit the archaeologist stereotype to a tee (no one Roger had ever known in the field looked and acted like Indiana Jones). The nerdy fellow was skinny, his head covered with a floppy, olive-drab hat. He wore thick glasses and a rumpled tan suit. On his wrist was a battered Timex with a large chipped dial, the sort an archaeologist from the 1930s might sport.

During the break, they introduced themselves.

"Trevor Hall," he said, shaking hands.

"Roger Fanning."

Hall lifted an eyebrow at the name, apparently impressed. He explained he'd read the archaeology blog Roger and Della posted, which devoted much space to the plight of the Lascaux caves. Hall complimented them on raising awareness of the problems facing the site and on encouraging donations. Hall was from Seattle. He'd come here to attend the conference and spend some weeks hunting for other, undiscovered decorated caves—a popular pastime of both professional and amateur archaeologists.

His eyes grew wistful. "I thought I had a good lead. But, nope. And I've been so excited. I was so excited."

This happened a lot in the field, like fishermen talking about the one that got away.

Hall continued, "I was hiking in the valley up the road and I met this farm boy who told me he'd overheard somebody talking about a small cavern near Loup that might've had some paintings in it."

Many decorated caves were found this way—by locals hiking or bicycling through the countryside. The Lascaux caves were discovered, in 1940, by four French students and, the story went, a dog named Robot.

"Loup?"

"That's right. It's a small town about fifteen miles from here. He didn't know anything more and couldn't remember who'd mentioned it. I've spent the last week searching every acre around the damn town. Nothing." He had to leave this afternoon; the hunt was over. "No Carter moments for me," he said with a sour smile. "Never had one. Maybe I never will. Oh well."

Referring to Howard Carter, the archaeologist who, in 1922, discovered the tomb of King Tutankhamen in Egypt, perhaps the most famous archaeological find in history.

Roger had never heard that phrase before: "A Carter Moment." But he and Della certainly knew the concept well—making a discovery that captured the world's imagination and put you, as an explorer, on the map.

They referred to such a coup in a rather more understated way: making "a significant find."

The conference resumed and Roger returned to his seat, half-heartedly watching the speakers. He was distracted as one word kept circling through mind: *Loup, Loup, Loup.*

Della and Roger Fanning had come to the field of archaeology from different routes.

Roger had been involved in archaeology all his life. The son of an academic (Roger Sr. specialized in Middle Eastern studies), the boy would often spend time with his parents when Dad was on digs in Jordan, Yemen, and the Emirates. It was natural that he would follow a similar path, though as he grew up he found he preferred the rather easier lifestyle an archaeologist experiences in Europe to the arduous—and often dangerous—world of the Middle East.

He got a job as a professor at his father's alma mater, Grosvenor College in central Ohio, and spent three or four months a year in the field, specializing in archaeological sites in France, Germany, and Italy.

It was there that he met Della, ten years ago. The young woman was in a dull marriage and had a dull job in public relations, and she had returned to school to get her MBA. But, on a whim, she'd decided to take Professor Fanning's Introduction to Anthropology. Della loved the field, changed majors, and went on to get her master's in the subject.

After graduating, she left her old life behind, divorcing her husband and quitting her office job. She and Roger soon married; their honeymoon was spent in a tent, at a newly discovered prehistoric site near Arles Amphitheater, in France.

Childless—hard with all the travel—they devoted their life to archaeology and caught the attention of the academic community, publishing important papers and making some solid discoveries. They were popular at the conferences, being charming and witty . . . and it didn't hurt that they had nearly model-quality looks.

Still, that significant find continued to elude them.

This was a constant disappointment, a vexing tarnish on their reputation. The failure also hurt their bottom line. Unlike academia in, say, medicine or physics or computer science, archaeology didn't offer any hope for corporate income from consulting or patents. But if you discovered something big, something that made the press, your university might double your salary—afraid you'd go elsewhere—and your lecture fees would skyrocket. If you could put sentences together—and both Della and Roger were solid writers—you had the chance of publishing a best-selling book (and if you were as good-looking as the Fannings, TV bookings were a possibility).

But as Roger was waiting to meet Della in the small park outside the conference hotel, he kept wondering: Was this their opportunity?

As soon as she joined him he told Della about Trevor Hall.

"Hm," she said, smiling. "Hidden treasure. He has no idea who told this boy about the cave?"

"No, he would've tracked him down if he could. The poor guy's spent a week slogging through the countryside."

Roger reached into his backpack, found the guidebook about the region, and flipped to the map. She scooted close. He scanned until he found Loup, a small town in the middle of farmland. "There."

"That's not cave geology," she said, brows furrowed.

"No, it's not."

Caves form because of volcanic, seismic, or erosive activity—usually from water. The caves in this region fell invariably into this last category. Certainly a river carving out caves might have dried up eons ago, but the odds were that caverns large enough to support habitation would be closer to a water source, and there were none anywhere near Loup.

Roger began looking farther afield, following the Dordogne River, a long and wide waterway that ran for hundreds of miles, a likely source of other caves, but archaeologists for hundreds of years had scoured the river's banks. Roger concentrated his search on smaller tributaries, and those near where they were now.

He cocked his head and squinted. "My God, look." He took a mechanical pencil and circled what he stared at. It was a minuscule blue line, representing a creek, running from some rocky hills to another tributary that ran eventually into the Dordogne.

And the creek had a name.

Le Loue.

Pronounced in French exactly the same as Loup.

"*That's* what the boy told Hall. He misheard the word."

Della said, "It's only about fifteen miles from here."

They stared into each other's eyes. Roger said, "What do you say about a day in the country tomorrow?"

"I can't think of anything I'd rather do."

<hr />

Monday morning, they took a taxi from the hotel into a small village near Loue Creek.

They found a scruffy but quaint inn, squatting in a lot filled with enthusiastic grass and weeds, close to the narrow road. Its name was *L'Écureuil Roux*.

The Red Squirrel.

Sounded more like a British pub than a French country inn.

Roger asked for a room and the manager hemmed and hawed, though it was clear the place was virtually empty. He grudgingly took their credit card after saying that he preferred cash and cocked his head, gazing in anticipation. They took their bags to the room and returned to the lobby with their trekking backpack. They asked to borrow two bicycles for a ride into the country. He'd seen several bikes sitting in the tall grass behind the garage.

Twenty euros later—the rental fee—and he and Della were cycling in the direction of Loue Creek.

The lazy stream was situated in a shallow valley of rock cliff faces on one side and grasses, flowering trees and lavender, on the other. The road was on the rocky side, and they biked along the road paralleling it, seeing hardly a single person. A few old Peugeots and Toyotas cruised past, oblivious to the bikers. They stopped at every rock outcropping that might support a cave, but the only possibilities were mere fissures in the limestone, too narrow to fit through.

Della braked to a stop and looked around the rolling scenery. "Sun'll be down soon."

They were some miles from the hotel. But Roger was still feeling the excitement of the hunt. "Just one more. Over there." He pointed to large crescent of stone that jutted off the road, thirty feet above the creek, covered with rocks, boulders, and gravel. Leaving the bikes at the top, they made their way to the base of the cliff face. At first, Roger was skeptical, thinking that the place was too near both the road and the waterway; surely a hiker or a boater would have discovered a cave long ago. But he saw at once that covering a view of the base of the outcropping was a thick tangle of brush and branches. They donned leather gloves and started to clear it away.

"Look!" he said, staring at what they'd revealed: a tunnel, three by four feet around, extending about a yard into the rocky interior, which was blocked by a pile of gravel and dirt. Roger crawled forward on his hands and knees and cleared away enough debris that there was so he had opened an eight-inch gap at the top.

Behind: blackness, from which issued damp, musty air.

A cave.

"Oh, honey!" Della joined him, getting as close as she could into the narrow opening. She handed him a flashlight and he clicked it on, then aimed the beam into the opening.

"My God. Yes!"

You couldn't see much of the cave from this angle through the tiny opening, but there was no doubt that Roger was looking at a portion of a cave painting. A horse, he believed.

"Take a look."

They changed position, and she too examined the walls. "Oh, Roger. I can't believe it!" She scooted higher on the pile of gravel. "I can't see in any farther." She played the light on the sliver of the painting.

They backed out and studied the obstructing pile of stone and gravel. He said, "I'd guess an hour or so to clear enough so we can get inside. It's too late to do anything more now. We'll come back in the morning."

He put his arms around her, kissed her hard.

A significant find . . .

At last.

Though, of course, there was one more matter to be addressed.

"It's a crisis of conscience. Pure and simple. What are we going to do?"

"I'm not sure. I'm really at a loss," Della was saying.

Now, Monday night, they were in the lounge of the inn, debating.

Stretching till a bone popped, he said, "There are two sides to it. You know, one says do the right thing. But it's not as easy as that."

"And sometimes you have to choose what looks like the wrong thing, if it's for the greater good."

"Do you think that's what we should do?"

They were interrupted by the innkeeper, a smirky, condescending smile on his face. "Is there something else you'd like? Another bottle of wine? Whiskey? Food?"

The shifty guy, always trying to make an extra buck.

"*Non, merci.*"

The man pouted and didn't leave until Della said, "*Bonne nuit.*"

Roger waited until the man was gone and then mused, "Doing the right thing."

As with many dilemmas, their crisis of conscience was quite simple: Whether or not to give Trevor Hall credit.

For his Carter Moment, his significant find.

Roger remembered the man's morose expression when he said that he hadn't had any great discoveries.

Maybe I never will. Oh, well . . .

Then her voice grew soft. "We haven't even published for a year, honey."

It *had* been a dry spell for their career recently. And the trips to Europe for digs and conferences were paid for largely by the couple themselves; the travel expenses provided by the university were minuscule. They'd just moved into a larger house, and the mortgage payments were quite the burden.

The discovery of a new decorated cave would make huge difference in their lives.

After a moment she asked softly, "Would Hall even know?" She shook her head. "Sorry. I shouldn't have said that."

Roger shrugged. "I introduced myself. He'd find out."

Crises of conscience can rarely be sidestepped.

They fell silent, the room filling with ambient noise—a creak from upstairs, an owl in the distance, the staccato snap of the licking flames.

Roger explained his thoughts: This was the real world. If Hall had the mettle to stick it out, he probably would have found the cave. If he'd thought more cleverly—like he and Della did—he would have found the cave.

She added, "And he didn't need to give you any information. If he was that concerned about getting credit he could have kept quiet and come back again."

"True. You're right. And, dammit, if it wasn't for us, there'd never *be* a discovery in the first place."

And yet Hall's face had seemed so wistful.

Include him or not?

Crisis of conscience . . .

And as with most such predicaments, the solution was easy and comforting.

Kick the can down the road.

"Let's decide in the morning."

"I think that's best," she said.

He kissed her shampoo-fragrant hair and they climbed the creaky stairs to their room.

⚬━┼━⚬

Roger awoke at six thirty, Tuesday morning, filled with intense energy.

He roused Della and, for a change was not moved to begin caressing and kissing, as often in the morning. He rolled quickly from the bed and showered, not bothering to shave. She too arose, showered and dressed quickly. They dressed in jeans, T-shirts, sweats, and jackets; even shallow caves could be quite chilly. On their feet were comfortable hiking boots.

Into the backpack, Roger placed the folding shovel, gloves, the camera, flashlights, a sketchpad, and pens, and energy bars and bottles of water.

In ten minutes—having had only coffee for breakfast—they were bicycling down the road, under an overcast sky. Soon they arrived at the cave.

Roger half expected to find it jammed with other archaeologists, or at least guarded by Trevor Hall. But, no, the place was deserted.

They left the bikes at the top of the outcropping, wove through the piles of loose stone and gravel, and made their way down the steep hill. Using the short camping shovel, Roger had cleared enough debris to allow them access.

Breathing fast from the exertion—and the excitement—he turned to his wife. "Ready?"

"Let's do it."

With some effort, they slipped through the gap and into the cave.

It was about thirty feet long, twenty wide, and ten high. The floor was flat—limestone, as most of them here—without standing water or pits. The ceiling was intact. These were instinctive observations—for safety—and once satisfied the place was structurally sound, they turned to the wall containing the fragment of image Roger had seen yesterday. It contained dozens of paintings.

"Oh my God," Della whispered.

Roger was unable to speak.

He had never seen any cave paintings this brilliant and well-defined. It was as if the chamber had been hermetically sealed since their creation and no moisture or gasses had entered to bleach or damage the art.

She gripped his arm.

The style was clearly Paleolithic, similar to that of the paintings at Lascaux: the figures were rendered in dark outline and filled in with red, beige, and sienna colorings. There were a number of animals, mostly cattle and a few horses. Curiously, though the diet of the tribes in this region was primarily reindeer—the piles of bones told this story—there were no depictions of this creature, either at Lascaux or here.

What was most astonishing, however, were not the animals but a series of paintings of humans in the middle of the wall.

This took Roger's breath away.

Della could only stare in shock.

Human figures were rare in Lascaux and other Upper Paleolithic caverns in this area, and when they did appear, they were rendered as stick figures. Anthropologists believed that this was due to some taboos or primitive religion proscriptions against representing humans.

But here the pictures of people were as carefully done as the animals: outlined and then filled in. These would be *Homo sapiens*, anatomically similar to humans today (as opposed to Neanderthal and *Homo erectus*, humanlike species that died out before the cave-painting years of the Upper Paleolithic era). The artist (presumably male, though not necessarily) was primitive stylistically but had made an attempt at perspective and three-dimensional representation. They had crudely drawn facial features and wore clothing that was baggy and brown, hides presumably.

Roger whispered, "This might be the first attempts to authentically represent humans."

"Maybe we've found a new tribe altogether."

He nodded. "Drawing humans like this means maybe they'd discarded at least one primitive taboo. God, we could be looking at a radical step forward in behavioral modernity."

This was the developmental state that set *Homo sapiens* apart from earlier and nonhuman species: the ability to think abstractly, create art, make and execute plans and engage in symbolic acts. These paintings suggested that perhaps behavior modernity might have been achieved earlier than believed, among some tribes at least.

"This is it," Roger said, choked with emotion.

A significant find. . . .

Which begged the question that had been consuming them both.

They looked at each other and she nodded. "We tell him. Trevor Hall."

Roger smiled. "We have to, yes."

She grinned as well.

Do the right thing.

The crisis of conscience had been resolved.

Roger felt in his gut a swelling relief.

And, hell, they'd get *some* credit. After all, the Fannings were the ones first into the cave. But they'd share the find equally with Hall, write the paper together, appear at the press conference together. Their success would be diminished some, but they could sleep at night.

"Let's get some pictures and get back to the hotel. I don't have Hall's number, but I know he's from Seattle. We'll find him."

"Roger? Shine the light here."

He swept the beam past her and the illumination splayed over the mottled gray wall. The image she was pointing at was in the center, where the humans and animals were depicted together. She indicated a man standing beside a dozen cattle. At his feet was a crude image of a black cat. The Upper Paleolithic era had its share of lions and leopards and other big cats in this region. The animals we know as house cats existed but were far more common in Northern Africa than in Europe.

"And, my God, Roger . . . Look at the cattle!"

He understood, and whispered, "They're domesticated."

Domestication of what we know as farm animals—raising and slaughtering them, rather than hunting—was just beginning around this era. But nearly all the Lascaux and other cave paintings around this time in prehistory, depicted animals being hunted; these were clustered in what seemed to be a herd. The man, near whom the cat was standing, seemed to be looking over the creatures. He had a full beard and was balding.

"A cowherd?" Roger asked.

"It might be. Astonishing to find organized animal farming that long ago. This is a first too."

"And look to the right," Roger said.

Della played her flashlight beam over the images adjacent to the cowherd. It depicted him once again but this time standing with a woman, with long straight hair. The cat was at their feet.

"A depiction of what might be a domestic union."

"Look, Roger—the paintings're to be sequential. They're telling a story, like panels of a cartoon."

More evidence of advanced behavioral modernity at a surprisingly early era.

They turned to the next painting in the sequence.

This showed the woman from the second panel, with the long hair, now standing beside a third figure—a clean-shaven man. The balding, bearded man stood by himself, some distance away, the cat still at his feet.

Roger and Della moved farther to the right and looked at the final painting in the center panel. It showed the balding man, along with the cat, standing on a small hill, alone.

"Something's odd," Della said. Frowning, she walked close and touched the picture.

"Honey!" Roger whispered urgently. You should never touch anything painted at an archaeological site with unprotected fingers; oils can ruin the fragile works. This was one of the first rules of archaeology.

Her face alarmed, she turned to her husband. "What do you think these were painted with?"

"Charcoal, pigments?"

"No, take a close look."

Roger walked up and removed from the backpack a folding magnifying glass. He leaned close and examined the image of the bearded man and hillock of earth he stood on. He shook his head and sighed. "Goddamnit."

"A hoax," she asked.

He nodded. "It's acrylic. Probably done in the last year or so."

"Somebody's having a laugh."

There was a long history of fake archaeological finds—the Cardiff Giant, the Michigan relics, the Piltdown Man. Some were done for profit, some to boost an explorer's prestige, some simple pranks.

"So close," Roger said, sighing.

Della shook her head and laughed, gazing at the picture. "Funny. We used to have a black cat."

"Really?" Roger asked absently. He was getting the camera out to take pictures. He'd send them to Trevor and report what the find had turned out to be.

"Fred, my ex, and I did, around the time I went back to school."

"Cat, hm? What happened to it?" Roger asked absently.

"Her. Fred got her in the divorce. Fine with me. I didn't fight it."

Roger knew Della felt guilty about running off with her professor. Taking her ex's cat would be pretty low.

Her face tightened into a frown. "And you know? The cattle?" Nodding at the herd painting on the wall. "Fred and I lived near that dairy farm." Her breath was coming fast. "And he was balding and had a beard. . . . Roger, this is odd." She gripped his arm. "What did Trevor look like?"

"Slim, fifties. No beard." But Roger thought instantly: *Razor.*

"Bald?" she asked.

"Hat."

"You never met Freddy, but you saw pictures."

"Years ago, maybe."

Della asked, "Did he wear an old watch?"

"Yes, a Timex, I think. Gold colored."

She gaped. "It was his father's. He never took it off!"

So her ex pretended to be this Trevor Hall. Roger looked at the painting. Freddy by himself, Freddy with Della, Freddy nearby when Roger and Della together. "Son of a bitch. He leads us to this great find, we announce it and it turns out to be fake. We end up with egg on our face."

Della asked, "Did he really think we'd go public with something like this, before we checked it out? That was—" Her voice ended in a gasp.

She was looking at the last panel of the paintings.

Freddy standing over the hill.

A burial mound.

"Oh, Jesus. Get out! Now!"

But before they took one step forward, there came a rumble from overhead. No, no . . .

It would be, Roger knew in despair, a truck or tractor fitted with a bulldozer blade, Freddy behind the wheel, shoving the boulders and gravel atop the outcropping to the edge. Just seconds later the downpour poured into the tunnel, sending clouds of dust into the cave and cutting off the light from outside.

Roger and Della began to choke.

There was a pause, then more debris crashed down, as Freddy backed up and eased to the edge once more, continuing to seal them in the tomb.

"No! Freddy! No!"

But no shouting, no screaming, however loud, could penetrate stone and earth.

"Phone!" Della cried.

They both grabbed their mobiles and tried to call. But there was no signal.

Of course not. Freddy had planned it all out. He would have been thinking of this for years, probably from the day he'd learned of the affair. He would have seen months ago on their blog that Roger and Della would be attending the conference at Lascaux, and started his plans. He'd found the perfect cave, trucked stone and gravel to the hill above it, studied the original paintings and mimicked them in his drawings here. He then signed up for the conference under the name Trevor Hall and waited until he could get to Roger alone and plant the seed of the hidden cave.

"Honey," she said in a raw, panicked voice that echoed through the small chamber.

"It's okay." He shone a beam on the entrance. "It's mostly gravel, I think. We can dig our way out. It'll take some time. But we can do it."

They propped the flashlights up, pointed toward the pile of rock, and began to grab the larger pieces and fling them aside and dig away at the gravel with the small shovel.

They got about two feet forward when Roger felt himself growing dizzy from lack of oxygen.

"I don't think . . ." Della began.

"It's okay. We're making good progress." He began choking as he inhaled the dusty, thinning air. Not enough, not enough. . . . It was like drinking salty water when you were thirsty. "We'll just take a break. Need some rest. Just for . . . just . . . for a bit."

He lay back against the wall. Della dropped the rock she held and crawled to him, flopping to the floor, resting her head against his shoulder, gasping.

One flashlight faded to yellow and went out.

A moment later he felt his wife go limp.

Good, good, Roger thought, his thoughts growing fuzzy. *Conserving her strength.*

He said, "We'll just take . . . a . . . little . . . rest."

Did he say that before?

He couldn't remember.

"Just five . . . minutes. We'll just rest a little. We're as good as out already. Just . . . some . . ."

His head lolled back against the rock.

Roger stared at the remaining flashlight, the beam turning to yellow, then dimming, amber. Like the sun growing low on the Valley of the Kings in Egypt, where Howard Carter had found Tutankhamen's tomb.

Just a few more minutes and we'll get back to work. It's going to be fine.

He said this to Della. Or maybe he didn't.

The light went out, and blackness filled the cave.

JOE R. LANSDALE *is the author of more than forty-five novels, twenty-five novellas, and four hundred short pieces, including fiction, nonfiction, poetry, essays, and reviews. He has written screenplays, and TV and comic scripts. He is Co-executive Producer on the Sundance TV show,* Hap and Leonard, *based on his Hap and Leonard series of crime novels. Other films and TV episodes have been made from his work. Among them,* Cold in July, Bubba Ho-Tep, *and* Incident On and Off a Mountain Road, *which was made for the Showtime TV series* Masters of Horror. *He has written for* Batman: The Animated Series, *as well as* Superman: The Animated Series. *He has received more than twenty-five writing awards and recognitions, including ten Bram Stokers, the Grandmaster and Lifetime Achievement Award from the Horror Writers Association, the Edgar from the Mystery Writers of America, the Spur from the Western Writers of America, and numerous others. He lives in Nacogdoches, Texas, with his wife, Karen, along with a cat and a very nice pit bull.*

The Haircut by Norman Rockwell

CHARLIE THE BARBER

BY JOE R. LANSDALE

harlie Richards, who thought of himself as a better-than-average barber, was lean and bright-eyed, with a thin smile, his hair showing gray at the temples. He loved to cut hair, and he loved that his daughter, Mildred—Millie to most—worked with him. They were the only father-and-daughter barber team he knew of, and he was proud of that. He was also glad that she lived at home with him and her mother, Connie, at least for now.

Next year she was off to the big city, Dallas. Graduated high school a couple years back, hung around, cut hair, but now she was planning to attend some kind of beauty college where she could learn to cut women's hair as well. Planned to learn cosmetology too. Claimed when she finished schooling she could either fix a woman up for a night out, or spruce up a dead woman for a mortuary production. Charlie had no doubt that would be true. Millie learned quickly and was a hard worker.

Charlie snapped the towel loose from where it rested on his customer's neck, applied talc so liberally that particles floated in the air like an early-morning mist. As the man stood up and unlimbered his wallet from his back pocket and paid his bill, Charlie called out, "Next."

Outside of the customer Millie was finishing up in her chair, there were only two others left. Mr. Weaver, a retired postal worker who looked as if he was born to be old, and one a teenage boy, Billy Thompson, a young man known as a fine quarterback and a good kid.

As Charlie waited for his next customer to settle into the chair, Charlie glanced at Millie. She was tall and lean and pretty, with dark hair and dark eyes, like her mother. She was hard at work on her customer's mop, an eleven-year-old boy reading a comic book and chewing a mouthful of bubble gum.

Outside, the fall wind whistled. Leaves blew across from the park and rattled against the wide front window and the smaller windows behind the waiting chairs with a sound like someone wadding cellophane. It made Charlie feel nostalgic. It was that kind of day when he had his first date with Connie, some many years before the war, back when he was a young barber and she worked as a secretary at a used-car lot.

Their first date was a picnic in the park, but the fall leaves blew so furiously that day, they had to go to his barbershop to escape them. That shop had been smaller than the current one, a place he shared with a tire repair business. He had a corner, more or less, and he could hear the hydraulic car racks lifting and dropping, hoisting cars in and out of the pit where the tires were taken off, replaced, rotated.

In the corner of the shop, their hamburgers and colas resting on top of the magazine table, they ate, and finally, surprising to both of them, they had kissed. The moment their lips parted, they both knew. It was like a movie. Something like that happened, you didn't fight it. They had been inseparable ever since.

Except for the war.

He didn't like to think about the war. His quick smile went away then. It was better to not think on it too much.

Millie finished with the kid, and he stood up from the chair and fished a dollar from his pocket and paid her, then he was out, passing outside the big window of the shop like a windblown specter.

Charlie glanced at the clock. It was near five. He would cut Billy's hair, and Millie would cut Old Man Weaver's white ring of fuzz, and that would be it for the day.

Millie patted the back of her chair like a pet, said, "Mr. Weaver, you're next."

Old Man Weaver rose slowly from the waiting chair, placed the copy of *Life* he had been reading on the table, and moved toward her as if wading through drying cement. Charlie wished he would hurry, because they had a rule. You came in the door before five, they stayed to give you a haircut. But at five they locked the door and pulled the window blind over the big window and closed the curtains over the smaller ones, and when they finished with any late arrivals, they left.

Charlie considered locking the door right then, but it was still a few minutes to five, and he wanted to keep his ritual. But at five on the dot he would wander over to the door and turn the sign and flick the lock.

He let his mind drift to the thought of a cold beer and then dinner. Connie was making pot roast tonight.

Billy came and sat in Charlie's chair. They exchanged a few pleasantries about football, and then Charlie went to work. Billy's hair was a little tricky, due to a front and back cowlick, but Charlie had enough practice now to make the cowlicks lay flat. The trick was not to cut the licks too close. Did that, they stood up like spikes.

As for Old Man Weaver, his hair, though short, was actually trickier. Cut it too close, he complained; didn't cut it enough, he complained. Sometimes, when you got it just right, he complained. Millie usually had better luck with the old man, so Charlie was glad he had gravitated to her chair.

Charlie touched the electric razor switch, and nothing happened. The clippers were dead as last July. He had used this Chic brand clipper so long, it had almost become a friend. It had sputtered and warned of its upcoming demise a few times recently, but now the inevitable had happened.

Charlie unplugged it, feeling as if he were unplugging a friend from an iron lung, and allowed it to check into that great barbershop in the sky, via the waste basket near his barber chair.

Charlie said, "Hold a moment, Billy."

Already Charlie was starting to sweat. He had to do something he dreaded, something he thought about correcting by changing where he kept his new equipment at the ready, but so far he hadn't. To do so was to admit something he didn't want to admit. To do so was to let the war and the past win.

Seemed silly when he thought about it, but not when he was confronted with it. He had to go to the back and open the storage closet door and go inside, reach on the top shelf for the new electric clippers. That wasn't the problem, it was the confined space. It was dark in there until he stepped inside and reached up and pulled the cord that activated the light. But even then, those walls seemed close and the light seemed dim and it felt like ages before he turned off the light and was out of there.

His walk to the storage room was his own personal Bataan Death March. When he arrived at the closed door, it seemed to him that he was willingly opening the door to hell. It was then that he told himself each time that he had to find shelf space in an open part of the shop, keep supplies out of the closet, and to hell with trying to beat this thing.

But he never made those changes. That would be giving up.

Charlie took a deep breath and felt the sweat on his forehead and palms bubble up and grease him.

I can do this, he told himself. It is not a hut on Palawan. It is not a tight grave.

Charlie opened the door and looked across the six-foot length to the rows of shelves at the back. On the top shelf was the box that contained the clippers. He had the man who brought the supplies put them there, perhaps as a kind of test to himself. He couldn't really see them in the darkness of the closet, but he could visualize them and their location clearly.

In the prison camp, the shelter, as it was called, had been about the same size as the closet. It was dug into the side of the rocks, and part of it was made of wood. It was where he was kept with two other soldiers, a very tight living arrangement. There were other shelters and other prisoners, but that shelter was where he and his two companions were kept. It was bad then, but now that the war was over, the memory of it was worse; his mind wore it like a torture device.

One night the Japanese decided to rid the camp of prisoners. Orders from on high. They boarded up the narrow one-way exit to the shelter and set it on fire. Smoke filled his lungs and heat licked at his flesh. He and the others had rushed the door, the only way out, and slammed against it with their shoulders, knocking it loose.

When he and his two companions were outside, there had been bayonets, and gasoline was tossed on them. He was able to dodge being lit on fire, but his companions did not. Their bodies were licked by orange tongues of fire that slavered up gasoline as well as flesh. Even now, if he closed his eyes, he could still see them, bright torches running wildly, falling down to be consumed by spirits of fire. The stench of their deaths was still in his nostrils.

Shelters were blazing. Men who had remained trapped inside the other shelters were screaming like women. Charlie tried to escape but was bayoneted in the abdomen. The pain consumed him and he passed out. He awoke to darkness all around, the sound of scraping. He could barely breathe. Didn't have the strength to move. A great weight was resting on him. Gradually he realized his fate. They thought him dead and were burying him alive.

Then there was a call to dinner. He knew that call. He had heard it many times, and it was not for the prisoners. It was for his tormentors. When the soldiers got around to it, they would bring bowls of buggy rice cooked to the consistency of a loose bowel movement to the prisoners. Tonight, however, even that was finished; he and his fellow prisoners had been served their last meal.

When the dinner call came, the soldiers stopped burying him, tossed their shovels aside, and went away, assuming what they thought was a dead body would be there when they came back.

Charlie found that he could still breathe because the dirt was loose on his face, his nose and mouth were exposed to the air.

He managed to wiggle his head loose, opened his eyes.

It was still night. He had not been out long. It was darker than before, without the bright light of burning shelters and bodies. It was as if during his time unconscious, the night had fallen down on him like an avalanche. The soil was tight and damp against his body. He could only move his feet and hands a little. He wiggled them, flexed his fingers until they begin to come free of the dirt, and he could sit up and scrape it off his lower body with his hands. He had not been buried deep, but another five minutes of shoveling and there would have been no escape.

As he came free from the grave, the pain in his abdomen intensified. He couldn't pull his legs loose. He bent forward and dug the dirt from around his legs. A hand rose up between his feet, the fingers spread, as if reaching for something. One of his comrades was lying across his legs. A dead comrade.

Charlie worked himself free. His wound and the exertion it took to free himself sapped him, but he forced himself to crawl out of the grave. The dirt had actually filled his wound and stopped the bleeding. A silver lining.

Only strong enough to crawl, he reached the jungle, lay there for a while. He could hear the Japanese laughing and enjoying themselves back at the camp. Someone was singing. It was like when American soldiers told him how they enjoyed cutting trophies off Japanese soldiers, ears and noses, and sometimes genitals. War was not a friend to human kind. It changed you, even if you thought it didn't.

But he wasn't thinking about that then. Fear gave him strength to keep crawling. He crawled into a thickness of trees, headed toward where there would be rocks by the sea. He had gone only a few feet into the trees, when his hand landed on something. It was a boot and there was another boot, and legs. Charlie looked up, and looking down at him, was a Japanese soldier. The man had a rifle in his hand with a bayonet on it. He raised the rifle. There was a flash of gritted teeth, and then . . . Slowly he pulled the rifle away and stood with it clasped to his chest.

The soldier squatted on his haunches, put his face close to Charlie's lifted head. Charlie couldn't really see the soldier's features. It was too dark.

The man studied him only briefly, then rose and stepped aside. Charlie started crawling, expecting the bayonet, but that didn't happen. When Charlie had the courage to turn and look back, the soldier was still there, and he motioned with his hand, a waving motion, an invitation for Charlie to proceed, and then the soldier walked away, favoring a limp.

Charlie started crawling again. After a short time he stopped to lie on his belly and rest. It occurred to him later that the soldier may have been hiding from what had been going on in the camp, not wanting to be involved, probably in shock. Whatever his reasons, he had spared Charlie.

In time, Charlie managed to reach the rocks, even stand and stagger. There were the bodies of American soldiers in the rocks and along the shoreline. A number had made it this far only to be caught and killed, burned alive or bayoneted.

Charlie stayed in the rocks awhile, and it was at that point that he couldn't think about what had happened afterward any longer. He had to jump over that memory and let his mind go to a day later, when he was found by Filipino civilians who treated his wounds and helped him survive.

He was one of a very few who lived through the massacre at the interment camp of Palawan, but he had brought it home with him along with the darkness and confinement of the shelter and the grave.

And now he stood before the closet, its interior like a dark memory he had to enter into.

It's a closet, he told himself, but recognition of what it truly was turned into cold comfort when he had to go inside.

Way he went in there, every time, was he remembered before the war, when he was a young barber, the first head of hair he cut. It was a young boy who his mother brought in. The boy had long locks, and he was a fighter in the chair, oversize and strong for his age.

If it hadn't been his first official given haircut, he might have told them to walk, but he had to start somewhere, and why not some place difficult. So he concentrated on holding the boy's head firmly and talking to him softly, clipping away with the old-fashioned squeeze clippers. Trying to cut the boy's hair was like conducting a bombing raid. He dove the clippers down when the kid quit moving, clipped, then waited until a new target presented itself. It took him an hour to cut the child's hair. From then on, even in war, when he needed to concentrate, he first focused on that unruly kid's noggin, a dive of the clippers, and then he took a deep breath and was ready for whatever was at hand. It was simple and silly and to some degree effective.

Charlie imagined the boy and opened the door to the dark closet, felt the walls move in close, the ceiling fall down, the floor rise up.

Entering the closet quickly, he grabbed the cord, turned on the light, but even with it brighter in there, it was for him bright like the first flames of the fire the soldiers lit up the shelter. He froze, and his nostrils filled with smoke and burning flesh.

Again, he thought of that kid, his first haircut. It gave him enough focus to reach the clippers off the shelf, pull the light cord . . . Oh hell, the horrid dark, and then he made for the light of the doorway, a finer light, and was out of there, almost at a run.

At home, at night, he had to sleep with the lamp on by his bed. Connie had grown accustomed to him rising up at night, saying, "Don't do it," over and over. Then she would touch him, and then she would hold him, and it would pass. For a time.

Back at his barber chair, Charlie plugged in the clippers and went to work. Millie paused in cutting Old Man Weaver's hair, said, "Dad, are you hot?"

"What?" he said.

"You're sweating."

"Oh," Charlie said, reached up and wiped his forehead with the sleeve of his barber's coat. "I'm all right. It's warm in the back."

Millie nodded, then smiled, and that made a lot of things okay.

Charlie turned his attention back to Billy's hair, the clippers hummed pleasantly while he cut, and now again he paused them and used the scissors from his coat pocket to clip at the cowlicks. The scissors worked better for that, keeping the licks even with the rest of the cut. When he felt he had the problem hair controlled, he returned the scissors to his pocket, picked up the clippers again, and went at it.

He and Billy talked about sports some more, Billy's family. Old Man Weaver and Millie talked about the weather, the tomato festival earlier that year, and about how Weaver's granddaughter had gone off to Tyler to teach high school history. It was the usual barbershop experience, and Charlie enjoyed it.

Charlie was almost finished with Billy's hair when the bell over the door clanged, and two young men entered.

One was nice-looking in a street-tough kind of way, and the other wasn't so nice-looking. He had a face that looked as if it had been set on fire with a blowtorch and the flames had been beat out with a garden rake.

Charlie could feel their attitude right away. It went before them like trucks pulling trailers. They sat in waiting chairs, reached magazines off the table, started thumbing through them. Now and again they looked up at Millie, and that bothered Charlie.

Charlie understood Millie was pretty. He understood that, as a dad, he was overprotective, and he knew nearly every male below the age of forty who came into the shop took note of her, and a lot of them above the age of forty. But these boys made him start to hurry Billy's cut. He almost decided to break a long-standing rule and tell them he was closing up and they had to go.

Old Man Weaver was finished. He climbed down from his chair, paid up, and went out. After he was gone, Millie turned the sign on the door from OPEN to CLOSED.

She walked to the big window and looked out. "You fellows walked here?" she said, turning to look at them.

"Yeah," said Inflamed-face. "We like to walk."

"Walking's good for you," said Nice-looking. "I read that in a magazine, maybe in a barbershop. I forget."

"I don't recognize either of you," she said.

"Visiting relatives," said Nice-looking.

"Who would that be?" Billy said.

"Don't be nosy," said Nice-looking.

"Sorry," Billy said. "Didn't mean nothing by it."

"Don't mean we didn't take something from it though, does it?" said Inflamed-face.

"Let's stay civil," Charlie said. "It was an innocent question."

"Yeah, that's right," said Inflamed-face, "civil. That's how we want to be. Civil."

Millie went back to her chair, said, "Who's next?"

"That will be me," said Nice-looking.

"I got to let him cut my hair?" Inflamed-face said, "and you get the good-looking girl?"

"Get what you deserve in life," said Nice-looking.

Nice-looking put the magazine on the table and climbed into Millie's chair.

"How would you like it?" she said.

"Like it is, only shorter."

Millie went to work. Charlie continued to cut hair, but he checked on Inflamed-face from time to time, glanced over at Pretty Boy in Millie's chair.

"Barbers, they do right smart business in a small town, don't they?" Inflamed-face said.

"We do all right," Charlie said.

"I'm thinking you might do better than that. Bet you bring in plenty. Men got to get their hair cut to stay respectable, don't they? You like them respectable, don't you, Dad?"

Charlie paused the clippers, looked at the one with the wrecked face. "Let me explain this where you understand it. Don't call me Dad, and leave my shop. Both of you. I don't like the way you talk."

"Well, that's all right, because we don't like the way you talk," said Inflamed-face, and he didn't move. Nice-looking stayed in Millie's barber chair.

"Want me to go with my hair partly cut?" said Nice-looking. "I can't do that."

"Yeah, you can," Charlie said.

Millie had ceased to run the clippers and had stepped back from the chair. Nice-looking didn't get up. He said, "Tommy, lock the door."

Inflamed-face, Tommy, stood up and locked the door. He went over to the big window and pulled down the blind. He started for the smaller windows.

"What the hell do you think you're doing?" Charlie said.

"We're helping you close up," Nice-looking said. "Finish the haircut, doll."

"You're leaving," Charlie said. "Buy yourself some clippers and do it yourself."

"I could do that," Nice-looking said, "but I won't."

Nice-looking stood up from the barber chair and opened his jacket. There was a .45 automatic in his waistband, a military pistol.

"What's this all about?" Charlie said.

"Easy, Dad," Millie said.

"Yeah," Inflamed-face said. "Easy, Dad."

"You got some money here, and we need it," Nice-looking said. "I think that's the best way to stuff in a nutshell, though sometimes I like to talk and couldn't put it in a bushel basket. Today, though, I'm feeling less talky. Here's so you rubes will understand us. We'd like your money. We'll take the money, and we'll hole up here for a while."

Tommy laughed.

Nice-looking eased the pistol out of his waistband and held it alongside his leg, tapping his thigh gently with the barrel. "You're all right with that, aren't you . . . Dad?"

"Take the money and go," Charlie said. "Take it all, but leave."

"Naw," said Nice-looking, "we kind of got a situation on our hands. Made a run at the bank here. Didn't work out so good. Cop came in while the gal was handing me the money; someone yelled. I had to shoot the cop, and Tommy here had to shoot the one who yelled."

"Didn't have to shoot anyone after you killed the cop," Tommy said. "Just wanted to."

"I stand corrected," Nice-looking said. "Okay. Here's how we start. Give us the money, Dad. Now."

"And you," Tommy said, pointing at Billy. "You got some money, don't you?"

"Enough for a haircut," Billy said.

Tommy grinned. "Like the old lady who peed in the ocean said, every little bit helps."

Billy stood up and fished in his front pocket and came up with a few dollar bills. Tommy came over and took them. "Hell, you got enough for a haircut and a shave. If you shaved. Go over there and sit in a chair and be still. You get nervous, we'll shoot you and tell God you died."

Billy went over and sat in one of the customer chairs.

"Now you, doll," Nice-looking said. "Finish cutting my hair. And you, Dad, you sit in the barber chair and be nice, or we won't be nice. Dig? Same goes for you, what is it, Billy?"

Charlie moved around to the front of the chair and sat in it. He could see Billy in the chair across the way. Billy was fuming. Charlie feared he might do something silly.

"I'm thinking I'll give you a haircut," Tommy said to Charlie, and wandered behind the chair where Charlie sat. "Little off the top first, then maybe I'll part your hair with a bullet. I got a gun too, Dad."

Tommy turned his attention to Millie, standing with the clippers in hand. Nice-looking had climbed back in the chair. "And you, girlie," Tommy said. "We might do some hair parting of a different kind with you."

"Leave her alone," Charlie said, and he moved to come out of the chair.

Tommy slapped Charlie over the ear. Charlie's head rang like a bell. "You shut up, Dad, unless you want to get the party started."

"Let her and the boy go," Charlie said. "Keep me. They won't say a word."

Tommy slapped him over the ear again. Charlie winced.

"Like we believe that," Nice-looking said, leaning back in the chair, shifting into a comfortable spot, resting the gun on his knee. "No one leaves. Not until we leave. Besides, you people make nice company, don't they, Tommy?"

"Damn nice company," Tommy said. "I think girlie could be nicer company then these two though."

Billy started to rise out of his chair, Charlie lifted a hand off his knee and patted the air. Billy stopped trying to rise up.

"Thatta boy," Tommy said. "You get excited, want to play the hero, you'll get dead."

Billy's face turned bright red, but he kept his seat.

Nice-looking turned in the barber chair and looked at Millie.

"You don't look like any barber I ever had," he said. "Look here, girlie. I'm going to need you to say a word or two. Not too much, but you can say something."

"Something," Millie said.

"Oh, a smart-ass," Tommy said. "We can fix that."

"Naw, it's all right," Nice-looking said. "I like them a little feisty. It's more fun to bring them down. The higher something is, the more fun to watch it fall. You got a purse, doll?"

Millie nodded.

"I want to hear you say it."

"Yes. I have a purse."

"That's good. You got any money in it?"

"A few dollars."

"Tell them what you think about that again, Tommy."

"Like the old lady that peed in the ocean," Tommy said. "Every little bit counts."

"That's your cue, doll," Nice-looking said. "Give me your purse."

Millie turned and reached under a shelf and brought it out. Tommy came over and took it, as he did, he ran his hand over her hand. Millie recoiled.

"Ah now, sweet girlie, I'm not so bad," Tommy said.

"Yes he is," Nice-looking said. "He's bad."

Tommy took Millie's chin in his hand and said, "I think you ought to give me a kiss."

Tommy snickered, let her go, went back to stand behind Charlie. He began looking through the purse. After a few minutes he found a small wallet. He dropped the purse and opened the wallet. He took out some bills and put those in his pocket, tossed the wallet on the floor with the purse.

"Where's the barbershop money?" Tommy said, leaning over Charlie's shoulder.

"Behind you, in the shelf, a cigar box," Charlie said.

"No cash register?" Tommy said.

"No," Charlie said.

"You see a cash register, Tommy?" Nice-looking said.

"No."

"Then what's the point in asking?"

Tommy shrugged, found the cigar box, opened it, thumbed through it. "What, a hundred dollars, some change? You might as well take Green Stamps."

"That's all we have," Charlie said.

"What's in the back?" Tommy said.

"Barber supplies, bathroom, back door, and the parking lot."

"Money?"

"No," Charlie said.

"Had to leave our car behind," Nice-looking said. "Or someone's car. We stole it. Now we got to have another one, so that one in the back I saw, that yours?"

Charlie nodded.

"We'll be taking it," Nice-looking said. "Having the keys is better than hotwiring some car. Neither of us are too good at it. Give me the keys."

"They're on that hook by the front door," Charlie said.

"Tommy," Nice-looking said, "get those keys."

Tommy got them, gave them to Nice-looking, who was holding out his hand. Nice-looking shoved the keys into his coat pocket.

"Finish my hair, doll," Nice-looking said.

Millie lifted the clippers and began to cut. Her hands trembled slightly.

⚬━┼━⚬

When Millie finished cutting Nice-looking's hair, he climbed out of the chair, looked in the mirror. He went over to the shelf in front of the mirror, found a comb and a bottle of red hair oil. He dripped a bit of oil into his palm, slicked his hair back with it, combed it.

"We could just lay low here awhile," Tommy said.

Nice-looking nodded.

"We could, but they don't go home, and we're here, someone might come looking for them."

91

"Hadn't thought of that," Tommy said.

"Ask me if I'm surprised."

Tommy's forehead wrinkled. "You don't have to talk that way."

"I don't have to is right," Nice-looking said.

"Now, we're going to need the three of you to go in the back."

Charlie and Billy stood up from their seats, and Mille started to follow.

As Millie passed and came up close to Charlie, Tommy said, "Honey, I'm going to need to pinch that butt. I been wanting to do that since we got here."

Tommy reached out to pinch her, and when he did Charlie stepped back and hit him in the face with an elbow. It was a sharp blow and Tommy staggered, his nose spouting blood.

Nice-looking moved quickly, slammed the gun barrel into the side of Charlie's head. It was a good blow, but Charlie only moved a little. Nice-looking seemed surprised by that. He started to hit Charlie again, but now Tommy was there, and he had drawn a small revolver from inside his coat. He said, "Let me do it."

"All right," Nice-looking said.

Tommy brought the revolver around to hit Charlie, and when he did, Billy grabbed Tommy's wrist, yelled, "Stop it."

Tommy jerked his hand free, pointed the revolver.

Nice-looking said, "Don't make noise unless you got to."

"I got to," Tommy said.

"No you don't," Nice-looking said.

"Okay," Tommy said, and stuck the pistol in his waistband, reached into his pants pocket, pulled out a knife, and clicked it open.

Before Billy could move, Tommy stabbed him in the gut. Billy fell back against the barber chair. Charlie grabbed him, pulled Billy away from Tommy, stepped in between them.

Billy sagged to the floor. Blood leaked out of him like spilled motor oil.

"Better move, 'cause I'm not finished, and I can cut you too, old man," Tommy said.

"I been cut," Charlie said.

"That's enough," Nice-looking said. "Got time for that later, we want it. Get them in the back. Might want them for hostages, and if we do, it's best they're alive. Except Billy there. I don't want him. He don't look so good, and he's wet. We'd just be dumping him beside the road somewhere, have to clean up after him."

"Cowards," Millie said. "You sorry cowards." Her body shook.

"Easy, baby," Charlie said.

"Yeah," Nice-looking said. "Easy, baby."

"In the back, now, and get that son of a bitch off the floor, or I'll finish him here," Tommy said.

Charlie bent down, slipped his arm under Billy's arm, lifted him up. "Sorry, son," Charlie said in his ear.

"I ain't," Billy said, but he had turned pale and his face was beaded with sweat.

Charlie grabbed the barber towel off the back of his chair, folded it and pushed it against Billy's wound. "Hold it there, son, press tight."

Billy pressed on the towel. When he did, he groaned. The towel began to turn red.

Millie came around and got on the other side of Billy, and they helped him walk to the back.

⊶

"It's not so bad," Billy said, as they went.

"Good," Charlie said, but from experience, he knew Billy was wrong. A stab like that felt like a punch in the gut at first, but then it felt like the fires of hell blazing through your belly. Pain would come, and Billy was leaking a lot of blood; his life was running out of him like water down a drain.

"It'll be okay, Billy," Millie said.

When they got to the rear of the shop, Nice-looking went to the back door and cracked it open. He looked out for a short time, then eased the door shut.

"There's a park back there," Nice-looking said. "There's a lot of people out there. Go out with them, someone might look and know better."

"What now?" Tommy said.

"Billy there, he isn't going, that's for sure. Put them in that closet, let me think on it."

A great shadow moved inside of Charlie. Of all the damn things, a confined space. It was one thing to will himself to grab clippers off a top shelf, but to be closed in, that was beyond what he could manage.

Charlie glanced at Millie. Her eyes were wide, her lips tight and thin. He knew that look. He had seen it on the face of soldiers about to enter into battle; he had seen it every day on the faces of his fellow prisoners.

Tommy got a chair from the front of the shop while Nice-looking pointed his gun and a smile at them. Tommy brought a customer chair in, placed it by the closet, opened the closet door. "All of you, get inside."

"Dad," Millie said.

Charlie hadn't moved. He still had one arm around Billy, Millie on the other side.

"Inside, I said."

With more will than Charlie thought he possessed, he began to trudge toward the dark opening.

I'll be all right with the light on, he told himself. *It won't be good, but it won't be as bad. As long as I have a light, that will make it better.*

At the doorway, looking into the darkness, Charlie almost broke and ran, but he couldn't do that. He couldn't. Not with Millie and Billy there. He had to go inside. As they entered the closet, he reached up quickly, pulled the cord, and turned on the overhead light. They eased Billy to the ground with his back against a shelf.

"No," Tommy said, and he entered into the closet, hopped up and broke the light with his pistol. "Let's keep it dark. And you, girlie, we get ready, we'll take you with us. We can have a party somewhere."

Tommy stepped back, framed by the light of the outside room, and closed the door, plunging them in the darkness. Then they heard Tommy scraping the chair across the floor, sticking it under the doorknob to hold them in.

Charlie took a deep breath. All he could do was sit on the floor of the closet and tremble. He knew he was in the closet, but he felt he was in the grave.

Why can't I move? he thought. *Why can't I do something? I did something then. Why can't I now?*

Because you know how it could end, for you and Millie and Billy, but you know too it will end that way anyway. You know what you did back then, and if you let yourself loose, you may do what you did before, and that's not how you want to be. Not like that. Never like that.

"Dad?" Millie said.

She touched his arm. He was embarrassed that she would feel it trembling, and that he was already so beaded with sweat his clothes were wet.

"What do we do, Dad?"

He thought about that first haircut again, but that still wasn't working. That worked when he knew he could leave, but now the dirt seemed to press against him, and if he broke from the grave, it would be dark, and there was the woods, the soldier and the rocks, and then there was what he had done.

Charlie told himself, you got to stop worrying about what you did, think about that thing you did instead, let it come out, let that rage rush to the surface like a missile. He could hear the soldiers talking outside of the shelter. No. Not the shelter. It was the thugs, and they were talking outside of the closet. Just a damn closet, not a shelter, not a grave.

"I go outside with the girl," Charlie heard Nice-looking say. "We go cool, and she drives the car around front and we pick you up there."

"I don't know," Tommy said.

"You don't know what?"

"What if you keep going?"

"Why would I do that? You got the money in your pocket, right?"

"Yeah, but what if you just kept going anyway? You and her. You could have some fun with her, dump her somewhere, keep driving. And here I'd be."

"I wouldn't do that to you, Tommy."

"Wouldn't you?" Tommy said.

Then they must have moved across the room, because all of a sudden, they couldn't hear them anymore.

Inside the closet, Charlie felt Millie push up against him, grab his arm, and hold it. "Oh, Dad. What if they take me?"

"It'll be okay," Charlie said. A kind of cool had settled over him, and it made the sweat on his body turn cold. He remembered something. The scissors in his barber coat. He reached and took them out.

And then he let himself remember how it was, how he had crawled and then hid in the rocks. The part he wouldn't let himself think about before, he thought about now. It was the part about where the soldier who had let him go, came back later, maybe an hour later. Charlie had reached the rocks by then and he could hear the pounding of the surf and through a split in the rocks he could see other rock heaps and the sand on the beach, and it was all bathed silver by the moonlight.

There was a soldier with a rifle and bayonet walking along the beach, looking left and right, crouched a little. The soldier had a limp like the man who had let him go. He had no doubt it was the same man.

Charlie didn't know if the soldier had been sent to look for stragglers, or if he had thought about what he had done, letting a prisoner go, felt bad for it, and had come to finish Charlie off.

A rage swelled up in Charlie, and though his wound was bad, he felt strong then. The dirt in the wound had lessened the flow of blood and clotted it, and Charlie was touched with madness. It was like a crawling thing inside of him; a den of twisting, poisonous reptiles. He had picked up a rock then. It was heavy and one end was a little sharp, and he could hold it firmly in his hand.

The soldier worked his way among the rocks, holding his bayonet-tipped rifle at the ready. The moonlight danced on the blade. The soldier passed the split in the rocks where Charlie hid in shadow, and before the soldier could look his way, Charlie sprang.

Charlie had felt in that moment like a panther. He landed on the soldier, knocked him to the ground. The soldier squeaked like a rat. The rock went up and the rock came down. A wet warmness splashed against Charlie. Some of it splashed into his mouth, and it was hot and coppery, and it tasted like vengeance, and the rock went up and the rock came down, and there was a sound like someone stepping on egg shells after a while, but still the rock went up and the rock came down.

Straddling that soldier, the one who had let him go, all he could think about then was the months of cruelty, the beatings, the starving, the fires, and bayonets. The rock went up and the rock went down.

When Charlie paused from exhaustion, the soldier no longer had a head. It was a puddle of blood mixed with sand and bone fragments. The light of the moon had changed, and the shadows were different, and the shadows covered Charlie and the dead soldier. Charlie realized he had been striking the soldier for a long time. He could hardly move, he was so exhausted. In that moment Charlie knew what was inside of him, and it had gone on beyond the need to kill the man. It had turned into the same kind of wicked vengeance as the American soldiers he knew who had cut pieces off dead Japanese soldiers and kept them as souvenirs, or who mutilated bodies, or enjoyed burning men with flamethrowers. The same sort of men he had been captured by. The same kind of man he had become.

Charlie sprang up and rushed the closet door. There was a jar to his shoulder, and he was bounced back, but he went at it again, and this time he heard the chair scrape and go scuttling along the floor. Charlie let what was inside of him come out in full, the thing he feared and had tamped down after that time with the soldier in the rocks. The door sprang open as the hinges creaked out of the wall. Charlie stumbled out into the light with the scissors clutched in his fist, slamming into something, and that something was Tommy.

Charlie hit him like an express train. Tommy went back and tripped over the chair Charlie had dislodged, smacked his head hard on the floor, and his gun came loose from his hand and went skittering across the tile floor.

Nice-looking, standing near the back door, panicked, fired his gun. The shot missed Charlie, slammed into the wall, but Charlie felt the bullet ruffle his hair. Nice-looking was trying to fire again, but the gun was jammed, and he was struggling with it, and Charlie was coming, the scissors raised.

Nice-looking let out a noise that reminded Charlie of the soldier that night, and then Charlie was on him.

The scissors flashed (the rock went up, the rock went down) and there was a scream, and at first he thought it was Nice-looking, but then realized it was him, and that what was coming out of him was pure rage. Blood spattered against his face, and for a moment he was in those rocks, and then he heard Millie scream, and he was sure this time it was her, not him.

"Dad, don't, please don't," she said, and her voice broke through the roar in his ears. He sagged slightly. The haze in front of his eyes faded.

Looking down at Nice-looking, who he was straddling, his hand raised with the bloody scissors in his fist, he saw that he had stabbed Nice-looking through the cheek and had struck him in the shoulder and chest. He could see the swelling red spots there, leaking through Nice-looking's shirt and jacket, streaming down his face and onto the floor. Nice-looking was crying like a child.

When Charlie looked back over his shoulder, he saw that Millie had picked up Tommy's revolver, and was pointing it at him. Tommy was in a heap on the floor, but he was starting to stir.

Charlie stood up. He put the scissors in his barber coat pocket, picked up Nice-looking's gun where it lay next to him on the floor. He saw the problem, worked with it briefly, cleared the chamber. It was the same kind of gun he had carried in the war.

He pointed the gun at Nice-looking, stepped back where he could see both of the men. "Don't get up, punk," he said to Nice-looking. "And you, Tommy, get over here and sit down beside him. You can hold hands if you like."

"I'm hurt," Nice-looking said, and he whimpered after saying it, like a mistreated dog.

"Yeah, you are," Charlie said. "But believe me, if not for Millie, you'd be dead."

And he would have, and worse. Charlie would have let what was inside of him keep coming out, like that time with the soldier in the rocks, but Millie's voice had cut through it all, and even the burning need to kill had been defeated by that small but wonderful thing. His daughter's voice.

I didn't kill because I didn't need to, Charlie thought. *I am human. I am a husband and a father. I gained control. That was war, and that was then and this is now.*

Tommy shuffled over, still looking dazed. He sat on the floor by Nice-looking. He didn't look up to see that Charlie was smiling at him.

Charlie took a deep breath. The demons were still there, but they were smaller now, and maybe in time he could defeat them, or at least make them so small as to no longer matter. He wasn't fixed, and maybe never would be, but he was better and felt as good as he had felt in a long time.

"Millie, darling," Charlie said, pointing the gun at the pair on the floor. "Go up and call some law, and tell them to send an ambulance for Billy. Everyone lives today."

GAIL LEVIN *writes artists' biographies, art history, and fiction; curates exhibitions; and exhibits her own art. A native of Atlanta, Georgia, Levin is now distinguished professor of art history, American studies, and women's studies at the Graduate Center and Baruch College of the City University of New York.*

She is the acknowledged authority on the American realist painter Edward Hopper. In 2007, the Wall Street Journal *chose her* Edward Hopper: An Intimate Biography *(1995, second expanded edition, 2007), as one of the five best portrayals of artists' lives, going back in its selections to 1931. Focused on women artists, the subjects of her other biographies include Judy Chicago and Lee Krasner.*

Red Cannas by Georgia O'Keeffe

AFTER GEORGIA O'KEEFFE'S FLOWER

BY GAIL LEVIN

I am so excited that Georgia O'Keeffe has finally agreed to meet with me! Getting her to come around wasn't easy. At first she wouldn't even reply to my letters. I kept at it. You know, persisted. Finally, I reached her secretary on the phone. When I did get word from O'Keeffe, she complained that there had been too many interviewers over the years. When I asked, she admitted that most of them were male journalists.

As far as I could tell from digging through files of old clippings, there's been a veritable avalanche of requests. I can see why some of the results put her off. Take Henry Tyrrell, of the *Christian Science Monitor*. Already in 1917, he embroidered: "Miss O'Keeffe looks within herself and draws with unconscious naiveté what purports to be the innermost unfolding of a girl's being, like the germinating of a flower . . ." She was having none of that. She could have taken offense at being called naive. Does her resentment still fester? Does memory make her so tough: "Why should I do this?" O'Keeffe had asked me when I requested an interview. I said, "Because I am a woman. I don't see art the way those men do."

I wrote to her how the paintings in her retrospective made me see in a whole new way. They moved me from the abstract geometry that I had studied in art school to finding subjects in nature. I started to see the world differently. Everywhere I looked, I began finding metaphors for the feminine.

As I changed my own work to bring out the feminine in nature, I went on to apply my discoveries to writing about O'Keeffe. I published this piece as a review of her recent show in the magazine *Womansplace*. Not wanting to alarm her, I haven't mentioned that I share the journal's feminist perspective, which some, I suppose, might call "radical." We want to change the art world and the larger society. We seek to eradicate male patriarchy and supremacy. We women must have our share of power.

To my mind, O'Keeffe's art and career embodies that power. When I saw for myself the strength of female forms in her large painted flowers, like *Red Canna* from the early 1920s, I knew one of these flowers would be perfect for the cover of my book on women artists, soon to go to press. The publisher warned me that O'Keeffe has so far withheld permission to reproduce her copyrighted images in all such contexts—those where the book is not entirely about her. But I am determined to change her mind. I need to get her to lend me a color transparency of one of her flower paintings and to give me permission to reproduce it.

I suppose you could see me as a revolutionary on a noble mission. I must convince O'Keeffe that her work has been transformative for my whole generation. I intend to get rid of that old saw that sneered at ladies painting flowers. "Lady Flower Painters" were only fit to decorate silk fans, sniffed Charles Dickens. Jo Hopper, married to that unreconstructed Victorian, Edward, used to complain how he disparaged her, O'Keeffe, and women artists in general as "Lady Flower Painters." Against that stereotype, O'Keeffe's flowers look epic. They must speak for and to women everywhere. But how am I going to get her to realize that? It's a small victory that she has at least agreed to meet with me.

Now that I am about to speak with her face-to-face for the first time, I am feeling a bit anxious. In the course of setting up this meeting, I picked up hints from others that she might not be so agreeable. I suspect that convincing

O'Keeffe to give me permission to reproduce one of her flowers in my book will take some effort. But I consider these paintings to be some of the most important by anyone—ever! They prefigure feminist art being done today. I mean my own and my contemporaries'.

So, mulling over all this in my mind, I finally arrive, after driving for two days alone in the sun, all the way from Venice Beach in Southern California, across the Arizona dessert, to Abiquiu, in northern New Mexico. Here O'Keeffe lives below the spectacular Sangre de Christo mountain range. It does not take much imagination to see that these colorful rocky forms that she paints in her landscapes already look like female forms and contours. Even the rosy tone of the weathered stone cliffs and buttes evokes flesh.

I can barely contain my excitement. At the door, I meet O'Keeffe's assistant, who seems a bit too stern. She takes my bag and tersely informs me, "No cameras, no recorders allowed."

I try to put aside the assistant's gruff manners so that I can approach O'Keeffe with the sense of awe that I feel. I see her as a role model for all women artists. I hope that she is a harbinger of my own future success. I see palpable strength both in her pictures and in her career in an art world where men still call the shots. Now eighty-six, O'Keeffe appears confident. More than half a century has passed since she first exhibited her drawings, then her watercolors, and oil paintings in New York. By now, she knows that she has earned the acclaim she has received. As praise builds, it confirms her greatness as the artist of her generation.

I am thrilled but surprised to see O'Keeffe in person: her skin is lined with fine wrinkles. While her hair is mostly gray, pulled back and pinned up in a severe bun, her brows are still thick and dark. She wraps her fragile thin frame in elegant black. Both her face and her body echo her austere surroundings, plain white adobe walls. She does not even display her own art. O'Keeffe seems to emanate a sense of control over this spartan environment. The effect, perhaps knowingly orchestrated, is intimidating.

O'Keeffe greets me, asking, "Good afternoon. How was your trip?"

I respond, "Miss O'Keeffe, thank you so much for seeing me. It is a great honor to meet you. You have so inspired me as an artist that I have brought some photographs of my own paintings to share with you."

O'Keeffe's reply stuns me: "I cannot see them. My sight is too weak now. I am told that I have a specific kind of eye problem, and there is nothing that anyone can do for it. That's what the people that think they know tell me. So I just decided to get on with it. I am making ceramic sculpture now. It won't bother you that I cannot see so much, will it?"

Taken aback, almost embarrassed, I reply: "I did not know. I am so sorry. I love your art. Your paintings have so inspired me."

"Virginia Goldfarb. Where did you get that name?" O'Keeffe changes the subject. "Is it like so many of these other women who have been taking geographic place names for themselves? Wanda Westcoast, Judy Chicago, Lita Albuquerque, or even that man, Robert Indiana?"

"No. My parents named me Virginia after my mother's mother, named Virginia. I was actually born and raised in San Francisco."

Seeming to relax a bit, O'Keeffe elaborates, "My own given name was bestowed at birth. I wasn't born anywhere near Georgia, but in Sun Prairie, Wisconsin. I don't like gimmicky names. If one's work is strong, such names are unnecessary."

The sting of skepticism lingers. I sense that I need to do more to soothe her doubts, but what? Winning her over feels like a struggle. "Miss O'Keeffe, I saw your show at the Whitney Museum and loved it! You are a role model for feminist artists of my generation."

"What do you mean by 'feminist artists'?" O'Keeffe snaps. I sense that she does not want to be reduced to anybody's feminist. She seems to doubt that I or any other feminists understand what she faced and how she coped.

"I am referring to women who make art about the experience of being female; women who call attention to the issues of gender and gender inequality."

To this, O'Keeffe, replies, "I supported women's suffrage. I belonged to the National Women's Party. I believe in women making their own living."

"I am also talking about women who have responded to new books like *Our Bodies, Ourselves*. Feminism encourages women to take pride and full ownership of their bodies. Such awareness informs feminist art."

At this O'Keeffe bristles, "I hear from a friend that one of these 'feminists' paid a lot of money to take out a full-page ad in a prominent art magazine. She wore only a pair of sunglasses and posed nude, holding a large dildo against her body, trying to attract attention to herself and her art."

I know the artist whom she is talking about. Her antics created a sensation but did nothing for feminism. Before I can figure out what to say, O'Keeffe elaborates, "Some have had the nerve to compare the aggressive sexuality of her pose to the photographs that Stieglitz took of me and included in a show of his photography. This is absurd! I was in an intimate relationship with Stieglitz! I don't want to see that transformed into a cheap template for this young woman's narcissistic strategy to promote herself. Stieglitz himself insisted, 'Each time I photograph I make love.'"

About that I wish that she had said more. I want to ask O'Keeffe about her relationship with Stieglitz. I am curious about how she managed to juggle his roles as the art dealer that he was for her and others, as a photographer, but then as her lover, and then her husband. Better not to go there. After all, Stieglitz, who was more than two decades older than O'Keeffe, has been dead for more than a quarter of a century. Besides, some say that he cheated on her. She is surely not going to want to relive the love affair, the marriage, his flirts with others, betrayals, her abrupt departure alone for New Mexico.

I've read that she puts great value on Stieglitz's own art—his photography. I'm sure that Stieglitz's close focus on photographing O'Keeffe—her art, her face, her hands, and her nude body—changed the trajectory of her life and career. I decide to ask her about that instead: "You were the subject of some of his most famous work. Was that difficult?"

"Stieglitz's idea of a portrait was not just one picture," explains O'Keeffe. "His dream was to start with a child at birth . . . As a portrait it would be a photographic diary. It took a lot of patience—posing for him. He would go on shooting me for hours and hours. I had to learn to hold still for what seemed like an eternity."

What that makes me wonder, I don't think I'd better inquire, so I change the subject. "Miss O'Keeffe," I venture, "you remember being in the Museum of Modern Art's second show in 1929? They called it 'Nineteen Living Americans,' but you were the only woman. How did that feel?"

"Yes I recall. You might know that Alfred Barr was the curator, but not that he didn't pick the artists for that show. The museum's trustees actually voted. You might think that nineteen is an odd number, but that's all that they could agree upon—not fifteen or even twenty. Some of the trustees, like Duncan Phillips, for example, already collected my work and that of other artists chosen. Each trustee wanted to promote *his* own artists. Thanks to Stieglitz most of them knew my work well. Some of them collected it."

"So the trustees did not know or like work by other women?"

"Maybe not well enough. Maybe not in the same way."

"Miss O'Keeffe," I ask boldly, about to read her a critic's comment on her work. "I am sure that you remember Paul Rosenfeld? He once described your work as 'spiritualizing' your 'sex.' He wrote: 'Her art is gloriously female. Her great painful and ecstatic climaxes make us at last to know something the man has always wanted to know . . . [t]he organs that differentiate the sex speak.'"

"This is false! Paul's words were often overly reductive. I hear that feminists are now making similar silly claims. One supposedly says that her art—her abstract flowers—represent 'active vaginal forms,' while she dismisses my ear-lier flower forms as 'passive.' News of this young woman trying to promote her art by putting mine down irritates me. What irks most is her cheeky attempt to usurp my place in history, all the while making use of what I invented. Why are these youngsters so fixed on fiddling with flowers?"

"Many of us view your paintings of large flowers as true icons of feminism. We appreciate the flower's metaphoric identity as a reproductive organ. We champion you as our foremother. There are so many kinds of flowers in your paintings: calla lilies, Oriental poppies, jack-in-the-pulpit, jimsonweed, iris, and red cannas. They have become our positive symbols, our revolutionary images."

"Poppycock! This is all too much," O'Keeffe groans.

"I must have agency over my body," I assert, somewhat defensively. "I'm okay with using my existence as a form of resistance. I need an emphatic symbol for that resistance." What, I wonder, would get her to see her work from our point-of-view? O'Keeffe does not view her flowers with the same gendered gaze as we do. Whatever they once might have seemed to her, by now, after decades of denial, she insists that they are just her close observations of nature, recorded with her particular elan, pizzazz, or whatever you want to call it. She considers herself beyond feminist stereotypes, above the fray.

"How do you choose your subjects then?" I try once more to tame her. "What is your relationship to nature?"

"I was taught in school to paint things as I saw them. But that seemed so limiting! If one could only reproduce nature, and get results always less spectacular than the original, why paint at all?" She looks at me as if I had to understand.

I try again, "But as a woman, how did you see yourself differently than men?"

"I was constantly experimenting. Eventually, I made up my mind to forget all that men had taught me and to paint exactly as I felt."

"Oh, yes!" That's it, I thought and burst out: "I want to know more about your flowers and female imagery, about their link to female sexuality, to female agency."

"You look at my flower and you think you see what I see and you don't," she demurs.

"What," I ask, "about all those images with central cavities and inner spaces?"

"Cavities: That sounds like the dentist! I have painted some interior spaces, such as the view from my own home, the East River seen from inside the apartment in the Shelton. All that concrete and those tall buildings—"

Oh no, I interrupt: "I meant that the flowers seem like metaphors for female anatomical forms, for women's sexuality."

"What metaphors? My work is as objective as I can make it! I suppose that the reason that I got down to an effort to be objective is that I didn't like such interpretations people tried to pin to my images." She continues, "I just learned about some feminist showing slides of my work along with those of other artists at a women's arts festival at some Ivy League university. She had the nerve to argue that these women—from myself to Louise Bourgeois to some Miriam Schapiro—all made art with the same kind of repeated patterns! Imagine: circular, organic, so-called 'biomorphic apertures.' Those openings are supposed to indicate women's preoccupation with their own inner spaces! What a ridiculous premise," O'Keeffe concludes, looking at me with suspicion.

I desperately try to shift the focus: "Why did you decide to paint your flowers so large?"

"Everyone has many associations with a flower. You put your hand to touch it, or lean forward to smell it, or maybe touch it with your lips almost without thinking, or give it to someone to please them. But one rarely takes the time to really see a flower. I have painted what each flower is to me and I have painted it big enough so that others would see what I see."

Finally, I cut to the chase: "I love your flowers and would like your permission to reproduce one in color in my book."

"What is your book?"

"My book surveys important women artists who paint."

"What is its exact title?"

"The title is: *Treasury of Great Women Painters from the Renaissance to the Present.*"

I now see that O'Keeffe is visibly annoyed. She does not want me or anyone else to put her in a limiting category. She raises her voice and shouts at me, "I am not a woman painter!"

I feel devastated as O'Keeffe stands up and indicates that the interview is over. She glares. "Just do *your* work. Leave mine alone."

WARREN MOORE *is professor of English at Newberry College, in Newberry, South Carolina. When not discussing Chaucer or Samuel Johnson, he is the author of* Broken Glass Waltzes, *a novel, and a number of short stories, including "Office at Night" from* In Sunlight and Shadow. *He lives in Newberry with his wife and daughter.*

He wishes to thank his parents for introducing him to Dali's work, and Susan Frommeyer, MD, for technical advice.

The Pharmacist of Ampurdan Seeking Absolutely Nothing by Salvador Dali

AMPURDAN

BY WARREN MOORE

Alan Bowling was walking again. The golden light of the Colorado autumn played across the rusts and browns of the ground beneath him. Behind him, the city. The air was cool here, away from the shops, the school, the fringes of the city of Ampurdan.

Alan didn't know why the city—pfft, *city*. Don't put on airs; at most, a town, really—was named Ampurdan. He had read that the word was an old name for a place in Spain, now called Emporda. He himself privately called it "Ampersand," a place between two other places, connecting them by force of . . . by force of what? How did an ampersand connect things, other than by the will and in the mind of the person connecting them? The *and* of the ampersand, the conjunction, was between whatever two things the speaker, the thinker, chose to conjoin. And since in Alan's life, the only conjunctions he saw were the compounding of day upon day, there seemed to be little sense of a period to this place, to this life. Merely a string of days becoming ellipsis, until one day each inhabitant reached an end of words.

If I keep thinking like this, I'm liable to lapse into a comma, Bowling thought, and smiled at the joke. He knew he wouldn't tell it to anyone else, not when he was back at work, not at the grocery later. It would have been too hard to explain, for something barely clever.

A few minutes before, he had seen another walker—perhaps a tourist? Alan laughed, although only the dust could hear him. This was no place for tourists, not because it was rugged, or crime-ridden, or much of anything, really, but because it *wasn't* much of anything—only a river and flat ground and the town that grew around the river. There was a mountain, but it was too far away to bring people to the city for the view. There were gullies here and there, but not the canyons people might explore. There were shops, a few restaurants, a couple of doctors, Alan's pharmacy. There were people, of course, but the same sort of people one might find anywhere, doing the things people had always done—eating, working, mating, growing, or dying.

And walking. Alan had been walking for a long time. Enough years ago that he didn't recall exactly why, he had walked away from the pharmacy one afternoon. Afternoons were slow times—his assistant, Marshall, and the technician could handle any customers—and he felt the urge to be somewhere other than behind his counter. So he told Marshall he was going out for a smoke (Why? He didn't smoke, but that first time, he felt as though he should give a reason.), and he walked away from the shop and into the countryside. It was three hours later when he returned, and if Marshall looked at him oddly, he didn't say anything about it, nor did he when Alan did the same thing a few days later, and again a few days after that.

Eventually, it just became a part of the routine. If Marshall speculated about Alan's peregrinations, he never said anything. Perhaps for a time he thought that Alan had a woman in one of the houses or apartment blocks, but he never asked, and Alan never said.

There was no woman, of course. Not that Alan was immune—he had dated on occasion, and he had a good job, owning his own store—he could have been a catch. And indeed, once, there was a woman. Her name was Carolyn, and she had dark hair and fair skin, with eyes the color of glass found in the desert. She might have been one he wanted, but she chose another. And a few years later, after her husband Derek had died, and while her name would sing in Alan's head, but before he could quite reach to her, she chose still another. And with time, she and her new husband left, and Alan no longer knew where they were, only where he was—in Ampurdan, in the city around which he would walk.

In fact, Alan couldn't really say why he had begun to walk those years before, and he couldn't say why he did it now, years later. Sometimes there was a satisfaction in feeling the ground beneath his feet, in knowing he had traveled a certain distance in a certain time. (Had he traveled? He remembered a physics lecture from college: "Work is force over distance. You may apply a great deal of force," the professor said. "You may grow very tired. You may strain your muscles and tear your ligaments. But no matter how much force you apply, if the recipient of the force ends where it began, you have ultimately done no work." At the end of each walk, Alan would be back at the drugstore, among the pills from the pharmaceutical companies and the chemicals he had for the rare occasions when he might need to compound a prescription himself. Had he traveled?)

Other times, people would see him headed to the outskirts of the city, to the federal land where the road ended and there was only land and sky, and they would say to him, "Ah, Dr. Bowling! Walking for your health, I see." And Alan would smile, glancing down a bit, half raising his hand, and keep walking, and the people he passed would congratulate themselves for their alacrity, but Alan knew that wasn't why he was walking either. It was good for him, true—certainly that's what the doctors said, and it kept him trim. But he never thought of that as a reason, never mind *the* reason, that he did it. He did it, because . . .

He did it because.

And that seemed like enough, most days, and when it didn't, he might not walk that day. And today, as he walked, the air was cool enough on his face that the hair on the back of his neck raised just slightly.

Carolyn's lips had felt cool like that, once, before she told Alan that she was going to accept Derek's proposal. Alan congratulated her automatically, and told her he wished them happiness. Maybe they had happiness, before the cancer took Derek. Maybe she had happiness now, with another man.

After a time, Alan turned back toward the town, toward his work, the prescriptions that needed filling or refilling, the customers he saw more or less often, depending on their health. As he moved back to the fringe of the town and the road to the shopping district, he saw a little boy. As he walked closer, he recognized the child as Jordan Hopkins; Jordan's parents ran a teacher's supply store in what passed for a downtown. He asked Jordan about his recent sore throat, and Jordan said he was fine and had missed only a couple of days of school but had been okay in time for the school carnival. *Score one for Zithromax*, Bowling thought, and smiled.

"What are you doing?" the boy asked him.

"Going back to work," Alan said. "I've been walking."

"Were you looking for something?"

"I don't think so."

"If I were walking, I think I'd look for something."

"Like what?"

"Treasure? Monsters?" Jordan thought for a moment. "Something."

"Well, I've never seen either of them around here, but if I do, I'll let you know. But you shouldn't try looking for the monsters, I think. You could get in trouble."

"I won't get in trouble," Jordan said. "I'm magic."

"All the same, best to avoid the monsters." The boy shrugged. As he started to walk again, Bowling said, "There's a good thing about looking for nothing much."

"What?"

"You're pretty much guaranteed to find it." But the child was already turning away, and Alan Bowling made his way back to the drugstore.

That night, after he had washed his dinner dishes and ironed the next day's clothes, Alan Bowling thought of Carolyn. It was something he did from time to time, almost never on purpose.

He would lie in bed, listening to the stereo playing Glenn Gould playing Bach, letting his mind wander before he slept, and sometimes he fell asleep right away, and other times he would think of the next day's tasks at work. But there were times he would think of Carolyn, not quite with regret, but with wonder at the choices he had made, and that she had made, and how their lives intersected and then veered away. He didn't know what it was about Bach that called her to mind—her tastes ran more to Piazzolla—but it did. Perhaps it was the interthreading of Bach's lines, echoing from left to right hand and back, always elegant, wasting nothing.

He thought of the months after she had chosen Derek. He had forced him-self to be gracious—Ampurdan was a small town—and he had never been one for being obviously unhappy. But as day wound into day, songs would play on the radio—not "their song," they had never really had such a thing, but still a song that would make her reverberate in his mind—or he'd see a picture in a magazine of a woman tilting her head a certain way, or a shard of stained glass that called her eyes to mind, and his breath would catch with sorrow. Anything could remind him of her, and everywhere was her absence.

But as months faded one into another, Alan learned that even in a small town, it wasn't so hard to avoid seeing people he didn't want to see. And with time, he grew used to the way things were, as the tongue grows used to the gap where a tooth used to be. But not always. There were still nights where he wondered if things could have been different, if he had met her sooner, if he had said something or not said something else, how decision had led to decision after decision.

Years can pass that way, and they had, until one day, Browning received a compounding request from an oral chemotherapy suspension—it was some-times necessary, when a chemotherapy patient couldn't take a pill or capsule, but it was uncommon, because the drugs didn't last as well in that form.

He looked at the order, and saw the patient's name: Derek Lipton. He looked at the prescription again: etoposide, and as he read, he saw the diagnosis of acute myeloid leukemia. Browning was surprised; AML generally didn't hit this early. Still, it was bad news, with a cure rate below 50 percent, and the fact that Lipton was having to take his chemo this way didn't bode well either. In fact, it might be best for Lipton if he just—

Got it over with? Browning shook his head and got to work.

Each week, the scrip would come in; each week, Alan Browning would prepare it. As the weeks went by, Browning wondered if Lipton received his medication at the hospital, or if Carolyn gave the etoposide to Derek herself. He wondered how long Lipton would last, how hard it was for Carolyn, if she still hoped he might get better, or if there had been much hope at all.

It had to be hard for her, he thought. And when he thought of it as a way to make things easier for both Carolyn and Derek, well, it didn't seem so bad, did it? And a man in Lipton's condition wouldn't get too close a look, after . . . well, after. Browning remembered a poem:

Now view yourself as I was, on the spot—
With a slight kind of engine. Do you see?
Like this . . . You wouldn't hang me? I thought not.

And in fact, they didn't. Indeed, it appeared that no one even checked—Browning wouldn't have been surprised if Derek had been a DNR. He saw Lipton's obituary in the paper and thought about the appropriate interval for consoling Carolyn.

He had begun walking around that time.

And he was walking still, years later. Once he got into the habit, he guessed, it carried on from inertia.

After Derek had died, Alan had imagined that he might encounter Carolyn on an afternoon, moving around the city as one does, or more to the point, as two might. And one afternoon, he did see her as he walked.

She was sitting on a bench at a park, talking to a man in a suit. And from that day, he wouldn't have been able to say why, but Alan Browning knew his chance had never arrived and never would. It had been futile—the aches after she had chosen Lipton, the waking nights, the last times he had filled Derek's prescription. All he had done was set Carolyn down a different path to a different man, a man who wasn't him and who never would be. He may even have eased her way.

He turned back to the pharmacy and never walked back to that park, even after he read about the second wedding. Instead, his walks ranged in the opposite direction, crossing the flat brown earth at the city's edge and beyond. He would try to blank his mind as he stepped, focusing only on the length of his stride, the intake of breath. He counted steps as if the process were a mantra.

And as the months and years passed, he managed to put the thoughts of what he had done somewhere deep inside himself. If someone had asked him—but no one would, because no one knew—he might have said that he had forgiven himself for a moment of human weakness. He had done a lot of good before and after that moment, after all. And really, perhaps he had even helped Carolyn (Oh, Carolyn!) and Derek Lipton, with Annandale's "slight engine." The words *Annandale* and *Ampurdan* blended somewhere below the surface of his mind. Annandale Ampurdan Ampersand Carolyn—they fit the rhythm of his steps, even though he didn't hear the beat as he walked.

He settled into the route where he had seen Jordan Hopkins, and would occasionally see the boy, throwing a ball into the air and catching it, watching ants conduct their business, or doing the other things that young boys do to fill their afternoons. Usually they would smile and nod, but occasionally Alan would ask him if he had found treasure. The boy would say no, not today.

"How about monsters?"

"No, not them either."

"Well, it's not all bad then, is it?"

The boy would shrug and toss his ball again. "Have *you* found any monsters, Dr. Bowling?"

"No, I don't think so. But I haven't been looking for them either."

"What have you been looking for?" Toss. Catch.

"I've told you before—when you're looking for nothing in particular . . ."

"You can count on finding it," the boy finished. Toss. Catch. And Alan Bowling would make his way back to work and finish the day and go home and listen to music or work a chess problem and might not think of the Liptons at all.

And the years passed, and an older Alan Bowling turned the store over to an older Marshall, who was still younger than he was. Jordan Hopkins had grown up, and was away at pharmacy school, of all things. Bowling secretly hoped that the boy would return to Ampurdan and take over the store one day, but he really didn't expect it. When people left Ampurdan— those who could—they tended not to return.

Carolyn hadn't (Oh, Carolyn!). Was she still alive? Bowling didn't know. A phrase of Bach might still call her to his mind, but it was the memory of a memory. He remembered the coolness of her lips, and the desert glass of her eyes, glass that reflected him, placed him outside but had never held him within. Or those may have been what he thought he should remember, and it was the memory of the *should* that he held and summoned from time to time.

But he still walked most days. The climate in Ampurdan was dry most of the time, and the afternoons were still pleasant enough for an old man's walks. And it was on one such walk when he saw a stir of motion—a bird, a fox, a rodent? He was never sure—and he misstepped and his ankle twisted and he pitched into a gully worn into place by rains long gone.

He felt the hip go when he hit the bottom, and the pain took his breath away as he drew his hand across the dust and pebbles to his side. But there wasn't pain below that. He tried to roll from his left side to something like a seated position, and that was when Alan Browning felt, then saw the blood on his hand. He looked farther down and saw the bend—no, the angle—in his thigh, and the rhythmic darkening of the ground around the leg.

He remembered anatomy from his freshman year: femoral artery; very dangerous, a man could bleed to death quite swiftly unless a tourniquet was applied. Browning reached for his belt, but he was very old and very tired, and his fingers didn't want to listen to him anymore. And Browning knew it, and he didn't really mind, because he had walked a long time over many years.

He suddenly felt cold, and he blinked hard, and for a moment he thought he saw Carolyn sitting at the gully's edge, perhaps some gray in the dark hair, eyes somewhere between blue and violet. *It's good of you to be here at last*, he thought, or said, or thought he said, but then he blinked again, and saw Derek Lipton, and slips of prescription papers, and then the man from the park, and then Jordan Hopkins, and then Carolyn once more (Oh, Carolyn!). And then he swallowed, and they were all gone, and he was just an old man dying at the bottom of a gully in Ampurdan, and there was nothing after the ampersand with no more will to connect things, and as things turned gray and faded further, he realized that he had found what he had been looking for all along.

Absolutely nothing.

DAVID MORRELL *is the author of* First Blood, *the critically acclaimed novel in which Rambo was created. He holds a PhD in American literature from Penn State and was a professor in the English department at the University of Iowa. His numerous* New York Times *bestsellers include the classic espionage novel* The Brotherhood of the Rose, *the basis for the only television miniseries to be broadcast after a Super Bowl. An Edgar and Anthony finalist, an Inkpot, Macavity, and Nero recipient, Morrell has three Bram Stoker Awards and the Thriller Master Award from International Thriller Writers. Bouchercon, the world's largest conference for crime-fiction readers and authors, gave him its Lifetime Achievement Award. Visit him at www.davidmorrell.net.*

Cypresses by Vincent van Gogh

ORANGE IS FOR ANGUISH, BLUE FOR INSANITY

BY DAVID MORRELL

Van Dorn's work was controversial, of course. The scandal his paintings caused among Parisian artists in the late 1800s provided the stuff of legend. Disdaining conventions, thrusting beyond accepted theories, Van Dorn seized upon the essentials of the craft to which he'd devoted his soul. Color, design, and texture. With those principles in mind, he created portraits and landscapes so different, so innovative, that their subjects seemed merely an excuse for Van Dorn to put paint onto canvas. His brilliant colors, applied in passionate splotches and swirls, often so thick that they projected an eighth of an inch from the canvas in the manner of a bas-relief, so dominated the viewer's perception that the person or scene depicted seemed secondary to technique.

Impressionism, the prevailing avant-garde theory of the late 1800s, imitated the eye's tendency to perceive the edges of peripheral objects as blurs. Van Dorn went one step further and so emphasized the lack of distinction among objects that they seemed to melt together, to merge into an interconnected, pantheistic universe of color. The branches of a Van Dorn tree became ectoplasmic tentacles, thrusting toward the sky and the grass, just as tentacles from the sky and grass thrust toward the tree, all melding into a radiant swirl. He seemed to address himself not to the illusions of light but to reality itself, or at least to his theory of it. The tree is the sky, his technique asserted. The grass is the tree, and the sky the grass. All is one.

Van Dorn's approach proved so unpopular among theorists of his time that he frequently couldn't buy a meal in exchange for a canvas upon which he'd labored for months. His frustration produced a nervous breakdown. His self-mutilation shocked and alienated such one-time friends as Cezanne and Gauguin. He died in squalor and obscurity. Not until the 1920s, thirty years after his death, were his paintings recognized for the genius they displayed. In the 1940s, his soul-tortured character became the subject of a best-selling novel, and in the 1950s a Hollywood spectacular. These days, of course, even the least of his efforts can't be purchased for less than three million dollars.

Ah, art.

It started with Myers and his meeting with Professor Stuyvesant. "He agreed . . . reluctantly."

"I'm surprised he agreed at all," I said. "Stuyvesant hates Postimpressionism and Van Dorn in particular. Why didn't you ask someone easy, like old man Bradford?"

"Because Bradford's academic reputation sucks. I can't see the point of writing a dissertation if it won't be published, and a respected dissertation director can make an editor pay attention. Besides, if I can convince Stuyvesant, I can convince anyone."

"Convince him of what?"

"That's what Stuyvesant wanted to know," Myers said.

I remember that moment vividly, the way Myers straightened his lanky body, pushed his glasses close to his eyes, and frowned so hard that his curly red hair scrunched forward on his brow.

"Stuyvesant said that, even disallowing his own disinclination toward Van Dorn—God, the way that pompous asshole talks—he couldn't understand why I'd want to spend a year of my life writing about an artist who'd been the subject of countless books and articles. Why not choose an obscure but promising neo-Expressionist and gamble that my reputation would rise with his? Naturally the artist he recommended was one of Stuyvesant's favorites."

"Naturally," I said. "If he named the artist I think he did . . ."

Myers mentioned the name.

I nodded. "Stuyvesant's been collecting him for the past five years. He hopes the resale value of the paintings will buy him a town house in London when he retires. So what did you tell him?"

Myers opened his mouth to answer, then hesitated. With a brooding look, he turned toward a print of Van Dorn's swirling *Cypresses in a Hollow*, which hung beside a ceiling-high bookshelf crammed with Van Dorn biographies, analyses, and bound collections of reproductions. He didn't speak for a moment, as if the sight of the familiar print—its facsimile colors incapable of matching the brilliant tones of the original, its manufacturing process unable to re-create the exquisite texture of raised, swirled layers of paint on canvas—still took his breath away.

"So what did you tell him?" I asked again.

Myers exhaled with a mixture of frustration and admiration. "I said, what the critics wrote about Van Dorn was mostly junk. He agreed, with the implication that the paintings invited no less. I said, even the gifted critics hadn't probed to Van Dorn's essence. They were missing something crucial."

"Which is?"

"Exactly. Stuyvesant's next question. You know how he keeps relighting his pipe when he gets impatient. I had to talk fast. I told him I didn't know what I was looking for, but there's something"—Myers gestured toward the print—"something there. Something nobody's noticed. Van Dorn hinted as much in his diary. I don't know what it is, but I'm convinced his paintings hide a secret." Myers glanced at me.

I raised my eyebrows.

"Well, if nobody's noticed," Myers said, "it *must* be a secret, right?"

"But if *you* haven't noticed . . ."

Compelled, Myers turned toward the print again, his tone filled with wonder. "How do I know it's there? Because when I look at Van Dorn's paintings, I *sense* it. I *feel* it."

I shook my head. "I can imagine what Stuyvesant said to that. The man deals with art as if it's geometry, and there aren't any secrets in—"

"What he said was, if I'm becoming a mystic, I ought to be in the school of religion, not art. But if I wanted enough rope to hang myself and strangle my career, he'd give it to me. He liked to believe he had an open mind, he said."

"That's a laugh."

"Believe me, he wasn't joking. He had a fondness for Sherlock Holmes, he said. If I thought I'd found a mystery and could solve it, by all means do so. And at that, he gave me his most condescending smile and said he would mention it at today's faculty meeting."

"So what's the problem? You got what you wanted. He agreed to direct your dissertation. Why do you sound so—"

"Today there *wasn't* any faculty meeting."

"Oh." My voice dropped. "You're fucked."

Myers and I had started graduate school at the University of Iowa together. That had been three years earlier, and we'd formed a strong enough friendship to rent adjacent rooms in an old apartment building near campus. The spinster who owned it had a hobby of doing watercolors—she had no talent, I might add—and rented only to art students so they would give her lessons. In Myers's case, she had made an exception. He wasn't a painter, as I was. He was an art historian. Most painters work instinctively. They're not skilled at verbalizing what they want to accomplish. But words and not pigment were Myers's specialty. His impromptu lectures had quickly made him the old lady's favorite tenant.

After that day, however, she didn't see much of him. Nor did I. He wasn't at the classes we took together. I assumed he spent most of his time at the library. Late at night, when I noticed a light beneath his door and knocked, I didn't get an answer. I phoned him. Through the wall I heard the persistent, muffled ringing.

One evening I let the phone ring eleven times and was just about to hang up when he answered. He sounded exhausted.

"You're getting to be a stranger," I said.

His voice was puzzled. "Stranger? But I just saw you a couple of days ago."

"You mean two weeks ago."

"Oh, shit," he said.

"I've got a six-pack. You want to—?"

"Yeah, I'd like that." He sighed. "Come over."

When he opened his door, I don't know what startled me more, the way Myers looked or what he'd done to his apartment.

I'll start with Myers. He had always been thin, but now he looked gaunt, emaciated. His shirt and jeans were rumpled. His red hair was matted. Behind his glasses, his eyes looked bloodshot. He hadn't shaved. When he closed the door and reached for a beer, his hand shook.

His apartment was filled with, covered with—I'm not sure how to convey the dismaying effect of so much brilliant clutter—Van Dorn prints. On every inch of the walls. The sofa, the chairs, the desk, the TV, the bookshelves. And the drapes, and the ceiling, and except for a narrow path, the floor. Swirling sunflowers, olive trees, meadows, skies, and streams surrounded me, encompassed me, seemed to reach out for me. At the same time, I felt swallowed. Just as the blurred edges of objects within each print seemed to melt into one another, so each print melted into the next. I was speechless amid the chaos of color.

Myers took several deep gulps of beer. Embarrassed by my stunned reaction to the room, he gestured toward the vortex of prints. "I guess you could say I'm immersing myself in my work."

"When did you eat last?"

He looked confused.

"That's what I thought." I walked along the narrow path among the prints on the floor and picked up the phone. "The pizza's on me." I ordered the largest supreme the nearest Pepi's had to offer. They didn't deliver beer, but I had another six-pack in my fridge, and I had the feeling we'd be needing it.

I set down the phone. "Myers, what the hell are you doing?"

"I told you."

"Immersing yourself? Give me a break. You're cutting classes. You haven't showered in God knows how long. You look like hell. Your deal with Stuyvesant isn't worth destroying your health for. Tell him you've changed your mind. Get an easier dissertation director."

"Stuyvesant's got nothing to do with this."

"Damn it, what *does* it have to do with? The end of comprehensive exams, the start of dissertation blues?"

Myers gulped the rest of his beer and reached for another can. "No, blue is for insanity."

"What?"

"That's the pattern." Myers turned toward the swirling prints. "I studied them chronologically. The more Van Dorn became insane, the more he used blue. And orange is his color of anguish. If you match the paintings with the personal crises described in his biographies, you see a corresponding use of orange."

"Myers, you're the best friend I've got. So forgive me for saying I think you're off the deep end."

He swallowed more beer and shrugged as if to say he didn't expect me to understand.

"Listen," I said. "A personal color code, a connection between emotion and pigment, that's bullshit. I should know. You're the historian, but I'm the painter. I'm telling you, different people react to colors in different ways. Never mind the advertising agencies and their theories that some colors sell products more than others. It all depends on context. It depends on fashion. This year's 'in' color is next year's 'out.' But an honest-to-God great painter uses whatever color will give him the greatest effect. He's interested in creating, not selling."

"Van Dorn could have used a few sales."

"No question. The poor bastard didn't live long enough to come into fashion. But orange is for anguish and blue means insanity? Tell that to Stuyvesant and he'll throw you out of his office."

Myers took off his glasses and rubbed the bridge of his nose. "I feel so . . . Maybe you're right."

"There's no maybe about it. I *am* right. You need food, a shower, and sleep. A painting's a combination of color and shape that people either like or they don't. The artist follows his instincts, uses whatever techniques he can master, and does his best. But if there's a secret in Van Dorn's work, it isn't a color code."

Myers finished his second beer and blinked in distress. "You know what I found out yesterday?"

I shook my head.

"The critics who devoted themselves to analyzing Van Dorn . . ."

"What about them?"

"They went insane, the same as he did."

"What? No way. I've studied Van Dorn's critics. They're as conventional and boring as Stuyvesant."

"You mean the mainstream scholars. The safe ones. I'm talking about the truly brilliant ones. The ones who haven't been recognized for their genius, just as Van Dorn wasn't recognized."

"What happened to them?"

"They suffered. The same as Van Dorn."

"They were put in an asylum?"

"Worse than that?"

"Myers, don't make me ask."

"The parallels are amazing. They each tried to paint. In Van Dorn's style. And just like Van Dorn, they stabbed out their eyes."

I guess it's obvious by now—Myers was what you might call "high-strung." No negative judgment intended. In fact, his excitability was one of the reasons I liked him. That and his imagination. Hanging around with him was never dull. He loved ideas. Learning was his passion. And he passed his excitement on to me.

The truth is, I needed all the inspiration I could get. I wasn't a bad artist. Not at all. On the other hand, I wasn't a great one either. As I neared the end of grad school, I had painfully come to realize that my work would never be more than "interesting." I didn't want to admit it, but I'd probably end up as a commercial artist in an advertising agency.

That night, however, Myers's imagination wasn't inspiring. It was scary. He was always going through phases of enthusiasm. El Greco, Picasso, Pollock. Each had preoccupied him to the point of obsession, only to be abandoned for another favorite and another. When he'd fixated on Van Dorn, I'd assumed it was merely one more infatuation.

But the chaos of Van Dorn prints in his room made clear he'd reached a greater excess of compulsion. I was skeptical about his insistence that there was a secret in Van Dorn's work. After all, great art can't be explained. You can analyze its technique, you can diagram its symmetry, but ultimately there's a mystery words can't communicate. Genius can't be summarized. As far as I could tell, Myers had been using the word *secret* as a synonym for indescribable brilliance.

When I realized he literally meant that Van Dorn had a secret, I was appalled. The distress in his eyes was equally appalling. His references to insanity, not only in Van Dorn but in his critics, made me worry that Myers himself was having a breakdown. Stabbed out their eyes, for Christ's sake?

I stayed up with Myers till 5:00 A.M., trying to calm him, to convince him he needed a few days' rest. We finished the six-pack I'd brought, the six-pack in my refrigerator, and another six-pack I bought from an art student down the hall. At dawn, just before Myers dozed off and I staggered back to my room, he murmured that I was right. He needed a break, he said. Tomorrow he'd call his folks. He'd ask if they'd pay his plane fare back to Denver.

Hungover, I didn't wake up until late afternoon. Disgusted that I'd missed my classes, I showered and managed to ignore the taste of last night's pizza. I wasn't surprised when I phoned Myers and got no answer. He probably felt as shitty as I did. But after sunset, when I called again, then knocked on his door, I started to worry. His door was locked, so I went downstairs to get the landlady's key. That's when I saw the note in my mail slot.

> *Meant what I said. Need a break. Went home.*
> *Will be in touch. Stay cool. Paint well.*
> *I love you, pal. Your friend forever.*
>
> *Myers*

My throat ached. He never came back. I saw him only twice after that. Once in New York, and once in . . .

Let's talk about New York. I finished my graduate project, a series of landscapes that celebrated Iowa's big-sky-rolling, dark-earthed, wooded hills. A local patron paid fifty dollars for one of them. I gave three to the university's hospital. The rest are who knows where.

Too much has happened.

As I predicted, the world wasn't waiting for my good-but-not-great efforts. I ended where I belonged, as a commercial artist for a Madison Avenue advertising agency. My beer cans are the best in the business.

I met a smart, attractive woman who worked in the marketing department of a cosmetics firm. One of my agency's clients. Professional conferences led to personal dinners and intimate evenings that lasted all night. I proposed. She agreed.

We'd live in Connecticut, she said. Of course.

When the time was right, we might have children, she said.

Of course.

Myers phoned me at the office. I don't know how he knew where I was. I remember his breathless voice.

"I found it," he said.

"Myers?" I grinned. "Is it really—*How are you? Where have*—"

"I'm telling you. I found it!"

"I don't know what you're—"

"Remember? Van Dorn's secret!"

In a rush, I did remember—the excitement Myers could generate, the wonderful, expectant conversations of my youth—the days and especially the nights when ideas and the future beckoned. "Van Dorn? Are you still—"

"Yes! I was right! There *was* a secret!"

"You crazy bastard, I don't care about Van Dorn. But I care about you! Why did you—I never forgave you for disappearing."

"I had to. Couldn't let you hold me back. Couldn't let you—"

"For your own good!"

"So you thought. But I was right!"

"Where are you?"

"Exactly where you'd expect me to be."

"For the sake of old friendship, Myers, don't piss me off. *Where are you?*"

"The Metropolitan Museum of Art."

"Will you stay there, Myers? While I catch a cab? I can't wait to see you."

"I can't wait for you to see what I see!"

I postponed a deadline, canceled two appointments, and told my fiancée I couldn't meet her for dinner. She sounded miffed. But Myers was all that mattered.

He stood beyond the pillars at the entrance. His face was haggard, but his eyes were like stars. I hugged him. "Myers, it's so good to—"

"I want you to see something. Hurry."

He tugged at my coat, rushing.

"But where have you been?"

"I'll tell you later." We entered the Postimpressionist gallery. Bewildered, I followed Myers and let him anxiously sit me on a bench before Van Dorn's *Fir Trees at Sunrise.*

I'd never seen the original. Prints couldn't compare. After a year of drawing ads for feminine beauty aids, I was devastated. Van Dorn's power brought me close to . . .

Tears.

For my visionless skills.

For the youth I'd abandoned a year before.

"Look!" Myers said. He raised his arm and gestured toward the painting. I frowned. I looked.

It took time—an hour, two hours—and the coaxing vision of Myers. I concentrated. And then, at last, I saw.

Profound admiration changed to . . .

My heart raced. As Myers traced his hand across the painting one final time, as a guard who had been watching us with increasing wariness stalked forward to stop him from touching the canvas, I felt as if a cloud had dispersed and a lens had focused.

"Jesus," I said.

"You see? The bushes, the trees, the branches?"

"Yes! Oh God, yes! Why didn't I—"

"Notice before? Because it doesn't show up in the prints," Myers said. "Only in the originals. And the effect's so deep, you have to study them—"

"Forever."

"It seems that long. But I knew. I was right."

"A secret."

When I was a boy, my father—how I loved him—took me mushroom hunting. We drove from town, climbed a barbed-wire fence, walked through a forest, and reached a slope of dead elms. My father told me to search the top of the slope while he checked the bottom.

An hour later, he came back with two large paper sacks filled with mushrooms. I hadn't found even one.

"I guess your spot was lucky," I said.

"But they're all around you," my father said.

"All around me? Where?"

"You didn't look hard enough."

"I crossed this slope five times."

"You searched, but you didn't really see," my father said. He picked up a long stick and pointed it toward the ground.

"Focus your eyes toward the end of the stick."

I did . . .

And I've never forgotten the hot excitement that surged through my stomach. The mushrooms appeared as if by magic. They'd been there all along, of course, so perfectly adapted to their surroundings, their color so much like dead leaves, their shape so much like bits of wood and chunks of rock that they'd been invisible to ignorant eyes. But once my vision adjusted, once my mind reevaluated the visual impressions it received, I saw mushrooms everywhere, seemingly thousands of them. I'd been standing on them, walking over them, staring at them, and hadn't realized.

I felt an infinitely greater shock when I saw the tiny faces Myers made me recognize in Van Dorn's *Fir Trees at Sunrise*. Most were smaller than a quarter of an inch, hints and suggestions, dots and curves, blended perfectly with the landscape. They weren't exactly human, although they did have mouths, noses, and eyes. Each mouth was a black, gaping maw, each nose a jagged gash, the eyes dark sinkholes of despair. The twisted faces seemed to be screaming in total agony. I could almost hear their anguished shrieks, their tortured wails. I thought of damnation. Of hell.

As soon as I noticed the faces, they emerged from the swirling texture of the painting in such abundance that the landscape became an illusion, the grotesque faces reality. The fir trees turned into an obscene cluster of writhing arms and pain-racked torsos.

I stepped back in shock an instant before the guard would have pulled me away.

"Don't touch the—" the guard said.

Myers had already rushed to point at another Van Dorn, the original *Cypresses in a Hollow*. I followed, and now that my eyes knew what to look for, I saw small, tortured faces in every branch and rock. The canvas swarmed with them.

"Jesus."

"And this!"

Myers hurried to *Sunflowers at Harvest Time,* and again, as if a lens had changed focus, I no longer saw flowers but anguished faces and twisted limbs. I lurched back, felt a bench against my legs, and sat.

"You were right," I said.

The guard stood nearby, scowling.

"Van Dorn did have a secret," I said. I shook my head in astonishment.

"It explains everything," Myers said. "These agonized faces give his work depth. They're hidden, but we sense them. We *feel* the anguish beneath the beauty."

"But why would he—"

"I don't think he had a choice. His genius drove him insane. It's my guess that this is how he literally saw the world. These faces are the demons he wrestled with. The festering products of his insanity. And they're not just an illustrator's gimmick. Only a genius could have painted them for all the world to see and yet have so perfectly infused them into the landscape that *no one* would see. Because he took them for granted in a terrible way."

"No one? *You* saw, Myers."

He smiled. "Maybe that means I'm crazy."

"I doubt it, friend." I returned his smile. "It does mean you're persistent. This'll make your reputation."

"But I'm not through yet," Myers said.

I frowned.

"So far all I've got is a fascinating case of optical illusion. Tortured souls writhing beneath, perhaps producing, incomparable beauty. I call them 'secondary images.' In your ad work, I guess they'd be called 'subliminal.' But this isn't commercialism. This is a genuine artist who had the brilliance to use his madness as an ingredient in his vision. I need to go deeper."

"What are you talking about?"

"The paintings here don't provide enough examples. I've seen his work in Paris and Rome, in Zurich and London. I've borrowed from my parents to the limits of their patience and my conscience. But I've seen, and I know what I have to do. The anguished faces began in 1889, when Van Dorn left Paris in disgrace. His early paintings were abysmal. He settled in La Verge in the South of France. Six months later, his genius suddenly exploded. In a frenzy, he painted. He returned to Paris. He showed his work, but no one appreciated it. He kept painting, kept showing. Still no one appreciated it. He returned to La Verge, reached the peak of his genius, and went totally insane. He had to be committed to an asylum, but not before he stabbed out his eyes. That's my dissertation. I intend to parallel his course. To match his paintings with his biography, to show how the faces increased and became more severe as his madness worsened. I want to dramatize the turmoil in his soul as he imposed his twisted vision on each landscape."

It was typical of Myers to take an excessive attitude and make it even more excessive. Don't misunderstand. His discovery was important. But he didn't know when to stop. I'm not an art historian, but I've read enough to know that what's called "psychological criticism," the attempt to analyze great art as a manifestation of neuroses, is considered off-the-wall. If Myers handed Stuyvesant a psychological dissertation, the pompous bastard would have a fit.

That was one misgiving I had about what Myers planned to do with his discovery. Another troubled me more. *I intend to parallel Van Dorn's course*, he'd said. After we left the museum and walked through Central Park, I realized how literally Myers meant it.

"I'm going to southern France," he said.

I stared in surprise. "You don't mean—"

"La Verge? That's right. I want to write my dissertation there."

"But—"

"What place could be more appropriate? It's the village where Van Dorn suffered his nervous breakdown and eventually went insane. If it's possible, I'll even rent the same room he did."

"Myers, this sounds too far out, even for you."

"But it makes perfect sense. I need to immerse myself. I need atmosphere, a sense of history. So I can put myself in the mood to write."

"The last time you immersed yourself, you crammed your room with Van Dorn prints, didn't sleep, didn't eat, didn't bathe. I hope—"

"I admit I got too involved. But last time I didn't know what I was looking for. Now that I've found it, I'm in good shape."

"You look strung out to me."

"An optical illusion." Myers grinned.

"Come on, I'll treat you to drinks and dinner."

"Sorry. Can't. I've got a plane to catch,"

"You're leaving *tonight*? But I haven't seen you since—"
"You can buy me that dinner when I finish the dissertation."

I never did. I saw him only one more time. Because of the letter he sent two months later. Or asked his nurse to send. She wrote down what he'd said and added an explanation of her own. He'd blinded himself, of course.

> *You were right. Shouldn't have gone. But when did I ever take advice? Always knew better, didn't I? Now it's too late. What I showed you that day at the Met—God help me, there's so much more. Found the truth. Can't bear it. Don't make my mistake. Don't look ever again, I beg you, at Van Dorn's paintings. Can't stand the pain. Need a break. Going home. Stay cool. Paint well. Love you, pal. Your friend forever,*
>
> *Myers*

In her postscript, the nurse apologized for her English. She sometimes took care of aged Americans on the Riviera, she said, and had to learn the language. But she understood what she heard better than she could speak it or write it, and hoped that what she'd written made sense. It didn't, but that wasn't her fault. Myers had been in great pain, sedated with morphine, not thinking clearly, she said. The miracle was that he'd managed to be coherent at all.

> *Your friend was staying at our only hotel. The manager says that he slept little and ate even less. His research was obsessive. He filled his room with reproductions of Van Dorn's work. He tried to duplicate Van Dorn's daily schedule. He demanded paints and canvas, refused all meals, and wouldn't answer his door. Three days ago, a scream woke the manager. The door was blocked. It took three men to break it down. Your friend used the sharp end of a paintbrush to stab out his eyes. The clinic here is excellent. Physically your friend will recover, although he will never see again. But I worry about his mind.*

Myers had said he was going home. It had taken a week for the letter to reach me. I assumed his parents would have been informed immediately by phone or telegram. He was probably back in the States by now. I knew his parents lived in Denver, but I didn't know their first names or address, so I got in touch with information and phoned every Myers in Denver until I made contact. Not with his parents but with a family friend watching their house. Myers hadn't been flown to the States. His parents had gone to the South of France. I caught the next available plane. Not that it matters, but I was supposed to be married that weekend.

La Verge is fifty kilometers inland from Nice. I hired a driver. The road curved through olive-tree orchards and farmland, crested cypress-covered hills, and often skirted cliffs. Passing one of the orchards, I had the eerie conviction that I'd seen it before. Entering La Verge, my déjà vu strengthened. The village seemed trapped in the 19th century. Except for phone poles and power lines, it looked exactly as Van Dorn had painted it. I recognized the narrow cobbled streets and rustic shops that Van Dorn had made famous. I asked directions. It wasn't hard to find Myers and his parents.

The final time I saw my friend, the undertaker was putting the lid on his coffin. I had trouble sorting out the details, but despite my burning tears, I gradually came to understand that the local clinic was as good as the nurse had assured me in her note. All things being equal, he would have lived.

But the damage to his mind had been another matter. He'd complained of headaches. He'd also become increasingly distressed. Even morphine hadn't helped. He'd been left alone only for a minute, appearing to be asleep. In that brief interval, he had managed to stagger from his bed, grope across the room, and find a pair of scissors. Yanking off his bandages, he'd jabbed the scissors into an empty eye socket and tried to ream out his brain. He'd collapsed before accomplishing his purpose, but the damage had been sufficient. Death had taken two days.

His parents were pale, incoherent with shock. I somehow controlled my own shock enough to try to comfort them. Despite the blur of those terrible hours, I remember noticing the kind of irrelevance that signals the mind's attempt to reassert normality. Myers's father wore Gucci loafers and a gold Rolex watch. In grad school, Myers had lived on a strict budget. I had no idea he came from wealthy parents.

I helped them make arrangements to fly his body back to the States. I went to Nice with them and stayed by their side as they watched the crate that contained his coffin being loaded into the baggage compartment of the plane. I shook their hands and hugged them. I waited as they sobbed and trudged down the boarding tunnel. An hour later, I was back in La Verge.

I returned because of a promise. I wanted to ease his parents' suffering—and my own. Because I'd been his friend. "You've got too much to take care of," I had said to his parents. "The long trip home. The arrangements for the funeral." My throat had felt choked. "Let me help. I'll settle things here, pay whatever bills he owes, pack up his clothes and . . ." I had taken a deep breath. "And his books and whatever else he had and send them home to you. Let me do that. I'd consider it a kindness. Please. I need to do *something*."

True to his ambition, Myers had managed to rent the same room taken by Van Dorn at the village's only hotel. Don't be surprised that it was available. The management used it to promote the hotel. A plaque announced the historic value of the room. The furnishings were the same style as when Van Dorn had stayed there. Tourists paid to peer in and sniff the residue of genius. But business had been slow this season, and Myers had wealthy parents. For a generous sum, coupled with his typical enthusiasm, he had convinced the hotel's owner to let him have that room.

I rented a different room—more like a closet—two doors down the hall and, my eyes still burning from tears, went into Van Dorn's musty sanctuary to pack my dear friend's possessions. Prints of Van Dorn paintings were everywhere, several splattered with dried blood. Heartsick, I made a stack of them.

That's when I found the diary.

During grad school, I had taken a course in Postimpressionism that emphasized Van Dorn, and I'd read a facsimile edition of his diary. The publisher had photocopied the handwritten pages and bound them, adding an introduction, translation, and footnotes. The diary had been cryptic from the start, but as Van Dorn became more feverish about his work, as his nervous breakdown became more severe, his statements deteriorated into riddles. His handwriting—hardly neat, even when he was sane—went quickly out of control and finally turned into almost indecipherable slashes and curves as he rushed to unloose his frantic thoughts.

I sat at a small wooden desk and paged through the diary, recognizing phrases I had read years before. With each passage, my stomach turned colder. Because this diary wasn't the published photocopy. Instead, it was a notebook, and although I wanted to believe that Myers had somehow, impossibly, gotten his hands on the original diary, I knew I was fooling myself. The pages in this ledger weren't yellow and brittle with age. The ink hadn't faded until it was brown more than blue. The notebook had been purchased and written in recently. It wasn't Van Dorn's diary. It belonged to *Myers*. The ice in my stomach turned to lava.

Glancing sharply away from the ledger, I saw a shelf beyond the desk and a stack of other notebooks. Apprehensive, I grabbed them and in a fearful rush flipped through them. My stomach threatened to erupt. Each notebook was the same, the words identical.

My hands shook as I looked again to the shelf, found the facsimile edition of the original, and compared it with the notebooks. I moaned, imagining Myers at this desk, his expression intense and insane as he reproduced the diary word for word, slash for slash, curve for curve. Eight times.

Myers had indeed immersed himself, straining to put himself into Van Dorn's disintegrating frame of mind. And in the end he'd succeeded. The weapon Van Dorn had used to stab out his eyes had been the sharp end of a paintbrush. In the mental hospital, Van Dorn had finished the job by skewering his brain with a pair of scissors. Like Myers. Or vice versa. When Myers had finally broken, had he and Van Dorn been horribly indistinguishable?

I pressed my hands to my face. Whimpers squeezed from my convulsing throat. It seemed forever before I stopped sobbing. My consciousness strained to control my anguish. ("Orange is for anguish," Myers had said.) Rationality fought to subdue my distress. ("The critics who devoted themselves to analyzing Van Dorn," Myers had said. "The ones who haven't been recognized for their genius, just as Van Dorn wasn't recognized. They suffered . . . And just like Van Dorn, they stabbed out their eyes.") Had they done it with a paintbrush? I wondered. Were the parallels that exact? And in the end, had they, too, used scissors to skewer their brains?

I scowled at the prints I'd been stacking. Many still surrounded me on the walls, the floor, the bed, the windows, even the ceiling. A swirl of colors. A vortex of brilliance.

Or at least I once had thought of them as brilliant. But now, with the insight Myers had given me, with the vision I'd gained in the Metropolitan Museum, I saw behind the sun-drenched cypresses and hayfields, the orchards and meadows, toward their secret darkness, toward the minuscule twisted arms and gaping mouths, the black dots of tortured eyes, the blue knots of writhing bodies. ("Blue is for insanity," Myers had said.)

All it took was a slight shift of perception, and there weren't any orchards and hayfields, only a terrifying gestalt of souls in hell. Van Dorn had indeed invented a new stage of Impressionism. He'd impressed upon the splendor of God's creation the teeming images of his own disgust. His paintings didn't glorify. They abhorred. Everywhere Van Dorn had looked, he'd seen his own private nightmare. Blue was for insanity, indeed, and if you fixated on Van Dorn's insanity long enough, you, too, became insane. ("Don't look ever again, I beg you, at Van Dorn's paintings," Myers had said in his letter.) In the last stages of his breakdown, had Myers somehow become lucid enough to try to warn me? ("Can't stand the pain. Need a break. Going home.") In a way I'd never expected, he had indeed gone home.

Another startling thought occurred to me. ("The critics who devoted themselves to analyzing Van Dorn. They each tried to paint in Van Dorn's style," Myers had said a year ago.) As if attracted by a magnet, my gaze swung across the welter of prints and focused on the corner across from me, where two canvas originals leaned against the wall. I shivered, stood, and haltingly approached them.

They'd been painted by an amateur. Myers was an art historian, after all. The colors were clumsily applied, especially the splotches of orange and blue. The cypresses were crude. At their bases, the rocks looked like cartoons. The sky needed texture. But I knew what the black dots among them were meant to suggest. I understood the purpose of the tiny blue gashes. The miniature anguished faces and twisted limbs were implied, even if Myers had lacked the talent to depict them. He'd contracted Van Dorn's madness. All that had remained were the terminal stages.

I sighed from the pit of my soul. As the village's church bell rang, I prayed that my friend had found peace.

It was dark when I left the hotel. I needed to walk, to escape the greater darkness of that room, to feel at liberty, to think. But my footsteps and inquiries led me down a narrow cobbled street toward the village's clinic, where Myers had finished what he had started in Van Dorn's room. I asked at the desk and five minutes later introduced myself to an attractive, dark-haired, thirtyish woman.

The nurse's English was more than adequate. She said her name was Clarisse.

"You took care of my friend," I said. "You sent me the letter he dictated and added a note of your own."

She nodded. "He worried me. He was so distressed."

The fluorescent lights in the vestibule hummed. We sat on a bench.

"I'm trying to understand why he killed himself," I said. "I think I know, but I'd like your opinion."

Her eyes, a bright, intelligent hazel, suddenly were guarded. "He stayed too long in his room. He studied too much." She shook her head and stared toward the floor. "The mind can be a trap. It can be a torture."

"But he was excited when he came here?"

"Yes."

"Despite his studies, he behaved as if he'd come on vacation?"

"Very much."

"Then what made him change? My friend was unusual, I agree. What we call high-strung. But he *enjoyed* doing research. He might have looked sick from too much work, but he thrived on learning. His body was nothing, but his mind was brilliant. What tipped the balance, Clarisse?"

"Tipped the . . . ?"

"Made him depressed instead of excited. What did he learn that made him—"

She stood and looked at her watch. "Forgive me. I stopped work twenty minutes ago. I'm expected at a friend's."

My voice hardened. "Of course. I wouldn't want to keep you."

Outside the clinic, beneath the light at its entrance, I stared at my own watch, surprised to see that it was almost eleven thirty. Fatigue made my knees ache. The trauma of the day had taken away my appetite, but I knew I should try to eat, and after walking back to the hotel's dining room, I ordered a chicken sandwich and a glass of Chablis. I meant to eat in my room but never got that far. Van Dorn's room and the diary beckoned.

The sandwich and wine went untasted. Sitting at the desk, surrounded by the swirling colors and hidden horrors of Van Dorn prints, I opened a notebook and tried to understand.

A knock at the door made me turn.

Again I glanced at my watch, astonished to find that hours had passed like minutes. It was almost 2:00 A.M.

The knock was repeated, gentle but insistent. The manager?

"Come in," I said in French. "The door isn't locked."

The knob turned. The door swung open.

Clarisse stepped in. Instead of her nurse's uniform, she now wore sneakers, jeans, and a sweater whose tight-fitting yellow accentuated the hazel in her eyes.

"I apologize," she said in English. "I must have seemed rude at the clinic."

"Not at all. You had an appointment. I was keeping you."

She shrugged self-consciously. "I sometimes leave the clinic so late, I don't have a chance to see my friend."

"I understand perfectly."

She drew a hand through her lush long hair. "My friend got tired. As I walked home, passing the hotel, I saw a light up here. On the chance it might be you . . ."

I nodded, waiting.

I had the sense that she'd been avoiding it, but now she turned toward the room. Toward where I'd found the dried blood on the prints. "The doctor and I came as fast as we could when the manager phoned us that afternoon." Clarisse stared at the prints. "How could so much beauty cause so much pain?"

"Beauty?" I glanced toward the tiny gaping mouths.

"You mustn't stay here. Don't make the mistake your friend did."

"Mistake?"

"You've had a long journey. You've suffered a shock. You need to rest. You'll wear yourself out as your friend did."

"I was just looking through some things of his. I'll be packing them to send them back to America."

"Do it quickly. You mustn't torture yourself by thinking about what happened here. It isn't good to surround yourself with the things that disturbed your friend. Don't intensify your grief."

"Surround myself? My friend would have said 'immerse.'"

"You look exhausted. Come." She held out her hand. "I'll take you to your room. Sleep will ease your pain. If you need some pills to help you . . ."

"Thanks. But a sedative won't be necessary."

Clarisse continued to offer her hand. I took it and went to the hallway.

For a moment I stared back toward the prints and the horror within the beauty. I said a silent prayer for Myers, shut off the lights, and locked the door.

We went down the hall. In my room, I sat on the bed.

"Sleep long and well," Clarisse said.

"I hope."

"You have my sympathy." She kissed my cheek.

I touched her shoulder. Her lips shifted toward my own. She leaned against me. We sank toward the bed. In silence, we made love.

Sleep came like her kisses, softly smothering.

But in my nightmares, there were tiny gaping mouths.

Sunlight glowed through my window. With aching eyes, I looked at my watch. Half past ten. My head hurt.

Clarisse had left a note on my bureau.

> *Last night was sympathy. To share and ease your grief. Do what you intended. Pack your friend's belongings. Send them to America. Go with them. Don't make your friend's mistake. Don't, as you said he said, "immerse" yourself. Don't let beauty give you pain.*

I meant to leave. I truly believe that. I phoned the front desk and asked the concierge to send up some boxes. After I showered and shaved, I went to Myers's room, where I finished stacking the prints. I made another stack of books and another of clothes. I packed everything into the boxes and looked around to make sure I hadn't forgotten anything.

The two canvases that Myers had painted still leaned against a corner. I decided not to take them. No one needed to be reminded of the delusions that had overcome him.

All that remained was to seal the boxes, to address and mail them. But as I started to close the flap on a box, I saw the notebooks inside.

So much suffering, I thought. So much waste.

Once more I leafed through a notebook. Myers had translated various passages. Van Dorn's discouragement about his failed career. His reasons for leaving Paris to come to La Verge—the stifling, backbiting artists' community, the snobbish critics and their sneering responses to his early efforts. *Need to free myself of convention. Need to void myself of aesthete politics, to shit it out of me. To find what's never been painted. To feel instead of being told what to feel. To see instead of imitating what others have seen.*

I knew from the biographies how impoverished Van Dorn's ambition had made him. In Paris, he'd literally eaten slops thrown into alleys behind restaurants. He'd been able to afford his quest to La Verge only because a successful but very conventional (and now ridiculed) painter friend had loaned him a small sum of money. Eager to conserve his endowment, Van Dorn had walked all the way from Paris to the South of France.

In those days, you have to remember, this valley was an unfashionable area of hills, rocks, farms, and villages. Limping into La Verge, Van Dorn must have been a pathetic sight. He'd chosen this provincial town precisely because it was unconventional, because it offered mundane scenes so in contrast with the salons of Paris that no other artist would dare to paint them.

Need to create what's never been imagined, he'd written. For six despairing months, he tried and failed. He finally quit in self-doubt, then suddenly reversed himself and, in a year of unbelievably brilliant productivity, gave the world thirty-eight masterpieces. At the time, of course, he couldn't trade any canvas for a meal. But the world knows better now.

He must have painted in a frenzy. His suddenly found energy must have been enormous. To me, a would-be artist with technical facility but only conventional eyes, he achieved the ultimate. Despite his suffering, I envied him. When I compared my maudlin, Wyeth-like depictions of Iowa landscapes to Van Dorn's trendsetting genius, I despaired. The task awaiting me back in the States was to imitate beer cans and deodorant packages for magazine ads.

I continued flipping through the notebook, tracing the course of Van Dorn's despair and epiphany. His victory had a price, to be sure. Insanity. Self-blinding. Suicide. But I had to wonder if perhaps, as he died, he'd have chosen to reverse his life if he'd been able. He must have known how remarkable, how truly astonishing, his work had become.

Or perhaps he didn't. The last canvas he'd painted before stabbing his eyes had been of himself. A lean-faced, brooding man with short, thinning hair, sunken features, pallid skin, and a scraggly beard. The famous portrait reminded me of how I always thought Christ would have looked just before he was crucified. All that was missing was the crown of thorns. But Van Dorn had a different crown of thorns. Not around but *within* him. Disguised among his scraggly beard and sunken features, the tiny gaping mouths and writhing bodies told it all. His suddenly acquired vision had stung him too much.

As I read the notebook, again distressed by Myers's effort to reproduce Van Dorn's agonized words and handwriting exactly, I reached the section where Van Dorn described his epiphany: *La Verge! I walked! I saw! I feel! Canvas! Paint! Creation and damnation!*

After that cryptic passage, the notebook—and Van Dorn's diary—became totally incoherent. Except for the persistent refrain of severe and increasing headaches.

I was waiting outside the clinic when Clarisse arrived to start her shift at three o'clock. The sun was brilliant, glinting off her eyes. She wore a burgundy skirt and a turquoise blouse. Mentally I stroked their cottony texture.

When she saw me, her footsteps faltered. Forcing a smile, she approached.

"You came to say good-bye?" She sounded hopeful.

"No. To ask you some questions."

Her smile disintegrated. "I mustn't be late for work."

"This'll take just a minute. My French vocabulary needs improvement. I didn't bring a dictionary. The name of this village. La Verge. What does it mean?"

She hunched her shoulders as if to say the question was unimportant. "It's not very colorful. The literal translation is 'the stick.'"

"That's all?"

She reacted to my frown. "There are rough equivalents. 'The branch.' 'The switch.' A willow, for example that a father might use to discipline a child." She looked uncomfortable. "It can also be a slang term for penis."

"And it doesn't mean anything else?"

"Indirectly. The synonyms keep getting farther from the literal sense. A wand, perhaps. Or a rod. The kind of forked stick that people who claim they can find water hold ahead of them when they walk across a field. The stick is supposed to bend down if there's water."

"We call it a divining rod. My father once told me he'd seen a man who could actually make one work. I always suspected the man just tilted the stick with his hands. Do you suppose this village got its name because long ago someone found water here with a divining rod?"

"Why would anyone have bothered when these hills have so many streams and springs? What makes you interested in the name?"

"Something I read in Van Dorn's diary. The village's name excited him for some reason."

"But *anything* could have excited him. He was insane."

"Eccentric. But he didn't become insane until after that passage in his diary."

"You mean his *symptoms* didn't show themselves until after that. You're not a psychiatrist."

I had to agree.

"Again, I'm afraid I'll seem rude. I really must go to work." Clarisse hesitated. "Last night . . ."

"Was exactly what you described in the note. A gesture of sympathy. An attempt to ease my grief. You didn't mean it to be the start of anything."

"Please do what I asked. Please leave. Don't destroy yourself like the others."

"*Others?*"

"Like your friend."

"No, you said 'others.'" My words were rushed. "Clarisse, tell me."

She glanced up, squinting as if she'd been cornered. "After your friend stabbed out his eyes, I heard talk around the village. Older people. It could be merely gossip that became exaggerated with the passage of time."

"What did they say?"

She squinted harder. "Twenty years ago, a man came here to do research on Van Dorn. He stayed three months and had a breakdown."

"He stabbed out his eyes?"

"Rumors drifted back that he blinded himself in a mental hospital in England. Ten years before, another man came. He jabbed scissors through an eye, all the way into his brain."

I stared, unable to control the spasms that racked my shoulder blades. "What the hell is going on?"

I asked around the village. No one would talk to me. At the hotel, the manager told me he'd decided to stop renting Van Dorn's room. I had to remove Myers's belongings at once.

"But I can still stay in *my* room?"

"If that's what you wish. I don't recommend it, but even France is still a free country."

I paid the bill, went upstairs, moved the packed boxes from Van Dorn's room to mine, and turned in surprise as the phone rang.

The call was from my fiancée.

When was I coming home?

I didn't know.

What about the wedding this weekend?

The wedding would have to be postponed.

I winced as she slammed down the phone.

I sat on the bed and couldn't help recalling the last time I'd sat there, with Clarisse standing over me, just before we'd made love. I was throwing away the life I'd tried to build.

For a moment I came close to calling my fiancée back, but a different sort of compulsion made me scowl toward the boxes, toward Van Dorn's diary. In the note Clarisse had added to Myers's letter, she'd said that his research had become so obsessive that he'd tried to re-create Van Dorn's daily habits. Again it occurred to me—at the end, had Myers and Van Dorn become indistinguishable? Was the secret to what had happened to Myers hidden in the diary, just as the suffering faces were hidden in Van Dorn's paintings? I grabbed one of the ledgers. Scanning the pages, I looked for references to Van Dorn's daily routine. And so it began.

I've said that except for telephone poles and electrical lines, La Verge seemed caught in the previous century. Not only was the hotel still in existence, but so were Van Dorn's favorite tavern, and the bakery where he had bought his morning croissant. A small restaurant he favored remained in business. On the edge of the village, a trout stream where he sometimes sat with a midafternoon glass of wine still bubbled along, although pollution had long since killed the trout. I went to all of them, in the order and at the time Van Dorn recorded in his diary.

Breakfast at eight, lunch at two, a glass of wine at the trout stream, a stroll to the countryside, then back to the room. After a week, I knew the diary so well, I didn't need to refer to it. Mornings had been Van Dorn's time to paint. The light was best then, he'd written. And evenings were a time for remembering and sketching.

It finally came to me that I wouldn't be following the schedule exactly if I didn't paint and sketch when Van Dorn had done so. I bought a notepad, canvas, pigments, a palette, whatever I needed, and for the first time since leaving graduate school, I tried to create. I used local scenes that Van Dorn had favored and produced what you'd expect: uninspired versions of Van Dorn's paintings. With no discoveries, no understanding of what had ultimately undermined Myers's sanity, tedium set in. My finances were almost gone. I prepared to give up.

Except . . .

I had the disturbing sense that I'd missed something. A part of Van Dorn's routine that wasn't explicit in the diary. Or something about the locales themselves that I hadn't noticed.

Clarisse found me sipping wine on the sunlit bank of the no-longer-trout-filled stream. I felt her shadow and turned toward her silhouette against the sun.

I hadn't seen her for two weeks, since our uneasy conversation outside the clinic. Even with the sun in my eyes, she looked more beautiful than I remembered.

"When was the last time you changed your clothes?" she asked.

A year ago, I had said the same to Myers.

"You need a shave. You've been drinking too much. You look awful."

I sipped my wine and shrugged. "Well, you know what the drunk said about his bloodshot eyes. 'You think they look bad to you? You should see them from *my* side.'"

"At least you can joke."

"I'm beginning to think that *I'm* the joke."

"You're definitely not a joke." She sat beside me. "You're becoming your friend. Why don't you leave?"

"I'm tempted."

"Good." She touched my hand.

"Clarisse?"

"Yes?"

"Answer some questions one more time?"

She studied me. "Why?"

"Because if I get the right answers, I might leave."

She nodded slowly.

Back in town, in my room I showed her the stack of prints. I almost told her about the faces they contained, but her brooding features stopped me. She thought I was disturbed enough as it was.

"When I walk in the afternoons, I go to the settings Van Dorn chose for his paintings." I sorted through the prints. "This orchard. This farm. This pond. This cliff. And so on."

"Yes, I recognize these places. I've seen them all."

"I hoped if I saw them, maybe I'd understand what happened to my friend. You told me he went to them as well. Each of them is within a five-kilometer radius of the village. Many are close together. It wasn't difficult to find each site. Except for one."

She didn't ask which. Instead, she tensely rubbed her arm.

When I'd taken the boxes from Van Dorn's room, I'd also removed the two paintings Myers had attempted. Now I pulled them from where I'd tucked them under the bed.

"My friend did these. It's obvious he wasn't an artist. But as crude as they are, you can see they both depict the same area."

I slid a Van Dorn print from the bottom of the stack.

"*This* area," I said. "A grove of cypresses in a hollow, surrounded by rocks. It's the only site I haven't been able to find. I've asked the villagers. They claim they don't know where it is. Do you know, Clarisse? Can you tell me? It must have some significance if my friend was fixated on it enough to try to paint it twice."

Clarisse scratched a fingernail across her wrist. "I'm sorry."

"What?"

"I can't help you."

"Can't or won't? Do you mean you don't know where to find it, or you know but you won't tell me?"

"I said I can't help."

"What's wrong with this village, Clarisse? What's everybody trying to hide?"

"I've done my best." She shook her head, stood, and walked to the door. She glanced back sadly. "Sometimes it's better to leave well enough alone. Sometimes there are reasons for secrets."

I watched her go down the hall. "Clarisse . . ."

She turned and spoke a single word: "North." She was crying. "God help you," she added. "I'll pray for your soul." Then she disappeared down the stairs.

For the first time, I felt afraid.

Five minutes later, I left the hotel. In my walks to the sites of Van Dorn's paintings, I had always chosen the easiest routes—east, west, and south. Whenever I'd asked about the distant tree-lined hills to the north, the villagers had told me there was nothing of interest in that direction, nothing at all to do with Van Dorn. What about cypresses in a hollow? I had asked. There weren't any cypresses in those hills, only olive trees, they'd answered. But now I knew.

La Verge was in the southern end of an oblong valley, squeezed by cliffs to the east and west. I rented a car. Leaving a dust cloud, I pressed my foot on the accelerator and headed north toward the rapidly enlarging hills. The trees I'd seen from the village were indeed olive trees. But the lead-colored rocks among them were the same as in Van Dorn's painting. I sped along the road, veering up through the hills. At the top, I found a narrow space to park and rushed from the car. But which direction to take? On impulse, I chose left and hurried among the rocks and trees.

My decision seems less arbitrary now. Something about the slopes to the left was more dramatic, more aesthetically compelling. A greater wildness in the landscape. A sense of depth, of substance. Like Van Dorn's work.

My instincts urged me forward. I'd reached the hills at quarter after five. Time compressed eerily. At once, my watch showed 7:10. The sun blazed crimson, descending toward the bluffs. I kept searching, letting the grotesque landscape guide me. The ridges and ravines were like a maze, every turn of which either blocked or gave access, controlling my direction. That's the sense I had—I was being controlled. I rounded a crag, scurried down a slope of thorns, ignored the rips in my shirt and the blood streaming from my hands, and stopped on the precipice of a hollow. Cypresses, not olive trees, filled the basin. Boulders jutted among them and formed a grotto.

The basin was steep. I skirted its brambles, ignoring their scalding sting. Boulders led me down. I stifled my misgivings, frantic to reach the bottom.

This hollow, this basin of cypresses and boulders, this thorn-rimmed funnel, was the image not only of Van Dorn's painting but of the canvases Myers had attempted. But why had this place so affected them?

The answer came as quickly as the question. I heard before I saw, although hearing doesn't accurately describe my sensation. The sound was so faint and high-pitched, it was almost beyond the range of detection. At first, I thought I was near a hornets' nest. I sensed a subtle vibration in the otherwise still air of the hollow. I felt an itch behind my eardrums, a tingle on my skin. The sound was actually many sounds, each identical, merging, like the collective buzz of a swarm of insects. But this was high-pitched. Not a buzz but more like a distant chorus of shrieks and wails.

Frowning, I took another step toward the cypresses. The tingle on my skin intensified. The itch behind my eardrums became so irritating that I raised my hands to the sides of my head. I came close enough to see within the trees, and what I noticed with terrible clarity made me panic. Gasping, I stumbled back. But not in time. What shot from the trees was too small and fast for me to identify.

It struck my right eye. The pain was excruciating, as if the white-hot tip of a needle had pierced my retina and lanced my brain. I clamped my right hand across that eye and screamed.

I continued stumbling backward, agony spurring my panic. But the sharp, hot pain intensified, surging through my skull. My knees bent. My consciousness dimmed. I fell against the slope.

It was after midnight when I managed to drive back to the village. Although my eye no longer burned, my panic was more extreme. Still dizzy from having passed out, I tried to keep control when I entered the clinic and asked where Clarisse lived. She had invited me to visit, I claimed. A sleepy attendant frowned but told me. I drove desperately toward her cottage, five blocks away.

Lights were on. I knocked. She didn't answer. I pounded harder, faster. At last I saw a shadow. When the door swung open, I lurched into the living room. I barely noticed the negligee Clarisse clutched around her, or the open door to her bedroom, where a startled woman sat up in bed, held a sheet to her breasts, and stood quickly to shut the bedroom door.

"What the hell do you think you're doing?" Clarisse demanded. "I didn't invite you in! I didn't—!"

I managed the strength to talk: "I don't have time to explain. I'm terrified. I need your help."

She clutched her negligee tighter.

"I've been stung. I think I've caught a disease. Help me stop whatever's inside me. Antibiotics. An antidote. Anything you can think of. Maybe it's a virus, maybe a fungus. Maybe it acts like bacteria."

"*What happened?*"

"I told you, no time. I'd have asked for help at the clinic, but they wouldn't have understood. They'd have thought I'd had a breakdown, the same as Myers. You've got to take me there. You've got to make sure I'm injected with as much of any and every drug that might possibly kill this thing."

The panic in my voice overcame her doubt. "I'll dress as fast as I can."

As we rushed to the clinic, I described what had happened. Clarisse phoned the doctor the moment we arrived. While we waited, she put disinfectant drops in my eye and gave me something for my rapidly developing headache. The doctor showed up, his sleepy features becoming alert when he saw how distressed I was. True to my prediction, he reacted as if I'd had a breakdown. I shouted at him to humor me and saturate me with antibiotics. Clarisse made sure it wasn't just a sedative he gave me. He used every compatible combination. If I thought it would have worked, I'd have swallowed Drano.

What I'd seen within the cypresses were tiny gaping mouths and minuscule writhing bodies, as small and camouflaged as those in Van Dorn's paintings. I know now that Van Dorn wasn't imposing his insane vision on reality. He wasn't an Impressionist, after all. At least not in his *Cypresses in a Hollow*. I'm convinced *Cypresses* was his first painting after his brain became infected. He was literally depicting what he had seen on one of his walks. Later, as the infection progressed, he saw the gaping mouths and writhing bodies like an overlay on everything else he looked at. In that sense too he wasn't an Impressionist. To him, the gaping mouths and writhing bodies were in all those later scenes. To the limits of his infected brain, he painted what to him was reality. His art was representational.

I know, believe me. Because the drugs didn't work. My brain is as diseased as Van Dorn's . . . or Myers's. I've tried to understand why they didn't panic when they were stung, why they didn't rush to a hospital. My conclusion is that Van Dorn had been so desperate for a vision to enliven his paintings that he gladly endured the suffering. And Myers had been so desperate to understand Van Dorn that when stung, he'd willingly taken the risk to identify even more with his subject until, too late, he had realized his mistake.

Orange is for anguish, blue for insanity. How true. Whatever infects my brain has affected my color sense. More and more, orange and blue overpower the other colors I know are there. I have no choice. I see little else. My paintings are *rife* with orange and blue.

My paintings. I've solved another mystery. It always puzzled me how Van Dorn could have suddenly been seized by such energetic genius that he painted thirty-eight masterpieces in one year. I know the answer now. What's in my head, the gaping mouths and writhing bodies, the orange of anguish and the blue of insanity, cause such pressure, such headaches that I've tried everything to subdue them, to get them out. I went from codeine to Demerol to morphine. Each helped for a time but not enough. Then I learned what Van Dorn understood and Myers attempted. Painting the disease somehow gets it out of you. For a time. And then you paint harder, faster. Anything to relieve the pain. But Myers wasn't an artist. The disease had no release and reached its terminal stage in weeks instead of Van Dorn's year.

But *I'm* an artist—or used to hope I was. I had skill without a vision. Now, God help me, I've got a vision. At first, I painted the cypresses and their secret. I accomplished what you'd expect. An imitation of Van Dorn's original. But I refuse to suffer pointlessly. I vividly recall the portraits of midwestern landscapes I produced in graduate school. The dark-earthed Iowa landscape. The attempt to make an observer feel the fecundity of the soil. Second-rate Wyeth. But not anymore. The twenty paintings I've so far stored away aren't versions of Van Dorn either. They're my own creations. Unique. A combination of the disease and my experience. Aided by powerful memory, I paint the river that flows through Iowa City. Blue. I paint the cornfields that cram the big-sky rolling country outside town. Orange. I paint my innocence. My youth. With my ultimate discovery hidden within them. Ugliness lurks within the beauty. Horror festers in my brain.

Clarisse at last told me about the local legend. In the Middle Ages, when La Verge was founded, she said, a meteor streaked from the sky. It lit the night. It burst upon the hills north of here. Flames erupted. Trees were consumed. The hour was late. Few villagers saw it. The site of the impact was too far away for those few witnesses to rush that night to see the crater. In the morning, the smoke had dispersed. The embers had died. Although the witnesses tried to find the meteor, the lack of the roads that now exist hampered their search through the tangled hills to the point of discouragement. A few among the few witnesses persisted. The few of the few of the few who had accomplished their quest staggered back to the village, babbling about headaches and tiny gaping mouths. Using sticks, they scraped disturbing images in the dirt and eventually stabbed out their eyes. Over the centuries, legend has it, similar self-mutilations occurred whenever someone returned from seeking the crater in those hills. The unknown had power then. The hills acquired the negative force of taboo. No villager, then or now, intruded on what came to be called the place where God's wand touched the earth. A poetic description of a blazing meteor's impact. La Verge.

I don't conclude the obvious: that the meteor carried spores that multiplied in the crater, which became a hollow eventually filled with cypresses. No—to me, the meteor was a cause but not an effect. I saw a pit among the cypresses, and from the pit, tiny mouths and writhing bodies resembling insects—how they wailed!—spewed. They clung to the leaves of the cypresses, flailed in anguish as they fell back, and instantly were replaced by other spewing anguished souls.

Yes. Souls. For the meteor, I insist, was just the cause. To me, the effect was the opening of hell. The tiny wailing months are the damned. As I am damned. Desperate to survive, to escape from the ultimate prison we call hell, a frantic sinner lunged. He caught my eye and stabbed my brain, the gateway to my soul. My soul. It festers. I paint to remove the pus.

I talk. That helps somehow. Clarisse writes it down while her female lover rubs my shoulders.

My paintings are brilliant. I'll be recognized as a genius, the way I had always dreamed.

At such a cost.

The headaches grow worse. The orange is more brilliant. The blue more disturbing.

I try my best. I urge myself to be stronger than Myers, whose endurance lasted only weeks. Van Dorn persisted for a year. Maybe genius is strength.

My brain swells. How it threatens to split my skull. The gaping mouths blossom.

The headaches! I tell myself to be strong. Another day. Another rush to complete another painting.

The sharp end of my paintbrush invites. Anything to lance my seething mental boil, to jab my eyes for the ecstasy of relief. But I have to endure.

On a table near my left hand, the scissors wait.

But not today. Or tomorrow.

I'll outlast Van Dorn.

JOYCE CAROL OATES *is the author of, most recently,* A Book of American Martyrs *(novel) and* The Doll-Master *(stories). Her story in* In Sunlight and Shadow, *titled "The Woman in the Window," has been selected for* The Best American Mystery Stories 2017. *She is currently Visiting Distinguished Writer in the Graduate Writing Program at New York University.*

Les beaux jours by Balthus

LES BEAUX JOURS

BY JOYCE CAROL OATES

Daddy please come bring me home. Daddy I am so sorry.

Daddy it is your fault. Daddy *I hate you.*

Daddy, no! I love you Daddy whatever you have done.

Daddy I am under a spell here. I am *not myself* here.

This place in which I am a captive—it is in the Alps, I think. It is a great, old house like a castle made of ancient rock. Through high windows you can see moors stretching to the mountainous horizon. All is scrubby gray-green as if undersea. The light is perpetual twilight.

Dusk is when Master comes. I am in love with Master.

Daddy, no! I do not love Master at all, I am terrified of Master.

He is not like *you*, Daddy. Master laughs at me, taunts me, twines his long thin icy fingers through my fingers and sneers at me when I whimper with pain.

Why did you come crawling to us, ma chere, *if now you are so fearful?*

Daddy please forgive me. Daddy do not abandon me.

Though it was your fault, Daddy.

Though I can never forgive *you.*

It is called by two names. *Le grand chalet* is the official name.

Le grand chalet des ames perdues is the unofficial, whispered name.

Indeed it is *tres grand*, Daddy. The oldest part of *le chalet* dating to 1563 (it is said: such a time is not possible for me to imagine) and the desolate windswept land that surrounds it like a moat so vast that even if I could make myself small as a terrified little cat, if I could squeeze out one of the ill-fitting windows to escape across the moor, Master's servants would set his wolfhounds after me to hunt me down and tear me to pieces with their sharp ravenous teeth.

Or, if Master is in a merciful mood, and not a mood of vengeance, the servants might haul me back squirming in a net to throw down onto the stone floor at Master's feet.

So I have been warned by the other girl-captives.

So I have been warned by Master himself not in actual words but in Master's way of laying a finger against the anxious little artery that beats so hard in my throat, with just enough pressure to communicate—*Of all sins, ma chere, betrayal is the unforgiveable.*

I am not sure where *Le grand chalet des ames perdues* is but I believe it to be somewhere in eastern Europe.

A faraway place where there is no electricity—only just candles—tall, grand candles of the girth of young trees, so encrypted with melted and hardened wax that they resemble ancient sculptures hacked out of molten stone. What shadows dance from such candles, leaping to the ceiling twelve feet overhead like starved vultures spreading their mammoth wings, you will have to imagine, Daddy—*le chalet* is nothing like the apartment in which we'd lived on Fifth Avenue at Seventy-Sixth Street, overlooking Central Park from the twentieth-third floor, though (as Mother said) those rooms were haunted too, and the souls that dwelt there wandered *lost.*

Here are six-foot fireplaces and great, soot-begrimed chimneys in which (it is whispered) girl-captives shriveled to mummies are trapped in their foolish yearning to escape Master. *Which is why Master is furious when smoke backs up*

*into the room and a beautiful stoked fire must be extinguished so that the chimney
can be cleared.*

A faraway place, Daddy. Where the automobiles are very old but elegant
and stately and shiny-black as hearses.

There is no TV in *le chalet*. Unless there is a single TV in Master's quarters
which none of us has ever been allowed to glimpse as none of us has ever been
brought into Master's quarters but this is not likely as Master scorns the *effete
modern world* and even the *20th century* is vulgar to Master as a sniffling,
snuffling, sneezing girl.

But there is an old radio—a "floor model." The servants call it a "wireless"—
in Master's (downstairs) sitting room where we are brought sometimes if we
have pleased Master that day in his studio.

In Master's studio it is often very drafty. Wind like cold mean fingers
pries through the edges of the tall windows and strokes and tickles us, and
makes us shiver and our teeth chatter for we are made to remove our clothing
quickly and without protest and to cover our shivering naked bodies with
silken kimonos that are too large for us, and fall open no matter how tightly
we tie their sashes.

In *le grand chalet* we are often barefoot for Master is an admirer (he has
said) of the *girl-child-foot*.

Also, the bare *girl-child-foot* cannot easily run through brambles, thorns,
pebbles outside the chalet walls.

In Master's studio we are made to pose by sitting very straight and very still
for hours or by standing very straight and very still for hours or (some of us,
the most favored) lying with naked legs asprawl or aspread on *chaises longues*
and our heads flung back at painful angles. And some of us, rumored to be
the most favored, made to pose by lying very still on the freezing-cold marble
floor in mimicry (Master says) of *le mort*.

It is forbidden to observe Master at his easel. It is forbidden to glance even
fleetingly at Master contorting his face in a paroxysm of anguish, yearning,
ecstasy as he crouches at the easel only a few feet away from us scant of breath,
weak-kneed. For art is a brutal master, even for Master.

Sometimes, Master, who is the very essence of gentlemanly decorum,
curses his brushes in a language most of us do not know. Sometimes,
Master throws down a brush, or a tube of paint, like a furious child in the

knowledge that someone (an adult, a servant) will pick it up for him, at a later time.

Fortunately, the marble floor beneath Master's easel is covered with a stained canvas.

It is shocking to us to glimpse Master's many tubes of paint, which appear to be flung haphazardly onto a table beside his easel; myriad tubes of paint, of which most are very messy, some are skeletal and squeezed nearly dry, a few are plump and newly purchased; for elsewhere in *Le grand chalet* all is chaste and orderly as a geometrical figure.

Master's studio with its high ceiling and white walls is one of the most famous artists' studios in the world, it is said. Long before the oldest of us was born, the studio existed at *Le grand chalet des ames perdues*, and of course, long after the youngest of us will pass away, Master's studio will endure for it is enshrined in legend, like Master himself who (it is said) is one of the very few living artists whose work is displayed in the Louvre.

Master has shunned fame, as Master has shunned commercial success, yet, ironically, Master has become famous, and Master has become one of the most successful painters of what is called the "modern era"; his paintings are unusually large, fastidiously painted and repainted, formal, rather austere, "classic"—even if their subjects are nude or minimally dressed young girls posed in languid postures.

Master insists upon the impersonality of art. Master has chosen to live far from the clamor of capital cities—Paris, Berlin, Prague, Rome. Master scorns the elite art world even as Master scorns the media that nonetheless pursues him with *paparazzi*. Master is revered for the severity of his art and for his perfectionism: Master will spend years on a single canvas before releasing it to his (Parisian) gallery. With each of his rare exhibits Master has included this declaration:

LIFE IS NOT ART

ART IS THE LIFE OF WHICH NOTHING IS KNOWN

TURN YOUR EYES TO THE PAINTINGS

"THE REST IS SILENCE"

Yet, the media adores Master as a *nobleman-artiste living in reclusive exile in a romantic and remote corner of Europe.*

In Master's studio time ceases to exist. In Master's studio the spell suffuses me like ether. My arms, my legs, my supine being on the green sofa—so heavy, I cannot move.

Master has posed my arm in a tight sleeve, Master has tugged open the tight bodice so that my very small, right breast is exposed; Master has positioned my bare legs just so, and Master has placed on my *exquisite girl-child-feet* thin slippers made of the most fragile satin, one could barely walk in them across a room; Master has fastened a necklace around my neck, of small gems worthy of an adult beauty (as Master has said: the necklace may have belonged to one of Master's wives).

And Master has given me a little hand-mirror in which to gaze, mesmerized at what I see: the pretty-doll face, the pert little nose, and pursed lips that are *me*.

How did I come to this captivity?—I think of nothing else.

Daddy, I ran away from you. I ran away from *her*.

Yet first it was with Mother, those restless hours in the great museum visible from our Fifth Avenue windows. Mother in dark glasses so that her reddened eyes were not exposed and no one who knew her (and knew you) would recognize her. Mother pulling my sister and me by our arms, urging us up the grand stairs, in seek of something she could not have defined—the consolation of art, the impersonality of art, the escape of art.

The mystery of art, which confounds us with the power to heal our wounds, or to lacerate our wounds to greater pain.

Soon then, I slipped away to come alone. A novelty at the museum, a child so young—alone . . .

But I was mature for my age, and my size. It was not difficult for me to single out visitors whom I would approach in the usually crowded lobby to ask to purchase a ticket for me, and take me inside with them as if I belonged with them. . . . Of course, I gave them money for my ticket. Very cleverly, I even lent them Mother's membership card (appropriated for the occasion), to facilitate matters.

Usually it was women whom I approached. Not young, not old, Mother's age, not glamorous (like Mother) but motherly-seeming. They were surprised by my request at first, but kindly, and cooperative. It was not difficult to deceive these women that you or Mother were waiting for me in the café in the American Wing, and then to slip away from their scrutiny once we were inside.

Soon then in the great museum I began to linger before a row of paintings by the 20th century European artist whom I would come to know as Master.

What a spell these paintings cast! I could not know that it was the spell of enchantment and entrapment, of inertia, that would one day suffuse my limbs like an evil sedative. . . .

These were large dreamlike paintings executed with the formality, stillness, and subdued beauty of the older, classical European art Mother had professed to admire, yet their subjects were not biblical or mythological figures but girls—some of them as young as I was. Though in settings very different from the settings of my life the girls seemed familiar to me, more sisterly than my own sister who was too young and too silly for me and was always interrupting my thoughts with her chatter.

Especially, I found myself staring at a painting of a girl who resembled me, lying on a small sofa in an old-fashioned drawing room. (I did not yet know the word for such an item of furniture—*chaise longue*.) The girl was like myself yet older and wiser. Her eyebrows were thin as pencil lines artfully drawn while mine were thicker, yet not so defined. Her eyes were exactly my eyes!—yet wiser, bemused. Her coppery-colored, wavy hair resembled my own, though in an old-fashioned style. Her doll-like features, delicately boned nose and somber pursed lips—like mine, but she was far prettier than me, and more ethereal. And she was gazing at herself in a small hand-mirror with an expression of calm self-absorption—impossible for me, who had come to dislike my face, intensely.

What was strange about the painting was that the girl on the sofa seemed to be totally oblivious of another presence in the room, only a few feet away from her: a stooped young man stoking a blazing fire in a fireplace, that so pulsated with heat and light you could nearly feel it, standing before the painting.

In fact, when you approach the painting from a little distance it is the "blazing" you first see that leaps out to strike your eye, before you see the small supine figure on the sofa gazing dreamily at her reflection.

Isn't that strange, Daddy? Yet, if the girl on the sofa is a girl in a dream, and the dream of the girl is her pretty-doll face, it is natural that she is unaware of another presence, even close by; the stooped figure is male but it is *stooped*, a servant surely, and not Master.

Each day after school I came to the museum. Each day I lingered longer by this painting—*Les beaux jours*. At first I'd thought that the title might mean *The Beautiful Eyes*—but *jours* means "days," it is *yeux* that means "eyes."

And so the title is—*The Beautiful Days*.

Days of enchantment, entrancement. Not yet days of entrapment.

Beautiful days of perfect calm, peace. Enough just to gaze into the little hand-mirror and to pay no heed to your flimsy satin slippers that will impede your flight if you try to escape and to the hot bright-blazing fire being prepared a few feet away by a stooped and faceless servant.

Other paintings by the artist whose name I must not speak—(for to speak of Master in such a way is forbidden to us, as to the servants of *le grand chalet*)—were fascinating to me as well and any one of these might have held me captive: *Therese revant—Jeune fille à sa toilette—Nu jouant avec un chat—La victime—La chambre.*

Faintly, I could hear their cries. The captive-girls in the paintings who were (not yet) myself.

So faintly, I could pretend that I had not heard. Glancing around at others in the museum, casual visitors, uniformed guards who took little notice of me, a child of eleven seemingly alone in the gallery, shivering with apprehension—for what precisely, I could not have guessed.

(And what is there to say of the museum guards?—did they not hear, either? Had they grown indifferent, bored with beauty as with suffering, as if it were but mere paint on canvas, a veneer and not a depth? *Will they not hear me, when I cry for help?*)

Outside the museum, the clamor of New York streets. Tall leafy trees, the enormous green park. On Fifth Avenue taxis queuing up at the curb in front of the museum, at the foot of the great pyramid of stone steps.

Vendors' carts, stretching along the block. These are owned exclusively by US veterans, it is decreed. The smell of hot meats is almost overwhelming to us, who are faint from malnutrition.

Our apartment at Fifth Avenue and Seventy-Sixth Street. Overlooking the park from the twenty-third floor. So high, we heard nothing. No sounds lifted to our ears from the street. When I pressed my hands over my ears, I did not hear sobbing. I did not hear even my own sobbing, or the wild beat of my heart.

Eleven on my last birthday. When you were still living with us, Daddy, though often you stayed away overnight. And your promise was—*Darling of course I am not leaving you and your sister and your mother; and even if I left—temporarily!— your mother, that would not mean that I was leaving you and your sister. No.*

But when you left we were made to move to another apartment on a lesser street, on a lower floor. You left us for another life, Mother said. She wept bitterly. She inhabited her (sheer) nightgown for days in succession.

Men came to stay with Mother but never for long. We heard their loud barking laughter. We hear the clatter of glasses, bottles. We heard our mother's screams.

We heard the men depart hurriedly in the early hours of the morning: stumbling, cursing, threats. Laughter.

Jenny whispered wide-eyed—*One of them will murder her. Strangle her.*

(You are thinking that is not likely, a child of eight or nine would say such a thing? Even in a whisper, to her eleven-year-old sister? Do you think so, Daddy? Is that what you have wished to think?)

(A daddy is someone who wishes to think what protects him. Not what protects his children.)

We knew nothing of adult lives. Yet, we knew everything of adult lives.

We watched TV. Late-night when we were supposed to be in bed, the volume turned low. We were thrilled that women with disheveled hair and mascara-streaked faces wearing sheer nightgowns were raped, strangled, murdered in their beds. NYPD detectives stared rudely at their naked bodies. Photographers crouched over them, bending at the knees so that their groins were prominent.

But Mother did not die, as you know. Mother's screams prevailed. Even here, in *le grand chalet*, I hear those screams at a distance. Unless they are the screams of my sister-captives, muffled with cushions or the palm of Master's hand.

The men brought whiskey, bourbon. Cocaine.

Out of Mother's refrigerator, soft, smelly brie. Hard Italian provolone. Snails and garlic, hot butter. They ate greedily. They ate with their fingers.

We ran away to hide, we hid our eyes. Nothing so disgusted us as snails like the tiny ridges of flesh between our thin girl-legs we could not bear to touch even in the bath, the sensation came so strong.

Daddy, you dared not touch us there. In those days when you were a new, young daddy, and you bathed us. When we were very young girls, scarcely more than toddlers, babies. That long ago, you have (probably) forgotten.

Daddy, we have not forgotten. How your eyes glistened with knowledge of what lay secret and hidden between our legs that you did not (allow yourself to) touch.

Master touches us everywhere. Of course, Master touches us *there*.

Daddy why did you go away. Why was your life not *us*.

Mother never knew how once, we saw her—the girl slipping from your lap, giggling.

Young enough to be your daughter, Mother had accused, furious. I wanted to protest—I am your daughter!

It had been an accidental encounter. Jenny and I had been delivered too early to the apartment by your private car, or your friend had stayed too late. Slipping from your lap giggling and blushing, stammering—*Oh hey. Don't think badly of me. I am not a bad person. . . .*

She'd been drinking. Both of you drinking. It was surprising to us, she was so tall, and not so thin, not so very pretty really, and not (probably) so young as Mother believed her to be though much younger than Mother of course.

Her tight, short skirt pulled up from her fleshy thighs. The front of her shirt pulled open.

Not a bad person. Please believe me!

In the great museum quickly I made my way up the grand steps, along the high-ceilinged corridors, to the dimly lighted gallery that contained Master's paintings.

Unerring through the maze of the museum like a blind child navigating by smell, or touch. And there it was, suddenly before me—*Les beaux jours.*

Stunning to me, nothing ever changed in the painting. The girl lying on the green *chaise longue* with legs askew, the girl gazing at herself in the little hand-mirror. The girl so like myself yet older and wiser than I, and (seemingly) content with that knowledge.

The girl oblivious of the hot bright fire blazing only a few feet from her.

For the first time I heard the faint, yearning voice, or voices—*Hello! Come to us.*

Or did they cry—*Help us* . . . .

On weekday afternoons the gallery was often near-deserted. Visitors trooped through the special exhibits but did not make their way to this gallery.

No one heard the cries. Except me.

How strange, the museum guards never heard. As the stupefying dullness of their guard-lives had made them incapable of seeing the wonder of Master's art though it was hanging before them, triumphant and transgressive.

Which is why it is so lonely, Daddy. If *you* do not hear.

And back in the apartment which was on a floor lower than the twenty-third but still high above the pavement, high enough to stir dread in the pit of my belly, I crawled out onto the dwarf-balcony, I dared to lean over the railing that was encrusted with pigeon droppings, waiting for you to discover me, Daddy, and scold me as (rarely) you'd done—*What are you doing! Get back in here, darling!*

Master never scolds. Master (rarely) betrays emotion in our presence for we do not merit emotion only just vexation, disappointment, displeasure.

Daddy, come soon! I am afraid that if Master is displeased with me, if Master becomes bored with me, that Master will dispose of me as he has disposed of the others.

So lonely! Yet, I love Master. I love this heavy spell that falls upon me in Master's studio even when my limbs ache and my neck strains to bear the weight of my head, posed and unmoving for hours.

If you do not come to bring me home, Daddy. If you abandon me to Master I will sink ever more deeply into the spell, and Master will tire of me, and a collar will be fastened around my neck, and a chain to the collar, to bind me fast in the lowermost dungeon of *le chalet.*

Come to us, help us.
  Help us, come to us.

As I drew nearer the paintings in the great museum the spell began to work upon me. Like ether, in the air.

There was no guard near. No other visitors. Trembling I leaned close to whisper, *Yes! I will come to you.*

For what I could see of the drawing room of *Les beaux jours* was very beautiful to me, if strange and sepia-colored, not altogether clear as the details of a dream are not altogether clear and yet seductive, irresistible.

More and more in the lonely afternoons after school I found myself in that other world. I did not (yet) realize it was Master's world, for you do not see Master in the paintings, you see only yourself painted with such ardor, such yearning, such desire it is like nothing else in the world you have ever known, or could imagine.

Each of the girls, in each of the paintings: their stillness, their perfection. For even the awkward girls, even the girls whose doll-faces were hidden from view, were cherished, beloved. That, you could feel.

Without you in my life, Daddy, there was not a promise of such happiness anywhere I knew.

Come to us, you are one of us—the voices whispered; and my reply was—*Yes. I am yours.*

⚬—⟡—⚬

Ma chere, bienvenue!—so Master greeted me.

Ma belle petite fille!—Master exclaimed in delight at the sight of me as if he had never seen anyone so exquisite.

For I had been discovered by a servant wandering lost and tearful in one of the dim-lighted corridors of the great old house I did not (yet) know was *le grand chalet des ames perdues.*

Master made me blush, and my heart beat so rapidly I could not breathe, covering my face, my hands, my bare arms with his sharp damp stabbing kisses that left me faint.

How far you have come, ma chere!—*across the great ocean, to your master.*

I could not (yet) know that each of the girl-captives was greeted so lavishly by Master, and made to feel *You are the one. Only you.*

⚬—⟡—⚬

In that other life it had come to be, I could not bear to look at myself in a mirror.

For when you'd left us, Daddy, you took away with you so much—you could not know how much.

But in Master's studio, posed by Master on the green *chaise longue* I am allowed to see that my face is not homely, not despised, but a pretty doll-face. I love gazing into the mirror that Master has given me, at the pretty doll-face.

It is like sleep, gazing at the doll-face. Very hard to wake up, to look away from the doll-face. My lips scarcely move—*Is this* me? The wonder of it is hypnotic, like caresses that never cease.

Though I know—I think—there is someone in this room with me . . . It is heat that I am beginning to feel, an uncomfortable rising heat in this drafty place.

The heat of a *blazing fire*. Somewhere close by.

Master tugs at my tight-fitting sleeve, pulling it off my shoulder to expose my right breast that is small and hard as an unripened apple. The skirt of this (tight) dress which I have been given to wear is very short, and falls back to reveal much of my legs. In other paintings, in other rooms, the stark white of my little-girl panties is revealed as Master has positioned my legs, spread my legs just so. But in this painting you cannot see the narrow band of white cotton between my thighs.

In Master's studio time ceases to pass. In Master's studio we never age. That is the promise of Master's studio.

Master laughs at us but not unkindly. *You know you have come to me of your own volition, do not be hypocritical,* mes cheres. *Hypocrisy is for* les autres.

Long hours we must pose. Our lives spill out before us heedless as spools of thread rolling across a slanted marble floor. Some of us are new to *le grand chalet*, some of us have been here entire lifetimes. For long hours we must pose in the drafty studio or we will not be given food. We must not interrupt Master's concentration for Master will be choked with fury, and Master will punish by withholding his love.

To quench our terrible thirst we are given small sips of water by a servant who crouches at our side. Master is particularly furious if we beg to be "excused" to use a bathroom.

Water-closet is the word they use here. I am embarrassed at this word. The flushing mechanism is very old-fashioned, pulled by a chain. Old pipes clang and shudder in the great old house like demons.

You disgust me. You!—Master's thin nostrils quiver with indignation.

It is hard to live in a body, we have learned. The body betrays the pretty-doll face and makes of its prettiness a mockery.

Bitterly Mother told us, as soon as she'd become pregnant for the first time, it was the end of your love for her, Daddy. My belly, she said. My breasts. So big, swollen. No longer a girl, he'd felt betrayed. Poor man was not *turned on.*

We did not want to hear this! We were too young to hear of such ugliness.

Of course, the marriage continued. Your father would not have admitted even to himself the limits of his—of a man's—desire.

❦

And one day Master selects me for a special scene to which he will give the title, succinct and appalling—*La victime.*

I am hoping that you will see this portrait, Daddy. It is the very painting I had seen on the wall in the museum, without guessing that the girl lying in a limp, lifeless pose does not merely resemble me *but is me.*

La victime is not so dreamlike and beautiful as other paintings of Master's, that are more celebrated. *La victime* is the blunt, irrefutable image—the *girl-victim.* Patiently, almost tenderly Master urged me to the floor, to lie on my back on a stone slab; almost lovingly Master molded my bare limbs, turned and positioned my head with his steely-strong fingers.

In *La victime* I am not so pretty, I think. I am very pale—as if bloodless. Nor am I provided with a little hand-mirror in which to admire my pretty-doll face. My eyes are shut, the vision has faded from them. Except for thin white cotton stockings and tiny, useless slippers I am nude—*naked.*

Slowly as if in a trance Master executes this portrait. After long hours, when Master has finished for the day, and exited the studio in wraithlike silence, I am roused from a comatose state by one of the servants, a dwarf-woman who flings open heavy drapery to let in sunshine like a rude blow—*Wake up, you. Don't play games. You're not dead—yet.*

When first I arrived at the chalet, I was treated like a princess.

As, when I was born, and for years when I was your only child, Daddy, I was treated like a princess by you.

Lilies of the valley in a vase, in my room at the chalet. Beside my bed which was perfectly proportioned for a girl of eleven. Sweet fragrance of lily-of-the-valley which is mesmerizing to me even now, to recall.

A woman-servant bathing me, washing my hair and brushing it in slow fierce strokes as Master looked on with approval.

Tres belle, la petite enfant!

And sometimes, at first, in those early *beaux jours* I'd thought would continue forever, Master took the hairbrush from the woman-servant, and brushed my hair himself.

And sometimes, vaguely I recall—Master bathed me, and put me to bed.

I am ashamed to confess, Daddy—I did not really miss you then. I did not think of you. It was only Master of whom I thought.

In Master's studio Master wears a smock that is stark-black like a priest's cassock. By the end of each day Master's smock becomes stained with paint, and so, each morning, Master must be provided with a fresh clean black smock.

On his slender feet, black silk slippers in which Master moves silently as something that is upright, a wraith.

I have never looked fully at Master's face, Daddy—it is not allowed. And so I have not really seen Master except to know that he is older than you, and very dignified, with a pale austere face like something that has been sculpted, and not mere flesh like other, lesser beings.

(Has your face grown coarse, Daddy? I don't want to think so.)

(*I will not think so* though Mother tried to poison us against you.)

Some of us have come to realize that Master does not love us because we are not Master's children. This was hard to comprehend, and hurtful, and yet it is obvious: none of us, Master's girl-captives, are the children of Master's loins. For Master's own precious seed (it is said) was not spilled carelessly into the world but planted well, and thrived, and Master has a son, a singular being (it is said) whom we will never see, for he lives in Paris and is, like Master, an *artiste* though not a world-famous *artiste* like Master.

Wildly it is said, Master's son will one day come to *le grand chalet* to free his father's girl-captives, for Master's son does not approve of Master's way of art.

Yet the years pass, and Master's son does not appear.

Instead, photographers dare to journey to this remote region in eastern Europe, somewhere beyond the Alps. There are reporters, would-be interviewers. Master has instructed his servants to turn away most visitors from the gated entrance of *le chalet* but from time to time, unpredictably, for it is Master's way to be unpredictable, Master will allow one or another stranger entry, if he (or less frequently, she) is working for an impressive publication, or is a fellow *artiste* with impressive credentials.

These privileged individuals are not allowed beyond the formal rooms of the great old house. Servants observe them carefully at all times and (it is said) Master's wolfhounds are stationed at a little distance, charged with watching the strangers' every move and poised to attack if a signal is given.

Most visitors see only opulently furnished rooms with heavy furniture, heavy Persian carpets, heavy velvet drapes of the hue of burst grapes, that have faded in swaths of sunshine, unevenly. They are allowed to photograph Master in such settings, which Master prepares in every detail, as in a stage set, for Master takes (occasional) delight in such scenes; in Master's apprentice years, Master was at the periphery of the Dadaist movement, and was a close friend of Man Ray; visitors are forbidden to photograph begrimed marble floors, cracks and water stains in ceilings, a patina of dust on Master's antique Greek statuary, the shocking interior of a *water-closet*. Except on very special occasions when Master's studio has been scrupulously prepared for such an invasion—a German public television documentary, an American celebrity interviewer for prime-time American TV—they are not allowed in Master's studio.

Very graciously Master answers questions at such times that have been approved by Master beforehand. For Master is the most eloquent of *artistes*, whose every remark is carefully shaped, like poetry.

Art is not the truth. It is art that shapes truth.
Art is not "beauty"—art is greater than beauty.
Art is the shadow of life that soars above life, and can never be contained by (mere) life.

At such times no one hears our cries from the back rooms of the chalet, or the (terrible, unspeakable) dungeons in the cellar.

Master has many of us here, Daddy. Of our free choice we came to Master, and to Master we surrendered our freedom like children who have no idea what they are doing. You cannot blame the servants for laughing at us—one day *ma cherie*, the next *ma prisonnier.*

In many rooms of the chalet Master has imprisoned us. Some of us are "servants"—that is, slaves. Some of us have collars around our necks, attached to chains. We are made to eat leftovers from bowls on the floor, as Master laughs at our desperate animal hunger.

Mes cheres, you are petit cochons are you? You are not angels! We know this.

Especially, no one hears our cries from the dungeons. The locked chambers, which servants avoid. Here is a smell of rusted iron, cobweb. No one wishes to hear, invited to a spare but elegant tea with Master in the most opulent of the front rooms, where a (piano) is displayed, reputedly once owned by Beethoven.

No one wishes to penetrate the mystery of *le grand chalet* despite rumors that have circulated for decades in such European capitals as Paris, Berlin, Prague, Rome. No one has the courage to confront Master, to risk Master's wolfhounds and servants and throw open the locked doors of the house, to release Master's girl-captives from their misery.

Help us! Please help us.

Release us from Master. . . .

In the most notorious of the dungeon rooms girls have died in their chains, their bodies shriveled like the corpses of the elderly. These were once living girls, girls with pretty-doll faces and coppery-colored, wavy hair, withered to the size of four-year-olds.

We who are still living beg for food which Master's servants give out grudgingly for Master is very clever, and very cruel, restricting the household food so that the more that is given to the girls, the less the servants will have for themselves.

Like all tyrants, Master knows how to set individuals against one another— *It is a finite universe in which we live. The more you give away, the less you will have. Give away too much, and you will starve.*

I am ashamed to say, Daddy—at the very start I was ignorant, and naive, and had no idea what lay in store. As a new arrival I was treated like a princess, and so I took pity on some of the other girls, who had been here longer, and seemed to be less favored than I was; I gave them food of mine, for each of my meals was a small feast, and I could not finish so many delicacies. You know, we can be generous when our bellies are stuffed, and so I was generous, but this did not last beyond a few months. It would not have seemed possible that Master would so turn against me, after he had so flattered me. This was my error, Daddy. But having come here at all, having lingered so long in front of *Les beaux jours* until one day I found myself inside the painting, in the drawing room with the blazing-bright fire, giddy with happiness—already that was my error, for I could not so easily crawl back out of Master's house and into my old, lost life.

You begin by being adored. In Master's adoration, you bask in your power. But it is a short-lived power for it is not yours, it is Master's. That is the error.

And then one day a camera crew arrives at the chalet in a modern-looking vehicle—a *minivan*. Strangers from London are welcomed into the chalet. There is a silken-voiced interviewer, himself a *celebrity of the art world*.

How renowned Master has become! How many honors has his art garnered! Major museums have hosted major exhibits. His name is "known"—by the discerning few, if not the multitudes. He has outlived all of his great contemporaries—he has outlived many younger artists, whose names will never be so extolled as his; he is an elderly man revered like a saint. With age his face has only grown more beautiful, and what is *aged* in his face—discolorations, lines—can be disguised by makeup, that makes of the sallow skin something marmoreal; his somewhat sunken eyes are outlined in black, each lash distinct. His thinning silvery hair is combed elegantly across his high skull. In his black cassock of the finest linen Master is a priest of art—the highest art.

Master says—*But we live for our art. There is no life except our art.*

The interviewer says—*Excuse me, sir?—I think I hear something—someone . . .*

(For the interviewer has heard us. He has heard us!)

But Master says laughingly—*No. You are hearing just the wind, our perpetual wind from the mountains.*

(Wind? These are cries, and not the wind. Not possible, these cries are but *wind*.)

The interviewer hesitates. The silken-voiced interviewer is at a loss for words, suddenly chilled.

Master says more forcibly, though still laughingly—*This is a remote region of Europe,* mon ami. *This is not your effete "civilization"—your Piccadilly Circus, Hyde Park, and Kensington Gardens. I am very sorry if our melancholy wind that never ceases distracts you and makes you sad!*

Master is so very charming speaking with a mock British accent, no one detects the quaver in Master's voice that is a sign of incipient rage; but the interviewer exchanges glances with his assistant and does not pursue this unwelcome line of questioning.

It is so: Master is a great artist. A great genius. To genius, much is allowed.

As other interviews have proceeded at *le chalet*, this interview proceeds without further interruptions: just one hour, but a priceless hour, to be scrupulously edited, and not to be broadcast on the BBC without the approval of Master and Master's (powerful, Parisian) gallery.

But the silken-voiced interviewer disappoints Master by declining his invitation to stay for tea, pleading exhaustion. And he and his crew must hurry away in the *minivan*, to catch a flight back to "effete" London.

Well! There is some laughter. There are handshakes.

Master has been placated, maybe. But Master is still irritable, and (as some of us know) still dangerous.

In the nether regions of the chalet we tell ourselves that the celebrity-interviewer from London heard us, and understood—it is not possible that he did not understand. One need only examine Master's famous paintings to understand. He will seek help for us, he will save us.

Such tales we tell ourselves to get through the long days and interminable nights in *le grand chalet des âmes perdues.*

Wind on the moors, wind from the mountains. Perhaps the mountains are not the Alps but the Carpathians.

It is not so far a distance to come, Daddy! Please.

It is not too late yet, Daddy. I have not yet been dragged to the lowermost dungeon, where the door is shut upon us, and we are forgotten.

You have not forgotten me, Daddy. I am your daughter. . . .

In *Les beaux jours* you will see me for I am waiting for you there. Come to the museum! Come stand close before *Les beaux jours* where I await you.

Help! Help me!—I whisper.

If I could call out more forcibly I am sure that someone would hear me. A visitor to the museum, one of the vacant-eyed guards. They would wake from their slumber. They are all good people, I know—at heart, they would *help me if they could.*

If you could, Daddy. I know you would help me. Will you? It is not too late.

I have set aside the little hand-mirror. I have gazed enough at the pretty-doll face. Sometimes I can see—almost see—out of the frame, Daddy—and into the museum—(I think it must be the museum: what else could it be?)—in the distance, on the other side in the land of the living—slow-moving figures, faces.

Daddy, are you one of them? Please say *yes.*

If I had my old strength I could crawl out of the frame, Daddy. I would do this myself, and would not need you. I would crawl out of the drawing room, and I would fall to the museum floor, and I would lie there stunned for just a moment, and maybe someone, one of you, Daddy maybe you, would discover me, and help me.

Or maybe I would simply regain my breath in the land of the living, and my strength, and manage to stand on my weakened legs, and walk away, leaning against the wall—past rows of paintings in hushed galleries—to the familiar stone steps, where Mother would pull Jenny and me, gripping our hands in hers—and I would make my way to the front entrance of the great museum, and more steps, and so to Fifth Avenue and the clamor of traffic and life—if I had my old strength—almost . . .

Daddy? I am waiting. You know, I have loved only you.

THOMAS PLUCK *has slung hash, worked on the docks, trained in martial arts in Japan, and even swept the Guggenheim Museum (but not as part of a clever heist). He hails from Nutley, New Jersey, home to criminal masterminds Martha Stewart and Richard Blake, but has so far evaded capture. He is the author of* Bad Boy Boogie, *his first Jay Desmarteaux crime thriller, and* Blade of Dishonor, *an action adventure which BookPeople called "the* Raiders of the Lost Ark *of pulp paperbacks." He shares his hideout with his wife and their two felines. Joyce Carol Oates calls him "a lovely kitty man."*

Find him at www.thomaspluck.com or on Twitter @thomaspluck.

La Vérité sortant du puits by Jean Léon Gerome

TRUTH COMES OUT OF HER WELL TO SHAME MANKIND

BY THOMAS PLUCK

T he cracking of the skulls was performed by a practiced hand. The bowl separated from the eye sockets and teeth. These were no virgin cannibals like the lost colonists of Roanoke, with their hesitation marks. Whatever people had done this had done it before, and had perhaps been doing it for a very long time.

Devin cupped the skull in his palm, reminded of how Danes toasted before a drink.

Skål.

It meant bowl, as in drinking cup.

Emma Frizzell had taught him that. And she had invited him here, ostensibly for his knowledge of the Bronze Age tribes who had pillaged and slaughtered throughout the area, but also for the funding that attaching his name to the dig would bring. Critics, including Emma, claimed Devin's books contained more cherry-picking and cocktail-party conversation fodder than real science, but they fueled great interest in the field, and with that came grants from billionaires' pet nonprofits, the lifeblood for a science that generated little corporate funding.

"Looks like you've found another unlucky bunch who met my boys the Kurgans," Devin said, hefting the bone bowl in his hands. He was tall and dusty blond with smooth, telegenic features.

"We're not so sure," Emma said, gesturing at students working with brush and screen and trowel in the neatly dug trenches, staked and lined and flagged. "It's similar to the Herxheim site and the Talheim Death Pit in some ways, but very different in others. There's what we call the well, for instance, which is more of a trash midden. It's unlike anything we've found in the LPK sites before. We're eight layers down and still hitting finds." The LPKs, or Linear Pottery Culture, had built small agricultural settlements all over Germany. Until the Kurgans found them.

Emma squinted at the sun's halo behind his head. She'd sprouted since their time as schoolmates, long-limbed but thick in the hips, dark curls tied with a red bandanna. With her lips drawn back over a cracked front tooth, she resembled one of the skulls herself.

"Any female victims?"

"None yet." Little red flags waved in the breeze, one for each corpse. "All men and boys, killed in the same ritual manner. The bones flensed with knapped chert blades." Crude-looking neolithic knives, but sharp enough that modern surgery had been performed with them, and sturdy enough to chisel open skulls, with help from a hammer stone.

"Enslave the women, slaughter the vanquished," Devin said. "The cannibalism is a new angle, but I'm sure there's an explanation. A famine caused by drought. Or maybe just to plunder further, they began viewing the conquered as meat on the hoof."

The Kurgans were named after the burial mounds they left scattered in their wake, each topped with a man-shaped, carved stone menhir. A single leader buried with his sacrificed harem, his trusty copper blade, and a handful of decorative fetishes to aid him in the afterlife.

Devin admired their pluck, the first humans to practice tribal warfare. Some theorized that *Homo sapiens* had dealt it to their bulkier cousins *neanderthalensis*, but there was no clear evidence. The Kurgans had left plenty: entire villages massacred, with the male bodies strewn about and the women taken. The same old story, still happening today. Less often, if you believed the statistics, which Devin did not. To him, civilization was a thin veneer over humanity's violent history, and he felt he protected his viewers and readers by reminding them that it was human nature to want what you did not have, and in men's nature to take it if they could.

"Professor Frizzell!" A student with a beard stood and waved. "Ade found another one of the, uh, things."

Emma bared her cracked-tooth smile. "Tell me what you think after you've seen the whole site."

"Oh, I will." He handed her the skullcap. "*Skål.*"

The find was not a skull, but a small stone figure. Adriane, a thick-armed woman with Marcia-from-*Peanuts* glasses, handed it up. "Careful, Bracken."

Bracken had runner's legs and held the fetish in a white gloved hand as Emma brushed the dirt away, baring a crude human figure carved from serpentine. It had a nondescript face, one arm raised, breast jutting below it, the other hand between her legs.

Devin peered over her shoulder. "Must be a fertility fetish."

The brush revealed a leaflike object between the object's thighs.

"She's holding a sword," Emma said.

"Looks more like an exaggerated vulva. Wasn't the Venus of Willendorf found not far from here?"

"Yes, but it's dated twenty-five thousand years earlier," Emma said. The Willendorf Venus had enormous breasts and hips, and gave birth to theories of a prehistoric matriarchal culture. "Look at her pose. One arm thrust high, the other low. Triumphant."

Devin frowned. The work was rough, the rock encrusted with dull bloodred. Little florets of bluish stone grew at the gouges for eyes, mouth, and crotch.

"Red ochre," Devin said. "That's usually on . . ."

"Gifts for the dead," Bracken said, gently blowing dust from the figurine's armpit. "To uh, appease them."

"I'm quite aware."

The hungry dead might mistake it for blood, and be sated. But here, so many had been slain that a little symbolic blood could never please them all.

Devin reached out. "May I?"

Emma found him a glove, and Bracken handed him the relic. It was cold from being in the earth. Eyeless, with a hungry red mouth. "This isn't Kurgan. Or it's something we've never found before."

"We've found several. I sent one for spectrum analysis. The blue is vivianite."

"Does the water have a high iron content?" Devin asked. Vivianite formed when phosphate-rich flesh bonded with ferrous minerals.

"Not too much," Emma said, placing the find in a plastic zip bag. "But blood does."

She always had an answer. Devin left her to catalog the find, and climbed the hill that the excavation had cut in half, and watched the little red pennants wave on the stakes that demarked where skeletons had been found. The human body barely held two gallons. But there had been many. Fields of rich green grew between the dig site and the quaint village up the road. Well fertilized.

Devin wondered if she'd invited him to extend an olive branch.

In ancient history class, when Dr. O'Dell was off on one of his wild tangents, scolding them for thinking that Vikings wore horned helmets, Devin had tried to score brownie points, repeating what his father had told him after a business trip to Copenhagen: that Danish people cheered with *skål*, because their Viking forebears had drunk mead from the skulls of their enemies.

Young Emma had laughed in her little huff, looked up from her book, and said, "Actually, it means *bowl*."

Right, Mr. O'Dell said. *The Vikings were raiders, but rape and pillage were not their whole lives. That image came much later, distorted by our own cultural lens. . . .*

Fat little know-it-all Frizzell beamed and went back to her book, showing off that she knew the material and could pick through O'Dell's scattershot lectures and read at the same time. She stood out as a braniac in their magnet school. Rumor was she had been accepted at Princeton, but her parents wouldn't let her go until she was seventeen. The next day she tried to palm off a copy of *The Long Ships* on Devin and he'd taken it to stop her from yammering and avoiding his eyes.

The excavation was far from Denmark, though still in Viking country. The bowled skulls and cracked bones of the slaughtered village of Hexenkeller predated Beowulf and his thanes by at least five millennia. The Kurgan hypothesis was O'Dell's, and as his successor, Devin had championed it with his pop-science books on human prehistory and his lost mysteries show on cable: the Kurgan people had used their technological supremacy to spread their culture, including the language known as Proto-Indo-European—a distant predecessor of modern tongues—across Europe and the subcontinent. It neatly explained the single origin of the root language and the sudden disappearance of the neolithic tribes.

Emma climbed up beside him and pointed to a stake with a blue flag marker not far from the top of the halved mound. "That's where they hit the first kurgan stone. Fifty yards from the well. This was slated for an industrial park, away from the village. They cut through and hit the gravestones."

Seven kurgan stones was another anomaly. They had been removed to a museum, and he'd stopped to see them on the way from Frankfurt in his rented BMW. Typical warrior markers, seven men, each carved with mustache and sword. They should have found a bevy of skeletal female companions. But only men, all but seven stripped of flesh, skulls uncapped. A handful also trepanned, with a hole in the front, as if they had been born with a unicorn horn and had it snapped off.

"Any weapons?"

"Seven Kurgan scythes," Emma said. "The defenders, if that's what they were, had only chert blades and hammer stones."

"And what's in the well?"

Emma shrugged. "We're only calling it a well. We aren't sure what it is. Organic material, but no bones. The blades are in the climate-controlled shed with the generator." She showed him.

The blades had taken damage. If the marks on the skulls weren't clearly from stone blades, he'd have assumed the scythes had been used on a beheading spree. He snapped pictures with his phone.

"What do you think?"

"It's . . . interesting." Devin slipped off his brown tweed coat. "I'd like to see the well. Get my hands dirty."

"Lani's got the well, but you can sift."

Devin hadn't worked a dig since college, and it felt good to shake a screen, sifting for beads, teeth, and bone fragments. He found none in the rich soil. After an hour he put down his sifter and looked down the pit. A slender figure squatted at the bottom, troweling dirt into a bucket with a thin rope tied to the handle and leading to the top, where it was slung over a small pulley. The stones of the well's edge were ragged and unshaped, meticulously stacked together and cemented with daub, a beehive mound with the top cut off.

"Hello down there."

A girl with a buzz cut peered up. "Bucket's not full yet."

Flat stones were piled beneath the pulley, the rope coiled on top. "This was enclosed, wasn't it?"

"Yup."

"How do you get down?"

"Footholds," Lani called, with unhidden exasperation.

He peered over the edge and sent a pebble tumbling. "My bad!"

She covered her head, then swore as it ricocheted off her forearm. "Fuck! If you're so damn curious, I'll show you."

She bounced on her heels to limber up, then jumped, feet landing on thicker stones on opposite sides. She balanced, then spidered her way up to the top, gripped the cross brace and swung over the rim without spilling a stone.

"Like that."

"Impressive."

She pointed to a growing quail's-egg lump near her elbow, skin split in the center. "Could've cracked my head open. Fuckers are sharp."

"I'll make it up to you." He held out his hand. "Devin Jarrett. *Lost Finds of the Ancients?*"

She shrugged. "Then bring me a bottle of the good stuff, rich boy. I take apologies in Scotch."

Hard nut to crack. "Will the Macallan suffice?"

She scoffed. "I drink Islay. Like a shovel full of peat in your face. Work in the dirt, might as well drink it too." She pulled a bottle of Volvic mineral water from the shade and chugged from it.

She'd been working hard, and the scent from her unshaved armpits was strong but not offensive, rather like the strong whiskey she favored.

"Done."

"If the doc says it's okay, I'll help you down, if you change out of the monkey suit."

"Tomorrow. I've got to check in."

"Bring the Scotch tonight. Ade's making gumbo. You don't want to miss it."
She pulled up the bucket and went to sifting.

The camp was far enough from the nearest hotel that the students slept in tents, and Emma and Adriane in their own small caravans. If he filmed the show—and it looked exceedingly likely he could sell the episode to his showrunner—they would ship his fitted Benz MaxiMog truck and trailer, and film filler shots of it pulling off the nearby autobahn and rocking into camp. It was part of the image, the dapper Indiana Jones who wore suede-elbow tweed jackets and carried a multitool instead of a whip and top-break Webley revolver, a styled coif in place of the fedora. And he needed a good show, something new, to kick off the next season.

He located the luxury B and B his assistant had booked, a Bavarian cottage right out of a snow globe, with a ZIMMER FREI sign in the window in Gothic letters.

He dropped off his bag and asked for the nearest outdoor shop and the best liquor store. Both were located in the town square between an old church and a tourist trap called the Hexenkeller Witch Museum, little more than a repurposed barn packed with torture implements that might have been antique carpentry tools to the untrained eye. He paid ten euro to examine their foot press and a Pear of Anguish, a studded cast-iron grenade the size of a human fist. The torturer would cram it into the orifice of choice, then turn a knob that expanded it like a cactus flower in bloom, cracking the jaw or splitting the flesh. Much more advanced than the stone skull-crackers buried outside town.

The tour guide, an elderly German man with rheumy blue eyes, told him the town's name meant Witches' Cellar, after the small alp to its north that protected it from harsh winds. The winds howled around the pointed hat of the alp like a shrieking woman. "The witch of the mountain used to whisper through the shutters, make wives kill their families, and run to the forest to live like wolves."

"She's quiet now?" Devin grinned.

He waved a hand at the executioner's blades and torture devices. "We killed all the witches."

Devin took a brochure for Violet. Outside, he wondered if there was something in the soil in this part of the world. Other than the bones.

It was a mere hour's drive to the Bergen-Belsen memorial, where little Anne Frank lay buried with thousands more. Not a place he'd wanted to visit, but his showrunner and lover, Violet, had family who died there, and he'd accompanied her pilgrimage. There had been a weight of human suffering in the air that tugged down at his innards like fishhooks, and he felt some of the same in Hexenkeller. At the museum, but more so at the dig, where hundreds had died terribly. Devin felt it at similar sites across the world, but never spoke of it. Just swallowed a chalky Xanax and soldiered on.

In the outdoor store he purchased cargo pants and a button-down shirt that could take roughing up, and in the liquor store he found a Riesling to bring home to Violet, a bottle of a ginger schnapps called Ratzeputz for the comic value—it probably did taste like a rat's putz—and a bottle of ridiculously overpriced Scotch whiskey the wizened shopkeeper kept behind the counter. On the drive back he left the windows down. The evening wind was cool and smelled of fresh cut grass. He listened for the banshee howl but heard only his tires on the asphalt.

The diggers sat on stones around a cook fire where gumbo bubbled in a cast-iron pot. Adriane ladled the heady stuff into tin bowls, while the interns sipped bottles of local beer.

". . . fertility was worshipped long before agriculture," Emma said. "They transposed the two later. Our goddess doesn't seem to signify either."

Bracken raised a beer. "Mr. Jarrett."

"I found an artifact in town," Devin said, and slipped the bottle out of the bag, tilting it so the fire reflected off the gold foil sword on the label. "A twenty-five-year, made with peat from a bog on Islay, where a Bronze Age leaf blade was found."

"Nice," Lani said, and patted the flat stone beside her.

Adriane thrust a bowl into his hands and they ate and drank, shielded from civilization by a ridge of alps on one side and forest on the other, a scrim of lights only visible when Devin stood to fill their plastic cups with Scotch. After a taste, Lani tapped cups with him and said all was forgiven.

"Tell me your theory about the fetish," Devin said, and savored the briny smoke of the whiskey.

Emma nursed a bottle of mineral water. "I don't think we'll ever know, barring an extraordinary find."

"Come on. I told you what I thought."

"Still Kurgan raiders, even with seven stones on one mound. Have you ever seen that before?"

"This was bigger than most of their conquests. They lost more men. You've found enough bones."

"But there's cannibalism," Adriane said, wiping her bowl clean with a hunk of bread. "The Kurgans didn't practice it. They bound and killed their captives."

Devin shrugged. "They got hungry. Bad harvests."

"My theory is ritual sacrifice," Emma said. "The victims were malnourished. We found signs of anemia in the bone development. Brains are a great source of fat, for nourishment. Would explain the cracking."

"And the holes?"

"Healed over," Adriane said. "Your garden-variety neolithic trepanation." Nearly 10 percent of skulls from the stone age period had such holes, either to relieve pressure from head wounds, or for some unknown rite.

"I read about a guy who did it to himself," Bracken said. "Like a third eye. Said it felt like . . . enlightenment."

"Or maybe he's just got a hole in his head," Adriane said.

Emma went on. "We found one woman in the mound. One woman, seven men."

"A Kurgan shield maiden. Like the new data on the Vikings." Archaeologists neglected to sex the skeletons in many Viking-era burial tombs, and had assumed warrior meant male. After further study, nearly half were found to be skeletons of women, with healed-over cuts in the bones to signify wounds in combat.

"We're unsure where she was, originally. The backhoe did some damage. And there were no battle scars on her."

Devin smiled. "Maybe a queen? Evidence of that primal matriarchy you were so fond of in school."

"No shit, you believed that?" Lani snorted and covered her mouth.

A log cracked in the fire pit.

The fire flickered off Emma's glasses. "I was caught up in the wave of the time. The theory that before humans understood lineage, there was a polyamorous, egalitarian utopia, and when men figured out that sex made babies, they put us in chains. It's a pleasing fiction, to imagine a Garden of Eden where women ruled, but there's no evidence for it."

"But it's almost a universal," Devin said. "The Greeks had the Amazons."

"What matters is the story being carried down across so many cultures," Emma said. "What does it mean? I like to think it's a seed of guilt in the collective unconscious. Boys growing up, seeing their mommies subservient. Wondering why she can't be free like they are."

"Maybe we were once," Lani said. "I mean, the hand that rocks the cradle rules the world, right?"

Adriane rolled her eyes. "Wait until you have kids."

"Not happening." She finished her dram and held out her cup.

Devin refilled hers and his own, sitting closer. "Maybe women did rule once. Maybe you should again. The Venus fetishes, like the Willendorf, are dated fifteen thousand years before agriculture. There's so little known of that era, who's to say it didn't happen?"

"Because it's bullshit." Emma smirked. "It's always a joke. Women ran things before there was anything worth ruling, and then men showed us how to *get things done*. It's patronizing, and it assumes to be female is to be nurturing, peaceful, and kind. For every heavy-breasted fertility goddess, there's a Morrigan or a Kali, a bringer of death. The fetish we found here isn't the barefoot and pregnant kind, she holds up her fist. The question is, was it in triumph, or in warning? Did they worship her, or appease her?"

A breeze whipped up, and Devin suppressed a shiver. Thinking of the Hindu death goddess Kali, with her necklace of shorn penises.

"What was the condition of her skull? This queen you found."

"We don't know," Adriane said.

"No head," Lani said. "Creepy."

"We're still looking," Emma said. "The excavators violated the integrity of the mound. My guess is they found bones and kept digging anyway, until they hit the first stone marker and damaged their equipment. So some of the bones and relics may be gone or destroyed."

Devin frowned. "Yet you're sure it's female?"

"Hips wider, for the birth canal. But no pockmarks indicating tears of the labral ligaments. Whoever she was, she never gave birth. Which rules out your queen mother idea."

"Unless it was Caesarian."

Lani snorted.

"I'm not suggesting she survived the procedure," Devin said. "But it's possible she died during childbirth, and bore a chieftain's son."

"Maybe a virgin sacrifice," Bracken said.

"She has no healed-over battle scars," Emma said. "But was killed with metal weapons. And not eaten. No flensing marks. I doubt she was the sacrifice. I think she was a priestess of some kind."

"A shaman for whatever the fetishes represent."

"We're waiting on carbon dating, but many of the bones in the channels are older than she is. The burial mound came after. Whoever built it capped the well with trash and stones and buried it at the northern terminus of the mound."

Devin squeezed his cleft chin. "I'm the first to admit when I'm wrong," he said, and offered to refill cups. Adriane demurred, and headed to her tent.

Bracken and Lani began cleaning up. "We've got this," Emma said. "You two worked hard today."

The two shrugged and wandered to their tents. Devin pitched in to not feel like a heel. When they were done he poured himself a dram. "Do you still drink?"

"I'll answer, if you tell me when you became British."

Devin smiled. "My showrunner demanded I go to a voice coach. Apparently it's gold with viewers. Now it's second nature." He held out the bottle.

"Just a sip."

She led him to the well's edge, where moonlight cast deep shadows. The pit's darkness was abysmal, and conjured Nietzsche's admonishment about gazing into such things. They looked anyway. The dank smell of cold stone had a tang through it, metallic. Like hands sweaty from the jungle gym in the school playground.

A tingle, low inside. "Lani reminds me of you. Then."

Emma grunted. "She's barely older than this Scotch. And she's nothing like me. She's smarter than either of us were."

"I was foolish, I know." They had fumbled with each other at a graduation party at his house when his parents were away. And never spoke of it after. Devin nearly thought he'd dreamed it, because she was gone in the morning.

"What I mean is, she doesn't need an old man to coach her."

So that's what was on her mind.

"Not this again. O'Dell may have been a sexist dinosaur, but you can't have expected me to throw away my opportunity on principle. He chose me."

Emma held up a callused palm. "Whoa. I asked you here because you know the Kurgans, and I thought the site could use some exposure. Not to dredge up high school. I'm happy how my career turned out, thank you. I enjoy working in the field, and I hate cameras. If you've got some guilt you want to work out? Don't do it on my account."

In the dark, her eyeglasses were two black scutes that rendered her eyes invisible.

"I was a young ass," he said, and put his hand on her shoulder.

"And now you're an old ass. Sober up before your drive."

She left him at the pit. He stumbled to the rental and waited for the fuzz in his head to fade. Despite studying the past, he spent little time dwelling on his own. One marriage, two kids. A two-apartment, three-year relationship with his showrunner Violet, which was open as long as they were both discreet.

At the *Zimmer frei* he had asked for a queen bed in case Emma had other reasons for asking him here. The hosts had left expensive milled soaps, and a silky body lotion. He made use of the latter coupled with memory.

His father had been away on business and his mother was "playing cards with the girls," which meant Devin had the house for the night. He called friends who called friends, and brought weed and girls and two-liter bottles of Coke that were half filled with vodka. Abigail Kane would only come if she could bring Emma, so he relented, and she sat silent for once, while the rest of them played "have you ever?" until the vodka-and-Coke was gone, then raided the liquor cabinet and watched a tape of *Blue Velvet* and passed out all over each other on the sectional.

Devin had woke to laughter and his parents' bedroom door clicking shut. He got up to chase them out and quiet Emma Frizzell climbed over him, pressing his hands to her breasts, kissing him with vodka-slicked lips. She was so white her skin seemed to glow in the static of the television. Her breasts were bigger than those of the girls he'd been with at that time so he kissed them and imagined Abby Kane's face, and when he was rock-hard he gave a downward nudge on the back of her neck. *I need this.*

He insisted until she unbuckled his jeans and took him in her mouth. She wasn't a girl to fuck and talk about, but if she wanted to blow him, who was he to tell her no? Her combination of prissy inexperience and eagerness was a memory he returned to often, something he would ask countless interns and prostitutes to mimic. When he finished she padded to the sink with her hand cupped to her mouth, and he tucked away his cock and feigned sleep.

He'd expected her to curl next to him, head on his lacrosse-toned shoulder, but heard only huffs of indignity. Through his eyelids he imagined her fat little fists clenched in pique, until the soporific effects of orgasm and liquor lulled him to true slumber.

Tonight, the cotton ball of moon outside his window solidified into Emma through his closed eyes, soft and white, stalking atop the mound, a night dog sniffing prey. A naked woman sprung from the shadows, tattoos down her rangy limbs, blue and ochre. His skin turned to gooseflesh. The faceless woman held one hand high, and the other held a copper sword between her thighs. She raised the blade and his rear puckered as she dragged the edge up his member.

Devin woke with a gasp, gripping himself so tightly his fingernails left crescents in the skin. He hunched in pain beneath the fat moon's glare. He clasped the window shutters, then washed himself and returned to sleep.

In the morning he passed Bracken running on the shoulder as he drove to the site, and found Adriane tending a skillet of bacon and a pour-over coffeepot shaped like a wide-mouthed flask. Bracken jogged in, shirtless and sheened with sweat.

"That coffee smells heavenly." The continental breakfast at his lodging was meager.

She poured boiling water over the grounds and acknowledged him with a grunt.

"Did I say something wrong last night?"

"Just monthlies," Adriane said.

Lani held out a mug. "Mine's two weeks early. Fucking bullshit."

"You're synced," Bracken said, grinning. "I grew up with my moms, grandma, and my older sister. They synced up sometimes."

"Ugh," Lani said. "Creeps me the hell out. Here comes Emma, let's see if it's all three of us."

Emma looked past them. She scratched the wisps of hair on the back of her neck. "Which one of you took the fetish?"

Adriane handed out black coffees. "I left it in the collection shed."

"I'll go look," Bracken said. "Long as there's bacon when I get back."

Emma studied the trenches through the steam rising from her cup.

"I didn't touch it," Devin said softly, behind her.

She put one arm akimbo to block him, and he nearly spilled his coffee. "You're an ass, but you're not that stupid."

After their quick meal Lani brought him to the pit, smirking at his tourist-trap hiking gear. "How much did that cost you?"

She showed him the foot holds in the pit, and tied the rope off and lowered it down the pulley. "Doc Frizz gets on my back for rock climbing it. But you're too tall. Brack can't do it either. This was built when people were shorter."

Devin avoided the well-worn footholds on the top. The arch of the foot and pebble-shaped toes were evident in the carved stone. Another lost mystery. Who stands at the top of a well? The lower sets were crude, for climbing. The rope burned his soft hands despite using every step. He hit bottom with a grunt and barked his scalp on a stone. He clutched his head and fell back against the wall, blinking, seeing nothing but darkness, no stars.

He clutched for the Xanax bottle he knew was in his tweed suit.

Once, during a lacrosse match, he'd bumped heads with a teammate so hard that he'd briefly gone blind. He panted, breaths echoing off the close walls of the pit. The dank heady scent now coppery with blood. When his vision returned, the opening above resembled a full moon.

"You okay?"

"Cut my head." He pressed his palm to his scalp and felt blood pulse from the wound. Pattering on the floor like a leaky showerhead. "Need a bandage."

Lani tossed down her bandanna. "Keep pressure on it and breathe slow. I'll get the kit. I'm a medic for search and rescue."

He wadded the fabric, gritted his teeth through the pain. The hooks dragged down his guts. He clenched his eyes shut, and red welled through the deep blue. The wind keened across the stones above, whirled down to tickle his hackles.

A long minute and Lani rappelled down, calves and hamstrings flexing. She squeezed down beside him with a penlight. "Let me check your pupils. I heard you whispering to yourself." She took his head in her hands and swabbed the cut with alcohol which stung like a bastard. He grimaced into her shoulder, tasted her salt.

His father would faint at the sight of his own blood, and Devin had been terrified of inheriting the same unmanly affliction; the first time he skinned his knee crashing his bicycle, he'd been relieved, watching the blood well through the skin. His mother wasn't home, so he cleaned it in the sink and picked the stones out with her fingernail scissors.

"Don't think you need stitches," Lani said, dabbing, penlight in hand. "But you should work topside. We'll hoist you up."

"I'm all right," he said, knowing the blackout was a mild concussion, like it had been on the lacrosse field, but not wanting to lose face. He let her tie the rope around his hips and climbed his way out with Bracken holding the rope, braced against the well stones.

He drank a bottle of water. He said he'd work slow, lowering the bucket for Lani and sifting what she dug. Bracken did most of the work.

"Sending up," Lani called, and Bracken pulled up the bucket, spread its contents on the sifter, and shook it as Devin picked through pebbles for chips of bone.

"We found the fetish," Bracken said. "After we scoured pretty much every-where, the doc walks out of her trailer with it. Must've had a brain fart."

"What do you think of the site?" Devin asked, eyeing a shard that could've been a tooth, but was only quartz. He tossed it in the discard pile.

"I'm just a second-year student, but looks like sacrifice to me. Like when they got overpopulated, they came here and had a feast. The layers, we haven't narrowed down the aging, but this wasn't one big slaughter. The doc thinks they did this every few years, to cull, maybe."

"Just the men."

"Well, you know. You don't need a lot of males to reproduce. Like drones in a beehive. You want more, for genetic diversity, but you don't need that many of us." He grinned. "My dad was just a sperm donor."

"He left? I'm sorry."

"No, nothing to be sorry about. He was a literal sperm donor. Moms said, why go to a bank when you can buy local? I'm the product of artisanal free-range man juice, from an athletic Silicon Valley tech guy. I saw him on weekends growing up. We still hang out, run together. Got a half marathon in New Orleans next month."

Devin frowned, then counted how often he'd seen his own father, and said nothing.

"Hey, did you dream last night? Real weird, like?"

"I thought you did more than dream, the way she hangs on you. Lucky young sod."

Bracken grinned and looked away. "It's not like that."

"We got something, Brack! Get the doc!" Lani's voice echoed up from the pit.

Something turned out to be teeth. A crescent of them, from the lower jaw. Adriane was the best digger but disliked heights. Lani rigged her in the rope and they eased her down. She spent the rest of the day freeing a jawbone from the packed humus.

"This is the best preserved find yet," Emma said, examining the mandible, wearing gloves. "We'll have to take much more care in the well. Don't want to risk stepping on anything. It's too tight down there. We'll rig a harness and work in shorter shifts."

Adriane had bared the rest of the skull. Lani climbed down with a digital camera and showed them photos on its screen. Two eye sockets filled with rich earth, staring up from the pit.

Emma measured the jaw with a caliper. "Adult female." The lower incisors were well-worn, as were the pointed canines. The molars were not. "I think we found her head."

They celebrated with dinner on Devin's expense card, at the local rathskeller. Roasted pig knuckle, wurst in curry sauce, local beer and wine. Devin drove them back to camp, where Adriane started a fire and they poured Scotch into coffee mugs.

They drank and huddled around the fire, warmed by the meal, the liquor, and the elation of the discovery.

"Looks like it was Kurgans after all," Emma said. "Someone cut her head off and dumped it down a well."

"And buried the rest of her with seven warriors."

"Maybe she was defiled later. The dating's not in."

"That puts the damper on the mother goddess crap. Even guys with serious mommy issues don't want to behead her," Lani said.

Bracken grinned.

"Even if matriarchal prehistory is a crock, I'd be willing to give it a try," Devin said. "You couldn't muck it up much worse than we have."

Emma shrugged. "History's full of horrible women."

"And that's what we know," Adriane said. "We tend to be left out of the record."

"Countess Bathory," Lani said. "Bathed in the blood of young girls, to stay young. Don't get any ideas."

Adriane huffed. "That's a myth, but I might try some on my ashy elbows. German air is dry as hell."

"Delphine LaLaurie," Bracken said. "She was a serial killer in New Orleans. I've been to her house. She tortured her, uh, servants." He looked into his cup.

"And we're not so weak," Emma said. "If women had an innate hatred of war and genocide, we would have stopped it."

"They did in *Lysistrata*."

"And Spartan women told their boys to come back with their shields, or carried on them."

Devin tilted his head. "It's nice to think about, anyway."

"Of course it's nice to imagine a polyamorous paradise," Adriane said. "It's only recently in most cultures that women have had any choice in their mates. Makes you wonder about sexual selection. If we'd have evolved differently, if parents didn't choose their children's mates for thousands of generations."

"I was chosen," Bracken said.

"We all know the story, turkey-baster boy." Lani elbowed him.

"I'm more interested in what we've been learning by tracing mitochondrial DNA," Emma said. "Sexual selection isn't a hard science."

"Speaking of hard science, I once heard a biologist say evolution selected the shape of the human penis, so it could scrape out a previous mate's, uh, semen." Bracken grinned into his cup.

"You're done," Emma said.

Lani snorted. "Whoever came up with that idea needs to study bonobos. They've got plenty of competition, and they're hung like this." She held out her pinky finger.

"And you're done, too. Don't need my students falling in a trench and breaking their neck. Not on my watch."

Lani wandered off with Bracken, snorting and laughing, and Adriane retired to her tent. Emma permitted herself a last sip. "I can't tell you what to do, but you shouldn't drive tonight."

"I wasn't planning on it."

Her eyes were hidden by the fire flicker on her glasses, but he could tell they held no welcome.

"I'll nap it off. Spare a pillow?"

She smirked and rolled up her coat, left it on a rock.

Alone with the crackling fire, Devin imagined what it would be like to live in the village before the Kurgans wiped them out. Something he did out loud on his television program, narrating the low-budget reenactments. Explaining how though we might look the same as our forebears, the "yawning chasm of the ages" made us practically different species. Language separated us, but also beliefs lost to time.

The darkness hid terrors, and the night sky held a thousand eyes of jealous and ruthless gods who demanded sacrifice. Even the Christian one had asked that of Abraham, as a test. We sacrifice our children to different gods now.

Mammon, for instance. Devin had wanted the best for his children, but split with his ex over pushing them to compete to get into the city's best pre-K programs. He'd recalled when his mother sat him down after two years in the magnet school. *We expected more of you. Look at your father. You're tearing his heart out.*

He never wanted his children to feel how he had that day. Didn't she think he could provide for their children? Let them live. *You never know what might happen,* his ex had said. Meaning he might die young of a heart attack like his father.

Devin had been on his first book tour. By the time his mother called, the old man was a buried artifact for future archaeologists to find. *I didn't want to upset you, now that you've finally found your way.*

Devin snorted awake. The fire was reduced to embers. Laughter echoed from the dig. He buttoned his coat against the chill wind.

His head was fuzzy, his cock painfully erect. A carefree groan came from afar. He stepped closer, following the lines of cord to avoid a fall. The moon had lost a sliver and rode low in the sky. He'd been out for hours. And missed something good.

Boots in the dirt, socks as well. Bare footprints on the paths. He could use another hour of sleep, but a little voyeurism might perk him up for the drive home.

Lani would be on top, of course. Lean and tattooed. His cock led him like a dowsing rod.

No silhouettes writhed in the tents. The muted sounds came from below. His multitool had a small penlight, and he used the beam to follow the path through close dirt walls toward the well.

A low moan, pleasure with a hint of pain, from around the earthen corner. He leaned to see.

Instead of tan tattooed skin, pale flesh glowed from above the pit.

Emma frog-squatted on the edge of the well, bare feet planted in the footholds. Naked but for smudged handprints that marred her skin.

"Where are your glasses? You'll fall in."

"I've been in." Her smile a wide drunken rictus, she rocked to a silent rhythm. Breathing in little huffs, wisps in the chill. He stepped closer.

She laughed at the tent in his pants. "So desperate. Just like you were then."

"Hey. You wanted *me*."

"Of course I did."

She was in the most unflattering of positions, hunkered and leaning, drooping like those outrageous Venus fetishes. Her eyes slick little stones in the light. His hand crept like a spider, unbuckled his pants.

She beckoned him closer.

Her curls were untied, snaking over her shoulders. Closer, he saw the handprints weren't dirt but smears of blood. Her handprints and others, patterned like cave pantings. Blood pattered into the pit from between her legs.

He gaped. She laughed her awkward little heave, and swung the chert knife. He stumbled back and twine snapped.

He hit the opposite edge of the earthen wall. He heard his leg snap, the blessed chill of shock blunting the agony as he crumpled into the trench. Alone with the wind's keen and the white blur of the moon.

Feet slapped the dirt beside him. He blinked and the moon became Emma, in a crouch.

"I need help," he croaked.

"Always what *you* need. Do you remember now?"

Sweating with Emma outside O'Dell's office, watching through the frosted glass while the professor consoled Tara Branigan, their only competition. Tensing as the stoic valedictorian scurried out the door and down the hall as if wounded. Devin's heart had pounded and he sank his fingers into Emma's soft white forearms like clay.

Don't fuck this up for me. I need this.

No tears. Her fists knotted in rage. Her shoes slapped the institutional gray floor and she fled. O'Dell squinted out the cracked door, waved him in with a conspiratorial smile. *No Frizzell? Emotional girl.*

"I'm sor—"

Emma cupped sticky fingers to his lips. "She's a blood goddess. You fed her. Woke her." She patted her belly, low. "She thanks you."

He gripped her arm. "You *will* get me out of here!"

She stabbed the stone blade into the meat of his thumb. He tore it open yanking away, stared at the gaping red mouth in his skin.

"She showed me what was before. The Kurgans, and their mounds? They aren't monuments to warriors." Huff. "They're wards, to keep things *in*. Her. Us."

The multitool had landed just out of reach. He clawed for it, and she thumped his ruined leg. The pain wrenched his eyes shut.

My cattle you were, and so you shall return.

The blue-ochre witch from his dream spoke behind his eyes. He screamed. Blood washed down the eyeless face, and her shriek became a cackle.

"You need some of us to breed!"

Laughter from above. Lani and Adriane leered down with blood-slicked faces.

"She chose," Lani said. "You're meat."

Bracken cowered at their feet, naked and stunned. A neat hole in his forehead trickled blood down the bridge of his nose.

"She says it's better if you do it before puberty," Adriane said. "Stone Age lobotomy."

Emma gripped him by the hair and pressed the skull cracker to his temple.

Devin whimpered as the flaked stone razored into his flesh. "Tell me your name!"

"Mother," Emma said, and swung the hammer stone.

S.J. ROZAN's *work has won multiple awards, including the Edgar, Shamus, Anthony, Nero, Macavity, and the Japanese Maltese Falcon, and S.J. was recently given a Life Achievement Award by the Private Eye Writers of America. She's written thirteen books under her own name and two with Carlos Dews as the writing team of Sam Cabot, plus more than fifty short stories, and has edited two anthologies. S.J. was born in the Bronx and lives in lower Manhattan. Her newest book is Sam Cabot's* Skin of the Wolf. *www.sjrozan.net*

Under the Wave off Kanagawa (Kanagawa oki nami ura),
also known as the "Great Wave" by Katsushika Hokusai

THE GREAT WAVE

BY S.J. ROZAN

T he water's cool silk slipped past her shoulders, her breasts, her hips. Terence permitted her to swim whenever and for however long she wanted, in the tiled pool in the basement just outside her suite. He required her to swim nude, as she had done at the beginning, when she was here by choice and the smooth sluicing delight of her swims always brought her out joyful, aroused, and aching for him. Arousal, ache, certainly joy, were no more, but she was grateful for the sensation, however temporary, of fluid, enveloping protection.

She drew breath and dove. Powerful kicks and strong strokes propelled her through this underground underwater world, and though she still, always, felt a stab of despair when her fingers found the slick hard wall where the water ended, once she kicked off and turned she was again alone and almost free. Terence couldn't swim. Her life, her body, the place she now lived, he had and would continue to invade; but in the water she could be without him. She knew he was sitting forward in his rattan chair, watching her, and so when she resurfaced to swim laps she alternated the side of her breathing as she changed direction. The whole time she was in the pool she never saw him.

She swam as long as she could. He never hurried her. Some days she thought she could stay in the water forever, until night came and day again and night, until he grew weary and walked away, until he slowly rotted in place, until the walls of her luxurious prison crumbled and she stepped from the water into the sun.

Trying to make that longed-for absurdity come to life, she swam sometimes for hours. But eventually her arms would start to shake, her breathing became labored, and in the end she had to emerge. Always patiently waiting, Terence would enfold her in her oversize soft, thick robe. She'd fold her arms, hugging the robe's warmth to herself as she walked, a gesture he'd always found alluring. He'd admire her supple form—he was generous with compliments— and lead her to the spacious subterranean suite in which she'd made her home for two years, three months, and eleven days.

No, of course: *he'd* made her home.

She'd lie down on the silk sheets. He'd lean over and gently kiss her.

She knew what to do: what they'd done when she first came here, when the dark pull of him was thrilling, when the danger and the lure, when fear and love, wore one face.

Isakawa said the same of the sea. *If I could be elsewhere, I would not*, he'd told her. *But I am always afraid to be here.*

So after her swims she made love with Terence, however and for however long he wanted.

At first she had refused. No: at first, when he'd locked the door and told her she couldn't leave, an electric exhilaration raced through her. A new game, its imaginary stakes higher than they'd ever played for. The night he did that, their lovemaking was already finished. She'd thought they were both spent, but when he turned that lock, when he sat back down on the bed and gently, carefully explained that he could never lose her and so she must stay, she could feel her body flush, her skin begin to tingle. She played her role, he played his, and she reached heights that night she'd never known existed.

But when they were, truly, spent, he gave her his beautiful, sad smile, and went out, and locked the door.

For a day she thought it was part of the game. *It's going too far,* she said. *Let me out of here. I have things to do. I'll miss my plane!*

Yes, he said, *you'll miss your plane.*

This isn't fun anymore.

Fun?

Let me out.

I can't lose you.

You're serious.

Of course.

I am too. Let me out.

Nothing.

I'll come back. You know that.

You were leaving.

For three months! To Kyoto, to study! You can visit. Or even come with me. We talked about it.

You were leaving me.

No! She wasn't sure, at that moment, what her "no" meant.

He'd taken great care with the suite. Statues, prints, and scroll paintings from his collection, precious works, he'd placed them in her rooms for study, for contemplation. A bronze bodhisattva he knew she loved, Imari dishes, a perfect-register edition of Hokusai's "Great Wave." Hokusai, his many influences and his tragic life, would have been the subject of her dissertation. Terence knew this, and he brought her books, museum catalogs, art DVDs. Whenever he thought it time, or whenever she asked, he replaced works with new ones, to give her a different perspective, a change. Many works had traveled in and out of her prison in these two years, but the heavy bodhisattva and the Hokusai remained. She wouldn't part with them. From the bodhisattva she tried to learn patience, to study calm. Two or three times she waited through periods of weeks and then talked to Terence again, without heat, kindly, rationally, explaining how she loved him, how she'd always come back, how he'd never lose her but this was no life for her. He never believed her and of course by now he was right.

He was right, also, to give her the art in her rooms. Without it she'd have gone mad. Whenever he left her she selected a piece and centered her attention on it, searching for whatever it had to teach, fighting down the panic, the hopelessness, the fear. Concentrating some days on color, some on shape, some on line or on just one square inch, she worked as she had when she'd been a promising graduate student, and Terence her lover and wealthy patron.

And of all the works, the Great Wave was the one to which she returned most often.

The sliding, striped blues of the sea; the dots of white foam and the reaching fingers of spray; the calm peace of Mount Fuji, so small in the distance; the towering curve of the Wave itself, seemingly impossible to escape. A rogue, unexpected and unforecast, it had come from nowhere on a clear bright day to overpower and subdue the men in the small, shelterless boats.

The men: Nagano, Hirose, Kimura, Ikeda, Hirahara, Ozeki . . . She knew all their names. Isakawa, the lead man in the front boat, had told her. She'd learned who they were, and heard parts of their stories, over the two years she'd been here. Even the ones in Isakawa's boat, the ones the smaller wave obscured, she knew them all, where they'd come from, their fears and strengths, and though Isakawa wouldn't talk about either their situation or hers, she knew how desperately they longed to survive the Wave and get back home.

They were equally desperate, she trapped in her opulent underground cell, with every comfort but freedom, the men on the wild, open sea, cold and wet and with nothing weighty they could cling to.

It was after her first escape attempt that Isakawa told her the men's names, their stories.

In her first months here, after the talks with Terence, after he smiled sadly each time and shook his head, after she finally had admitted to herself persuading him was impossible, the idea came to her, so simple she was ashamed she'd not thought of it before. At the end of her swim one day, as he held out her robe, she clamped onto his arm, pulled and pushed and threw him into the pool. To the sound of his wild splashing, she took off, naked and dripping, up the stairs.

The door at the top was locked.

The key, where was the key? In Terence's own robe? She spun to look back to the pool and there was Terence, his breathing strained, his face blank, dragging himself out.

He took away the art, and all her clothes, leaving her nothing but white walls, white sheets. She couldn't turn the lights out. At intervals he came with rice in a white plastic bowl with a white plastic spoon. He didn't speak.

Finally he brought back a small scroll painting, hung it from a nail. The immensity of her gratitude frightened her.

She understood the lesson and things returned to the way they had been. When he rehung the Great Wave—the last piece he brought, in the slow process of restoring her prison—and he was gone and she was sitting in front of it, Isakawa, speaking for the first time, told her about his love for and fear of the sea.

Thrilled for a voice that wasn't Terence's, she asked Isakawa his name, asked him about the other men, asked about the rogue wave, asked whether they'd been through times like these before. About the Wave he refused to speak, and her imprisonment likewise was a subject from which he turned away. But over many weeks Isakawa told her about his wife and grown sons, with fishing boats and families of their own. He spoke about Nagano's three young daughters, and the flowering plum trees Hirose tended alone since the death of his wife, and the glorious autumn colors on the flanks of Mount Fuji visible from the village for which they'd been making when the Wave arose. She talked with Isakawa about the blue of the sea and the glowing white of the foam and the clear yellow sky and she realized that to rise against Terence as literally as the Wave was rising against the boats was her only chance.

The swims had made her strong, and the bronze bodhisattva was her first thought. She lifted it, tried its heft, but though it was not large it was solid and it was too heavy; she could carry it, but not swing it, not, she thought, dependably use it to cause damage or death. She surveyed the other works in her prison and tried to imagine their use and realized, finally, that the sole possibility was the only one framed in glass: the Great Wave.

Many times, she imagined the scene. She would be holding the print when Terence unlocked the door, perhaps to fetch her for her swim. Seeing what it was as she swung it, he'd be shocked for a moment, unable to move. She'd smash it into his face, and when the glass broke, she'd use shards of that, too, to destroy him. Then she'd take the key from his pocket and she'd be free.

I'm sorry, she said to Isakawa. *Please apologize to Nagano, to Hirose, to Kimura.* Because the print, of course, would also be destroyed, when she acted. *There are others*, she told Isakawa. *None that I've seen as perfect as this one, but many others. In the world. There, out there.*

He didn't reply.

In fact, from the day she decided that to be free she'd have to sacrifice the print, Isakawa didn't speak again.

She rehearsed the event in her mind, and she rehearsed the actions. She took the Great Wave off the wall, held it, swung it, rehung it, and studied it, waiting.

And when the day came that she decided was the one, she gripped the print and stood listening for the click of the lock.

The door opened, and—

She could not do it.

The perfect, sliding blues, the immaculate whites, Fuji in the distance, and all the men, all the boats; she held the print and couldn't lift it, swing it, crush him with it.

Terence looked at her, confusion showing.

It has a crack, she said. *The glass, here.*

I don't see anything.

I look at it for hours sometimes. I know every atom. The glass is cracked. If the crack gets larger it might tear the print. Please, take it to be reframed.

He saw no crack; there was no crack. But he smiled and said, *Yes, of course.*

And now there was nothing left.

The next time he came to take her for her swim she was ready, wrapped in her thick robe, sitting and staring at the wall where the Great Wave had hung. She stood, not too eagerly, so he wouldn't suspect. She walked with her arms folded, hugging the robe's warmth, and she asked Terence about the print, how the framer was doing, how soon it might come back. He told her it would be soon, and he must have seen nothing out of place because without incident they reached the end of the corridor that led from her prison suite to the pool.

She burst into a run. Not stopping to shed the robe, she leaped into the welcoming cold. Terence's shout echoed behind her, but was soon lost as water closed over her and the bodhisattva, hidden by artful draping of the robe and by her folded arms as she walked, tied around her waist with strips torn from the white silk sheets. The bodhisattva dragged and held her down. It was not, this beautiful bronze piece, heavy enough to keep her under if she fought against it, but she did not. She let it ballast her as she gulped in water, to weight her even more, and she fought her body's panic, its desperation for breath, while inwardly she laughed: breathing was how she'd always fought panic, before.

Through the water's flowing surface she could see Terence on the pool's edge, waving his arms, shouting, screaming. She couldn't hear him.

As the blackness seeped around the edges of her mind the voice she did hear, the last one, was Isakawa's.

We didn't make it home, he told her.

None of you? Nagano, to his babies? Hirose, to his trees? Kimura, Hirahara?
We didn't make it.

No, she said, this time fully understanding the meaning of her "no." *No, we didn't.*

New York Times *bestselling writer* **KRISTINE KATHRYN RUSCH** *writes in whatever genre she pleases. She's won awards in all those genres, and hit best-seller lists in most. She tends to mix genres, particularly in her science fiction. (Her Retrieval Artist series features mysteries set on the Moon.) Her mystery novels, published under the name Rusch, include* Spree *and* Bleed Through*. She's published several collections of her award-winning mystery stories, including* Secrets *and* Lies*, which collects her most acclaimed stories. She also writes mystery set in the 1960s as Kris Nelscott. Her latest mystery novel, published as Nelscott, is* A Gym of Her Own *from WMG Publishing. To find out more about all she does, go to kriswrites.com.*

The Thinker by Auguste Rodin

THINKERS

BY **KRISTINE KATHRYN RUSCH**

1970

L eo's blood, warm against her cold hands, steamed in the frosty night air.
Like hot coffee in a paper cup.

Lisa tried not to giggle, because she knew the giggle would be hysterical.
She ran a hand over Leo's face. He was leaning against the marble edge of the
empty pool surrounding the *Fountain of the Waters*, legs splayed, head pointed
toward Wade Lagoon.

Irv was just staring at him, and Helen—God knew where Helen had gotten
off to, because Lisa didn't. Her ears still rang from the explosion, which had
been louder than she had expected.

Cold night, dry night, and when that happened, sound traveled. Which
meant someone would be here soon to investigate.

Lisa peered over her shoulder, looking past the sculptures jutting out of
the fountain, saw light from the full moon glinting on the ice on the terrace.
The Cleveland Museum of Art formed the backdrop, big, rectangular, and

official, like some government office building. A man hunched near the stairs, facedown on the marble tiles.

Then she realized it wasn't a man at all. It was the statue, down, damaged, but not destroyed.

God, she thought it had been destroyed, the way the pieces had sailed by her, slamming into everything.

Slamming into Leo.

Irv was rocking, mouth working. He couldn't be hit, could he? He wasn't even looking at her.

She was covering one of the wounds on Leo's side with her hands. But his face was dripping, and she couldn't tell in the silver moonlight if his eyes were half-closed because he was unconscious or if they were half-closed because they were damaged.

"We have to get him out of here," she said to Irv. Her voice sounded tinny, flat, faraway. Her ears were plugged, her face aching from either the cold or shock or something.

Irv didn't even look at her. Maybe he couldn't hear her.

She grabbed him with one bloody hand. "Irv!" she shouted, then realized that was stupid.

People had to be running here. Someone had probably called the police by now.

And if they heard her shout, they would have a name.

But no one lived near the art museum, that she knew of anyway, and the students at Case Western University lived blocks away. Students wouldn't run toward the sound of an explosion, would they? They would think it was something planned.

She hoped.

Irv blinked, his eyes focusing on her.

She pointed forcefully at Leo, then carefully mouthed, *We have to go.*

Irv nodded. She had been right: he couldn't hear.

He slipped his arms under Leo, and lifted him easily.

"Where's Helen?" Irv asked.

Lisa shrugged and raised her hands in an *I don't know* gesture. She reached for Leo, wanting to stop the bleeding on his side, but that side was now pressed against Irv.

Lisa waved her hand toward the van, east of here, on one of the back streets near the university, which had seemed like such a good idea at the time.

So stupid now.

She hadn't expected pieces of the statue to go flying. Or rather, she had, but not at them. Leo had said they would be driving away by now. He had said they would be inside the van, where they could see it all, but not be near the explosion.

Lisa had asked specifically, because she didn't want to be nearby when the bomb went off. It was her worst nightmare—or damn near, anyway. Worst would have been pieces of her flying alongside pieces of the statue, like Diana in New York, identified by a piece of her thumb.

Her thumb.

Lisa shook her head, realized she was a little dizzy. She was probably in shock too. Not thinking clearly.

At least she was thinking clearly enough not to yell for Helen. Helen, whom she'd last seen raising a Magic Marker and grinning, saying, "There. *Now* it's done," and Leo saying, "C'mon, we gotta go," and Helen laughing, her familiar trill too loud in cold.

Now, Helen was missing, and Irv was trudging down the path like a soldier in a bad World War II movie, Leo's legs bouncing against his hips. Then Lisa shook her head again. All night—movie and TV references in her brain. Was that all she knew? Was that why she had done this? Had all those naysayers been right? Were kids—her generation—were they desensitized by all the violence in the movies, on television? Or was it the war? Or inspiration?

And God, she had to move. She had to find Helen.

Lisa looked down at the snow in the base of the fountain. A hole in the snow where Leo had been. A hole that was formed by his body, and probably melted by the hot blood leaking out of him.

They were leaving a trail, one the cops could track if she wasn't careful. If she didn't hurry.

Her hands were getting cold again, and they were clammy. Blood, clotting. Leo's blood. She hadn't worn gloves—she'd needed her fingers free, or so she had thought.

She bent down, grabbed a handful of dirty snow, used it to wipe off the blood, hoping that would be enough.

Then she walked toward the museum, afraid that she would see Helen downed, just like the statue, damaged and useless, ruined against the stones.

2015

First day on the job and Erika still stopped on the terrace near the statue of Rodin's *The Thinker* and stared up at its ruined legs. She ran her fingers across the bent edges, like she had done three times before: first, when she considered an internship at the Cleveland Museum of Art; second, the day before the application deadline; and third, the day she walked in for her interview.

Each time, the statue had caught her, made her hesitate. It reminded her of that vet who had shown up in her life-drawing class freshman year. She'd been nervous enough drawing naked human beings, but this guy—he had wheeled in on an ancient, rickety wheelchair, then stopped at the base of the platform where a naked man lay on a sofa.

The naked guy, maybe thirty, ripped and gorgeous, had nothing draping his privates. But he looked so bored, as if he spent all his time naked—and maybe he had.

Erika had heard the university paid good money for life models, particularly those who could sit still for more than an hour. No fidgeting, no shifting. She couldn't imagine doing anything like that, sitting naked in front of a circle of art students as they sketched each and every flaw.

Not that the guy on the divan had a single flaw—that she could see, anyway, and she had been looking closely at him.

Until wheelchair man had come in, screaming. He'd hoisted himself onto the platform, peeled off his prostheses, revealing ruined thighs, and then told the students staring at him in shock: *This is life*, this *is what the human form looks like*. Not *that*.

And he had looked at the life model with great contempt, as if the life model had been the one to hurt him.

Then the vet grabbed his prostheses, shoved them back on, and levered himself back into the chair. He had wheeled his way out, leaving her shaken.

Although the professor had given Erika her only A of that year. Because she couldn't get him out of her mind. So instead of drawing the life model as he was, she drew the life model and the vet, which, apparently, she had been supposed to do. The prof had actually invited the vet in. It had been a show, to remind the artists that life was more than perfection, that *art* was more than perfection.

But she liked the perfection, and the control that art gave her. Which was why the statue, this ruined Rodin, disturbed her so much.

Cast by Rodin himself, or at least, under his tutelage, the sculpture was one of the last he would ever make. It was sold directly to Ralph King, who donated it to the museum, and the museum in its infinite wisdom, had placed the bronze outside without properly protecting it.

It had a green patina now, one she hadn't wanted to touch the first time. But she still found her fingers moving upward, fingering the ruins, thinking about how art changed, how nothing was permanent, not even famous bronze sculpture that should have survived as the artist intended for centuries.

Today the bronze was cool. The summer sun hadn't yet warmed the metal like it had the day she interviewed. She let her hand slip off the statue itself onto the marble plinth. Marble always felt warm to her, comforting in its cold stone way.

Then she squared her shoulders and walked across the terrace. More steps, and she would be inside the beaux arts building that looked so early 20th century on the outside, and hosted some of the most transformative works on the inside.

Her stomach twisted. She still wasn't sure if museum work was for her. The internship would tell her that. She actually got one of the coveted curatorial internships, available only to graduate students. She was supposed to learn about the artwork and how to preserve it, but she would also work with the museum collections and help plan exhibitions, or so she was told.

Planning someone else's work because she couldn't see a future for her own.

She reached gigantic columns at the top of the stairs, her hesitant form reflected in the glass of the large door on her left. She ran a hand over her face, then glanced back at the ruined *Thinker*. He wasn't really Rodin's any more. He was a combination of Rodin's vision, the bad decision to keep him outside, and the vandalism. A different kind of art.

Art out of control.

If she stepped inside, her life would be all about control. Planning, work, classes, doing what someone else wanted.

If she walked away—then what? Fifty thousand dollars in student debt for no reason whatsoever.

If she ran away—well, she had nowhere to run to. She wasn't talented enough to strike out on her own, and she no longer had any dreams.

She winced at the thought, walked between the huge columns and headed for the center door, her face in the glass round and young and determined. Not showing her inner turmoil at all.

Not showing anything except an expression that already felt like it had been cast in stone.

1970

Everything had seemed so clear at midnight. At midnight, Lisa had had no idea she would be covered in blood, searching for Helen.

At midnight, Lisa had been sitting cross-legged on the floor in the back of the van.

And she had been terrified.

She should have trusted that emotion.

She had imagined their trip like the opening of that *Mission: Impossible* TV show—match touched to fuse, then a long, slow burn with sparklers, until everything turned white. She hadn't pictured the clunky alarm clock taped to three sticks of dynamite, and some kind of mechanism behind it all that would—Leo promised—ignite the entire thing.

Leo and Irv sat in the front seat, Irv behind the wheel because he was the best driver. And Helen beside her, head tilted back, eyes closed. Remarkably silent for a group that could talk late into the night. Everyone else seemed incredibly calm. Lisa had been the only one fidgeting. Probably the only one with regrets, already. Pre-bombing regrets.

A chill had settled into her bones, one she couldn't shake. She had spent days contemplating those sticks of dynamite, which, Leo warned, were dangerous all by themselves. She kept thinking about the town house bombing in Greenwich Village not quite three weeks ago. She kept replaying the news footage in her mind—March snow falling around the ruins of this swanky town house in the Village, firemen in their heavy winter coats and boots, smoke billowing out of the ruins.

Reports said that two women—one naked and screaming—escaped the rubble, went to a neighbor's, got clothes and food, and disappeared. Initially, Lisa had hoped that one of them had been Diana. Diana had recruited her. But four days after the bombing, the police had announced that Diana was among the dead.

The dead: two men, one woman. Rumor had it that the second man was Terry. Lisa had heard him speak more than once, those intense eyes focusing on her and her alone. He had reminded them all that Weatherpeople didn't kill. They were bringing the war home, yes, but not the death. Just the fear, and the destruction.

Then he had reminded everyone in that audience:

They'll come after us if we kill someone. Once we kill people, we can't go back.

Who would've thought that the people they'd kill would be their own?

Irv pulled the van onto one of the little side roads dotting the university. Lisa had attended classes around here, but it all looked strange to her in the dark. No streetlights, not back here, and just a bit of light dribbling from the buildings around her.

Irv shut off the ignition and the vehicle shuddered.

No one said a word.

Then Irv opened his door. The interior light came on—dammit, someone should have disabled it—and in the bright white glare, she saw just how frosty her breath was.

"Long way to walk," Leo said, voice low as if someone could overhear them. Maybe some student was walking the grounds this late, but she doubted it. It was midnight, although not as dark as she wanted. Clouds skated across the full moon.

"Yeah," Helen said, sounding confident as usual. No shiver in her voice, no hesitation. "I want to see this."

"I don't want to be close," Lisa said. "There'll be pieces."

She thought of Diana. Identified by bits. Tiny bits.

"Shrapnel," Irv said, and she thought she heard affection in his voice. "Just like 'Nam."

Always bringing them back to the mission.

Lisa glanced at the box, the bomb nestled inside, wrapped in blankets as a kind of cushion.

"Let's go," Irv said.

Irv opened the side door, letting in even more cold air. His eyes were bright, but his lips looked chapped. He *was* nervous, which was probably why he hadn't said anything on the drive over, why he was pushing them all now.

"We hurry, we screw up," Leo said.

"We go too slow," Irv said, "we miss our window."

It was midnight. The alarm clock was set for 12:30.

Lisa scrambled out of the van and stood behind Irv. Helen slid out after her.

Leo reached in for the box. He had made them all promise that he would handle the bomb, no one else. He had had a training session in bomb-making. He'd also read a few books, which was a few more than the rest of them had read.

Helen glanced at Lisa, then grinned. Lisa made herself smile back. Helen bounced on her toes, not from cold, but from excitement.

Lisa had seen it before. Helen had grabbed a helmet from one of the leaders on the Days of Rage, and stuck the bulky thing over her blond hair, then grinned, as if daring to them to take it off. That Chicago march—had tear gas, arrests, but those were expected. Lisa had avoided the tear gas, nearly got clubbed with one of the truncheons, and kicked a pig in the knee. He had squealed, doubled over, and then toppled, and she had felt powerful.

She didn't feel powerful now.

The clouds passed. Moonlight bathed everything in a clear, cold light. Helen's eyes glinted.

"Ready?"

Lisa nodded.

Leo cradled the box in his arms, as if it contained a puppy, not three sticks of dynamite. He started down the path, Irv beside him, walking like they were carrying an offering to an altar.

Maybe they were. An altar to the rich, the powerful.

The Cleveland Museum of Art, founded by Cleveland's wealthy, all their money made in oil and refining and railroads, the kind of men who were now "investing" in Vietnam, paying for the war, paying for kids to die.

Lisa nodded her head, hanging on to her resolve.

No one worked at the museum late. No one would be near the south entrance. Irv had checked on that. It was important to all of them that no one get hurt.

The air was dry and frigid. The edges of the wide path leading up to the south entrance hadn't been shoveled as well as it should have been. Ice-covered snow crunched as Lisa stepped on it, the sound like miniature explosions in the night.

The sound didn't seem to bother the others. They walked quickly, Leo breathing hard. The bomb didn't weigh that much, so he had to be nervous, more nervous than he was letting on.

Ahead, she could see the statue, sitting high on its base, contemplating all that was beneath. She'd had a tour of the museum not two weeks before. The guide had said that this sculpture, *The Thinker*, had been intended to be part of a Great Doorway for some other exhibition in France or somewhere. It was all supposed to illustrate Dante's *Inferno.*

The Thinker was supposed to be looking down, into the Gates of Hell.

From which Lisa, Leo, Irv, and Helen were emerging.

The clouds covered the moon again, dimming the eerie light. And Lisa swallowed some of the dry air. The statue almost looked alive, as if he actually saw them coming, as if he knew what they planned.

"How're we doing on time?" Leo asked, voice echoing across the icy white landscape.

"Plenty," Irv said as Helen said, "Ten after."

Neither of them looked at the time on the alarm clock, which Lisa wasn't going to point out.

They'd reached the long terrace in front of the huge staircase coming up from Wade Lagoon. The *Fountain of the Waters* had been shut off months ago, and looked barren, particularly in this light.

They had to cross the terrace, go up some steps, walk across more marble, and go up more steps before they even came close to the damn statue. It had never seemed so far away.

Lisa's mouth was dry, and she was cold, colder than she could ever remember being. She glanced at Helen, who grinned again, then held up two Magic Markers, fat and stubby.

"What's that for?" Lisa asked.

"We gotta state our intentions, right?" Helen said.

"We are." Leo half growled that sentence. "I'm carrying our intention."

His comment made Helen pout. Then her gaze met Lisa's again, and she shrugged prettily.

They climbed the last flight of stairs.

Leo bent over and set the box down. He looked like a penitent and *The Thinker* like a bored god who had seen it all. Lisa could almost hear him saying that nothing would catch his attention.

Then Leo would stand, smile, and say, *This will.*

It all happened in her mind in a flash. She made herself focus, even though this was the part that scared her the most.

Leo stood up with the bomb in his hands.

On TV, they had said that someone had crossed wires at the town house, that they hadn't known what they were doing, and just jostling the bomb they were making set off the explosion. Explosions—there had been three. Had Diana died in the first one? Or had she seen it, tried to get away, only to get caught by a secondary blast, all the other sticks of dynamite going up?

One cop had said that most of Diana had been vaporized. Lisa didn't want to be vaporized. She held her breath, so she couldn't see the warm air from her lungs turn into frozen water vapor in the ice-cold air.

Leo slid the bomb on the top of the pedestal, right beside *The Thinker*'s toes. *The Thinker*'s feet looked surprisingly lifelike. And she felt a half-hysterical giggle build. Would they identify *The Thinker* by pieces and bits? Would they figure out what happened to him by looking at a section of his toes?

"There," Leo said. "We have to go now."

"One second!" Helen's voice rang across the terrace. That was when Lisa realized Helen wasn't beside her. Irv was; he had watched Leo with the same intensity that Lisa had.

But Helen had moved, and Lisa hadn't even noticed.

Lisa stepped to one side, saw Helen crouched beside the large pedestal that the museum had placed the statue, the sharp smell of Magic Marker in the air.

She had written *Off the Ruling Class!* like the Black Panthers sometimes yelled *Off the Pigs*. Like that horrid Manson family had written *Death to Pigs* in blood at those murders last summer.

But all Lisa could think about was that Red Queen in Disney's *Alice in Wonderland*, who had scared the crap out of her as a little girl, screaming, "Off with their heads."

"Come *on*," Leo said, his voice reverberating against the ice and marble and columns.

Helen stood up, raised a Magic Marker like it was a flag, and said, "There. Now it's done."

Her grin chilled Lisa even worse, and *off with their heads* in the Red Queen's voice echoed in her mind, sounding ever so slightly deranged.

Helen, as the Red Queen.

Lisa shuddered. She hurried down the steps, and suddenly she had passed Leo, ending up behind Irv, who was moving fast.

"C'mon." Leo was clearly talking to Helen. "We gotta go."

Helen laughed. God, it sounded like a Disney villain laugh, out of control and crazy.

Irv reached out, grabbed Lisa's arm, and pulled her forward. She nearly fell. She wanted to shake him off, but she was afraid she would slip even more on the ice.

She heard crunching behind her, feet breaking ice, and Leo wasn't yelling anymore.

She wanted to turn, to see the fuse, lit and burning, as the flame crept its way to the bomb, even though she knew that wasn't how it worked. Her heart pounded, and she couldn't quite catch her breath.

She hadn't looked at her watch. They had enough time, right? They had to.

A clock somewhere on campus rang its half-past-the-hour bell.

If they kept going on the regular path, they might be in the bomb zone when the bomb went off. Lisa veered in the other direction, running for the Wade Lagoon. She wasn't sure what she was thinking: the Lagoon was iced over. But she had to get as far away from the museum as she could.

"We're not going to make it," Irv said, although she wasn't sure what "it" was, since they were no longer heading back to the van.

He grabbed her and yanked her toward the gigantic *Fountain of the Waters*. She tripped over the lip, where the pool was in the summer, and staggered onto even more ice.

The fountain itself provided little cover, but its base, with a bunch of steps, seemed okay.

She knelt on one of the steps (marble; *cold*), and put her hand on the edge, then squeaked with surprise. She had clasped an ice-cold fist.

She looked over, and saw a life-size boy, opening what looked like wings. He was naked and extremely realistic.

His face looked demonic in the shadows cast from the fountain itself.

The bomb hadn't gone off. She looked between the gigantic figure carved on her right and the fountain itself. The museum looked the same. *The Thinker* crouched in his usual contemplative position. No explosion. Nothing.

Except Leo, scrambling the last few yards toward them. He leaped over the lip of the pool, skated into place beside her, and crouched, covering his head with his arms.

Irv was already protecting his head.

She ducked too, wondering what the hell had happened to Helen.

Nothing happened. It was strangely quiet.

"Shit," Leo said, his voice muffled by his knees. "Shit, shit, shit."

He dropped his arms, rose up like Lisa had done a moment ago, and peered over the edge of the fountain, only his hands hadn't touched any of the figures.

"It should have gone off." Irv was looking up too.

Lisa brought her arms down, but she wasn't going to peer over that edge. They weren't far enough away.

"Give it a minute." She sounded steadier than she felt.

"What if it doesn't go off?" Irv glanced at Leo, who did not look back. "They'll find it."

"They've found other bombs," Lisa said. Why was she the calm one all of a sudden? "All the duds. It hasn't led them to any of us, not yet."

"I wonder if the clock just stopped. It's cold. The mechanism might not have worked." Leo stood up—

And that was when the world turned white. The fountain shook. Lisa toppled backward onto the ice. Then she heard it, the loudest sound in the universe. The sound felt physical, big and forceful, as if it could shove her around all by itself.

She got pelted by tiny bits of ice. Or something. Something fine. Like sand. The grit filled her mouth, her eyes, her nose. She coughed and couldn't hear it.

She rolled over so more junk wouldn't go in her face, but it seemed like the ice/sand storm had already ended. She sat up, then remembered the bomb, and thought she better crouch again.

Until she realized: it had gone off.

The world had gone weirdly silent. Irv had fallen over, and Leo—she couldn't see Leo.

She blinked her eyes. They felt gritty, as if she had just awakened. They were starting to tear, but the tears felt cold. She wiped a hand over her face, felt something wet, looked, realized that, yes, some of what hit her had been shards of ice.

But not all of it. She saw fine bits of metal glinting in the moonlight.

Her mouth tasted metallic. She spit, then spit again, looked, didn't see blood. Maybe she was okay.

Just shaken.

Irv was sitting up, looking stunned.

She still didn't see Leo.

She scanned, finally saw his form crumpled against the edge of the pool. She scrambled toward him, put a hand on him, felt something warm and wet and sticky, then smelled copper.

Blood.

"Leo," she said, but her voice sounded wrong. Far away. "*Leo.*"

She wanted to grab him, shake him, but she wasn't sure if she should. Then he moved, just a little, bringing a hand up toward his face.

The hand dripped.

She looked down, saw blood pooling from his right side.

He had been standing in the open when the bomb went off. Irv's voice, inappropriately cheerful, echoed in her head.

Shrapnel. Just like 'Nam.

She swallowed, knelt down beside Leo, and for the first time that night, wished she had more light.

She needed to look for the damage.

She needed to see if he was going to die.

2015

They assigned Erika the Yitzhak exhibit. She hadn't even known the exhibit was coming when she interviewed. She hadn't known anything about it until the morning of her hire, when they tried to explain the exhibit to her.

An Israeli artist, hired to—what, exactly?—do something with the Rodin.

It took half the day for Erika to understand that Nevet Yitzhak was going to do a multimedia installation about *The Thinker.* Or maybe two installations. No one was certain about that yet, although Yitzhak had to be, right? She was the one designing it all.

Only she was in Israel, supervising from afar.

And right now, Erika had to handle the camera crew here. Nice people, here to film the annual conservation of the statute. The ladders, the scaffolding, the proper placement of the camera. Erika did none of that.

Instead, she was in charge of snacks and bottled water. Mostly, she stood around, watching the conservators take their soft cloths and rub *The Thinker*'s damaged limbs. He hunched over as if he were protecting his own nakedness. Or maybe, he was pretending at practiced boredom, like that beautiful man she had been assigned to draw in that long ago life-drawing class, the class that the vet had interrupted.

The vet was foremost on her mind. Did he use a soft cloth on his damaged legs, or did he accept help? And if he did, did he look down and away, like *The Thinker*, or did he just accept the ministrations as part of his every day life?

She didn't know; she couldn't know. She didn't even know who the vet had been. She supposed she could have asked her professor. She had a hunch he did that little bit of playacting every semester, shocking his first-year students with a bit of street theater.

She wondered how many couldn't get that moment out of their minds for years afterward.

She sighed, made herself focus.

She was just a gofer, an unpaid gofer, who was gaining experience.

At watching someone else's art develop—concept to exhibition—without a single hands-on moment. Without a single thought.

1970

Irv, trudging away, holding Leo. Leo, who was bleeding too much.

Lisa glanced down the path. She couldn't see them any more. They had disappeared into the darkness. Their footprints were hidden by the broken ice on the path, but she had no idea if there would be a blood trail for when the police got here.

She also had no idea if there were sirens. She couldn't trust what she heard, because her hearing was weird. Usually when her ears were plugged, her breathing sounded too loud, but she couldn't hear her own breath. Just this strange ringing that sounded like a continual finger running around the surface of an expensive glass made of the finest crystal.

Something dripped on her upper lip. She rubbed her hand under her nose, felt something viscous, looked. Blood. Her nose was bleeding.

She was injured, but she had no idea how much. She knew nothing about concussive injuries. Nothing at all.

At least she wasn't dizzy—or that dizzy, anyway. She made herself walk up the stairs, because she didn't want to slip on the ice, and fall again. She didn't remember hitting her head, but that didn't mean she hadn't. She hit the ground pretty hard after the blast, and the pain hadn't yet registered.

She knew it would register soon.

He had toppled backwards, the statue. Falling behind the base. Helen's words stood out in stark contrast to the pale stone: *Off the Ruling Class.*

Off *The Thinker.*

Someone grabbed Lisa's arm, and she screamed. The scream ripped her throat, but she couldn't hear it, not really. She felt it, knew it had to be loud.

She yanked herself away and turned at the same time.

Helen stood beside her. Her face was smattered with something black or gray, as if she'd stood too close to a fire. The whites of her eyes looked astoundingly bright in the full moon. Her coat was tattered, and she was missing a boot.

But she grinned. She looked too happy. Much too happy.

"We have to go," Lisa said.

Helen tapped her ear. She couldn't hear either.

Lisa mouthed the words again, just like she had done for Irv.

Helen nodded, then pointed at the words on the base, and pumped her fist, like Muhammad Ali in one of his interviews.

Now, Lisa mouthed. She wanted to add that Leo was badly hurt but she didn't. She knew that Helen couldn't hear her.

Helen didn't seem to notice anything. Her bare foot was on the cold pavement, and one arm dangled at her side, not that she seemed to care. She looked inappropriately gleeful.

She walked over to the statue, braced herself on her bare foot, and kicked the statue with her booted foot.

Lisa grabbed at her, then pointed to the van.

Helen made a show of sighing, but she squared her shoulders, winced a little, and started marching forward. She didn't even look for the lost boot.

Lisa followed, feeling like the only sane one left in the group. It made her wonder what, exactly, someone sane would notice about her. The blood on her face? The way she took stairs, as if she had never seen them before? The look in her eyes?

She wasn't sure what that look was. It wasn't gleeful craziness like Helen's, and it wasn't fear, which Lisa had felt earlier. It was some kind of calm acceptance, some kind of weird feeling that she had stepped from a world she thought she understood into one so very different that she couldn't quite process it.

All she knew was that they had to leave. Maybe, if he had good sense, Irv had already driven Leo to a hospital.

Helen's mouth was moving. She was talking, but Lisa couldn't hear her. Not that Lisa was trying.

She put her hand on Helen's back and shoved her forward. If Helen didn't start moving faster, Lisa would leave her behind, tell Irv she couldn't find her, let Helen take the rap for the whole thing.

And, with that thought, anger flooded in. The group should have listened to her when Lisa mentioned the townhouse bombing. They should have given up this method of bringing the war home.

She should have listened to herself. She should have walked away long before this.

The statue wasn't the only one looking into the gates of hell.

She had descended into it, and she hadn't even known how.

2015

They had moved Erika from the Yitzhak exhibit to the centennial. Her supervisor had said she would learn more from handling all the program items for 2016, since the Yitzhak exhibit was well in hand.

Handling all the program items for the centennial year meant researching the museum's history for the birthday party and the official celebrations. She wasn't really handling any exhibits per se; she was planning a "birthday party" to commemorate the first day the museum's doors had opened, in June of 1916.

Lately, she had been inside the cool air-conditioning, sitting at the desk they had assigned her in the bowels of the museum, working on a computer that should have been upgraded five years ago.

Usually she worked in silence, but today, someone down the hall had a door open, and she could hear voices, raised and angry.

Angry voices were not normally part of the museum.

Finally, Erika couldn't take it any more. She picked up her mostly empty bottle of water, and walked toward the noise.

The door to the office was half-closed. Erika wasn't even sure whose office it was, because she had never been invited into the offices proper. The voices had lowered—or at least the speaking voice had.

It belonged to a woman.

". . . materials are wrong and you must change them," she was saying forcefully. "The bombing wasn't an act of vandalism."

"Well." The responding voice was male. "I'm afraid the statue *was* vandalized—"

"Vandals spray graffiti," the woman snapped. "They don't bomb a statue. You're trivializing the event."

Erika's breath caught. They were talking about *The Thinker*. They were talking about the upcoming installation. There were two installations now. One was called *The Antithinkers*, and the other, *Off the Ruling Class*.

"We're not trivializing anything," the man said. "When the final materials come out, you'll see. Nevet did a fantastic interview in which she called the 1970 bombing cultural terrorism and linked it to the destruction occurring all over the Mideast—"

"*Cultural* terrorism tries to wipe out the culture," the woman said, voice dripping with contempt. "That bombing was done by Weatherpeople. They didn't care about culture. They were political—"

"They were called the Weathermen," the man said. "And I agree, they were a terrorist group—"

"I didn't say they were terrorists." The woman lowered her voice. "You need to fix this. Give credit where . . ."

"What are you doing?"

It took a moment for that question to register. One of the volunteers stood in front of Erika, frowning. Clearly, she had been caught eavesdropping, but fortunately not by one of her bosses.

"Stepped out of my cubby to get some water." Erika lifted the mostly empty bottle. "What are they fighting about?"

"Nothing important," the woman said.

Erika recognized her; she came every Thursday. But if Erika had to say what the woman did, she couldn't. The woman was one of those mousy chubby types of indeterminate age, the kind everyone ignored.

The only reason Erika even noticed her was because her eyes were sharper than they should have been. This woman seemed to miss nothing.

"It sounds important," Erika said.

The woman gave her a condescending smile. "You'll understand some day."

Erika *hated* it when people said that. "Understand what?"

"Faulkner. 'The past is never dead. It isn't even past yet.'"

Erika stared at the woman. Had she just quoted a dead white guy?

Erika hated it when someone did that. It was so condescending.

She let out a breath, then pushed past the woman, and headed to the Provenance. They didn't like it when she came in and only bought a bottle of water, but she couldn't afford to eat lunch there half the time. She was still on a student budget, because no one paid her to be here. Even the bottle of water was expensive.

The past isn't dead. How stupid was that? Those people in the office were fighting about the wording for the upcoming exhibit, not what happened in the past.

Or maybe Erika was just feeling tired. Because all those articles she'd been reading—the ones from 1916—felt like they'd taken place thousands of years ago. The past truly did feel dead to her.

She rubbed a hand over her face, not sure how anyone could feel so passionate about an exhibit or two or three. She had become jaded working here: no one seemed to care about the art itself. Tourists wandered through too fast; students complained when they had to make a study of an existing painting; and the curators themselves seemed pulled in a thousand directions.

Even Erika wasn't enjoying the art. She didn't look at it anymore. And she couldn't remember the last time she'd touched *The Thinker*. Probably since his annual maintenance, when he'd looked just a little too much like the man in her memory.

Just a little too much like a living, breathing human being.

1970

The van was enveloped in its own exhaust, as if it was coated in the smoke of a recently extinguished fire.

From hell, probably.

Lisa shook her head at herself. About a block ago, she had gotten very, very cold, and even though she could see the van ahead, it looked very far away. Her limbs felt heavy.

Shock setting in.

She didn't dare let it.

Her ears hadn't entirely unplugged, but she thought the ringing was different. Not quite as loud. And something else had wormed its way in.

A siren?

She wasn't sure, but that would make sense.

She turned to see if Helen was reacting to the new sirens, but Helen wasn't reacting to much. She was limping now, and she had slowed down as well.

Lisa finally grabbed Helen's good arm and tugged her forward. The exterior of the van smelled like gasoline and carbon monoxide, a stench that normally made Lisa cough. She didn't even mind this time.

She just yanked down on the back-passenger door handle, and stepped into the back of the van, nearly kicking Leo.

He was sprawled on the floor where Irv had clearly dumped him. And, if Lisa had to guess, she'd guess that Leo hadn't moved since. The van's thin carpet looked dark and blotchy in the overhead light, and Leo looked gray.

Lisa had never seen anyone look gray before.

She reached out of the van to help Helen in, but Helen was gone. Again. Jesus. What was with—

And then the front-passenger door opened, where Leo had sat on their way here. Helen bounced in as if they were all going on a joy ride, the exhausted woman from the sidewalk gone.

Lisa pulled her door closed, then stepped over Leo to get to some boxes piled behind the passenger seat.

Leo didn't move as she stepped over him. He didn't flinch, he didn't try to protect his face.

He did nothing at all.

She knelt beside him, rather than sit on the boxes. The carpet was squishy with blood.

"We have to get him to a hospital," she said. Her voice sounded normal now. Or normal with a cold. Sound was still far away, but not quite as bad. Her ears had started working again.

"Screw that," Helen said. "They'll catch us if we go to a hospital."

"It's not a bullet wound," Lisa said. "It's—"

"Shrapnel." Irv said, as if he was speaking underwater. "It's shrapnel."

Bringing the war home, baby. Irv's voice again. Laughing as they placed the bomb into its box, hours ago—what felt like days ago. Weeks ago.

Years ago.

"So what?" Lisa said. "We can't help him ourselves."

"I'm thinking we go to Pittsburgh. No one will think twice about a guy like this in a hospital in Pittsburgh. They won't even know about the bombing." Irv had clearly been thinking about it while he waited.

"That's over two hours from here." Lisa put her hand on Leo's forehead. He didn't flinch at the chill of her skin. His skin felt cold too. Clammy.

His eyes were glazed.

"We have to get him help, *now*," Lisa said.

"He knew the risks," Helen said, using past tense.

Lisa looked at her. And Helen, the bitch, grinned, then shrugged.

"We agreed," Helen said. "No hospitals. No pigs. No help."

"We know anyone who can help with this?" Lisa's voice shook. Leo was still staring. He hadn't stopped staring. And she wasn't sure he was breathing. "No one in our group has this kind of medical training."

"It's one of the risks," Helen said. "And we agreed."

Sirens were growing closer.

"Pittsburgh," Irv said, and put the van in gear. It lurched forward, then he eased it away from the curb, like they'd been taught. Like *Leo* had taught them.

How not to look suspicious. Drive like a normal person.

But how did a normal person drive after a bomb exploded? How did a normal person drive when someone was dying in the back?

"Take him to a goddamn hospital," Lisa said.

"Pittsburgh," Irv repeated. "Pittsburgh."

It was clearly something he'd been saying to himself. A mantra.

He knew.

She knew too.

Leo was dead.

Friendly fire.

Or was it? The statue got off one shot before it toppled off its base, rolling until it was facedown on the terrace, limbs lost. One shot to hurt the enemy.

The statue wasn't dead, but Leo was.

And Lisa had no idea what to do about it.

2015

People still dressed up for this sort of thing. Or maybe the ruling class did.

Erika smiled to herself at the thought. She stood near the makeshift bar, near the dark blue exhibit wall. Museum patrons, volunteers, and students wandered through, picking up bits of cheese with toothpicks and eating tiny sausages. A few had a veggie-filled plate, and almost everyone carried a fake plastic wineglass.

Mostly, people clung to their food as they stared at the installations. More people were looking at *Off the Ruling Class* than *The Antithinkers*, apparently caring less about the history and the curation than the way the statue "reacted" to its own history.

Nevet Yitzhak had come up with something brilliant. The statue, animated, pondered his own destruction. Yitzhak made him real. He looked at a photo of his own body facedown on the terrace, and seemed stunned by it. Then he hid his face in his arms.

Erika had only watched *Off the Ruling Class* once. It brought tears to her eyes. It also made her use a different entrance to the museum every day. *The Thinker* had been alive enough for her. She didn't need to see him move in a piece of 3-D art. Now he seemed even more alive, judgmental, and just a little bit lost.

She didn't like to think of him as lost. His 3-D self had helped her find that spark again. She might not be able to draw to anyone's satisfaction except her own, but she could do other things.

She didn't have to restrict herself to the old ways, not when there were a hundred new ways to create art, just like Nevet Yitzhak had done. Exciting ways.

People were talking about this installation. Erika overheard bits and snatches of conversation all over the exhibit. Mostly, they talked about their emotional response, but she had overheard one of the directors talking to a local critic, heads bent together.

"It makes me think of what ISIS did in Palmyra," the critic had been saying as Erika passed, picking up stray programs.

"It's supposed to," the director had replied.

That stuck with her, primarily because she'd heard it before, and wasn't sure she agreed. She understood the global nature of the exhibit, and the way the Cleveland Museum of Art, one of the best museums in the world, wanted to keep its hand on the global stage.

But Erika found herself returning over and over again to the *Antithinkers*, the newspaper clippings, the decision to keep this casting of *The Thinker* damaged, to show what Sherman Lee, the director of the museum at the time, had said:

No one can pass the shattered green man without asking himself what it tells us about the violent climate of the USA in the year 1970.

Not Syria. Not the Middle East at all.

The USA.

There were terrorists here too, and apparently always had been.

Erika had spent half her work time investigating "weatherpeople," discovering that they were initially called the Weathermen like the man in the office had said, and then, right around the time of the bombing, becoming the Weather Underground—because they had all decided to disappear, go "underground."

They made no sense to her, these Weatherpeople. What was weird was that so few of them had gone to prison for what they had done. Some even taught at universities now—or had, before they retired. Hell, she could have had a Weatherperson for a professor and not even known it.

There was no proof that these Weatherpeople had been involved in the bombing of *The Thinker*, no real reason given for the destruction except four words, scrawled in some kind of marker. *Off the Ruling Class.* Which meant what, exactly? *The Thinker* hadn't been a member of the ruling class. In Dante's *Inferno*, he'd actually been a poet, at a time when poets weren't considered much of anything at all.

Erika's boss stopped at the bar, and asked for a bottle of water. Then she gave Erika a familiar look—one filled with disapproval.

"You should mingle," her boss said, and nodded toward a woman, standing alone near the *Antithinkers*.

Erika fake-smiled, then trudged over. That woman near the *Antithinkers* was the last person Erika wanted to talk to. Erika had noticed her coming in.

The woman was rich-woman thin, wearing a white designer dress that Erika had seen on one of those Fashion Week red-carpet videos. The woman's bony hands sparkled with a massive diamond-and-sapphire ring on her left hand, and a slightly less gaudy one on her right. The rest of her jewelry was tasteful though. She wore a flat gold necklace around the dress's collar, and matching gold earrings.

The gold set off the remaining blond in her white hair, which she wore at chin length, in one of those angular cuts that also spoke of money.

It wasn't the aura of money and comfort that made Erika want to talk to someone else, however. It was the woman's face. She had clearly been beautiful decades ago, but she was too thin now, which accentuated her high cheekbones, and made her carefully made-up eyes sink into their sockets.

When Erika had first seen her, Erika had thought that the woman looked like a walking skeleton who was trying to pass as a living person.

Seeing the woman up close didn't change Erika's mind.

The woman turned, and for a brief moment, her gaze fell on Erika. Then it moved past her. Erika turned enough to see that volunteer, the one who had quoted Faulkner, standing behind her.

The volunteer wore a blue silk dress that make her look like a badly dressed mother of the bride. Those sharp blue eyes, though, didn't look motherly. They were filled with something else, something vicious.

Erika stepped out of the way. Screw the boss. Erika wasn't going to talk to either of those two women.

But Erika couldn't bring herself to walk too far away. She stayed close enough that she could pretend she was just entering the conversation if the boss came by again.

The skeletal woman smiled at the volunteer.

"Well, look at us," the skeletal woman said, and Erika shivered. She recognized the voice. It belonged to the woman who had been arguing about the language of the exhibit a month ago. "Who'd've thought we'd be the ruling class."

The volunteer's lips thinned. Her cheeks turned a bright red—not from embarrassment, but from fury.

"We always were," the volunteer had that same tone she had used with Erika on that day.

They had known each other. No wonder the volunteer had quoted Faulkner. She might not have been talking to Erika at all, not really.

Erika took one tiny step back. Now she really didn't want to be part of this conversation.

The skeletal woman looked at the still images from the *Antithinkers.*

"I would have thought Irv would be here," she said. "But of course, he never did have the balls."

Then she tilted the glass of white wine she held in her right hand at the volunteer, and walked toward the stairs.

The volunteer didn't follow. Instead, she put the back of her hand to one of her cheeks, as if taking her own temperature.

"Who was that?" Erika asked before she could stop herself.

The volunteer blinked, as if she hadn't even realized Erika was there. Then the volunteer looked after the skeletal woman.

"Why, Helen, of course," the volunteer said softly. "She's the Red Queen. Always and forever, the Red Queen."

1970

The drive took forever. They arrived in Pittsburgh at four in the morning, and followed road signs that read HOSPITAL. The hospital the signs led them to looked as old as the art museum, and was in a scary part of the city.

Irv parked catty-corner from an entrance marked EMERGENCY. Then he got out and opened the side door. Lisa helped him slide Leo out, even though she knew it was pointless.

Leo was weirdly pale, and he hadn't blinked, not once since she got in the van.

Irv didn't say anything though, just carted Leo to those doors.

Lisa didn't help. She couldn't bring herself to. She knew there was no point in bringing him inside. She would never see him again, and if she let that thought in all the way, she might not ever recover.

So she slammed the van door shut, shoved her hands in her pockets, and started across the parking lot.

"Where're you going?" Helen yelled from the passenger seat.

Lisa didn't answer. She didn't know where she was going. She just knew she had to get away, had to leave now.

Maybe she would find a pay phone. Maybe she would call her dad and ask him to get her.

Maybe she would go home.

Then she let out a snort. Home. She could no more go home than the wild-eyed vets coming back from 'Nam could.

Besides, what would she say to her dad? *Hi, Daddy. I accidentally killed someone today, and I can't cope with that. Can I come home and pretend everything is normal? Is that all right?*

And what would her father say? Her conservative father, who always told her she should be grateful for what she had. Would he say, *Sure, honey. I'll be right there?* Or would he disown her?

She shook her head. The air was cold here, but not as bad as it had been in Cleveland.

It wouldn't be fair to call her father, to put everything on him. Besides, she had disowned him a year or more ago, when she thought being on the vanguard of a revolution would be fun.

Fun. With Leo staring at nothing, and Helen laughing like a demented doll, and Irv, as stone-faced as *The Thinker* himself.

Lisa marched away, realizing they had gotten what they wanted. They had brought the war home. But not in the way they expected.

Things never went the way anyone expected.

She had thought she might die tonight. She had thought they all might, if something went wrong. And she had expected the statue to be ruined.

But then what? A call to arms? A realization that the war was wrong? The end of the museum?

She hadn't thought things through. *They* hadn't thought things through. They had planned on adventure, on a statement, on sending a message.

Which they had.

She just wasn't sure, exactly, what the message had been.

JONATHAN SANTLOFER *is the author of the bestselling* The Death Artist *and the Nero Award–winning* Anatomy of Fear. *He is the coauthor, contributor, and illustrator of* The Dark End of the Street, *editor/contributor of* La Noire: The Collected Stories, The Marijuana Chronicles, *and the* New York Times *best-selling serial novel* Inherit the Dead. *His stories have been included in such publications as* Ellery Queen's Mystery Magazine, The Strand, *and numerous collections. He is the recipient of two National Endowment for the Arts grants, has been a visiting artist at the American Academy in Rome and the Vermont Studio Center, and serves on the board of Yaddo, the oldest arts community in the United States. Also a well-known artist, Santlofer's artwork is included in such collections as the Metropolitan Museum of Art, the Art Institute of Chicago, and the Newark Museum. He is editor of the forthcoming collection of stories and art on the subject of democracy to benefit the ACLU,* It Occurs To Me That I Am America, *Touchstone/Simon & Schuster, January 2018. Currently, he is at work on a new crime novel and his memoir,* The Widower's Notebook, *will be published by Penguin Books, spring 2018.*

The Empire of Light by René Magritte

GASLIGHT

BY JONATHAN SANTLOFER

t was true, she hadn't been feeling well, hadn't been herself, the headaches, the nausea, the slight vertigo. But she was fine. She'd always been predisposed to colds and flu, periods of time when she didn't feel quite right, *sensitive*, her mother used to say, and that was true. It was a virus, that's all, at least she'd thought so for the first few weeks. But now, after three months she wasn't so sure.

"Give it time, Paula, you know how these New York colds can linger, especially in winter," Gregory, her husband of six months, always so sweet, always trying to reassure her.

But what sort of cold lasted three months?

She'd finally gone to the doctor, tired of Gregory telling her to give it time. Gregory, who insisted she use his doctor, "the best in the city," an elderly man with cotton-candy white hair, who gave off a whiff of mothballs, his office somewhat down on its heels despite the lower Park Avenue address, the upholstery of the waiting room chairs worn, one actually splitting, the only other patient waiting, a woman who looked to be at least ninety and possibly blind, milky cataracts on her eyes that gave Paula a chill. No receptionist either, the doctor himself opening the door and escorting Paula into the examining room, reading aloud from the chart she had just filled out: "Thirty-seven, no history of serious past illness."

He was nice enough, Paula thought, and appeared to know what he was doing, the usual tests, blood pressure, heart and lungs, drawing blood. And she had to admit he was charming and talkative, plus they shared an interest in crime fiction—movies as well as books, her favorite genre since she'd been a girl—the two of them comparing classic and contemporary favorites throughout her examination.

Still, she'd complained to Gregory when she got home. "His office is a mess and he's so *old*." Her husband gave her a look that said, *Stop being a spoiled brat*, she'd seen it slide across his handsome face, before he tried to hide it. She knew the look, had seen it too many times in her life, and he was right: She *was* spoiled. The only child of successful artists who had given her everything—the best private elementary school, then boarding school. After that, her parents' money made it possible for her to attend prestigious art schools, undergrad and graduate, where she'd studied painting, though even she could see she was only adequate, that she would never be in the same league as her A-list artist parents. She'd rarely put brush to canvas since grad school, nowadays only puttered in her well-appointed studio, rearranging high-quality oils and pastels, the tubes of paint untouched, the pastel wrappers still intact.

Paula pulled herself out of bed, managed to brush her teeth, wash her face, run a comb through her hair, all of it an effort, then made her way down the lushly carpeted staircase of the Greenwich Village brownstone, her hand gliding along the mulled oak bannister. She'd always liked the feel of it, smooth and solid, something to hold on to, so few things in life felt like that. Except for Gregory, her rock, her protector.

The phrase *disappointing daughter* trickled into her mind like an inky stain, though surely her parents had never said such a thing—not to her face—always encouraging, doting on her the way all striving parents do, with expectations that she would be successful, *must* be successful, another thought they'd never expressed though she clearly felt, along with the feeling that she would never measure up.

Paula's fingers tightened on the bannister.

Her mother, a successful artist, one of the few who used pastel in a serious way, "that rare artist who brilliantly defies the limitations of her medium," so said the *New York Times* about her mother's first exhibition at the tender age of twenty-three. Paula had read the review so many times she could recite it by heart, along with others that traced the arc of her mother's remarkable career, one that had never taken a downturn, her work now valued in the high six figures, the best examples going for well over a million at auction.

It was the same for her father, whom just about every art magazine and periodical had dubbed "a genius," his major paintings—large invented narratives—were currently selling for even more than her mother's pastels. A fabulous pair, Paula the envy of her boarding school friends. "Your parents must be *so* cool," though she'd often wished for a housewife mom and an accountant dad.

A decade of great reviews for both parents, before Paula had ever been born.

An "accident," she'd overheard one day, her mother whispering to a friend after too many martinis, about the birth of her baby girl. Paula was five or six at the time and the word, *accident*, like a mole, burrowed deep into her psyche and made itself an uncomfortably permanent home.

Gregory, an aspiring artist himself, had been dumbstruck when she first told him who her parents were. Paula, equally dumbstruck by this incredibly handsome young man, an artist, flirting with her, at least it seemed so, his hand on her arm, her wrist, as he spoke, his blue eyes sparkling, that devastating smile she would come to love, along with the dimples on his perfectly stubbled cheeks.

Paula paused at the bottom of the staircase opposite the mirror, the one with painted reflections on its surface so that the viewer could not tell what was real and what was not, just one of a series of hand-painted mirrors her father had made. She caught her fractured reflection, large nose and square jaw, the resemblance to her father uncanny, his rugged good looks, which had never quite worked on a girl.

"Make your weakness your strength," her mother always said, assessing Paula's face as if it were a disjunctive Picasso portrait, tilting her head one way then the other, once suggesting a nose job, another time a chin reduction.

But Gregory found her attractive, always telling her she was "striking," though secretly Paula would have preferred beautiful, even settled for pretty.

How she loved showing him off, could feel peoples' eyes slide from Gregory to her and back. *She must have something to get him*, what they had to be thinking, though she didn't mind. After all, he was hers. And not just handsome, but *gorgeous*, everyone said so, and eight years younger than she, though she looked young enough, or had, before this lingering illness produced dark rings under her eyes and turned her skin pallid.

There had been a few boyfriends before Gregory, none who mattered or who'd hung around very long, something always wrong with them, or more likely, she thought, with her. But she was married now, and happy, something she told herself every day.

A note on the sleek kitchen island: *Darling, today is the day you are going to feel all better! I'll be home early. Love you, Gregory.*

Her husband, who had left their bed so quietly, careful not to wake her, so considerate, always taking care of her.

Paula read and reread the note, held it to her cheek. She pictured the studio she'd bought for her husband, a cavernous space in a converted industrial building. Though there'd been plenty of room in her brownstone—any room he wanted—but he said he couldn't paint at home, had to be out, needed his own space, and she understood though she'd have preferred to keep him close. And he deserved a good studio for his sweetness and devotion, the kindness and care he always showed toward her. A talented painter too, all he needed was a break, and he'd never gotten any, not with his blue-collar background and the state college with its so-so art department, though he never complained, except to fight her on buying the studio for him.

"I don't want you spending your money on me, Paula."

"Who else would I spend it on?"

Gregory's perfect jaw clenched as he told her he was happy to stay in his Lower East Side tenement, with the makeshift studio in the living room.

But Paula had prevailed.

The truth? She didn't like the idea of him keeping his apartment, any apartment. A separate studio was okay, but not an apartment he could escape to when he grew tired of her, and of course she worried he would, no matter how many times he reassured her, no many how many times he professed his love.

She pictured the look of absorption on Gregory's face while he painted, the sweat on his veined neck, the smell of him, the taste of him. For a moment all of her symptoms disappeared and she felt fine, the idea that Gregory was hers and that he loved her, was enough to cure her, at least for the moment.

She replayed the message from Dr. Silvershein, who confirmed she did not have Lyme disease, her self-diagnosis. After all, she'd spent the summer in her family's Rhinebeck home, and ticks were rampant in the area.

If not Lyme then how to explain the nausea, the aches and pains—the visions. The only way she could describe them. Seeing something one moment. Then not. House keys placed on the small mahogany table by the front door, suddenly gone. A necklace she was sure she'd put on top of her dresser, missing. Was she losing her mind? Was this illness a sign of early dementia?

The doctor had found nothing, her blood tests, all negative. He suggested she had a low-grade virus that would eventually go away or perhaps she was just tired, which annoyed her. How could she be tired, she didn't do anything. She was no longer painting, didn't have a job and didn't need one, thanks to her parents. All she did was lie around reading mysteries and thrillers. When she told Gregory the doctor's report he'd been so happy: *You see, darling, there's nothing wrong with you. It's just a bug.*

Another note tucked beside the teapot: *Drink this! XO Gregory.*

Paula lifted the top off the pot, eyed the tea, the brownish color murky and cloudy. Burdock Root, whatever that was, according to the tea bag label. Gregory had been coming home with holistic remedies since she'd gotten sick, one foul-tasting tea after another, along with his daily smoothies laced with kale, tofu, vitamins, and minerals, which he swore by, but no way Paula was drinking this awful-looking tea, plus it was cold.

She was about to pour it out when she pictured Gregory, how sweet and concerned he always was, and how he would give her that stern parental look—the one she'd seen often enough on her parent's faces.

She poured herself a cup.

It was tepid and acrid on her tongue. Two sips were more than enough, though she'd tell Gregory she'd drunk it all.

A moment later, it hit her, a slight blurring of vision, the room starting to spin.

Paula eased herself into a chair and waited until the spell, if that's what it was, passed. And it did, though her head had begun to throb.

She took deep breaths, then a few more sips of the tea, her hand shaking so that she almost spilled it.

What's wrong with me?

Should she call Dr. Silvershein and see him again, or maybe her old family doctor? But she'd had all the tests. Surely anything serious would have shown up.

Was it all in her head?

And if so, why? She'd never been happier, married to Gregory, someone who loved her for who she was, not who she could be or should be.

Another sip of the tea, so considerate of Gregory to have made it before he left.

She didn't want to bother him while he was working but the cell phone was in her hand and she had already hit autodial and the phone was ringing. Paula pressed the cell to her ear, waiting to hear her husband's voice and have him console her.

Voice mail.

When he was painting he often turned his phone off.

"Just calling to say hi," Paula said, affecting a lighthearted tone. She didn't want him to hear her desperation, her need. "Nothing important. I know you're working, no need to call me back. See you tonight. Love you."

She disconnected, her hand still shaking, but even hearing Gregory's voice on a machine helped to soothe her, a little, give her strength so that upstairs she took a detour into her studio. She hadn't stepped foot in it for months, but perhaps it was time to get back to work, something to distract her, to make her feel productive.

At first glance the studio looked as neat as ever, though on closer inspection she noticed several of her brand-new paint tubes were dented, as if squeezed, one leaking color around the cap, the label on others ragged.

Paula tightened the cap on the leaky tube. She must have been fiddling with it and didn't remember.

One more time she worried about her memory, her mind, but shrugged it off while she carefully arranged paint tubes around her palette like a prismatic color chart: yellows then oranges, then red; next purples and blues; finally blacks and whites. The act calmed her and it looked good. She did the same for her pastels, noting that some of the casings were torn or unraveled, a few of the pastels worn down, their tips crumbled and flaky, which surprised her; she was sure she hadn't used them either. Or had she? Damn it, she just couldn't remember.

On a shelf below the oils were bottles and tins of unused solvents, one with smudges of what looked like blue paint on its handle. Lifting it for a closer look, she saw they were fingerprints. *Hers?* When had she done that? And the cap was loose though, again, she had no memory of ever having opened it.

The idea that she was losing her mind was exhausting. Or was it the other way around: the exhaustion affecting her memory? Either way she'd had enough.

Back in her bedroom she sagged onto the bed and plucked her latest crime thriller off the stack on her beside table. A few pages and her eyes were already closing but she refused to give into the fatigue, sat up and pulled on clothes, a cashmere sweater, woolen slacks. She needed to get out, breathe some fresh air, that was all. Downstairs, she tugged on boots, wrapped a scarf around her neck, shrugged into her winter coat.

Outside there was frost on her brownstone windows, patches of snow and ice on the path, icicles hanging from the gaslight they'd installed after lobbying the city for months. It had been Gregory's idea, something old and romantic, and Paula loved the idea too.

She swiped an icicle off the wrought iron lamp, watched it splinter to the ground and shatter like glass.

That's when she noticed the gas lamp was casting black shadows onto an already dark sidewalk. She looked back at the house, also dark, and at the houses abutting hers, dark too, golden light smoldering in the windows.

But how could that be?

She looked up at puffy clouds in a bright blue sky.

She shuddered, closed her eyes and counted to ten. When she opened them nothing had changed: the houses still dark, the sky bright blue, the gaslight glowing.

She checked her watch: 10:16 A.M.

Beneath her feet, snow melted into puddles like a stop-action film. A moment later it solidified into ice.

Paula shivered, tugged her coat tighter, closed her eyes and counted again.

This time when she opened them everything was normal: the houses as bright as the blue sky, the patches of snow frothy around her boots. Everywhere she looked it was daylight, a sparkling winter day.

Paula's head was spinning again, and that feeling in the pit of her stomach like she was going to be sick.

She darted back to the house, slammed the door behind her, sagged against it trying to catch her breath, as if she'd run a long distance, not just a few yards.

What is wrong with me?

When the nausea passed and her breathing normalized she went to her laptop and googled her symptoms: dizziness, headaches, nausea, hallucinations. There were an infinite number of possibilities—anemia to high blood pressure, middle ear infections to heart disorders, diabetes to common anxiety—but surely any of those medical conditions would have shown up in her tests.

Anxiety: that was it! She'd always been nervous, anxious, easily upset.

She would ask the doctor for anti-anxiety meds and she'd be cured. Simple.

Why had she never done this before? She felt so much better.

She was about to call Gregory and tell him her latest diagnosis when she glanced back at the laptop and saw another category for dizziness and hallucinations: POISON.

Again, there were many, which she skimmed, stopping on the one most familiar to her—TOXIC ART SUPPLIES—then scrolled through a list of paints that contained heavy metals, solvents and varnishes that emitted volatile organic compounds referred to as VOCs, the toxic fumes from heated plastics and resins, deadly spray fixatives and modeling glues.

This was followed by a list of the most highly toxic paint pigments: Barium Yellow, Burnt or Raw Umber, Cadmium Red. She scrolled further: Chrome Green and Prussian Blue. Then: Manganese Violet, Naples Yellow, and Vermilion. She paused on Cobalt Blue then Flake White.

Paula knew all about Flake White, AKA Lead White, from art school—everyone had given it up in favor of the nontoxic Titanium—but other than the Cadmiums, she hadn't known the other pigments were dangerous, particularly Cobalt Blue.

But she *did* know about it, about toxins, didn't she? Something smeared across the back of brain like an underdeveloped negative that she could not decipher.

What was it?

Beneath the list of poisonous paints she read the warning: Inhaling or ingesting any of the above, even in small amounts, can result in dizziness, headaches, nausea, and in some cases, hallucinations. Large doses can be fatal.

Paula fingers trembled on the keyboard. Could she have poisoned herself with art supplies? But that didn't make sense; she hadn't been painting in years.

Then, like a wash of watercolor bleeding across her mind's eye the thought came to her: Gregory, who painted every day, who used oils and solvents, who often came home reeking of turpentine, his fingers stained with color, Cadmium Red, which he refused to give up ("There's no other red quite like it"), and Cobalt Blue, a staple of his palette. Plus, Gregory mixed his own colors, used a mortar and pestle to grind raw pigments into linseed oil. Something her father did on occasion to get "that special richness only hand-ground paints guaranteed," no matter how many times he'd been warned that inhaling the pigments or getting them on your hands where they could be absorbed through the skin, was dangerous. Her mother too, refused to wear a mask when using pastels, a particularly easy way to inhale toxic powders that escaped into the air while working. Both her parents seemed to think that stained hands and pigment-splattered clothing was the sign of a real artist, and apparently Gregory shared the myth.

Had she inhaled solvent fumes from his clothes, toxic paint from kissing his fingers?

She guessed it was possible, but enough to make her sick? This sick?

Paula sat back as another set of thoughts and pictures scudded across her mind: the teas and smoothies Gregory made for her every day, their odd, bitter taste, and the headaches and dizziness that often followed.

But it couldn't be.

Gregory loved her.

Or did he?

She saw it again, not a picture this time, just the hard, cold truth: a handsome young man who had married her for money. What else could he possibly see in her? She did nothing, wasn't beautiful nor brilliant, just unsuccessful Paula, dull and drab. Except for one thing: she was rich.

When they'd met, Gregory had practically nothing: the Lower East Side tenement and a part-time job painting walls in an art gallery; no family money, no prospects other than an art career that might or might not eventually take off, but when would that be, and how many art careers ever did?

Still, she fought the idea. She had been reading too many crime novels, that was all.

Gregory cared about her. He needed her, adored her.

But the thought soured fast. He needed her all right. For his brand-new studio and her beautiful brownstone, for everything that came with being her husband. There'd been no prenup, at the time she wouldn't consider humiliating him, would not taint their love.

Taint.

The word spiraled and took shape before her eyes, letters swirling into a liquid stream that dripped into cups of tea and dribbled into smoothies, then morphed into a kind of abstract Rorschach inkblot, then, a coiling snake, and finally, Gregory's handsome face: leering.

No.

Paula shook her head against the idea, the room spiraling, mind blurring. But when her mind cleared, the thought was still there and she knew it was true: Gregory was trying to kill her.

It was like that old black-and-white movie with Ingrid Bergman and Charles Boyer, the one where the husband tries to drive his wife crazy to get her money. What was the title? Paula thought a moment and it came to her: *Gaslight.* That was it.

Paula stood, her balance slightly off but her mind sharp now, determined. She pictured the dented paint tubes in her studio, the worn pastels, the can of solvent stained with blue fingerprints. How easy it had been to add a little solvent to her tea, some pastel flakes to her smoothies.

A perfect plan: Poisoning her with her own materials. Too smart to use his own.

She paced across the room and back, hands at her sides balled into fists. How could she have been so stupid, so vain, so trusting? She swiped tears off her cheeks, hadn't even noticed she'd been crying. But she would not allow herself to be sad.

No. She would get even.

And she knew how to do it.

She would take a page out of Gregory's book, but she had something even better. No crumbling bits of toxic cobalt pigment in his food, no solvent in his drinks. That would take too long. Not that she was in a hurry. She could take her time too, but she needed to use something tried-and-true; something tested.

Paula hadn't been down here in years, the place always gave her the creeps, the bare bulb dangling from a chain casting weird shadows, the greenish mold on the wall where water endlessly seeped and dripped, the low roar of the oil burner, the basement rarely frequented by anyone but the various tradesmen, Paula always hovering on the top of the stairs, hand ready at the door to escape, calling out, "Everything okay down there?" before she'd slip away and wait until they were finished. Her father promised to clean the place up, to have the mold taken care of, paint the walls, add decent lighting, but he never did, preoccupied with his artwork and gallery openings, parties with dealers and collectors, her mother the same.

How many times had she been left alone?

As a baby, then a toddler, she'd had a nanny, like most Manhattan kids of a certain class, a tall German woman, stern and unsmiling with closely set eyes and a hairbrush always at hand to be used as a threat, and more, an immigrant with family back in Munich but none here, who one day left without a word of goodbye, which surprised her parents, but not Paula, who, at seven, felt perfectly equipped to take care of herself. There'd been another nanny after the German, her parents had insisted, but she didn't last long, just a few weeks, there one day, gone the next. After that, her parents decided Paula should come directly to one or the other's studio, which she did a few times, but she preferred to stay alone in the big brownstone, and after a while her parents relented, the two of them so involved in their work they hardly noticed.

Paula slipped on latex gloves then made her way down the basement steps, the dripping sound echoing as she crept across the damp concrete floor to the metal cabinet tucked into a dark corner where her father stored old-fashioned art supplies he rarely used, Venice Turpentine, tubes of unstable "lake" pigments, encaustic wax, materials that needed to be kept cool.

There were several dead mice, mangy and shriveled, and Paula held her breath as she stepped over them and opened the cabinet door. The metal hinges squeaked and she shuddered as she pushed aside hunks of wax, bottles and tins, tubes of paint. The cardboard box was still there behind them, wrapped in heavy plastic, just as she remembered.

In the kitchen, as Paula set the box beneath the sink, behind a box of Brillo pads and a container of Comet, that underdeveloped image, the one she'd had a few days ago, streaked across her brain but this time she knew what it was, parts of the picture filling in. For several years she had seen it daily but then it faded. Until now.

Paula shut her eyes, but the picture loitered in her mind like a nightmare waiting to be acknowledged as real. She nodded, as if saying, *Okay, I see it, I know it, I remember—so what?*

She had stopped drinking Gregory's smoothies, had been pouring his teas down the drain for weeks, and was feeling better, stronger. Gregory seemed pleased, but she knew he was acting.

Tonight she would cook his favorite meal, beef bourguignon, chop mushrooms and onions, blanch bacon, sear the carefully cubed pieces of tenderloin, make her own gravy out of beef broth and corn starch.

With the box from the basement already on the counter, she slipped on gloves, found the tiny silver spoon her grandmother had bestowed upon her as a baby, and dipped it into the box of salt like crystals. She shook more than half of them back into the box; she only needed the tiniest bit, which she stirred into the stew.

It dissolved instantly. No color. No taste. No smell. Nor did it change the texture of any food or drink, the reason for its most common nickname: "The poisoner's poison."

"Wow," Gregory said. "This is delicious, but you shouldn't have worked so hard, darling."

"It was good for me to do something," Paula said, "and I like seeing you happy." She sat back and watched him eat two heaping portions while she picked at a salad, claiming she was still without appetite.

She'd made enough stew for two nights, and Gregory ate it heartily again the next.

It was a week later, when they were side by side in bed watching a *Law and Order* rerun that he complained of a headache and when he got up, had to stop and grab hold of the bedpost.

"Whoa," he said. "I'm dizzy."

"Maybe it's the two glasses of wine," she said.

"But I always have two glasses at dinner."

Paula held off for three days before adding a few flakes to the expensive Château Lafite Rothschild. Too bad she would not be able to drink it, though she knew Gregory could not resist. In the kitchen, she poured herself a glass from a different bottle, an everyday Merlot, then poured some of the Lafite Rothschild down the sink, as if her glass had come from it. A shame, she thought, to waste it, but one had to make sacrifices when it came to revenge.

Gregory had his usual two glasses then half of a third. "It's too good to waste," he said, drinking it down.

This was the easier way to do it, Paula realized, no laborious cooking, just a few drops of the salts in a wine bottle that Gregory was sure to drink, as he got drunker, blaming his slight vertigo on the wine, though it didn't stop him from drinking it.

About a week later he complained of his teeth hurting, and when he showed Paula the odd whitish spots on his nails she commented that it must be caused by one of his painting solvents or that "dangerous Cadmium Red," or perhaps he wasn't getting enough of some vitamin and should get something at the health food store, which he did.

It was when his hair started falling out, that he became alarmed. "It's in the sink and between my fingers when I smooth it back!"

"Ridiculous!" Paula said, examining his head carefully, noting the thin spots and the strands between her fingers when she ran her hand through his hair. "All men start to lose a little hair at your age. Maybe you should get that stuff, you know, Rogaine. They say it works."

Gregory bought it and used it religiously, diligently rubbing the foam into his scalp morning and night, and Paula watched, almost feeling sorry for him.

This could not go on much longer. Gregory had already gone to the doctor a few weeks ago—of course the doctor had found nothing—but now, he was planning to go again.

Paula knew the slow-acting poison was almost impossible to detect and so uncommon that doctors rarely even thought about testing for its presence. Plus the fact that rat poisons that contained thallium sulfate had been banned in the United States since the mid-seventies. She supposed her father had bought it back then to control the mice and occasional rats in their brownstone basement and forgotten about it. But she hadn't.

She remembered the day she'd found it, read the label, had researched what it was and what it could do.

Paula stopped doctoring the food and drink for a few days so that Gregory would feel better and think he was cured, before starting again. Then she added a bit more to a creamy fish chowder and to a sparkling Riesling wine, and when Gregory toppled over after dinner she helped him into bed and called the doctor.

"I see," she said, cell phone to her ear. "A stomach flu going around? But he's been sick on and off for a few days. . . . Okay, I'm sure he'll be fine too, doctor, but I'll make sure he sees you when he's stronger." Her voice filled with concern for Gregory's benefit and for the doctor's. She wanted Dr. Silvershein to remember she had called, concerned and worried, but not *that* worried.

It was time.

A pot of tea she insisted Gregory drink, one cup, then another.

Now there was vomiting and diarrhea, quite unpleasant, and Gregory complaining that he felt as if his feet were on fire.

She offered sympathy and an ice pack for his feet.

For two days he was like that, in bed and out, limping, almost sobbing at one point. She said she would call 911 if it got any worse, though she never did.

It pained her to see him like this, his muscular body feeble, his beauty ravaged.

Then she told him. Wanted him to know what she was doing and why. It was too late now, the poison had already done its damage, no way he'd be able to repeat what she said to him.

"I know what you were trying to do," she said. "Poisoning me with paints and solvents."

Gregory struggled to raise his head. "*W-what?*" The word croaked.

"You're after my house, my money. I *know* that, Gregory. I saw the proof. But I've stopped you."

"I would—never." His vocal cords constricted, every word like shards of glass in his throat, but he continued to speak, to beseech her. "I—love you, Paula. I—do. Don't you—know that?"

"Ha!" she cried.

Gregory managed to sit up. He took several breaths. "Paula—what—have you—done—to me?"

For a moment, the image of that underdeveloped negative was back in her mind, now sharp and clear, even the words sounded familiar.

"You were trying to kill me," she said, "so I'm killing you. It's only fair."

"You're—crazy!" he rasped.

"Me? Crazy! *Me?*"

Something inside Paula snapped and exploded, spots before her eyes, a tingling as if ants were crawling up and down her arms. She leaned in close to his face and screamed—"*You're* the crazy one! *You!* Not *me!*"—the picture burning in her mind along with those words—*accident, failure, worthless*—hammering inside her head. She reached out, hands, like claws, only inches from his neck, blind with rage, shaking with fury. Then she stopped, sucked in a deep breath then another. There was no reason for all of this fighting, this ugliness, it would all be over soon.

Gregory just looked at her, his face gaunt, his eyes rheumy. "How—could—you—possibly think I—would—ever . . . harm you?" Then his body shuddered and seized and his head fell back against the pillow, mouth twitching, a thin line of viscous drool sluicing over his chin.

When the heart failure came Paula was almost relieved; seeing her once beautiful and beloved Gregory suffering had not been much fun, no matter what he had done or tried to do.

When the emergency crew arrived and proclaimed him dead she cried real tears and wrung her hands until the ambulance drove away. Then she rid the house of the poison, threw away every plate, glass, cup, and utensil Gregory had eaten from, cleaned his bedsheets and threw away the towels she had used to mop up his vomit.

The Frank E. Campbell funeral home had been serving the city since the late 1800s, where such silent screen stars as Rudolph Valentino and Greta Garbo, politico Mario Cuomo, more recently the actor Philip Seymour Hoffman along with rap star The Notorious B.I.G., had been honored and eulogized in death.

Gregory, Paula decided, deserved to go out in style, the chapel choked with flowers, a blow-up of their wedding photo—Paula looking happy if plain, Gregory beaming and beautiful—framed by gladioli, greeted guests in the wide entryway.

Paula's face, dusted with white powder, was as pale as the moon against her black designer dress, expensive but appropriately simple. She wore the mask of widowhood seamlessly, her tears falling quite naturally. She really did love Gregory, no matter what, and she found it easy to nod and sniff when people offered their condolences—an Oscar-worthy performance that made her regret she had not considered a career in acting rather than trying to compete with her artistic parents.

The reception continued back at her home, the brownstone vying with the funeral home for flowers, finger foods laid out, tuxedoed bartenders serving expensive white wine and Perrier.

She'd had the place professionally cleaned though a slight antiseptic odor still hung in the air.

Paula took comfort in seeing the friends who had never believed how someone like her could possibly have snared a man like Gregory, sad and upset for her, along with the relatives who shook their heads and told her she was brave for the third time in her life.

She was only partially surprised to see the cotton-candy-haired man, as he had treated Gregory for several years.

"I am so sorry," the elderly doctor said, grasping her hand in his. "What a tragedy. Gregory was such an extraordinary young man, so talented and kind." He paused. "They're saying viral encephalitis, right?"

Paula nodded sadly. She knew that thallium poisoning was very often confused for the disease and, without sophisticated and specific laboratory instruments for testing the poison, would never be detected. Even so, she wasn't taking chances. There would be no autopsy, and she had scheduled Gregory's cremation for tomorrow.

"What a loss," Silvershein said, shaking his head. "If only I'd come when you called."

Paula shook her head too. "How could you have known? How could anyone have known it was so serious? You can't blame yourself."

"No," he said. "But he was so young, so talented, his whole life ahead of him, and he loved you so much, Paula, he told me so on his last visit, only a few weeks ago."

Paula wanted to scream at the doctor: *It isn't true—he was trying to kill me!*—but she remained composed. "Did he?" The words spoken so soft as a memory played in the back of her mind like a movie: Christmas vacation, her last year of boarding school. She'd brought a painting home, one she'd done in art class, something she had worked on for weeks and weeks to impress her talented parents, something she was proud of, her best painting ever. She saw it now, propped against the wall in her mother's large studio, her mother stepping close, then back, tapping her chin, striking a contemplative pose.

"It's good, Paula," she said, just a slight note of surprise in her voice.

Oh, the pride Paula had felt!

Then her mother moved in closer again, "But here and here"—she indicated areas of Paula's painting—"could use some work."

"How so?" Paula asked, though she'd wanted to yell, to howl and curse at her mother, who had already plucked a large brush from her palette and was mixing paint.

"This area here," her mother said. "You see, it needs a bit more color." And as she said so, added a brushstroke to the canvas. "And here—" She stopped, took up another brush, dragged it through a glob of paint on her palette, then dabbed it onto another spot of Paula's painting.

"See how much better it looks?"

Paula just barely nodded.

Again and again her mother mixed pigment and added strokes to the picture, lost in the act, oblivious to Paula, shrinking beside her, until half of the original image was gone, smothered under a layer of wet paint.

"Voilà!" her mother cried out.

Paula twitched a smile, then picked up the painting, wet paint glazing her fingers, brought it back to her bedroom, into the closet, and slammed the door. It was the last time she would ever show her mother anything.

But months later, Paula back home after the end of the school year, there it was, just where she'd left it, in the closet, exactly as she had painted it—not one of her mother's brushstrokes in evidence.

But how could that be?

Paula lifted the painting closer and studied the surface inch by inch. There were no signs of paint having been scraped off, or any added. The painting looked precisely the way she had painted it in boarding school, nothing about it changed or altered.

Paula couldn't believe it or figure it out, but then, as now, it no longer mattered.

"Oh yes," the doctor was saying, and Paula, unsure of what he meant said, "Excuse me?"

"Gregory, how much he loved you."

For a moment Paula was overwhelmed with grief and regret.

"It's how your mother died, isn't it?" the doctor said, "What?" Paula wasn't sure she'd heard him correctly. "I think so," she said, stifling a flinch. "I was away at boarding school when it happened."

"I see. And your father's death, coming just a few months later. What a shock that must have been for you." He squeezed her hand.

Paula took her time before answering, forcing her eyes to tear up. "Yes," she said. "I adored my parents."

"Such talented people," Silvershein said.

Paula's uncle, her father's younger brother, an aspiring writer, whom she hardly knew, who supported himself teaching junior high school, who had been standing close by, leaned in.

"They never really determined the reason for Anton's heart failure. I don't know why they put him in the ground so damn fast. Dead at forty-nine, my God."

Paula offered the man a solemn nod, then turned back to Dr. Silvershein when he said, "I saw the body."

"My father's?" Paula asked.

"No, Gregory's. As his internist all these years, the coroner called me out of courtesy, plus we're old medical school buddies."

"Oh?" Paula slid her hand from the elderly doctor's surprisingly firm grip.

"Do you mind hailing a cab for me," he asked.

"Of course not," she said, allowing him to take her arm. They moved slowly through the dwindling crowd of mourners, whispering condolences and nodding, as they headed toward to the door and out onto the street.

"Have you read Agatha Christie?" the doctor asked when they were halfway down the path. "Oh, of course you have, you said so when I first saw you in my office. One of your favorite authors since you were quite young, isn't that what you said?"

Paula opened her mouth but it took a moment to form the word. "Yes."

"What's the name of that Christie book, you know, the one where they think it's black magic but it turns out to be poisoning?"

Paula shrugged then waved a little too frantically to an oncoming taxi, which swerved and stopped at the curb.

"*The Pale Horse!*" Silvershein snapped his fingers. "That's it! Have you read it?"

"No," Paula said, her heart fluttering. "I don't think so."

"I'm sure you'd have remember, if you had. Oh well." He took hold of the cab's door handle, then stopped and turned back to her. "By the way, and I hope you won't mind, but I've taken the liberty of delaying Gregory's cremation, it won't be more than a day."

"But—why?" Paula glanced up, down, anywhere to avoid the doctor's eyes and when she looked back at the house it had suddenly gone dark, the sidewalk as well, though the sky was bright.

"Are you okay? the doctor asked.

"Oh—yes," she said, her eyes darting from the bright sky to the darkened houses and back.

"There was something about Gregory's nails," the doctor said. "I'm sure it's nothing but it's where chemical compounds, often overlooked in normal testing, collect, in the fingernails."

Paula's mind was scrambling, searching. "Oh, it must be from his painting," she said. "No matter how many times I told him not to, Gregory insisted upon using toxic paints, cadmiums and cobalts."

"Really?" said Silvershein. "Well, that can be tested for as well, but they wouldn't prove fatal unless Gregory ate a tube of the stuff. No, it can't be that."

He stopped and scratched his head. "The coroner is performing some specific tests I ordered right now."

Paula looked at the overhead clouds that cut across the daylight sky, then at the gaslight in front of her brownstone. It seemed to glow in the dark more intensely than ever.

JUSTIN SCOTT *is the author of thirty-seven thrillers, mysteries, and sea stories including* The Man Who Loved The Normandie, Rampage, *and* The Shipkiller, *which made the International Thriller Writers list in* Thrillers: 100 Must-Reads.

*He writes the Ben Abbott detective series set in small-town Connecticut (*HardScape, StoneDust, FrostLine, McMansion, *and* Mausoleum*), and collaborated with Clive Cussler on nine novels in the Isaac Bell detective series.*

The Mystery Writers of America nominated him for Edgar Awards for Best First Novel and Best Short Story. He is a member of the Authors Guild, the Players, and the Adams Round Table.

*Paul Garrison is his main pen name, under which he writes modern sea stories (*Fire and Ice, Red Sky at Morning, Buried at Sea, Sea Hunter, *and* The Ripple Effect*) and thrillers based on a Robert Ludlum character (*The Janson Command, The Janson Option*).*

Born in Manhattan, Scott grew up on Long Island's Great South Bay in a family of professional writers. His father, A. Leslie Scott, wrote Westerns and poetry. His mother, Lily K. Scott, wrote novels and short stories for slicks and pulps. His sister, Alison Scott Skelton, is a novelist, as was her late husband, C. L. Skelton. Scott holds bachelor's and master's degrees in history, and before becoming a writer, drove boats and trucks, built Fire Island beach houses, edited an electronic engineering journal, and tended bar in a Hell's Kitchen saloon.

Scott lives in Connecticut with his wife, filmmaker Amber Edwards.

PH-129 by Clyfford Still

BLOOD IN THE SUN

BY JUSTIN SCOTT

SUMMER, 1973
NEW YORK CITY

I f you can fly, then this roof is as good as any," Clyfford Still told Jimmy Camerano.

Jimmy was sitting on the edge of the parapet with one arm hooked around a masonry gargoyle and his legs dangling ninety feet above Tenth Street.

"Zoom from New York. Alight on a calmer island. Paint pictures undisturbed."

Still was Jimmy's hero, a unique painter, a founder of abstract expressionism, and a recluse who likened art galleries to brothels, museums to mausoleums, and most of his fellow artists to ambitious backstabbers. Tall, white-haired, and slick in a sharkskin suit, he stood inside the parapet, leaning on his elbows, peering down dubiously at Jimmy's landing zone.

It was a hot, sticky night. The city had emptied out. The antique and furniture shops were shut, the sidewalks deserted, curbs empty but for a single parked car near the middle of the block. The cops had driven by once, but hadn't noticed Jimmy overheard.

"If you can't fly, then this roof is sufficient for a killing nosedive. But I say, emphatically, art is a force for life, not death. A painter has to live a long time."

Jimmy was as low as he could ever remember. For all he knew he was falling already and didn't care. Meeting his hero for the first time face-to-face made surprisingly little difference.

"Live long for what?"

"To know that art is a matter of joy."

Easy for a god to say, thought Jimmy. In truth, he had known it himself, most of his life. Their eyes met and his mind flashed on an image of the older man wiping a dirty window with his handkerchief.

"For instance," said Still. "That street . . ."

Jimmy followed Still's gaze. He saw no joy in the dull light cast by a handful of windows and anemic street lamps. A man left the telephone booth on the corner and its light went out.

"That street needs a horse."

"What?" said Jimmy.

"What?" said Abby Whitlock, who had brought Still up to the roof and was standing beside him, safe inside the parapet.

Still said, "Jimmy, I see in your face I don't have the words to talk you off your ledge. Abby, I'm sorry." He turned abruptly and loped to the open stair hatch.

Abby called, "Where are you going?"

"I'll try to show him, instead." His crown of wild white hair floated down the steps.

Jimmy asked Abby, "Is it sheer coincidence that the god of the New York School, revered by Rothko, de Kooning, Pollack, Motherwell, and Newman—and worshipped by me since I was a kid—who split years before I hit town—shows up tonight of all nights on this roof of all roofs?"

"I called him," she said.

"Why?"

"Because I love you." Abby reached across to touch his cheek. He flinched, thinking she would try to grab him, and flung both arms around the gargoyle.

With a loud crack, it broke loose from the rotting cement, and rocked on the ledge, held in place only by its own weight.

Abby jumped back and opened both hands to show him she wouldn't grab him. Jimmy caught his balance on the ledge. He often wondered what went through people's minds when they fell from buildings. Now he knew. It would be all about context—suicides wondering why, murder victims still begging no, and sheer, heart-pounding disbelief for accidents.

"Why would Still come to you? He hates art dealers."

"He knows I take care of my artists. Even the ones I don't love."

"What does he think about my work?"

"I would never ask. If I ever used him for business, we wouldn't be friends."

"What kind of friends?"

"Don't be stupid."

"What did you tell him?"

"I told him you're sitting on a ledge. And I read him Bern's review."

"Burned by Bern," said Jimmy, speaking of backstabbers. "I always wondered if Bern would turn on me."

Anyone outside the bloodthirsty art business would have tried to console him with naive assurances that one vicious *New York Times* critic could not wreck a solid career.

But Abby knew the business. She owned both the Whitlock Gallery on Fifty-Seventh Street and the first uptown-gallery downtown branch in the SoHo district, and she had loved Jimmy too long and hard to sugarcoat what Bern Horne could do to an artist he chose to destroy.

"Bern can destroy your price," she admitted. "He cannot destroy your life, unless you let him. He can't destroy the work you've done. He can't destroy the work you do next."

"How can I show the work if I can't sell it?"

"Live long, like the man said. Your shot will come around again."

They stared down at the empty street, Jimmy on the parapet, Abby safe behind it, and argued. Abby was sunnily hardheaded, Jimmy desperate.

Clyfford Still suddenly appeared on the sidewalk.

"What's he carrying?" asked Abby.

"Gallon of paint and a wall brush." The paint was as white as his hair.

"Your old tools."

"Thanks for reminding me I can always go back to house painting."

Abby laughed. "I'll still represent you."

"Not for long."

She met his eye in silence.

He was not surprised she could not deny it.

Still put the paint and brush on the curb, and walked quickly to the phone booth. The light went on when he closed the door. He came out in a minute, hurried back, and picked up his paint.

Jimmy said, "Even if you did keep representing me, I cannot go back to handouts."

⊶—⊷

Fire Island, the summer of 1965, Abby Whitlock and Bern Horne searched beyond the boardwalk for the studio that they heard Jimmy Camerano had hidden in the empty sand dunes east of the Pines. He had built it of scrap lumber and tar paper that he had begged from the builder who paid him two dollars an hour to paint ceilings in beach houses. A good deal, he claimed, as he only needed a dollar a day for food, plus a little extra for ferry and train fare to New York, and brushes and paint on Canal Street. He had a skylight made of sheet plastic stapled over a hole in the roof, a car radio that ran off a six-volt battery, hurricane lamps, a bottled-gas refrigerator he had found in the dump, and a bedsheet draped over a canvas on an easel.

Bern—still trying to be a painter back then—asked, "How do you get through the winter?"

"I rent a loft on the Bowery."

"As posh as this?"

"Not quite."

Bern spotted a magazine print of a Clyfford Still painting that Jimmy had cut out of *Life* and taped to his rusty refrigerator. "*PH-129.*" Bern knew it well. A jagged snatch of red united a giant field of warring yellows. If Still ever titled a painting, instead of giving it a filing number, he could have named it *Blood in the Sun.*

He turned away from it abruptly and homed in on Jimmy's easel.

Without asking, he whipped off the bedsheet.

What jumped from the canvas was like a fist in his face. No wonder this guy living on scraps was sure of himself: he had more talent in his fingernail than Bern could dream of.

Bern counterpunched without even thinking about it.

"Just what the art scene needs, another lyrical abstract expressionist."

"What do you call it?" asked Abby.

"*Untitled 1*." Jimmy was not sure yet what to make of Bern, and much more interested in Abby-in-hip-huggers. Bern, who seemed disappointed that he didn't respond to the crack about his work, struck him as bold, rich, educated, and adrift. Abby had glittery blue eyes and black curly hair, the kind of easy walk that came from being sure about something, and a smile that made him feel like it was meant all for him.

"It's not bad," said Bern. "Not bad at all."

Abby said, "It's good."

Bern opened the rusty refrigerator. It was marginally cooler inside, he supposed, and held half a bottle of wine.

"I'll be back." He pushed out the screen door.

⊙━┼━◎

"Alone at last," said Jimmy.

Abby said. "We will never be friends if I sleep with you."

"What? Where did that come from?"

"I know your kind."

"What kind?"

"Italian. I've known Italians. You can't help yourselves."

"I'm not Italian. I'm American."

"You know what I mean. Didn't your father have girlfriends?"

"He did worse. He was a violent criminal. Threw people off buildings."

"I'm sorry—"

"Don't be. I wonder sometimes did he get the high out of it that I get out of painting?"

"I shouldn't have said any of that—but I wasn't kidding."

"Why do you want to be friends?"

"To help you."

"How are you going to help me?"

Abby Whitlock planted herself in front of *Untitled 1*.

She followed one rule when evaluating a painting: if she had trouble breathing, it was good. Bern was marginally right calling it derivative of Clyfford Still, but only marginally. It had its own passion.

"Who's going to sell it?"

"When I get enough work done, I'll find a gallery."

"You just did."

"You?"

"I will own a gallery on Fifty-Seventh Street."

Fifty-Seventh Street was Gallery Row, the pinnacle of art selling. She had made him a life-changing offer, and Jimmy Camerano managed to push an "Oh," out of stunned silence.

Bern Horne found his way back to the boardwalk, walked a mile to the harbor where they had a grocery and a liquor store, stole someone's red wagon to trundle his purchases back to the end of the boardwalk, scooped the bags into his arms and slogged through the deep sand, dodging poison ivy. Hot and sweating, job done, he stepped into the shack, only to be staggered by his second fist of the day.

Abby was mooning at Jimmy Camerano as if the painter, not *Untitled 1*, was the work of art. Not that she wouldn't covet the painting too. She was smart enough to see how good it was. But she wanted the whole package.

Jimmy looked mighty pleased. He had probably made the first move, cast the first look, the opening what-if glance. Abby was a one-man woman, by and large. Jimmy must have made the first move.

Heart churning, Bern stuffed cold cuts, beer, Coke, and wine into the refrigerator. His hands were shaking. He stacked cans of tuna, fruit and coffee and evaporated milk on a plywood shelf, and poured sugar into the near-empty jar in which Camerano hid it from the ants.

"I've been thinking," he said, at last. He stalked to the easel, which Jimmy had left uncovered. "Here's your problem."

"I don't have a problem."

The son of a bitch was so sure.

"You don't think you have a problem. But you're copying work the man did in 1949."

"I am not *copying* anybody."

"Maybe not like carbon paper. But Clyfford Still walks through the snow and you're trying to squeeze your feet in his footsteps."

Jimmy wasn't having any of that. "Nobody paints alone. You think these idiots doing pop would stand a chance if Edward Hopper didn't focus them on the Ashcan School?"

"I agree they're idiots. But they're not copying Hopper, or the Ashcan School."

"You can follow as long as you add."

Bern dragged him back to the refrigerator. "What made you cut this out? Why did you hang it here?"

"Because nobody can paint like that."

"That's what I'm saying,"said Bern. "The snow around his footsteps is never going to melt."

"Yeah? What if I add fire?"

Bern looked at Abby. She looked away. He wasn't "losing" her. He had already lost her to this talented bastard who was not only stealing his girlfriend, but had a far better chance than Bern ever would of filling Clyfford Still's footsteps, unless something derailed him.

He noticed what he hadn't earlier. Taped under *PH-129* it was a little squib scissored from last month's *New York Times*, date-lined Los Angeles. June 18, 1965.

The new Los Angeles County Museum of art opened today a exhibition titled, "The New York School: the First Generation," the first historical survey of the New York abstract expressionist group. Among artists whose work is represented are Jackson Pollack, Willem de Kooning, Franz Kline and Clyfford Still.

"Look at the last line," Bern said to Jimmy. "'Critics have argued that the museum's collection has some serious gaps.' You know what that means? There's room for your fire."

Jimmy puffed up at the flattery, as Bern thought he would. "That's what I mean," he said. "Everything doesn't have to be so-called new. There's room for great painting. Look at Jon Schueler."

Bern groaned theatrically. "Another derivative lyrical abstract expressionist."

"Jon Schueler can paint circles around Rothko."

"I agree," said Bern. "But he'll never get the chance to."

"We're all derivative. Schueler derives from Turner. The pop idiots derive from Hopper. Hopper derives from Sloan. Even Still is derivative."

"Who is Clyfford Still derivative of?"

"Still is derivative of Still."

Bern laughed. "Touché, Jimmy."

He found a church key and opened a couple beers. Abby drank wine.

They talked. The Vietnam War was heating up, but Jimmy had been drafted years before, straight out of high school, and Bern had 4-F knees, which made them immune to interruption.

"I'm getting out of painting," Bern said, suddenly.

Jimmy sounded appalled. "Stop painting?"

"Just in time. Pop art, kinetics, land art, op, photorealism are sweeping away ordinary painters. You don't have to worry, Jimmy. But all except the best are goners, they just don't know it, yet. I envy you, but I don't have the talent to stave off the inevitable."

"What will you do?"

Bern grinned. "I can always be a critic. Abby says I have a clever tongue, don't you, dear?"

Abby asked, "Is there a . . ." She gestured around the shack.

"Outhouse around back. It's clean."

As soon as she left, Jimmy asked, "Does Abby really own a Fifty-Seventh Street gallery?"

"She will."

"Wow. She offered to represent me."

"I'm not surprised. She has a terrific eye for what sells."

"Are you two . . . ?"

Bern had a sudden burst of hope, but it was false hope and he no choice but to swallow it. Abby was smitten and would do exactly what she wanted to. No matter how hard he fought for her, it wasn't his fight to win. All he could do was grieve and rage. He said, "Just on-and-off friends kind of forever."

"Can she afford to open her own gallery?"

"Show me a New York painter's girlfriend and I will show you a rich man's daughter whose mother died in childbirth or was a hopeless alcoholic." Bern rattled off names of girls Jimmy had been introduced to at exhibits, or heard about, or, in two cases, had things with too brief to know about their mothers.

"Which was Abby's mother?"

"Doesn't matter," Bern smiled, acting the part of the sophisticate delighting in the wonderful vagaries of New York art. "Same result. Artists' bills get paid. Fathers freak out. A good time is had by everyone else, for a while. And paintings get made."

He wondered which of them tore him up worse—Jimmy for taking her, or Abby for being taken. Happily, he wouldn't have to chose. What he did to one would be suffered by both.

⚬══╪══⚬

A year later Abby opened shop on Fifty-Seventh Street. With a head for business, a gift for making friends, and taste that matched New Yorks' hunger for things that seemed new, she did well. A year after that, she opened Whitlock SoHo downtown on Greene Street. Her father, a Cincinnati industrialist, blustered in one day and, instead of admiring the work for sale, demanded of the airy space, "What kind of business is this? Where are your assets?"

"Fifty artists who count on me."

"They're not an asset. They're a liability."

Abby said, "If they're a liability, they are a lucrative liability." She showed him the deed to the building, and told him she no longer needed her allowance. It had to be the greatest moment in her life, even though they both knew that certain funds had passed directly to her from her grandmother.

She watched Bern find a place in the world, too, converting slickly from almost-painter to freelance writer for *ARTnews*, *Art in America*, *Art International*, *Esquire*, and the *Partisan Review*. She cheered him on—one hand would wash the other—and tipped things his way with a dinner party that included an editor at the *Paris Review*. Bern's piece for that "in-est of in" magazines lauding "the raw joy" of pop art while skewering its existence got his photograph in the first issue of *New York* magazine: "Bern Horne, the charming young independent critic with an art dealer's flair for picking

267

winners, an art historian's knowledge of why, and an essayist's razor-sharp pen to explain it all in compelling prose."

When Abby caught wind that *New York* was going to offer him a regular column, she informed a friend at the *Times*, and the *Times* gave him a desk, which included a regular paycheck and expenses. The other New York papers printing art columns went bankrupt, and Bern was suddenly empowered to turn the winners he picked into rich celebrities.

Jimmy Camerano painted summers in his shack and winters on the Bowery. Abby waited until she had the clout to steer her bravest clients his way, and chose his best for a show at the Whitlock SoHo. The first sentence of Bern's *Times* review read, "Just what art needs, another lyrical abstract expressionist."

Jimmy dropped the paper on the floor and raised his fist to punch the wall. "Keep reading!" said Abby.

"It's revenge. That son of a bitch is getting back for you coming with me."

Abby said, "I would have thought so. I was really worried he would. But for some reason he didn't. I'm amazed, but wait until you hear the rest of it." She did not bother picking up the paper. She had memorized it.

"'Why, you might ask, do we need another Clyfford Still when we already have a perfectly splendid Clyfford Still? Good question. But you won't ask it when you see Jimmy Camerano's new show at Whitlock SoHo downtown on Greene Street. With emphasis on new. What a painter! The only question you will ask is how does he do it? How does he imbue a thirty-year-old movement with the freshness of a summer morning?'

"You're made, Jimmy."

⸺◆⸺

He had always been a worker. Now, not having to scramble for food and rent, his output soared. In less than a year he had finished enough paintings for Abby to pick from for a new show. Bern Horne loved it and said so in memorable prose in both the *Times* and the magazines. He included the next exhibition, which Jimmy turned out a year and a half later, in a roundup of top-selling young painters for *ARTnews*. When the Fire Island National Seashore condemned his shack in the dunes, Jimmy commissioned Horace Gifford to build a sleek studio-house farther out on the beach at remote Water Island. And when the landlord tried to jack up his rent on the Bowery, he bought the building.

After the renovation party, when everyone else had staggered home, and Abby had gone to bed, Bern asked, "Have you found time to work?"

"Not a lot. Renovating and building the house at the same time ate a lot of energy."

"Haven't you painted anything?"

"Some. But I'm not ready to show it."

"Do I have to beg?"

Jimmy flipped an electrical switch. The wall that cordoned off his studio glided magically open and lights flooded down his easels. Jimmy didn't know it, but Bern had already talked Abby into sneaking him an early look. He stalked among them, quickly.

"I see why you need a wall."

"What do you mean?"

"Not quite party fare, are they?"

"What are you talking about?"

Bern shoved his hands in his pockets, pivoted from painting to painting. "What the hell is this?"

"I'm stepping out."

"You're stepping *in it*. In my humble opinion."

"You're wrong," said Jimmy.

"And you're stepping backward. This is not you. This is not Jimmy Camerano. This is . . . I don't know what this is."

"Call it realistic," said Jimmy. "Figurative? Representational?"

"What made you think to go in this direction?"

"There's a bar on Avenue C. It's got a huge cellar, must have been a swimming pool, or something."

"I heard about it."

"Monday nights, three hundred representational painters show their stuff. Everyone has an opinion. I've seen it turn into fistfights."

"Representational is so old."

"It's so old, it's new."

"But you don't need this. You're made. You're loved. You're rich. You can sell every painting you ever make for the rest of your life."

Jimmy said, "You once told me don't step in Still's footprints. Remember? In the long run you were right. I can't keep doing the same stuff. This is what is coming out of me now."

"I would put it back if I were you. . . ." Bern looked around again. "Well, as you yourself said, at least there isn't a lot of it." Suddenly, his expression softened. "Oh, Jesus, Jimmy. I'm sorry. Don't listen to me. You have to follow your own . . . I don't know—gut, muse, instinct—you're a fine painter. You'll figure it out. . . ."

When he got to the door he could not resist turning around to say, "Kiss Abby good night for me, would you?"

He doubted Jimmy even heard him, so deep was the confusion gathering on his face.

Clyfford Still stepped off the curb, dipped his wall brush in the gallon can, bent his knees, lowered the brush to the street, and started walking.

Abby asked, "What is he doing?"

Jimmy pulled Bern's review from the pocket he had crumpled it into and smoothed the paper and read it silently in the city skyglow.

> Did I betray collectors who invested in Camerano's pictures? No. They are adults, and will likely continue to see beauty in their acquisitions. The best among them will wax philosophical: after all, in the dark of a sleepless night, what true art lover dwells on the cash value of his collection? But I will admit to artists and collectors alike, I was wrong. A stench wafts from Camerano's latest exhibition at the Whitlock SoHo—the stench of a rubber factory devoted to retreading used tires. (I used the word *latest* to mean "same as last show and show before that, etc.") If Camerano will never change—or at least try to grow—that's his business. But is it too much to ask him to stop pillaging Clyfford Still?

Bern Horne had set him up from the beginning. From the very beginning, he set him up to destroy him. And he'd been stupid enough to listen to him.

"What is Clyff doing?" Abby asked again.

Jimmy had already seen it in a glance. "He's painting a horse. He said the street needed a horse, so he's painting a horse. What I can't figure out is how's he going to deal with that car?"

The way the horse was taking shape, the line of the perfectly proportioned animal that stretched curb to curb, would stop abruptly where the single parked car blocked it.

"Why did I listen to Bern? Why did I throw away all my new stuff and go back to imitating Still?"

"You don't imitate," Abby said firmly. "Never say that."

"I didn't, at first. Later I did. That's why I had to change—Bern tricked me. But after eight years, I mean, Abby, how long . . . ?" His voice trailed off, his gaze fell to the street.

Abby tried to capture his attention with an up-from-under smile that asked, Wouldn't you remember me for eight years? But Jimmy was watching with quickening interest the closer Still got to the car. Suddenly his face lighted.

"Oh—*that's* what he's doing!"

Clyfford Still put a curl in the horse's tail so it swept over its back and all of a sudden it was cantering with joy. He perched the empty paint can and brush on an overflowing garbage can, fumbled keys from his pocket, climbed into the car, and drove away.

Abby reached over the parapet and laid her hand on Jimmy's shoulder. "You don't imitate."

"I enjoyed being liked. I got addicted to it."

"Who doesn't?"

Jimmy pointed at the horse. "Still doesn't."

"Good. Let's get a drink."

"What do you mean 'good?'"

"You got Still's message."

Jimmy Camerano turned to Abby Whitlock, but did not move from the ledge. "If I stopped painting, would you stay with me?"

"If I were blind, would I walk in traffic without a Seeing Eye dog? No. I wouldn't stay with you."

"If I didn't stop painting, but left New York to paint more, and better, would you leave New York with me?"

"No. I have two galleries and fifty crazy painters counting on me."

"Would you visit?"

She touched his face. "So often that you won't regret leaving."

Jimmy Camerano looked down at the horse. It was the most beautiful thing he had ever seen, and he never could have painted it. He braced his hands on the ledge. "What if I just step into the air?"

"Art will have lost a great painting for no good reason."

"Only one?"

"In the time that Clyfford Still wasted driving up from Maryland, tonight, he could have painted a great painting. Don't you owe it to him—and me—to get off the roof and back to work?" She flashed him the Abby smile and he thought, Still is right. I've never gone wrong going my own way.

"JUMP!"

Jimmy leaned forward to look down. Bern Horne was standing on the sidewalk, shouting through cupped hands. That's who Clyfford Still had telephoned, hoping Bern could help Abby talk him off the ledge if his horse didn't, but without a clue that Bern had his own agenda.

"JUMP!"

Leaning forward, Jimmy started to lose his balance.

"JUMP OR I'LL KILL YOUR NEXT SHOW TOO."

Jimmy Camerano threw his arms around the gargoyle. It tipped from the ledge, immensely heavy. He had a hundredth of a second to let go before it took him with it. But in that hundredth he saw another way. He pushed against the massive weight of the gargoyle, which lifted him back onto the ledge and altered its course, slightly, before it hurtled down.

What would his father shout to Berne?

"CATCH!"

SARAH WEINMAN *is the editor of* Women Crime Writers: Eight Suspense Novels of the 1940s & 50s *(Library of America) and* Troubled Daughters, Twisted Wives: Stories from the Trailblazers of Domestic Suspense *(Penguin). Her fiction has appeared in* Ellery Queen's Mystery Magazine, Alfred Hitchcock's Mystery Magazine, *and several anthologies, while her journalism and essays have appeared most recently in the* New York Times, *the* Guardian, *and the* New Republic, *as well as the anthology* Anatomy of Innocence: Testimonies of the Wrongfully Convicted *(Liveright). Weinman's book about the real-life abduction that inspired the novel* Lolita *is forthcoming from Ecco.*

Nude in the Studio by Lilias Torrance Newton

THE BIG TOWN

BY SARAH WEINMAN

You don't expect to see a portrait of your mother hanging on the wall of your gangster boyfriend's living room. Especially when that portrait shows your mother without a stitch of clothing on but for a pair of green heels.

"Where did you get that painting?" I asked, my voice more querulous than I wished. It was my first time in his house. I hesitated about a return visit even before seeing the portrait, but now I knew. I would not be back.

He turned to face the portrait. I looked at his back, the white collared shirt barely covering darkly matted hair. I'd run my hands through that broad, fleshy forest the few afternoons we'd fucked in a Ritz-Carlton hotel suite. Again I remembered what I found attractive about him: power, status, money. And what I found ugly: body, face, manner.

He turned around. "Bought it at an estate sale," he said, the Russian accent adding a nasal quality. "She reminded me of my wife."

A wave of nausea roiled my stomach. I wasn't sure if it was for my mother or for his wife.

"She's beautiful," I murmured.

"A lot more beautiful than Rosalie. Why am I talking about my wife? She's not here and you are."

He reached for my waist. I let him. And later, when he took me from behind on his king-size four-poster bed, I buried my face into the duvet and tried not to think that he was really thinking of the woman in the painting. My mother.

In that moment I changed my mind.

I would be back, but not to see him. I needed that portrait.

⁘

When I tell you about my mother it's from what others told me. She died a month after I was born. The stories varied: my father said it was a blood infection. His mother said it was a curse. My stepmother got a pained look in her eye if the subject ever came up. Which is to say, what little I knew amounted to nothing at all.

I didn't miss her until I was fifteen. I was too busy cooking, cleaning, ironing, looking after my younger siblings (we didn't speak of halves) and anything considered domestic work. I left school at twelve. It's what girls my age did. At fifteen my father and his wife wanted to marry me off to some local farmhand. He was nice enough. But the thought of bearing any of his children, let alone over a dozen, as was the custom in the small town of my youth, once caused me to bring up my dinner in an inconvenient setting. The other option, becoming a nun, was out of the question. Taking vows seemed even more repellent than marrying a farmer boy.

So I made my way to Montreal instead. That, too, was what girls my age did. But I also went because she did the same.

I didn't find her there, of course. She was dead. I found trouble instead. Just another Sugar-Puss on Dorchester Street, sleeping in SROs and walking the streets and hopping from nightclub to nightclub in search of men with money. Sometimes they congregated at the Chez Parée ready to throw dollar bills at the garter of Gypsy Rose Lee. Sometimes they haunted the Casa Loma hoping Duke or Miles might battle each other in a late-night jam session. Always they prowled, and I counted as prey.

The gangster I met in a different way. My newest flatmate was three days fresh into Montreal and looking for something silly to do one weekday afternoon. We went to the bowling alley on Sainte-Catherine, where you could get a lane for a dollar an hour. Halfway through our first game we realized the lane was hot. Or at least I did when I saw the gangster, mutiny flashing in his eye.

"You took our lane," he said. His accent wasn't as thick back then.

"We paid for it."

"That's always our lane."

"This time it isn't."

"Then we'll pay for it anyway." He waved over some other men dressed like him. He spoke words in his mother tongue and then, switching back to English, told me, "You better bowl good. There's money on you."

Sweat beaded on my flatmate's forehead. "There's *what*—"

"Shut up and bowl, Marie-Eve." She opened her mouth to try again and caught my glare. Her mouth closed shut.

We bowled. They bet. We were terrible. They howled with laughter. I cannot remember who won or lost. Afterward the men took us to the Crystal Palace and paid for every single one of our drinks. Marie-Eve moved out a week later, spooked by the experience. The same night I fucked the gangster for the first time.

I carried on this way for a while. Why not? It thrilled me to be seedy. So far removed from the little town of Tadoussac. There a future lacked any pleasure. Here the present was all pleasure. But the present never lasts. I wasn't even twenty and could feel the rot setting in.

There it remained until I saw my mother's portrait. I knew it was her from the single photograph I possessed, which I carried everywhere I went. Well-worn creases couldn't mask the life force of this woman, who couldn't have been more than twenty-two at the time. She, my mother, burned with future.

A future my birth snuffed out.

The oil portrait undid me as much for the surprise as for the expression. She looked hesitant. In-between. Vulnerable, not only because she was nude. I had spent my whole life knowing her to be an unsolved riddle. This clue, hanging in my boyfriend's house, gummed things up some more.

It added more variables to her story. And to mine. It made the rot inside me grow smaller and the shame grow larger.

I couldn't find my mother. But at the same time, I could.

He was gone when I woke. A note lay beside me: *Leave by ten*. The grandfather clock struck nine. Was this tacit permission, or carelessness? I shook off the thought. Of course he was careless, if he fucked his mistress in the bed he shared with his wife.

Broad daylight did me no favors, but a time window was a time window. How careless could I be, to snatch this painting off the wall? Could I be bold, but not too bold? I put on last evening's clothes, pretending not to care at my disheveled, cheap state, and went out into the main room.

Where I found I was not alone.

"Mademoiselle Cléa," said a voice I didn't recognize. Low. Deep. The barest trace of an Anglophone accent.

My name wasn't Cléa. My mother's was Clothilde. Close enough?

I said nothing, took in the stranger's appearance. Medium height, trim bearing, fedora loosely atop his medium brown hair. Bright green eyes compensated for the overall medium boil. The eyes made him, if not exactly attractive, more distinct.

He shook his head as if to erase a memory. "*C'est ma faute*," he said. "You cannot be her. And yet—" he flicked his head toward the painting.

"I don't know what you're talking about," I blustered.

The man's answering smile was vulpine, a word I never even knew existed until I moved to Montreal, seeing wolves in fancy clothing all across the city. "Of course you do. The resemblance is remarkable. Did Andrei realize this when he took you as a lover?"

There were many things I could say, none polite, most obscene, so I opted for silence.

"I was there, you know. At the bowling alley."

I felt the room temperature fall.

"He should have chosen the other girl, but he was drawn to you," the man continued, switching back to French. "Now I see why."

"I don't," I cut in. "Why does he have this portrait?" I hugged my arms around my chest. The dressing gown covered me fully and yet I felt stripped.

"Revenge," said the man. He took off his hat and placed it on the mantel near the painting. His hairline, to my surprise, did not recede but showed off corkscrew curls. As I stared, a flush went through his cheeks. "I don't usually take off my hat," he muttered.

"Why revenge?" I pressed.

"Because he wanted the artist and couldn't get her."

"The artist. Not the subject."

Back came the smile. "Well, you are correct. But mostly, the artist."

I looked again at the portrait of my mother. Clothilde. Hesitant, but I observed it differently now. In a manner that made me feel most uncomfortable. I dared not contemplate these thoughts. I shut them out.

But the man, whose name I still did not know, could read my roiling reveries. He could pluck them out of my mind and place them in between us, where they could live, smolder, ignite.

"*Dis-moi*," I whispered.

His voice went deeper, lower. "It is nearly ten. We must both leave."

"You must tell me!" I snapped in English.

"Apparently I must," he agreed. He grabbed my left arm. The shock of it jolted us both. A current went up to my shoulder, and I stared up at him, startled.

Realization dawned. "You were here for this, too. The painting." I stared directly at him. "Who was she to you?"

He said no more. He grabbed my arm again and I let him. I shut my eyes and when I opened them we were in his car. Both in the back seat. Someone else driving.

And then he spoke of the artist and her subject. The painter and my mother.

<hr>

The words were his. The story is hers.

History repeated itself in my mother. Clothilde. She, too, had been a country girl—from Saint Rivière, two towns over from Tadoussac—looking for something beyond the limited borders of the small town. She, too, had run away from a prospective marriage for adventure in the Big Town. It hopped and skipped in a different way the generation before, embers from the stock market crash making the miserable seek pleasure with desperation. It was, perhaps, more dangerous than now.

But she didn't get in trouble. Not exactly. Not right away. She worked hard cleaning houses, scrubbing floors, mopping kitchens, whatever it took to pay her way and send the rest back to the family. They were disappointed she didn't stay but eager to take her money, the only reason for contact. If she missed her parents and many brothers and sisters, Clothilde never let on. Supporting them was simply her duty.

One of her employers was not much older than herself. A woman, a mother, but not a housewife. She'd tried it out but her skills were wasted on a husband who didn't appreciate them. He was too busy spending money faster than they both earned. Their marriage ended with the crash. He left, broke and chastened, but she had a new mouth to feed: their little boy, born seven months later, whom he never saw and never supported.

So the woman recovered her best skills. Nothing to do with house chores. She didn't paint houses, she painted people. She'd done so before her marriage, and her subjects thought well of her work. A few paintings appeared in exhibitions, and other people bought them. The country was in a depression, like all the other countries around the world. But this woman did all right. Not well, because an artist struggles even when there is money coming in, but enough that she didn't worry too much about putting food on her little boy's table. Enough that she could hire someone else to do the chores.

She found Clothilde through a friend of a friend. Hired her the very next day. For nearly a year they barely spoke other than to give and receive instructions. One in particular: the woman wasn't to be disturbed while painting. Clothilde saw no problem. She felt nervous around the woman's portraits. They conveyed things she wasn't sure she liked. A keen way about the world. Secrets revealed, unbidden.

Clothilde felt her secrets might spill out if she became the woman's subject.

Then one morning, as Clothilde finished scrubbing the kitchen floors, she heard the woman scream. Worried, she breached the inner sanctum. The woman flashed angry eyes at first but then found her calm.

"I'm sorry. I shouldn't have reacted that way."

"What's wrong, madame?"

The woman shook her head. "It's nothing, really . . . oh, damn." Tears welled up in the woman's eyes. "It's not nothing. I'm about to lose a big commission. The person I was supposed to paint said no."

Clothilde said nothing, though she wanted to say everything. But better to let the woman go on when she was ready.

"It's daring, I know, to ask something like this of anyone, but when a commission like this comes in and I have my boy to take care of, I must do it—"

"I'll do it," Clothilde blurted out.

The woman stopped. She took in Clothilde, all of her. A gleam caught in her eye as she began to look at her entire figure. "Hmm" was all the woman said at first.

"If you don't want—"

"But I do. She looked a little like you. I think this will work. Do you realize what I want?"

"To stand in front of you for hours every day for days on end?" Clothilde may have been banned from the studio, but she had worked long enough to see the stream of subjects pour in on a near-daily basis.

The woman laughed, then clapped her hand over her mouth. "Yes, I suppose." She paused. "But it gets drafty here. Very cold. That might make you uncomfortable."

Clothilde was already uncomfortable. She had been the whole time. But she'd taken the job on a bold whim and now this was the next one, wherever it led.

"I understand," she said to the woman.

"No, I don't believe you do."

"I *do*." Now it was Clothilde's turn to stare openly at the woman. Taking the painter in from head to toe. Clothilde had never before regarded a woman so frankly. She feared the feeling but thrilled at it.

And the woman—Clothilde knew her name, would speak it in her mind, but never out loud, not even later, when it counted most—gave the only necessary answer:

"All right then. We'll begin tomorrow morning."

"You're the boy," I broke in. The car had pulled up to a fancy house. The kind you would see in Westmount, a neighborhood I did not frequent.

He had the grace not to be annoyed. "I am," he said.

"You're younger than I thought, then. I thought you'd be as old as—"

"Let's not speak of him right now." The door on his side opened. "Come with me."

"Where else would I go?"

"Back to his place." He stood on the sidewalk. I got out after him.

"I don't think so."

I followed him inside the house. Just as fancy as on the outside. Before I could stop myself I said, "Your father supported you then?"

"He raised me." The tone did not allow for argument. I was too cowed by the opulence, the kind that did not announce itself but simply existed, daring to be contradicted.

"And you inherited it all."

"Almost all. Not the painting." He directed me to sit in a plush chair across from him. I sat. He remained standing. "He didn't know it existed. Neither did I, till I met your boyfriend."

"You were going to tell me why he wanted the artist."

I could see he did not want to answer. He turned his head away from me at an angle, finding a spot on the floor more to his liking. Enough time passed that I thought he might not answer.

But it came, in a near whisper. "Because she said no. Men like him always hear yes, even when those saying it don't mean it." His head whipped up. Fury flickered into his green eyes.

"Don't judge me," I said.

"I'm not. The world works this way. I'm well aware. Morality is a costume to wear at convenient times. And when it's inconvenient, it's shed like a snakeskin."

The bitterness undid me. "Is that what your house is?" I waved around for maximum effect. "Another mask? I'm here and I don't even know your name."

"And I don't know yours. Unless it really is Cléa."

An impasse, then. The next generation on different sides of a painting, an unfinished story. One which I wanted an ending to, so very badly.

"How do you even know what your mother said to mine?"

He sat in the nearest chair, bowing his head again. "She told me, even when she knew it would hurt me."

When he picked up the thread again I understood the hurt.

The first morning Clothilde was indeed as cold as the artist warned. Goose bumps dotted her body as she posed with her arms up above her head, exposing her armpits. The hair on them, more than anything else, bothered her most. Not that the artist could see her entirety. She could put that away in a small, faraway corner of her mind, concentrating on banal thoughts like how much dust remained in the parlor to clean when this was done.

"Move your left arm a fraction to the right," the artist called out.

Clothilde did so almost automatically, but the act of doing so snapped her out of her domestic rumination. For the rest of the session she felt an overwhelming need to fidget. Itches begging to be scratched in places out of reach. Thoughts racing quickly.

And then, after interminable time passed, the artist clapped once. "*Voilà*," she cried, talking to the canvas. Then she moved her head so Clothilde could see her. A half smile played on the artist's lips.

Clothilde, insolent, spoke first. "We are done?"

But the artist, if she heard it, ignored it. The smile became a proper one. "Yes, Clothilde. See you tomorrow morning."

Clothilde escaped from the studio for her bedroom. When the door shut behind her she felt, as she always did, the lack of space, barely enough to fit herself, the twin bed, a closet, and a nightstand. But something else intruded further. She spent the night wondering exactly what it was, tossing and turning as an answer eluded her.

The answer remained out of reach with each successive painting session. The artist barely spoke except to give directions from her easel. Chin up. Eyes wider, no squinting. A shoulder up, then a shoulder down. Right leg turned out just so. Clothilde was so pliant she did not take in each command, she became them. By the end of each session, punctuated with another *Voilà!* from the artist, Clothilde hardly felt human—until, as she did every time, she kicked off the green shoes while fleeing the studio.

A week passed this way, then another. Outside of the studio Clothilde and the artist remained cordial, as much as giving and taking orders for domestic duties counted as such. But inside the studio was another matter. How could two women be cordial when hardly any speech passed between them? When for hours on end, one painted and the other remained as still as she could, and then when she could no longer, carried on nonetheless?

Three and a half weeks into the session, a shift.

They began in April, and now it was nearer to May. That month was Clothilde's favorite. The biting winter cold was no more and the scorching summer was weeks away. In between, the air smelled of promise and honeysuckle. Optimism pervaded the crowd thronging in Phillips Square or around the Main. It was a time when, perish the thought, the idea of reaching the top of Mount Royal seemed an enjoyable, not an unbearable, prospect.

And here Clothilde was, stuck inside this studio cage as her favorite month began. When the artist commanded, Clothilde did not yield. The "keep your shoulders level" prompted Clothilde to stick one out at a greater angle than normal.

The artist finally stood up, paintbrush thudding as it hit the floor.

"What is *wrong* with you? We're so close and now is the time you decide not to listen to me?"

Clothilde, as the artist raised her voice in frustrated anguish, closed her eyes, knowing it could not block out the sound but wanting to believe it could. After a beat, she opened them again. The artist faced her. Only inches separated their faces.

"I'm sorry," said the artist. Her voice caught as she recovered her normally medium-modulated tone. "You've been so good and have never complained once. I suppose I was shocked you finally did." A rueful chuckle followed a half gasp. And then, the artist's hand on her shoulder.

"Will you forgive me?"

Time seemed to slow down. Clothilde looked back at the artist and then, before she could let the impulse go, she reached for the artist's other hand, then placed it on her breast.

"I think so," said Clothilde. Then she leaned in and kissed the artist's mouth. Time stopped for a while. Clothilde felt warmth spread inside her and reveled in the taste of the artist's lips, like a mix of cherries and apples, and the feel of her hands moving about her body. As one hand crept lower and lower, pushing against Clothilde's mound, time started up again.

"I can't," the artist whispered, snatching her hand back.

This time it was she who fled the studio in a hurry. The paintbrush lay on the floor. Clothilde, still unclothed but now alone, ventured over to the easel to see what the artist left behind.

The painting was ready, at least to Clothilde's mind. And it felt as if she was seeing her inside self revealed to the outside. Or perhaps it was the artist's inner self.

Clothilde felt before she heard the intake of breath behind her. When she turned her head a fraction, she found two eyes staring up before a pair of feet scampered away from the door.

<hr>

"You saw what happened," I said.

The man did not answer. He did not have to. His face had turned stark white during the telling.

"How old were you? Four?"

"Nearly six, and I stopped being a child then."

"Did you know what you were seeing?"

He gave me a look of utter pity. My question was so foolish. But he answered, and it was the answer of a man who had not released his own anguish.

"I loved my *maman*, but my father happened to show up the following day. A whim, I suppose, since he had barely kept track of me for the previous year. He asked why I looked so sad and I told him. Before I could understand I was living with him and the roles reversed: I barely saw her for the next ten years. And never for very long. Not until after my father died."

I understood everything in that moment. Why he'd been at the bowling alley. Why he stayed in the gangster's orbit. Why he wanted that painting.

"It isn't for you; it's for her. She's still alive, isn't she?"

Again, he did not answer me directly. He rose from his chair and turned toward me. I realized, all of a sudden, we were very nearly the same height. In heels I would be taller. But it meant, when he took my hand with an intensity that betrayed him, I could close the gap between us and kiss him lightly with the barest of effort.

His hand in mine, he said, "We will go tonight for the painting."

And he told me his name: François.

I had wanted the painting all to myself because it hurt so much to see my mother there when I knew precious little about her. And now, thanks to François, I knew more, so much more—knowledge I wasn't asking for, but needed. And with that knowledge came the realization the painting wasn't mine and could never be.

But I could restore it to the person who needed it most.

For the next few hours François and I busied ourselves with other things. And, also, each other. I won't say it was transcendent, because that's a lie. But for the first time, I didn't hate myself after fucking. The lifelong grief I spent my whole life pushing away remained, but now I could accept it for what it was and not let it rule me.

We watched the sun set outside the kitchen window as we feasted on croque madame (courtesy of his chef, of course) and cheddar cheese and figs and fruit and then, when the light faded into night, we changed into all-black shirts and pants, donned black masks, and instructed his driver to stay home for the night.

"You've done this before?" I wondered.

He shook his head. "I've thought about it a lot. Came close once or twice. But it's a two-person job."

François drove smoothly out of the neighborhood, down Côtes-des-Neiges and away from the Main. Less than ten minutes later he pulled the car up a block away from the gangster's opulent manse. Close enough for a getaway, but not too close.

We stepped out of the car and I hesitated. "What's wrong?" he whispered.

"I don't know." I waited. Then I heard a wail in the distance.

"We should go," he said.

"Slowly."

We did. Creeping up along fences, averting our masked faces, but we needn't have worried. No one was out tonight. I stayed alert for anyone who might appear, but this was as clear a coast as one could have.

I stifled a laugh. So much had happened in such a short time. I felt drunk on information, on learning so much about my mother. Clothilde. She was younger than I when she encountered the artist. And there was so much still to know.

But not yet. We were upon the gangster's house. The front door would not do. François and I scurried toward the back, where both of us knew of another way in. Me, as the mistress. He, as the revenge-seeker.

The window was partway open. François pried it further and let me go first. We landed in the laundry room, and as soon as both of us thudded to the floor that sense of wrongness grew stronger.

"I hear something upstairs," I said.

François waved it away. "We're here, let's go. If we have to leave we'll know when."

The staircase from the laundry room shuddered with each one of our steps. My heart beat triple time at the thought of being discovered. François betrayed no emotion. He focused on silence and I tried to follow suit. When we reached the top of the stairs, he before me, together we pushed on the door.

It didn't budge.

"Is it locked?"

"*Je ne sais pas. Je pense que non.*" He furrowed his forehead, thoughts obvious: to kick the door or not to?

He tried pushing on it again. Still no good. There was nothing to do but kick it. No room for a running jump. Brute force or nothing at all.

François and I both hurled ourselves at the door.

It flew open.

A man's body lay on the floor at the end of the hallway.

And a woman stood over the body. Even from such a distance we could see the fury in her eyes as she held the gun between herself and the man, but also the sense of defeat.

François shut the door and scampered down the rickety stairs before I had a chance to take another breath.

"Get down here!" he growled.

I did.

Before long we were outside again, catching our breaths.

And as we made our way back to the car, taking a different and more complicated route four times as long, we heard the wail of police sirens, the screams of the gangster's wife as she resisted arrest, and the sad intonations of the officers reciting the arrest.

We were silent for the whole ten-minute drive. Then, as François parked the car in his driveway, he turned to me and removed his mask, resignation written all over his face.

"We won't get the painting tonight. But someday we will."

It took nearly nine months.

By then the gangster's wife, Rosalie in full and Risa to her intimates, was serving a five-to-fifteen-year prison term for manslaughter. Everyone wanted her to plead guilty because they feared what she would say in a trial, and what others would say about the gangster. Better to get her away from Montreal. Who knows why the gun went off and the gangster died?

Only when the police turned up at François's house three days later, looking for me, because Risa invoked my name in her statement in less than flattering terms, did it seem there might be a motive. I told the truth, leaving out the failed painting heist. They might check for signs of life in the laundry room, but having collared their woman, one with ugly secrets, I doubted they would follow up with us again.

By then François's house had become mine. I had as little to do as before but there was no longer a need to fill the aching void with bad sex and worse drugs. On the worst days, when I thought I might spirit myself away for good, François always caught me in time. There had not been any worst days in quite a while.

When the painting of my mother finally arrived I wasn't prepared. I kept myself ignorant of the negotiation process. Every time François returned from another meeting with Risa, he looked more ashen than before. I became so accustomed to this cycle that when the painting did return, covered in packing material, I did not recognize it for what it was.

Then François said we had a visit scheduled for the following morning. To deliver the package.

My eyes widened in alarm. "It's done?"

"It is." He gripped my hand. "It's time."

The driver took us and the painting there in just under an hour. A tiny village near Sainte-Agathe-des-Monts, populated by a few hundred. That was where the artist lived now. Where she'd lived for nearly my entire life.

François told me more about her in the car. How after she lost custody of him, she lost the will to paint for some years. And for Montreal, now associated with so many unhappy memories. She found the village by placing her finger on a map and tracing a circle exactly halfway. She gave herself a week, and if she abhorred it she could leave. She didn't. And then she painted again and restored herself in part.

The painting was exhibited only once, the year François turned eight. The gangster fell in love with it, or so he would boast to his drinking buddies, and doubled its asking price. It had indeed been a revenge of sorts. A pitying kind. For the artist had spurned the gangster's violent advances one night, a year before François was born. He never forgot, for women generally did not say no to him. And he thought, in his furious mind, that if he could possess her most daring portrait and that she must live off his largesse, then he had won.

The driver reached a dirt road. Turning left, we slowly approached a modest wood-paneled bungalow with a red-and-white roof. François took the painting out of the trunk and held it gingerly with both hands. I walked slightly behind him, holding nothing but my purse. There was no doorbell, so I rapped on the door for the both of us.

My breath quickened when the artist answered the door. I could not say why I felt her to be so familiar. She didn't resemble her son, not exactly, though her graying hair still curled around her face and she was nearly as tall as François. As she greeted us I sensed a keen intelligence that seemed kin to his. And when she smiled it matched her dancing eyes and dry wit.

François tore off the packaging and placed the painting on the closest easel. The house was so small the entire main room functioned as the artist's studio, with unfinished canvases loitering about in different parts of the room. She stared at her long-ago creation, the desire-filled nude clad in green heels. Then she looked up at me, astonished.

"Cléa!" she cried. Then she caught herself. A blush bloomed in both cheeks. She held up a hand to cover her face, then thought better of it.

"You look just like her."

I felt my entire self lighten. I felt my mother, the true Clothilde, of a secret name no longer secret, within me. And also within the artist, the woman she wasn't allowed to love.

There was nowhere else I wanted to be.

"I've been told that," I said in English. "My name is Aurelie."

LAWRENCE BLOCK *has written a surfeit of novels and short stories, along with half a dozen books for writers. Over the years, he has somehow contrived to edit a dozen anthologies, most recently* In Sunlight or in Shadow: Stories Inspired by the Paintings of Edward Hopper. *It was over forty years ago when he began chronicling the fictional life of Matthew Scudder, and the two have grown old together in seventeen novels and eleven shorter works.*

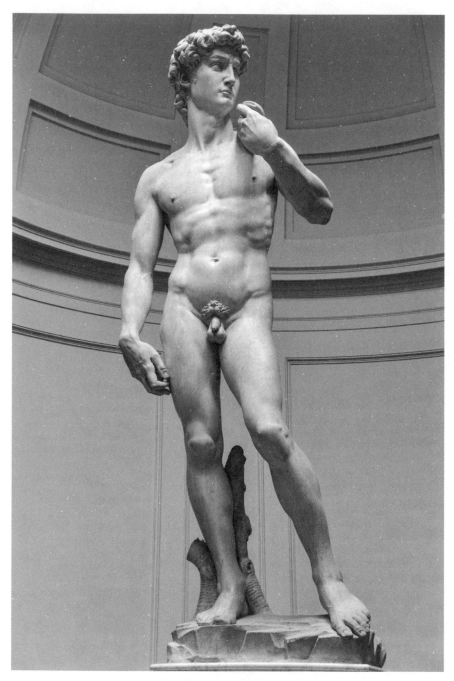

David by Michelangelo Buonarroti

LOOKING FOR DAVID

BY LAWRENCE BLOCK

Elaine said, "You never stop working, do you?"

I looked at her. We were in Florence, sitting at a little tile-topped table in the Piazza di San Marco, sipping cappuccino every bit as good as the stuff they served at the Peacock on Greenwich Avenue. It was a bright day but the air was cool and crisp, the city bathed in October light. Elaine was wearing khakis and a tailored safari jacket, and looked like a glamorous foreign correspondent, or perhaps a spy. I was wearing khakis too, and a polo shirt, and the blue blazer she called my Old Reliable.

We'd had five days in Venice. This was the second of five days in Florence, and then we'd have six days in Rome before Alitalia took us back home again.

I said, "Nice work if you can get it."

"Uh-uh," she said. "I caught you. You were scanning the area the way you always do."

"I was a cop for a lot of years."

"I know, and I guess it's a habit a person doesn't outgrow. And not a bad one either. I have some New York street smarts myself, but I can't send my eyes around a room and pick up what you can. And you don't even think about it. You do it automatically."

"I guess. But I wouldn't call it working."

"When we're supposed to be basking in the beauties of Florence," she said, "and exclaiming over the classic beauty of the sculpture in the piazza, and instead you're staring at an old queen in a white linen jacket five tables over, trying to guess if he's got a yellow sheet and just what's written on it—wouldn't you call that working?"

"There's no guesswork required," I said. "I know what it says on his yellow sheet."

"You do?"

"His name is Horton Pollard," I said. "If it's the same man, and if I've been sending a lot of looks his way it's to make sure he's the man I think he is. It's well over twenty years since I've seen him. Probably more like twenty-five." I glanced over and watched the white-haired gentleman saying something to the waiter. He raised an eyebrow in a manner that was at once arrogant and apologetic. It was as good as a fingerprint. "It's him," I said. "Horton Pollard. I'm positive."

"Why don't you go over and say hello?"

"He might not want that."

"Twenty-five years ago you were still on the job. What did you do, arrest him?"

"Uh-huh."

"Honestly? What did he do? Art fraud? That's what comes to mind, sitting at an outdoor table in Florence, but he was probably just a stock swindler."

"Something white-collar, in other words."

"Something flowing-collar, from the looks of him. I give up. What did he do?"

I'd been looking his way, and our glances caught. I saw recognition come into his eyes, and his eyebrows went up again in that manner that was unmistakably his. He pushed his chair back, got to his feet.

"Here he comes," I said. "You can ask him yourself."

○—→—○

"Mr. Scudder," he said. "I want to say Martin, but I know that's not right. Help me out."

"Matthew, Mr. Pollard. And this is my wife, Elaine."

"How fortunate for you," he told me, and took the hand she extended. "I looked over here and thought, What a beautiful woman! Then I looked again and thought, I know that fellow. But then it took me a minute to place you. The name came first, or the surname, at any rate. His name's Scudder, but how do I know him? And then of course the rest of it came to me, all but your first name. I knew it wasn't Martin, but I couldn't sweep that name out of my mind and let Matthew come in." He sighed. "It's a curious muscle, the memory. Or aren't you old enough yet to have found it so?"

"My memory's still pretty good."

"Oh, mine's *good*," he said. "It's just capricious. Willful, I sometimes think."

At my invitation, he pulled up a chair from a nearby table and sat down. "But only for a moment," he said, and asked what brought us to Italy, and how long we'd be in Florence. He lived here, he told us. He'd lived here for quite a few years now. He knew our hotel, on the east bank of the Arno, and pronounced it charming and a good value. He mentioned a cafe just down the street from the hotel that we really ought to try.

"Although you certainly don't need to follow my recommendations," he said, "or Michelin's either. You can't get a bad meal in Florence. Well, that's not *entirely* true. If you insist on going to high-priced restaurants, you'll encounter the occasional disappointment. But if you simply blunder into whatever humble trattoria is closest, you'll dine well every time."

"I think we've been dining a little too well," Elaine said.

"It's a danger," he acknowledged, "although the Florentines manage to stay quite slim themselves. I started to bulk up a bit when I first came here. How could one help it? Everything tasted so good. But I took off the pounds I gained and I've kept them off. Though I sometimes wonder why I bother. For God's sake, I'm seventy-six years old."

"You don't look it," she told him.

"I wouldn't care to look it. But why is that, do you suppose? No one else on God's earth gives a damn what I look like. Why should it matter to me?"

She said it was self-respect, and he mused on the difficulty of telling where self-respect left off and vanity began. Then he said he was staying too long at the fair, wasn't he, and got to his feet. "But you must visit me," he said. "My villa is not terribly grand, but it's quite nice and I'm proud enough of it to want to show it off. Please tell me you'll come for lunch tomorrow."

"Well . . ."

"It's settled, then," he said, and gave me his card. "Any cabdriver will know how to find it. Set the price in advance though. Some of them will cheat you, although most are surprisingly honest. Shall we say one o'clock?" He leaned forward, placed his palms on the table. "I've thought of you often over the years, Matthew. Especially here, sipping caffè nero a few yards from Michelangelo's *David*. It's not the original, you know. That's in a museum, though even the museums are less than safe these days. You know the Uffizzi was bombed a few years ago?"

"I read about that."

"The Mafia. Back home they just kill each other. Here they blow up masterpieces. Still, it's a wonderfully civilized country, by and large. And I suppose I had to wind up here, near the *David*." He'd lost me, and I guess he knew it, because he frowned, annoyed at himself. "I just ramble," he said. "I suppose the one thing I'm short of here is people to talk to. And I always thought I could talk to you, Matthew. Circumstances prevented my so doing, of course, but over the years I regretted the lost opportunity." He straightened up. "Tomorrow, one o'clock. I look forward to it."

⚬━⚬

"Well, of course I'm dying to go," Elaine said. "I'd love to see what his place looks like. 'It's not terribly grand but it's quite nice.' I'll bet it's nice. I'll bet it's gorgeous."

"You'll find out tomorrow."

"I don't know. He wants to talk to you, and three might be a crowd for the kind of conversation he wants to have. It wasn't art theft you arrested him for, was it?"

"No."

"Did he kill someone?"

"His lover."

"Well, that's what each man does, isn't it? Kills the thing he loves, according to whatsisname."

"Oscar Wilde."

"Thanks, Mr. Memory. Actually, I knew that. Sometimes when a person says whatsisname or whatchamacallit it's not because she can't remember. It's just a conversational device."

"I see."

She gave me a searching look. "There was something about it," she said. "What?"

"It was brutal." My mind filled with a picture of the murder scene, and I blinked it away. "You see a lot on the job, and most of it's ugly, but this was pretty bad."

"He seems so gentle. I'd expect any murder he committed to be virtually nonviolent."

"There aren't many nonviolent murders."

"Well, bloodless, anyway."

"This was anything but."

"Well, don't keep me in suspense. What did he do?"

"He used a knife," I said.

"And stabbed him?"

"Carved him," I said. "His lover was younger than Pollard, and I guess he was a good-looking man, but you couldn't prove it by me. What I saw looked like what's left of the turkey the day after Thanksgiving."

"Well, that's vivid enough," she said. "I have to say I get the picture."

"I was first on the scene except for the two uniforms who caught the squeal, and they were young enough to strike a cynical pose."

"While you were old enough not to. Did you throw up?"

"No, after a few years you just don't. But it was as bad as anything I'd ever seen."

⚬━⊱━⚬

Horton Pollard's villa was north of the city, and if it wasn't grand it was nevertheless beautiful, a white stuccoed gem set on a hillside with a commanding view of the valley. He showed us through the rooms, answered Elaine's questions about the paintings and furnishings, and accepted her explanation of why she couldn't stay for lunch. Or appeared to—as she rode off in the taxi that had brought us, something in his expression suggested for an instant that he felt slighted by her departure.

"We'll dine on the terrace," he said. "But what's the matter with me? I haven't offered you a drink. What will you have, Matthew? The bar's well stocked, although I don't know that Paolo has a very extensive repertoire of cocktails."

I said that any kind of sparkling water would be fine. He said something in Italian to his houseboy, then gave me an appraising glance and asked me if I would want wine with our lunch.

I said I wouldn't. "I'm glad I thought to ask," he said. "I was going to open a bottle and let it breathe, but now it can just go on holding its breath. You used to drink, if I remember correctly."

"Yes, I did."

"The night it all happened," he said. "It seems to me you told me I looked as though I needed a drink. And I got out a bottle, and you poured drinks for both of us. I remember being surprised you were allowed to drink on duty."

"I wasn't," I said, "but I didn't always let that stop me."

"And now you don't drink at all?"

"I don't, but that's no reason why you shouldn't have wine with lunch."

"But I never do," he said. "I couldn't while I was locked up, and when I was released I found I didn't care for it, the taste or the physical sensation. I drank the odd glass of wine anyway, for a while, because I thought one couldn't be entirely civilized without it. Then I realized I didn't care. That's quite the nicest thing about age, perhaps the only good thing to be said for it. Increasingly, one ceases to care about more and more things, particularly the opinions of others. Different for you, though, wasn't it? You stopped because you had to."

"Yes."

"Do you miss it?"

"Now and then."

"I don't, but then I was never that fond of it. There was a time when I could distinguish different châteaux in a blind tasting, but the truth of the matter was that I never cared for any of them all that much, and after-dinner cognac gave me heartburn. And now I drink mineral water with my meals, and coffee after them. *Acqua minerale.* There's a favorite trattoria of mine where the owner calls it *acqua miserabile.* But he'd as soon sell me it as anything else. He doesn't care, and I shouldn't care if he did."

Lunch was simple but elegant—a green salad, ravioli with butter and sage, and a nice piece of fish. Our conversation was mostly about Italy, and I was sorry Elaine hadn't stayed to hear it. He had a lot to say—about the way art permeated everyday Florentine life, about the long-standing enthusiasm of the British upper classes for the city—and I found it absorbing enough, but it would have held more interest for her than for me.

Afterward Paolo cleared our dishes and served espresso. We fell silent, and I sipped my coffee and looked out at the view of the valley and wondered how long it would take for the eye to tire of it.

"I thought I would grow accustomed to it," he said, reading my mind. "But I haven't yet, and I don't think I ever will."

"How long have you been here?"

"Almost fifteen years. I came on a visit as soon as I could after my release."

"And you've never been back?"

He shook his head. "I came intending to stay, and once here I managed to arrange the necessary resident visa. It's not difficult if there's money, and I was fortunate. There's still plenty of money, and there always will be. I live well, but not terribly high. Even if I live longer than anyone should, there will be money sufficient to see me out."

"That makes it easier."

"It does," he agreed. "It didn't make the years inside any easier, I have to say that, but if I hadn't had money I might have spent them someplace even worse. Not that the place they put me was a pleasure dome."

"I suppose you were at a mental hospital."

"A facility for the criminally insane," he said, pronouncing the words precisely. "The phrase has a ring to it, doesn't it? And yet it was entirely appropriate. The act I performed was unquestionably criminal, and altogether insane."

He helped himself to more espresso. "I brought you here so that I could talk about it," he said. "Selfish of me, but that's part of being old. One becomes more selfish, or perhaps less concerned about concealing one's selfishness from oneself and others." He sighed. "One also becomes more direct, but in this instance it's hard to know where to start."

"Wherever you want," I suggested.

"With David, I suppose. Not the statue though. The man."

"Maybe my memory's not all I like to think it is," I said. "Was your lover's name David? Because I could have sworn it was Robert. Robert Naismith, and there was a middle name, but that wasn't David either."

"It was Paul," he said. "His name was Robert Paul Naismith. He wanted to be called Rob. I called him David sometimes, but he didn't care for that. In my mind though, he would always be David."

I didn't say anything. A fly buzzed in a corner, then went still. The silence stretched.

Then he began to talk.

"I grew up in Buffalo," he said. "I don't know if you've ever been there. A very beautiful city, at least in its nicer sections. Wide streets lined with elms. Some fine public buildings, some notable private homes. Of course the elms are all lost to Dutch Elm disease, and the mansions on Delaware Avenue now house law firms and dental clinics, but everything changes, doesn't it? I've come round to the belief that it's supposed to, but that doesn't mean one has to like it.

"Buffalo hosted the Pan-American Exposition, which was even before my time. It was held in 1901, if I remember correctly, and several of the buildings raised for the occasion remain to this day. One of the nicest, built alongside the city's principal park, has long been the home of the Buffalo Historical Society, and houses their museum collection.

"Are you wondering where this is leading? There was, and doubtless still is, a circular drive at the Historical building's front, and in the midst of it stood a bronze copy of Michelangelo's *David*. It might conceivably be a casting, though I think we can safely assume it to be just a copy. It's life-size, at any rate—or I should say actual size, as Michelangelo's statue is itself considerably larger than life, unless the young David was built more along the lines of his adversary Goliath.

"You saw the statue yesterday—although, as I said, that too was a copy. I don't know how much attention you paid to it, but I wonder if you know what the sculptor is supposed to have said when asked how he managed to create such a masterpiece. It's such a wonderful line it would almost have to be apocryphal.

"'I looked at the marble,' Michelangelo is said to have said, 'and I cut away the part that wasn't David.' That's almost as delicious as the young Mozart explaining that musical composition is the easiest thing in the world, you have merely to write down the music you hear in your head. Who cares, really, if either of them ever said any such thing? If they didn't, well, they ought to have done, wouldn't you say?

"I've known that statue all my life. I can't recall when I first saw it, but it must have been on my first visit to the Historical Building, and that would have been at a very early age. Our house was on Nottingham Terrace, not a ten-minute walk from the Historical building, and I went there innumerable times as a boy. And it seems to me I always responded to the *David*. The stance, the attitude, the uncanny combination of strength and vulnerability, of fragility and confidence. And, of course, the sheer physical beauty of the *David*, the sexuality—but it was a while before I was aware of that aspect of it, or before I let myself acknowledge my awareness.

"When we all turned sixteen and got driver's licenses, David took on new meaning in our lives. The circular drive, you see, was the lovers' lane of choice for young couples who needed privacy. It was a pleasant, parklike setting in a good part of town, unlike the few available alternatives in nasty neighborhoods down by the waterfront. Consequently, 'going to see David' became a euphemism for parking and making out—which, now that I think of it, are euphemisms themselves, aren't they?

"I saw a lot of David in my late teens. The irony, of course, is that I was far more drawn to his young masculine form than to the generous curves of the young women who were my companions on those visits. I was gay, it seems to me, from birth, but I didn't let myself know that. At first I denied the impulses. Later, when I learned to act on them—in Front Park, in the men's room at the Greyhound station—I denied that they meant anything. It was, I assured myself, a stage I was going through."

He pursed his lips, shook his head, sighed. "A lengthy stage," he said, "as I seem still to be going through it. I was aided in my denial by the fact that whatever I did with other young men was just an adjunct to my real life, which was manifestly normal. I went off to a good school, I came home at Christmas and during the summer, and wherever I was I enjoyed the company of women.

"Lovemaking in those years was usually a rather incomplete affair. Girls made a real effort to remain virginal, at least in a strictly technical sense, if not until marriage then until they were in what we nowadays call a committed relationship. I don't remember what we called it then, but I suspect it was a somewhat less cumbersome phrase.

"Still, sometimes one went all the way, and on those occasions I acquitted myself well enough. None of my partners had cause to complain. I could do it, you see, and I enjoyed it, and if it was less thrilling than what I found with male partners, well, chalk it up to the lure of the forbidden. It didn't have to mean there was anything *wrong* with me. It didn't mean I was *different* in any fundamental way.

"I led a normal life, Matthew. I would say I was determined to lead a normal life, but it never seemed to require much in the way of determination. During my senior year at college I became engaged to a girl I'd known literally all my life. Our parents were friends and we'd grown up together. I graduated and we were married. I took an advanced degree. My field was art history, as you may remember, and I managed to get an appointment to the faculty of the University of Buffalo. SUNY Buffalo, they call it now, but that was years before it became a part of the state university. It was just plain UB, with most of its student body drawn from the city and environs.

"We lived at first in an apartment near the campus, but then both sets of parents ponied up and we moved to a small house on Hallam, just about equidistant between the houses each of us had grown up in.

"It wasn't far from the statue of David either."

He led a normal life, he explained. Fathered two children. Took up golf and joined the country club. He came into some family money, and a textbook he authored brought in royalties that grew more substantial each year. As the years passed, it became increasingly easy to believe that his relations with other men had indeed been a stage, and one he had essentially outgrown.

"I still felt things," he said, "but the need to act on them seemed to have passed. I might be struck by the physical appearance of one of my students, say, but I'd never do anything about it, or even seriously consider doing anything about it. I told myself my admiration was aesthetic, a natural response to male beauty. In youth, hormone-driven as one is, I'd confused this with actual sexual desire. Now I could recognize it for the innocent and asexual phenomenon it was."

Which was not to say that he'd given up his little adventures entirely.

"I would be invited somewhere to attend a conference," he said, "or to give a guest lecture. I'd be in another city where I didn't know anyone and nobody knew me. And I would have had a few drinks, and I'd feel the urge for some excitement. And I could tell myself that, while a liaison with another woman would be a betrayal of my wife and a violation of my marital vows, the same could hardly be said for some innocent sport with another man. So I'd go to the sort of bar one goes to—they were never hard to find, even in those closeted days, even in provincial cities and college towns. And, once there, it was never hard to find someone."

He was silent for a moment, gazing off toward the horizon.

"Then I walked into a bar in Madison, Wisconsin," he said, "and there he was."

"Robert Paul Naismith."

"David," he said. "That's who I saw, that's the youth on whom my eyes fastened the instant I cleared the threshold. I can remember the moment, you see. I can see him now exactly as I saw him then. He was wearing a dark silk shirt and tan trousers and loafers without socks, which no one wore in those days. He was standing at the bar with a drink in his hand, and his physique and the way he stood, the stance, the attitude—he was Michelangelo's David. More than that, he was my David. He was my ideal, he was the object of a lifelong quest I hadn't even known I was on, and I drank him in with my eyes and I was lost."

"Just like that," I said.

"Oh, yes," he agreed. "Just like that."

He was silent, and I wondered if he was waiting for me to prompt him. I decided he was not. He seemed to be choosing to remain in the memory for a moment.

Then he said, "Quite simply, I had never been in love with anybody. I have come to believe that it is a form of insanity. Not to love, to care deeply for another. That seems to me to be quite sane, and even ennobling. I loved my parents, certainly, and in a somewhat different way I loved my wife.

"This was categorically different. This was obsessive. This was preoccupation. It was the collector's passion: I must have this painting, this statue, this postage stamp. I must embrace it, I must own it utterly. It and it alone will complete me. It will change my own nature. It will make me worthwhile.

"It wasn't sex, not really. I won't say sex had nothing to do with it. I was attracted to David as I'd never been attracted to anyone before. But at the same time I felt less driven sexually than I had on occasion in the past. I wanted to possess David. If I could do that, if I could make him entirely mine, it scarcely mattered if I had sex with him."

He fell silent, and this time I decided he was waiting to be prompted. I said, "What happened?"

"I threw my life over," he said. "On some flimsy pretext or other I stayed on in Madison for a week after the conference ended. Then I flew with David to New York and bought an apartment, the top floor of a brownstone in Turtle Bay. And then I flew back to Buffalo, alone, and told my wife I was leaving her."

He lowered his eyes. "I didn't want to hurt her," he said, "but of course I hurt her badly and deeply. She was not completely surprised, I don't believe, to learn there was a man involved. She'd inferred that much about me over the years, and probably saw it as part of the package, the downside of having a husband with an aesthetic sensibility.

"But she thought I cared for her, and I made it very clear that I did not. She was a woman who had never hurt anyone, and I caused her a good deal of pain, and I regret that and always will. It seems to me a far blacker sin than the one I served time for.

"Enough. I left her and moved to New York. Of course I resigned my tenured professorship at UB. I had connections throughout the academic world, of course, and a decent if not glorious reputation, so I might have found something at Columbia or NYU. But the scandal I'd created made that less likely, and anyway I no longer gave a damn for teaching. I just wanted to live, and enjoy my life.

"There was money enough to make that possible. We lived well. Too well, really. Not wisely but too well. Good restaurants every night, fine wines with dinner. Season tickets to the opera and the ballet. Summers in the Pines. Winters in Barbados or Bali. Trips to London and Paris and Rome. And the company, in town or abroad, of other rich queens."

"And?"

"And it went on like that," he said. He folded his hands in his lap, and a little smile played on his lips. "It went on, and then one day I picked up a knife and killed him. You know that part, Matthew. It's where you came in."

"Yes."

"But you don't know why."

"No, that never came out. Or if it did I missed it."

He shook his head. "It never came out. I didn't offer a defense, and I certainly didn't provide an explanation. But can you guess?"

"Why you killed him? I have no idea."

"But you must have come to know some of the reasons people have for killing other people? Why don't you humor an old sinner and try to guess. Prove to me that my motive was not unique after all."

"The reasons that come to mind are the obvious ones," I said, "and that probably rules them out. Let me see. He was leaving you. He was unfaithful to you. He had fallen in love with someone else."

"He would never have left," he said. "He adored the life we led and knew he could never live half so well with someone else. He would never fall in love with anyone else any more than he could have fallen in love with me. David was in love with himself. And of course he was unfaithful, and had been from the beginning, but I had never expected him to be otherwise."

"You realized you'd thrown your life away on him," I said, "and hated him for it."

"I *had* thrown my life away, but I didn't regret it. I'd been living a lie, and what loss to toss it aside? While jetting off to Paris for a weekend, does one long for the gentle pleasures of a classroom in Buffalo? Some may, for all I know. I never did."

I was ready to quit, but he insisted I come up with a few more guesses. They were all off the mark.

He said, "Give up? All right, I'll tell you. He changed."

"He changed?"

"When I met him," he said, "my David was the most beautiful creature I had ever set eyes on, the absolute embodiment of my lifelong ideal. He was slender but muscular, vulnerable yet strong. He was—well, go back to the San Marco piazza and look at the statue. Michelangelo got it just right. That's what he looked like."

"And then what? He got older?"

He set his jaw. "Everyone gets older," he said, "except for the ones who die young. It's unfair, but there's nothing for it. David didn't merely age. He coarsened. He thickened. He ate too much and drank too much and stayed up too late and took too many drugs. He put on weight. He got bloated. He grew jowly, and got pouchy under his eyes. His muscles wasted beneath their coating of fat and his flesh sagged.

"It didn't happen overnight. But that's how I experienced it, because the process was well along before I let myself see it. Finally I couldn't help but see it.

"I couldn't bear to look at him. Before I had been unable to take my eyes off him, and now I found myself averting my eyes. I felt betrayed. I fell in love with a Greek god, and before my eyes he turned into a Roman emperor."

"And you killed him for that?"

"I wasn't trying to kill him."

I looked at him.

"Oh, I suppose I was, really. I'd been drinking, we'd both been drinking, and we'd had an argument, and I was angry. I don't suppose I was too far gone to know that he'd be dead when I was done, and that I'd have killed him. But that wasn't the point."

"It wasn't?"

"He passed out," he said. "He was lying there, naked, reeking of the wine seeping out of his pores, this great expanse of bloated flesh as white as marble. I suppose I hated him for having thus transformed himself, and I know I hated myself for having been an agent of his transformation. And I decided to do something about it."

He shook his head, and sighed deeply. "I went into the kitchen," he said, "and I came back with a knife. And I thought of the boy I'd seen that first night in Madison, and I thought of Michelangelo. And I tried to *be* Michelangelo."

I must have looked puzzled. He said, "Don't you remember? I took the knife and cut away the part that wasn't David."

It was a few days later when I recounted all this to Elaine. We were at an outdoor café near the Spanish Steps. "All those years," I said, "I took it for granted he was trying to destroy his lover. That's what mutilation generally is, the expression of a desire to annihilate. But he wasn't trying to disfigure him, he was trying to refigure him."

"He was just a few years ahead of his time," she said. "Now they call it liposuction and charge the earth for it. I'll tell you one thing. As soon as we get back I'm going straight from the airport to the gym, before all this pasta becomes a permanent part of me. I'm not taking any chances."

"I don't think you've got anything to worry about."

"No, because if you were going to develop the urge to sculpt, it would have happened by now. I'm a far cry from the innocent young call girl you met at Danny Boy's table all those years ago."

"Not such a far cry. You look as good to me now as you ever did."

"You know something? I know you're lying and I don't even care."

"I'm not, though. You're a few years older, and you don't look as fresh and dew covered, but if anything you're more beautiful now than you were then. And there's the fact that age cannot wither you, nor custom stale your infinite variety."

"You old bear. Shakespeare?"

"Antony and Cleopatra."

"Infinite variety, huh? I guess David's variety wasn't all that infinite. How awful though. How godawful for both of them."

"The things people do."

"You said it. Well, what do you want to do? We could sit around feeling sorry for two men and the mess they made of their lives, or we could go back to the hotel and do something life-affirming. You tell me."

"It's a tough one," I said. "How soon do you need my decision?"

PERMISSIONS

We gratefully acknowledge all those who gave permission for material to appear in this book. We have made every effort to trace and contact copyright holders. If an error or omission is brought to our notice we will be pleased to remedy the situation in future editions of this book. For further information, please contact the publisher.

Jill D. Block, "Safety Rules"
Remember All the Safety Rules by Art Frahm, 1953 (p. 2)
Oil on canvas, 29.5 × 33.5 in. (74.9 × 85.1 cm.). Private collection/Jill D. Block.

Lee Child, "Pierre, Lucien, and Me"
Bouquet of Chrysanthemums by Auguste Renoir, 1881 (p. 20)
Oil on canvas, 26 × 21 ⅞ in. (66 × 55.6 cm.). The Walter H. and Leonore Annenberg Collection, Bequest of Walter H. Annenberg, 2002.

Nicholas Christopher, "Girl with a Fan"
Girl with a Fan by Paul Gauguin, 1902 (p. 30)
Oil on canvas, 92 × 73 cm. Museum Folkwang, Essen, Germany.

Michael Connelly, "The Third Panel"
The Garden of Earthly Delights (third panel) by Hieronymous Bosch, ca. 1500–1505 (p. 48)
Oil and grisaille on wooden panel, Center panel is 7'2 ½ × 6'4 ¾ in. Each wing is 7'2 ½ × 3'2 in. Museo del Prado, Madrid, Spain.

Jeffery Deaver, "A Significant Find"
The Cave Paintings of Lascaux, discovered 1940 (p. 60)
Mineral pigments on cave walls. The Axial Gallery in the caves of Lascaux, France.

Joe R. Lansdale, "Charlie the Barber"
The Haircut by Norman Rockwell, August 10, 1918 (p. 78)

Gail Levin, "After Georgia O'Keeffe's Flower"
Red Cannas by Georgia O'Keeffe, 1927 (p. 100)
Oil on canvas, 36 ⅛ × 30 ⅛ in. Courtesy of the Amon Carter Museum of American Art, Fort Worth, Texas; 1986.11.

Warren Moore, "Ampurdan"
The Pharmacist of Ampurdan Seeking Absolutely Nothing by Salvador Dali, 1936 (p. 110)
Oil and collage on wood, 30 × 52 cm. Copyright © Peter Horree / Alamy Stock Photo.

David Morrell, "Orange Is for Anguish, Blue for Insanity"
Cypresses by Vincent van Gogh, 1889 (p. 120)
Oil on Canvas, 36 ¾ × 29 ⅛ in. (93.4 × 74 cm.). The Met, Rogers Fund, 1949.

Joyce Carol Oates, *"Les Beaux Jours"*
Les beaux jours by Balthus, 1944–1946, (p. 154)
Oil on canvas, 58 ¼ × 78 ⅜ in. (148 x 199 cm.). Hirshhorn Museum and Sculpture Garden, Smithsonian Institution, Washington, DC, gift of the Joseph H. Hirshhorn Foundation, 1966.

Thomas Pluck, "Truth Comes Out of Her Well to Shame Mankind"
La Vérité sortant du puits by Jean Léon Gerome, 1896 (p. 176)
Oil on canvas, 35.8 × 28.3 in. (91 × 72 cm.) Musée d'art et d'archéologie Anne de Beaujeu.

S.J. Rozan, "The Great Wave"
Under the Wave off Kanagawa (Kanagawa oki nami ura), also known as the "Great Wave" by Katsushika Hokusai, 1830–32 (p. 198)
Polychrome woodblock print; ink and color on paper, 10 ⅛ × 14 ¹⁵⁄₁₆ in. (25.7 x 37.9 cm). H. O. Havemeyer Collection, bequest of Mrs. H. O. Havemeyer, 1929.

Kristine Kathryn Rusch, "Thinkers"
The Thinker by Auguste Rodin, 1880–1881 (p. 208)
Bronze; overall: 72 × 38 ¹¹⁄₁₆ × 55 ¹⁵⁄₁₆ in. (182.9 × 98.4 × 142.2 cm.) The Cleveland Museum of Art, gift of Ralph King 1917.42.

Jonathan Santlofer, "Gaslight"
The Empire of Light by René Magritte, 1953–1954 (p. 236)
Oil on canvas, 76 ¹⁵⁄₁₆ × 51 ⅝ in. (195.4 × 131.2 cm.). The Solomon R. Guggenheim Foundation Peggy Guggenheim Collection, Venice, 1976, © 2017 C. Herscovici / Artists Rights Society (ARS), New York.

Justin Scott, "Blood in the Sun"
PH-129 by Clyfford Still, 1949 (p. 258)
Oil on canvas, 53 × 44½ in (134.6 x 113 cm). Copyright © 2017 Clyfford Still Museum, Denver, CO © City and County of Denver / ARS, NY.

Sarah Weinman, "The Big Town"
Nude in the Studio by Lilias Torrance Newton, 1933 (p. 274)
Oil on canvas, 203.2 × 91.5 cm. Private collection.

Lawrence Block, "Looking for David"
David by Michelangelo Buonarroti, ca. 1501–1504 (p. 292)
One single block of marble from the quarries in Carrara in Tuscany, 5.16 meters tall. The Accademia Gallery, Florence, Italy.